THE
WALSHES

THE COMING OF EVE

JOE CLARK

This book is dedicated to my wife, Anita,
with thanks for her love and support.

1

APRIL EMERGED FROM her office. She had just posted on her blog. Women had to keep the faith. Obama had won the nomination. Hilary Clinton would not be the first woman president of the United States. At least not yet. But the McCain-Palin ticket had to be defeated. This country could not survive four more years of Republican rule.

The kids were in bed. Lights out at eleven. No video games after dinner. JJ pushed the limit on that one. When he couldn't play actual games, he spent his time editing videos and creating music. Becky was a reader. Catherine Coulter and Patricia Cornwell were her favorite authors. Lucy Farinelli, Kay Scarpetta's niece, was her culture hero.

It was 11:13 p.m. on Saturday, June 7, 2008. The swim meet had gone well that morning. No firsts. JJ was nipped at the very end of the 25 free. Becky had led part of the way in the 100 medley but ended up third. The afternoon had been spectacular. Becky mowed the lawn because she got to drive the mower while her dad and JJ trimmed the edges. April took care of cleaning the house and picking up groceries.

They had capped off the evening with a little TV and Scrabble.

The living room was dark and quiet. No TV. He was in the kitchen which meant he had serious business to discuss. Things were tight but that had been going on for so long that it seemed normal.

April stopped at the edge of the kitchen and leaned against the doorway. That was the sexiest pose she could come up with. She put on her brightest smile. He was studying the Washington Post Jobs section. He looked up and smiled as he surveyed her lean 5 foot 8 frame. His deep voice ruptured the stillness. "We need to figure something out."

"I know." Her response was barely audible.

He looked back down and studied the job ads. He sighed. "I've got one more unemployment check coming and then we are on our own."

She frowned. "Joe, we've been on our own. Those checks barely pay for groceries."

"Then we'll have to find something to replace them or starve." There was a harsh edge to his voice.

"I can go full-time at the office," she suggested. "I'll probably have to do that anyway. They're getting rid of all the part-timers. Maybe I can find part-time work as a sales clerk. That will more than make up for the unemployment checks."

He walked over and put his arms around her. There was a lilt in his voice when he spoke. "You already have a full-time job. You're Becky and JJ's mother. You're also CEO of this household. That's at least a part-time job."

"The benefits are great but the salary is nothing to write home about."

He looked straight into her green eyes and ran his fingers through her auburn hair. He kissed her on the forehead. The deep, authoritative command returned to his voice. "I'm thinking about signing on with a temp agency," he said as if he had already made his decision. "There's plenty of work out there and those companies provide benefits."

She shook her head. Walking away from 15 years of career-building to become a hired gun seemed like an admission of failure. "I don't think that's a good idea. This whole financial mess will blow over in a couple of weeks. Then the real jobs will open up and you will be stuck doing temp work."

His face was stern. His voice strong. "I've got to get a paying job. When we divvied things up, I got responsibility for bringing home the big bucks. We were able to buy this house because of my salary. It's on me to come up with the money."

"And you will. You just need a little more time. Have you been to a hundred interviews yet?"

"Thirty or so."

"When you get to a hundred, I'll start to worry."

"We can't wait that long. We can't hold out for another six months the way we're going."

She pulled away and started walking across the kitchen. The gestalt struck her. She paused to take it in: the warm cherry wood cabinets set against the Arctic white of the walls; the granite countertop with its specks of pink and turquoise playing off the slate floor dappled with streaks of green, blue, pink, and mauve; the chrome jacketed dishwasher, oven, and refrigerator rising from the landscape like mountains. They had a beautiful home but it was the millstone that could drag them under.

She drummed her fingers on the counter-top. If she told him about her prospects, there would be hope. He would probably hang on for a while longer. But it might be a false hope. If she didn't tell him, he would do what he felt was necessary to take care of his family.

She turned back to face him. She had to smile. He was such a sweet, beautiful man: tall, muscular with sandy brown hair and hazel eyes. Fifteen years had passed since his last varsity basketball game. He was still trim and solid. His jaw-line was softer. He was starting to develop love handles. But he looked like he could step out on the court tomorrow and steal rebounds or make the sudden pivot to create an open shot. "I've been talking to Pat and I think he has something for me. I didn't want to say anything until I knew for sure. Give me some time to work with him before you make a decision."

Pat Connolly, her literary agent, hadn't been much help lately. But now he was acting as if he had something for her. She could push him to speed the process up. It would have to be something with an advance that would pay some bills while she was writing. He should be able to do that. She was, after all, a pretty good writer.

2

A PHONE MESSAGE was waiting for April when the Walshes returned from Mass the next morning. Pat needed to speak with her as soon as possible. She decided he could wait until after the family breakfast.

April went up to the room that served as her office to make the call. "Pat, what's up?"

"G'd day t' ye, lass. 'ow are ye doin' on this fine marnin'?" he said in that brogue of his.

"I'm fine, Pat. Thanks for asking. How are you?" She pulled out her notepad and drew a leprechaun with horns.

"Fine, lass. 'Tis a fine day."

"Yes it is. Can you tell me what you wanted to talk about?"

"Craig Robertson at the Times-Herald is lookin' for som'un to write a story." April sketched a man's head - balding, perpetual scowl, and a stogie.

She felt a thrill and worked to suppress the excitement in her voice. "What's the story about?"

"Prostitution. He wants an insider who thinks it should be legal."

"That doesn't sound like me." She wanted to discourage him without saying no. But she was already wondering if there was a way she could pull it off.

"If ye ha'some friends, ye can use their stories," he said brightly.

April jotted down, *Prostitute friends????* She cleared her throat and wondered out loud, "Why doesn't he put one of his staff reporters on it?"

"He doesn't want anybody directly connected t'the Times-Herald."

"But if I take an assignment from him, I will be directly connected to the Times-Herald," April objected.

"Y're to be a free-lance writer proposin' a series to him," Connolly explained as if the answer was obvious.

She scowled. "Plausible deniability. But why me?"

"Ye have written some stuff on social issues. They like what ye have t'say."

She took her time considering the proposal and then demanded, "I would need some money up front."

"'e's open to an advance."

"More than that. I'm going to have to take time off work to dig for fresh insights."

"I can get ye a book deal with a nice advance."

April jotted down, *Book deal!!!* She suppressed the emotions roiling inside. "I'll have to think about it," she said in her most unenthusiastic voice.

Before she could hang up, Connolly interjected, "Lass, it's my understandin' that Senator Muehlberg wants ye t'do this."

April gasped. "Oh."

"Can ye meet with Robertson tomorrow around 9?" Connolly asked hopefully.

"When did you find out about all this?" April demanded in a harsh voice. She should have at least a week to think through her approach and make arrangements.

"Friday. This is the first chance I've 'ad t'talk t'ye."

"You heard about it before Friday," April countered angrily. "You could have given me a heads up last week. You could have sent me a message or something on Friday."

"Can ye meet with him in the marnin'?" the agent pressed in a calm voice.

"Ten o'clock," April hissed. She closed her eyes, clenched her teeth, and shook her head. This was all very strange.

"I'll set it up for ten."

After the call, April went back down to her family. All eyes were on her as she descended the stairs.

She forced a smile. "It looks like I'm going to have a chance to write a major piece for the Times-Herald."

"That's great," Joe said. "But what's the downside?"

April cleared her throat. "They want ammunition to support legalizing prostitution. And," she hesitated, "they want it yesterday."

"Mom, you can't support making prostitution legal," Becky objected.

April shrugged. "That's the job, and I'm not really in a position to turn it down." She continued down the stairs and walked over to her husband.

Joe gave Becky a reassuring smile. "She's just going to lay the facts out."

"It's immoral and degrading," Becky objected.

April regarded her daughter with a faint smile. "It's also legal in many parts of the world."

Joe said, "If we legalize it, we can regulate it. We can require health care and benefits for the girls, We can also collect taxes to pay for some of the costs."

"I don't like it. It's a bad idea," Becky said with an air of finality.

"I'm still going to have to look into it and I will probably end up taking the assignment," April said. Her voice was flat, unenthusiastic.

April spent the afternoon and evening researching prostitution. She called Senator Anna Muehlberg to set up a meeting on Monday afternoon. Her brother, Bill MacMahon, agreed to meet her for lunch and give her a street lawyer's view on the issues.

3

CRAIG ROBERTSON WAS in the middle of five things when April showed up. He was scrunched over some papers. From behind, he looked like a big, lumpy medicine ball. The phone to his right caught April's attention. She wondered why he hadn't gotten himself a hands-free phone. It seemed he really liked doing things the old-fashioned way. He was a taskmaster somewhat softened by a kindly, old professor facade. April took a seat and waited.

When he finally turned around to discuss the new project, he greeted her with a big smile.

"Prostitution is spiking in Northern Virginia," he began. His voice was high and raspy. "There have been a lot of public nuisance complaints lately. We've run several articles on the sex slave trade and its impact on Fairfax and other communities in the area. We've run a couple of stories about runaways turning to prostitution and drugs. None of those articles dealt with the larger population of hookers."

He paused to take a deep breath. "I'm looking for a series that will put things in perspective and help us think about how to deal with the problem." He inhaled audibly.

Watching him struggle this way was painful. His lungs were compromised even though he had quit smoking twenty years ago. But he hadn't really exercised since he left the army. After he made editor, his aerobic exercise had been provided by either sex or stairs.

April forced herself to object. "We have laws against prostitution because we don't want it."

"Prostitution has been around for thousands of years. It isn't going away. It's time to stop kidding ourselves and make it legal." He took another heavy breath.

"You're willing to accept sex slavery and teenage girls forced to sell themselves just to survive?"

"Sex with underage girls is never going to be legal. The sex slave trade is a problem for the feds," Robertson sneered. "That leaves a bunch of hookers who are creating a nuisance because they are completely out of control."

April's jaw tightened. Her eyes narrowed. "Women who are doing what they have to do to survive," April countered angrily.

He leaned back in his chair to consider his answer. A smile played across his face. "Have you talked to those women? Are you sure that prostitution is their only alternative?"

April grimaced. "No. But I can't imagine any other reason why they would submit to something like that."

"I've talked to more than a few of them," Robertson rasped. "Some of them have not bothered to look into any other options. Some of them have walked away from good jobs to become dancers, strippers, and prostitutes."

"Really?" April rolled her eyes. She muttered, "I bet you know one personally."

Robertson grinned and chuckled softly. "I have spent some time with one woman who has an MS in biotechnology and walked away from a lab position at NIH because it was boring. She's a regular at the Camelot." He paused to inhale audibly.

"She's probably the only one in existence," April said sarcastically.

Robertson suddenly became serious. "When we had troops in Vietnam, there were two types of women who serviced the men: house girls and cyclo girls or prostitutes." He paused to let that sink in. "The house girls cleaned and washed clothes. They got a set wage from each GI they took care of. The cyclo girls provided socially unacceptable services but pulled in a lot more money." Robertson inhaled heavily. "The prostitutes were in it for the money. The house girls envied the money but wouldn't stoop to selling their bodies."

"And you think the same thing is going on here?"

"There are always women who look at the money and decide that they can put up with the shit." He grinned. He had gotten his punch line in.

April scowled. "But prostitutes are exploited and they probably end up getting the short end of the financial stick in the long run."

"Everybody is exploited. Food workers are exploited." Robertson glared at April. "Why do you think there are so many illegals in the food industry?"

"No idea," she sighed.

"They're the only ones who can live on that kind of income." Robertson flashed a bright, self-satisfied smile. He leaned forward to lecture April. "Waiters and busboys in chain restaurants are exploited. And they come from the same population as prostitutes. Clerical workers are exploited." Robertson paused for another breath. His voice was rising and the words were coming faster. "Hell, my sister is exploited and she's a project manager. Her salary is based on a 40-hour work week but she averages over 60 because that's what the job requires." He paused to catch his breath. "Cops are exploited. They spend a lot of time dealing with the same social deviants that prostitutes deal with. But the cops have to file reports and make court appearances on their own time without compensation."

April moistened her lips. She rubbed her hand on her skirt and realized that she was sweating. She closed her eyes and leaned back struggling for control. A scenario began to form in her mind. She cleared her throat. "So I'm a young woman with a high school diploma and my options are scrape by on what I can make as a waitress at Olive Garden or go for big bucks as a hooker. Which do I choose?"

"What do you think?" Robertson coaxed. He seemed calmer.

"My situation is tight but I don't feel exploited. I have a family that I love and that loves me," April said reflectively. "I am not tempted." She leaned forward and looked Robertson directly in the eyes. "Besides several women who lived the life have written books. They make it clear that prostitution is not what it's cracked up to be."

Robertson's eyes bored into her. She felt completely naked. He said dismissively, "Women continue to make it their career choice. I need someone to take a fresh look at the issue. Can I depend on you?"

April stammered, "I am not sure how I could come up with a fresh slant."

"What would Nellie Bly do?" he sneered.

"Join the inmates in the nut house?"

"Exactly." His voice was cold. His stare sent chills through her body.

April winced. "I don't see how I could do that."

"Well, see what you can do. I need your answer by Thursday morning."

Robertson returned to the work on his desk. The conversation was over.

April scowled at his back. This wasn't fair. It wasn't what he said but how he said it that left her shaking. She knew that she only had this shot because Anna had asked for her. If she didn't agree to the terms and conditions, Robertson would have somebody else on it before she got back to her car. She sat there struggling to respond. Nothing came out.

She stood and said, "Okay. I'll see you Thursday morning."

She walked out of the editor's office as calmly as she could. As she made her way to the car, she carried on a running debate. The answer was obvious. It was money. Money made the world go around. Money made secretaries get up and go to work at meaningless jobs. Money made waitresses hustle. They treated customers well because they needed the tips. Money made the editor and his sister put up with the shit.

Well, maybe not. Craig Robertson could retire any time he wanted. He didn't have to worry about money. And he didn't have to put up with the shit. She was not doing this for the money. While she couldn't afford to ignore the money, she was going to do it because she had to write. It was in her DNA. Cops were probably in the same boat. They needed the money, but they went to work because an inner force drove them. She should put that on her list of future projects - "The Soul of a Cop."

As she drove off to meet her brother for lunch, the trembling subsided. A smile crept across her face. She told herself that she just needed a few friendly prostitutes with good stories.

4

APRIL MET BILL for an early lunch at the Old Georgetown Grille in Bethesda, not far from his D.C. office. He was sitting at a booth against the wall to the right of the entrance absorbed in something on his cell phone. He had developed an intimate relationship with the device. Bill was energetic and compulsively active. The cell phone gave him access to a world of things to do. It held a small library of legal references as well as documents relating to cases he was working on. It provided him access to an online legal library. It kept a copy of his schedule and a list of contacts. The most important of those contacts was Mrs. Anita Smith. Her official title was receptionist but she ran the office for Bill.

April stood beside Bill for several seconds before he looked up and greeted her with a cheery, "So you're the new flack for the sex industry?"

"God! I hope not." April laughed. "I don't want to make a career of this." She hugged him and gave him a peck on the cheek.

He went back to his work. "Have you talked to her nibs yet?"

She took a seat across from him. "The senator is my next stop."

He looked up at his sister and smiled. She was bright and bubbly. "So, what can I do for you?"

"Fill me in on what's going on at home then give me some legal background on prostitution."

A waiter took their order. They caught up on family matters while they were waiting for lunch to be served. Bill's kids were growing like weeds. Will started playing baseball this summer. Carine was teaching Karen to play tennis. The little pumpkin could volley. Sort of. April smiled at the thought of her four-year-old niece hitting a tennis ball over the net with a racket that must be as big as she was.

Bill paused to study his sister with a severe look on his face. He asked in a concerned voice, "What about Joe?"

"He's hanging tough," she said bravely. She waited while the waiter put their food on the table. She took a sip of tea and ran her fingers through her hair before focusing her gaze on her brother. "He spends his days either researching job opportunities or running to interviews. He goes to a job fair about once a week. But there are a lot more unemployed engineers than there are jobs."

"How are you guys doing financially?"

"We're going to be okay," she assured him. "How about if you tell me what you know about making prostitution legal."

"It's going to happen. It's already widespread in Europe and Asia. Australia and New Zealand are reasonably satisfied with the results of their experiments.

The majority of Americans support legalization or at least decriminalization of prostitution just as long as it's kept out of sight." He looked around and said in a conspiratorial voice. "The problem is that we are stuck with our Christian ethics and the anti-sex crowd can be very vocal."

"Does Senator Muehlberg's bill stand a chance?"

Bill shook his head. "Not this year."

April ate a bite of salad. "So why the big push?"

Bill took a bite of his sandwich and chewed thoughtfully. "In cases like this, you have to keep pounding away until the barriers start collapsing."

"And the series that I'm supposed to write?"

"Push public sentiment in the right direction."

April pursed her lips and tilted her head. "What if I come to a different conclusion?"

"You won't." He smiled broadly. "You will get to know people who are getting a raw deal and you will come out swinging."

"I'm that predictable?"

"You are. Why do you think you were selected for this assignment?"

She nibbled on her salad. She stared at her brother while she chewed. The implication that she was an easy mark bothered her but she had already agreed to take on the assignment. "What's the legal situation?"

"A 2003 Supreme Court ruling that adults have a right to engage in private, consensual sex is the sleeping dog. The court did specify that its ruling did not apply to prostitution. But the only issue is money." Bill paused to chew on a mouthful of fries. "If John and Jane have a very cozy relationship that sometimes involves sex and one night Jane shows up sobbing that she has lost her job and doesn't have any money for food or rent," Bill explained. His voice was rising. His cadence was slowing for emphasis. He sounded professorial. "There are three possible outcomes. John comforts her and they end up sleeping together before she leaves to go back to deal with her problems. Or John hands her whatever money he has. She thanks him and gives him a hug and a kiss before disappearing into the night." Bill ate another mouthful of fries and took a drink of water.

April grinned suddenly. "But if she jumps in bed with him after she takes his money?"

"That could be prostitution and an illegal act." Bill chewed on a bite of his sandwich. "Eventually, the question will be put before a court: If it's legal to give somebody money and it's legal for two people to engage in consensual sex why isn't it legal to give somebody money and engage in consensual sex with that person?"

"It is silly when you put it that way. Anything else?"

He chewed another bite of his sandwich and washed it down with ice water. "There are a couple of court cases - one in California and one in New York. The California case is already a done deal. The California Supreme Court has ruled that the state cannot prevent a disabled man from hiring prostitutes who are willing to help him with his sexual issues."

April looked up at Bill. "And the New York case?"

"A couple of women performed oral sex in public and claimed that the acts were art which is covered by the First Amendment."

"So, charges against them will probably be dropped."

"You've got it."

She nibbled on her salad and sipped her tea. "What does Carine think about the situation?"

"Her specialty is managing businesses. She believes that prostitution should be a legal business. The issues for her are how to regulate it and how to manage it so it's profitable."

"I think Joe is broad-minded enough to be comfortable with it as long as he doesn't run into hookers when he's out with the kids."

Bill smiled and nodded. "Amen."

She took a big drink of tea. She sat back and savored the ice in her mouth while she studied her brother. "Are you going to introduce me to some hookers that I can build my story around?"

He grinned and nodded. "I have a client who is willing to meet with you."

She put her fork down and rested her chin on her hands. "Is she willing to work with me?"

He returned her gaze. He hedged, "You are going to have a sales job. She wasn't enthusiastic about the situation but if she does agree to help you, she will be a real asset."

April took a deep breath and sighed. Her voice was flat. "Can I meet with her tomorrow after I get off work? I have to put my ideas together for a Thursday morning meeting."

He smiled at her and called for the bill. "I'm pretty sure that I can arrange that. I'll get back to you."

5

THE SENATOR'S OFFICE was a simple, utilitarian place. It had an outer area for the receptionist and a small inner sanctum. The inner office housed the senator's desk and computer and a couple of chairs for visitors. Senator Anna Muehlberg was sitting at her desk when April knocked at the office door.

"Come in, my dear."

Senator Muehlberg was practically an aunt. She had worked with April's father when he was in the senate. April's parents had been strong supporters of Anna Muehlberg's senate campaigns. Over the years, the Muehlbergs and the MacMahons had grown very close. April had worked as an intern for Anna and her husband, Frank, during her last two summers in high school. Even at that time, April knew that she was not going to follow her father into law and politics. She was a writer.

April pulled a chair over and sat next to the senator's desk. "Thank you for seeing me."

Senator Muehlberg looked up from her work and smiled. "Of course. You are a very important person right now. When Craig mentioned that you might be available for this project, I was very excited. You have such a wealth of knowledge, intelligence, and writing skill that I knew you were the perfect choice."

"To be honest, I don't know a great deal about prostitution and what I do know is negative. I can't imagine why we are talking about legalizing it."

Anna Muehlberg swiveled in her chair to face April directly. She focused her bright, green eyes on her protégé. There was a faint smile on her face. "Well, my dear, criminalizing it certainly hasn't worked."

April was appalled. "Does that justify putting a stamp of approval on one of the most horrific lifestyles imaginable?"

"In a way, it does," Anna Muehlberg said calmly. "We can only solve a problem if we are willing to recognize and understand it. We can only help people if we approach them as friends and recognize their potential. That cannot happen as long as we insist that they are criminals who must be punished."

"Still it's repulsive. Just the thought of a woman doing something like that makes my skin crawl." April stopped short. She had just agreed to dive into that world to get a story for Craig Robertson.

"Like what, my dear?"

April just stared back. The words were there but she couldn't bring herself to say them.

"If lewd, lascivious behavior is so awful, I must confess to being a terrible person," Anna Muehlberg continued.

April recoiled. "You were a prostitute?"

"Oh heavens no. I have been happily married for most of my life. But Frank and I were quite adventurous in our younger days."

April closed her eyes and shook her head. "That's not the same thing."

Anna Muehlberg sat for a few seconds - her thin body ramrod straight. She was direct and unyielding but not confrontational.

"Prostitution has been part of human society as far back as we can document. Temples in India are decorated with pornographic art including depictions of groping, intercourse, and even fellatio," the senator said.

She pursed her lips and gazed at the ceiling behind April for several seconds before continuing. "We have inherited the Puritan approach to sex. But realize that even the Puritans had to make concessions. They had an official documented rule that said there was no sin if the first baby was born six months after the marriage."

"That doesn't necessarily imply prostitution," April countered in a stern voice.

"Not beyond reasonable doubt," the senator conceded. "But the circumstantial evidence is compelling."

"What about under-age girls? Aren't you opening the door for sex with minors who have run away from home or are out on the street without a real job for whatever reason?"

"Regretfully, that sort of thing is a problem," Anna Muehlberg sighed. "It will continue to be a problem whether or not prostitution is legalized. But we can develop a path out of prostitution and all that it entails to a normal lifestyle once prostitution is legalized."

"Women can already transition into normal lives. Some of them write books about their experiences."

"They are rare birds. I imagine that most women who have gotten out of prostitution have found some man who was ignorant of their past or so hard up that he had to live with the knowledge." Anna Muehlberg paused to study the ceiling again. "In my experience finding a 'legitimate' job after a few years of working as a prostitute is extremely difficult."

April digested that thought. "I suppose that you have worked with women who were trying to do just that."

"Yes"

"And that's why you have decided to push for legalization?"

"That and I am convinced that the whole issue is a charade." The senator paused.

April's eyebrows arched. She shook her head. Senator Muehlberg smiled and continued, "The only people who are brought to justice for violating laws against prostitution are poor people who can't afford good lawyers and politicians."

"I've read that men aren't convicted very often," April conceded.

"The ones who are convicted are poor blacks. Do you think that anybody but you would care if Joe slept with a prostitute on one of his business trips?"

April blushed. "His employer might."

"Yes, he carries around sensitive information that he might share in an unguarded moment. But there would be no reason to throw him in jail or even fine him as long as he was engaging in sex with a consenting adult."

"You seem to have all the angles covered." April scowled. Her tone was hostile. "What do you want from me?"

"I need you to meet these women, get their stories, and present them to the reading public in a compelling way."

April felt like she was being set up. She shrugged and turned to study the plaques on the wall. "You probably have all the stories you need."

"But I am not a writer," Anna Muehlberg said sharply. "And even if I was, much of what I know is protected by attorney-client privilege."

April turned back to look at her mentor. "Then what?"

"We use the response to your articles to get an issue on the ballot in November. We generate support of our proposed legislation."

"Bill says it's not going to pass this year," April objected.

"Bill is a lawyer. He is a talented politician like his father. He can't help worrying about things like that. I expect you to be a writer who puts her passions into words and lets the cards fall where they may."

Anna Muehlberg got up from her seat and walked around her desk. She led April to the door. "Are you clear on what I want?"

April was studying her feet. She nodded slightly. "Yes."

"Can you do it?"

"I don't know."

The senator pressed, "But you will try?"

"Yes," April said without enthusiasm. It didn't matter. Senator Muehlberg would get what she wanted.

Anna leaned in very close as she walked April to the door. She spoke in a low voice, just barely above a whisper. "There is one other thing that I want you to think about."

April stopped and turned to look at her. Their eyes locked. "In the 1920s between the two wars," Anna continued. "Things began to go very badly for Jews. Not for all Jews but for the majority. My great-grandfather was in the majority. He was not poor but he certainly was not well off. He sensed that the situation would get very bad unless something drastic was done. He decided that he had to move his family to America. This was not easy but my great-grandfather was a strong, resourceful man. He brought his family here. When they arrived, they had nothing but their strength, intelligence, and determination. They also had a connection with a man from the old country who had a farm in upstate New York. He gave them a place to live and a job. They were farmers for the rest of their lives. My grandmother did not go to school. She was educated by her mother. She saw to it that her daughter and her granddaughter were educated and given every opportunity to succeed in this country. That is why I am compelled to fight for these women. They are Americans living in America and they deserve a chance to succeed."

They shook hands. April walked out without looking back. She could feel the eyes of her friend following her all the way to the hallway exit.

6

APRIL PLOPPED DOWN on Joe's lap and gave him a kiss. He was deep into Paul Young's religious fantasy, "The Shack." He put his book down and gave her a kiss. "Long day?"

"Very long. I just got off the phone with Bill. He was giving me instructions for meeting a contact tomorrow after work."

"I gathered. So, you're going to do the story?"

She sighed. "I think I will. I still need to meet with Craig Robertson on Thursday morning and sell him on the concept. Then Pat has to get me the book deal he promised."

"Book deal?" Joe lifted his eyebrows in surprise.

"Honey, we have to pull in some serious money from this project. Newspaper writing is okay as long as it's steady. I get occasional assignments. If I am going to make a go of it, I need to be writing books that sell." She looked up at him hopefully.

"And you believe a book about legalizing prostitution will sell?"

"It will if I can put in enough sex and enough heart-tugging hard luck stories to drown out the legal mumbo jumbo."

"Will you be ready to do that by Thursday morning?"

"I will be ready to make my pitch to Craig and whoever Pat is talking to. Then I'll have to hope for the best."

He looked down at her and shook his head in disbelief. She grinned up at him.

He bent over and rubbed his cheek against hers. He kissed her on the neck. "Do you know how much I love you?"

"Yes."

He nibbled at her neck. "Really. Do you have any idea how crazy I am about you?"

She nuzzled against his neck and nipped his earlobe. "A real man would take me upstairs and show me."

He scooped her up in his arms and stood up. She laughed hysterically as he charged up the stairs. At the top of the stairs, she squealed, "The lights."

"What about them?"

He pushed the bedroom door open and shut it with his foot.

7

APRIL ARRIVED AT the Chevy Chase Playground at three sharp. She spotted her contact almost immediately. The woman was a redhead about 5 foot 7, wearing khaki shorts and a khaki shirt with a green neck scarf. She was attractive but not beautiful. Her almond shaped grey-green eyes were captivating. Her face was slightly rounded. Her nose was sharp like a pyramid lying on one side. She had a wide mouth with thin lips. She could have passed for April's twin except that she was younger by several years. April could feel herself being watched and evaluated as she made her way towards the woman.

"Bridget Allen?" April said as she extended her hand.

The woman looked directly at her for the first time. She reached out reluctantly and gave April a limp handshake. "I assume that you are Bill's big sister, April."

"Yes, I am Bill's sister but I am really here about a story that I am working on," April said awkwardly.

"About prostitution and why it should be legalized," Bridget said sarcastically.

"I'm sorry. I don't mean to be putting you down." The words tumbled out. April knew she had said the wrong thing and her delivery was atrocious. She must have sounded as awkward as she felt.

The woman looked away. She seemed distracted by something on the other side of the playground. "You are, " she said without looking at April. "But not in the way you think."

April took a deep breath. She was calm and confident when she spoke. "Okay. What am I doing wrong?"

Bridget turned to confront April. "You are the poster girl for the white, middle class, soccer mom and you don't have much use for women like me."

April bit her lip and ran her hand through her hair. "That's not true."

Too confrontational. She shifted her weight and crossed her arms to keep from fidgeting.

Bridget rolled her eyes. "My livelihood depends on my ability to read people quickly and accurately. I am very good at it. You are not that good at hiding your feelings."

April looked down at her shoes. "I am not at all comfortable with the idea of sex for pay."

Bridget turned to leave. She took two steps then she turned back and said, "Maybe you should tell your editor that you can't do this story because you are going to make everyone you talk to uncomfortable."

April could feel her story getting away from her. She stepped around in front of Bridget and looked straight into her eyes. She swallowed. "I'll have to work on that because I am going to do this story." Brave words but her voice was weak.

"You understand that I only agreed to meet with you because I owe Bill a favor or two," Bridget said. She shrugged. "I don't believe this is going to work. You are going to end up reporting what you see through rose-colored soccer mom glasses."

Bridget started to walk away. April caught her arm. She said in a conciliatory tone, "Can we at least arrange for an interview so I can hear your side of the story and try to get it right?"

Something snapped. Bridget's eyes widened in disbelief. "Hearing about it isn't enough. You will never understand unless you experience it."

April recoiled. She blinked and then stammered, "That's extreme. I have no intention of trying my hand at prostitution."

Bridget grinned fiendishly and chuckled. "Artists and writers prostitute themselves every day. You've probably sold some stuff that you weren't proud of to make a quick buck."

"That's not the same thing," April retorted.

Bridget sneered, "Is pumping out trash that much easier than giving some guy a blow job?"

April blushed. "I have a husband and children to think about."

Bridget folded her arms across her chest. She studied April with a look of utter disbelief for several seconds. Then she chided, "Bill told me you were pretty good at that sort of thing."

April could feel heat spreading from her stomach to her cheeks. That was too personal. How could her brother say something like that?

Bridget's upper lip curled into a sneer. She waved her hand dismissively. "I'm not interested in creating a soccer mom's version of me. I am not going to work with someone who won't meet me halfway."

April stepped closer to Bridget. "What do you want?"

"I am not a whore, harlot, or tramp. They are sluts. Prostitutes are a cut above whores because they are conducting business," Bridget said in a firm voice. She paused to assess April's reaction. "I am a cut above the common prostitute because I provide more than a quickie experience. I am a professional entertainer. I am a surrogate companion, friend, or wife. Sometimes, I am the ultimate social worker. I help people who are having difficulty dealing with normal, everyday, sexual relationships."

April nodded her approval. "I can write that but I am going to need a couple of interviews to get the details."

Bridget crossed her arms. Her jaw was tight. Her stare, fierce and direct. "First you are going to have to walk a mile or two in my shoes."

That was too much. Why couldn't the woman just tell her story?

April wanted to scream but she managed to answer in a relatively calm voice. "What do you have in mind?"

Bridget stepped back from April and relaxed a little. "Clubs in this area have amateur night contests generally on Friday nights," she said casually. "We'll go to a few of them. We can talk about your experiences. When I'm convinced you've got the idea, we can work on the next step."

April cocked her head and arched her right eye-brow. "Just take off my shirt? No touching?"

"You'll need to take off more than your shirt. There will be more than touching when they stick tips in your garter."

April's mind was racing. She could do it. She knew that. Nellie Bly would do it without a second thought. But April did not want to do it. The idea was repul-sive. Bridget smiled and chuckled softly. "Do we have a deal?" she asked.

"I'll have to think about it," April said very quietly.

"Don't take too long. I may change my mind," Bridget warned. "There's an amateur night a week from this Friday. That would be a good opportunity to get started."

Bridget studied April as if she expected a reply. When April said nothing, Bridget continued, "I have to go. I have to pick up my sons and take them home. Get back to me in a couple of days, if you want my help."

Bridget walked towards the community center without looking back.

8

APRIL REPLAYED WHAT had just happened as she watched her contact walking away. Finally, she muttered, "I'm going to kill my stupid ass brother."

She stalked back to her car, angrily pulled on her seat belt and started the engine. Then it occurred to her that she needed to think about her next move. She turned the car off, tilted her seat back, and closed her eyes.

You neglected to mention a few things, Bill. The woman has children. You told her about my sex life. What else?

Why that woman? Surely you've got other clients I could talk to. She owes you a favor? For what? What did you do?

The woman is intelligent. Brassy. She mixes in with all the other suburban mothers like she's one of them. How does she pull that off?

Maybe you got it right, Bill. But working with her is going to be a challenge. She wants topless dancing and blow jobs? Nellie Bly might do that but April Walsh is going to draw a line. But. But I can't come up empty. Getting up on a stage and dancing around topless might be okay as long as Joe doesn't find out. This Bridget woman is going to have to give me something first. I'll have to explain the rules.

April suddenly realized that she did not know how to get in touch with the woman. That meant getting contact information from Bill. She was going to need a separate cell phone for communicating with her contacts. It would have to be a "no contract" phone. She decided to pick one up at WalMart on her way home.

April brought her seat into the full upright driving position. She started her car and headed out into the traffic.

Purchasing the phone and getting it set up took over an hour. She registered it using her birth name, Yvonne MacMahon. That was a name she hadn't used since people started calling her April thirty years ago.

By the time she reached her house, she was gripped by the sense of being caught in a deep web of conspiracy. She didn't quite know how to react when Joe greeted her at the door.

"Are you okay?"

"Yeah. I guess," April said. Her chin was drooping toward her chest. Her eyes were fixed on the floor. "I've been lost in thought trying to work out this story."

"How did your meeting go?"

"Good but not great. We have some more negotiating to do before we get down to business." She gave Joe a wan smile and kissed him on the cheek. "I have to call Bill to find out how I get in touch with her."

She started up the stairs on the way to the room that served as her home office. Halfway up, she turned and said, "Joe, just so you know, if I do get this job,

I am going to be out at night a lot. That will be the best time to meet with the girls. I will probably be spending some time at clubs interviewing women and observing what goes on."

Joe grimaced. He didn't like the idea. Those clubs were no place for a woman like his wife. The women who frequented them were there for business. It wasn't a polite social gathering. But he said, "Okay."

She continued up the stairs to her office and shut the door. She placed a call. When Bill answered, she said, "What the hell were you thinking?"

"I just did what you asked. I set you up with a woman who could give you inside information on the sex industry in this area."

"Do you know what she expects me to do to get that information?"

"I knew that she was going to be a tough nut to crack."

"Do you know that she has a son?"

April sketched Bridget with her two sons.

"She has two sons, Bill and Alex. She's divorced. Her ex has disappeared."

"Where did she get the idea that I was good at giving blow jobs?"

April started sketching herself on her knees but she couldn't finish the sketch.

"I might have mentioned that you had a reputation."

"Hearsay," April objected. "Why did you tell her that and what else did you tell her?"

"I just told her enough to convince her that you were okay. She wouldn't have met with you otherwise."

"How bad am I?"

"Just typical college girl stuff. I told her you had a couple of semi-serious relationships before you started dating Joe and that the two of you have cleaned up your acts since you've been married."

"You brought Joe into this?" Her voice rose in alarm. She sketched Joe in and drew angry circles around him.

"No. No. Just a little background. He graduated a year ahead of you and took a job in DC so you two had a long-distance relationship while you finished up college in Emmitsburg."

"Why did you tell her that?" She sketched Bill with his neck in a hangman's noose.

"Don't worry. Nothing you did is going to shock her."

"I'm not worried about shocking her," April snapped. "Did you know that I am going to have to dance topless to get her cooperation?"

"No. We didn't discuss that."

"That was her condition. I need to get back in touch with her. Can you have her call me?" April gave him the number for her new cell phone.

"So you're going to do it?"

"I didn't say that," April snapped. "I said she should contact me. I need her to give me something before we move forward."

"Alright. I'll pass the message along."

"Bill, you have to be careful what you say." April's voice softened. "I don't want my family dragged into this. And I do not want Becky or JJ hearing tales about their mother."

"Okay. My lips are sealed. But, honestly, I don't see how there is going to be a connection between Bridget and your family," Bill protested.

"My editor wants me to be the next Nellie Bly. My contact wants me to walk a mile in her shoes," April said. She sketched a jet in a nosedive. "This could get very bad very quickly."

"Alright. I'll be careful. Let me get back to work."

"Take care."

9

APRIL SPENT THE morning putting together an outline and a rough draft of her article. She needed to offer a historical perspective, contrast the current situation in her own backyard with perceived success in other countries, and come up with some good stories to generate reader sympathy. Statistics from countries with legalized prostitution were not conclusive. The value of legalization was hotly debated in online posts. On the other hand, there was no evidence that tolerating prostitution had led to any serious problems. She could write a series supporting Senator Muehlberg's bill but Bridget Allen's story was only a starting point.

The call came in around eleven. It was Bridget. "So, you're going to do it?"

"I need some assurance that this is not going to be a wild goose chase. I have to come away with some significant material for my story."

"I guarantee that you'll get more material than you can use."

"That doesn't help. It's a nice promise but it doesn't give me a warm feeling." April sketched a picture of

Bridget arms crossed, chin pushed forward, and mouth clamped shut.

"What do you want?" Bridget sounded conciliatory.

"I want to know how you went from being a housewife with two children to being an entertainer in the sex industry." April wrote *The Many Lives of Bridget Allen* across the top of her pad.

"Didn't Bill tell you about that?" Bridget sounded surprised.

"No. He believes that you are going to tell me."

Bridget hesitated. "You have to promise that you will go with me to the amateur night a week from Friday."

"Why?" April drew a sheet with a hole and part of Bridget's face showing through the hole.

"I told you I don't want a soccer mom's version of me appearing in print."

"I will go with you if my editor approves my proposal. I need your story to show him that I can get some fresh insights."

"I can give you the short version now but if you want the whole story you will have to walk a couple of miles in my shoes."

"Give me the short version." April let her irritation show in her voice.

"I started working clerical jobs as soon as I graduated from high school. You know - secretary, receptionist, typist, whatever was available. When my husband and I were both working, we were making a go of it. Since the divorce, I have been on my own. My ex hasn't sent me a single check. You can't support yourself and two children on a secretary's salary. My parents helped to keep us afloat. One night, I was at a bar with some friends. It was amateur night. I decided to give it a try. I found out I was good at it and I kinda liked it. So, I turned pro. When I found out how the escort business worked at the Tahiti, I applied and went to work there. That's about it."

"I guess that's enough. Assuming the piece is approved, where should I meet you?" April sketched parents, kids, and Bill in a circle around the headshot of Bridget. They were all connected. April had to find out how.

"I plan to pick you up and make sure that you get home safely. Is that okay?"

"I'm trying to keep my family out of this. I'd rather meet you someplace else."

"Where?"

"There's a food court at the mall up the road from my house. I can sit there and sip coffee until you show up. Call this number and I'll come out to your car."

"That will work."

"What time?"

"Between seven and seven thirty."

"I'll be ready," April said as she wrote *Mall - Friday – 7*.

"Who is Yvonne MacMahon?" Bridget asked. "I guess that's your maiden name. Where did the Yvonne part come from?"

"Yvonne is my first name. No one has called me that since I was a child. April is the only name that I ever use."

"So now you can use Yvonne as your *nom de guerre*."

"That's a pretty fancy way of putting it. I'll give you a call in a couple of days and let you know for sure. I can't do anything without my editor's okay."

10

APRIL WOKE FROM a sound sleep at five on Thursday morning. She made coffee and reviewed her presentation. The typos and nits were easy to fix. The objections and questions that leaped out at her were more challenging. She researched and wrote out responses while she waited for the rest of the family to wake up.

April jumped when she heard Joe ask, "How are you doing?"

It was as if he had materialized out of thin air. She looked up and exhaled a long breath through her pursed lips. It took several seconds to reorient. "Struggling. I want to get this over with."

"Why don't you take a shower and get dressed while I make breakfast?"

"I'm still working things out. I'll eat later."

"Time to stop working," Joe said in a firm, commanding voice. "You had your presentation ready last night. Leave it alone before you ruin it."

"I fixed a few things this morning. Now I'm looking for holes."

"That's a waste of time and energy." He put his hands on her shoulders. His thumbs kneaded her tense muscles. "Your audience will always think of something that you didn't. Your best bet is to trust your instincts. You know the material well enough to come up with good answers."

Joe put his arms around her. He held his cheek against hers. She smiled. He repeated his instructions. "Go take a shower and join us for breakfast."

She was wearing a black pants suit with a white blouse. A pearl necklace and matching earrings offset the outfit. Joe said, "Good choice. You look great."

He held her chair for her and served her pancakes and coffee. She picked at the pancakes.

"Are you okay, Mom?" Becky asked.

"Yes. I just don't feel like eating."

"Are you scared?" JJ asked.

"I guess so," April said. "I don't know exactly how to describe it. 'Anxious' might be the best word."

"But they asked you to write the article," Becky objected.

"Yes, and they can always decide they made a mistake," April fretted.

"They wouldn't do that. Would they?" Becky said.

"I hope not. I won't know for sure until the meeting is over."

"Your mom is going to be okay. It's normal to be jittery before a big presentation," Joe said. He smiled reassuringly. "There are no guarantees but they should okay the project."

His confidence was infectious.

After Joe and the kids left for the pool, April went back to her presentation. She overruled herself on some of the earlier changes. *It's always best to stick with your first idea.*

The meeting minder on her cell phone put an end to the mental anguish. She drove over to the Times-Herald for her big meeting with Craig Robertson. Two other editors and four reporters sat in on her presentation. The editors questioned whether the story was worth printing. The reporters challenged her ideas and offered their own suggestions.

Robertson let the meeting run for ninety minutes. When it was over, he led April into his office. "You've got a good start," he rasped. "I am going to let you run with this. Make sure you address the objections."

"Thank you, sir." That was weak. April was exhausted and shaky.

"I need the story by early September."

"I can give you a story by then," April said in a high, anxious voice. "But it is going to take me some time to get in-depth material. I will need to find the right women and get close to them."

"You already have one." Robertson's lip curled into a sneer. He studied her with a wide-eyed stare.

"Yes, sir, and all that she has given me is a thumb-nail sketch," April said defensively. "She has made it quite clear that she is not going to open up until she is comfortable with me."

Robertson swatted her answer away. "Reporters deal with that all the time," He said as he turned back to the work on his desk.

"These women work very hard to keep their lives and their feelings hidden from the outside world." The words came out in a rushed jumble. April forced herself to slow down. "Their johns don't want to know what they feel. Their pimps don't want to know what they feel. They probably don't want to deal with their feelings. I have to believe that penetrating those barriers is going to take time."

Robertson pivoted back to face April. "Why do we care what they feel?" He was exasperated.

"Because Senator Muehlberg believes that we must make them people we care about instead of criminals who should be punished."

He shook his head in disgust. "I want a progress report in two weeks. We should meet again at the beginning of July."

April blurted out, "I'm going to need an advance because I'm going to take time off work to focus on this."

"I can get you five hundred."

"Make it a thousand to cover my salary for the first month."

He looked at her with that wide-eyed sneer again. Then he chuckled. "Alright one thousand. I'll get the check to you in a couple of days."

She nodded and beat a retreat to the door.

April found a corner table in the Starbucks across the street from the Times building where she could sip coffee and calm herself down. She checked in with her agent Pat Connolly to talk about publishers and that book deal. He had disappointing news. The publishers wanted more information. April would have to work up a presentation that he could pass along to the ones that had expressed an interest. It would be best if she could get the presentation to him by four so he could start distributing it.

She pulled out her laptop and went to work. She didn't want to deal with her family just yet.

When she finished the presentation for the unnamed publishers, she emailed it to Pat and gave him a call to let him know it was on the way. Then she went home to her family.

11

ON FRIDAY MORNING April walked into her boss' office and informed him that she would need to take a month off. He fired her on the spot. She could take as much time off as she wanted effective immediately. He didn't need her. He had one full-time position and three part-timers.

The next several days passed quietly. The weekend routines were normal. Saturday morning started off with a swim meet. Chores took up Saturday afternoon.

Owen Stewart showed up on Saturday evening to take Becky to the movies. It was her first real date. They had gotten to know each other through the swim team. Owen was a sweet, well-mannered boy. But he would be a freshman at Duke in the fall.

When Becky got home, April had her sit in the kitchen and talk about the date. Becky had more important things to discuss. "I've been researching prostitution," she began.

"And what is your conclusion?"

"It has replaced witchcraft as a way to deal with women who don't fit in."

"Really?" April suppressed a laugh.

Becky glared. "It's been going on for thousands of years all over the world. Doesn't that make it normal? Why are we making it illegal?"

"Interesting observation," April said.

"There are dozens of different types of prostitutes. If a man is rich enough, he can have his own private prostitute. She's called a mistress." Becky sounded as if she was lecturing one of her students.

"Yes. That is common knowledge," April conceded. "But we believe that sex should be associated with love. If you are paying for it or being paid for it, something is wrong."

"Why? Sex was around along time before love and marriage were invented."

"Robbery and murder have been around just as long. Do you want to make them legal?"

Anger flitted across Becky's face. She snorted. Then replied in a flat, controlled voice, "Prostitution doesn't really hurt anybody."

"It might if it's your husband who is paying another woman for sex," April countered in a calm, reasonable tone.

Becky was livid. "So that makes a prostitute a dangerous woman just like a witch?"

April was surprised by her daughter's ferocity. "Witchcraft, like all magic, is an illusion. It only works on people who believe. Marriage is a long-term relationship. It only works if both parties are fully committed."

"Marriage is another illusion that only works for believers," Becky shot back. She was still in full attack mode. "It's a control mechanism. Humans are not naturally monogamous."

"In this country, monogamy is the best way to form stable families that are capable of bringing children into the world and caring for them until they are able to take care of themselves," April said in her best parental voice. She knew she was coming across as condescending.

"Marriage isn't always a relationship between two people," Becky objected. "Polygamy is fairly common. In Europe, it is common for a man to have a relationship with one or more women besides his wife. In the Old Testament, Jacob had two wives. Abraham had concubines. David had multiple wives. Solomon, the wisest man in the world, had a hundred wives."

"Which is a good reason to question whether he was really wise," April deadpanned. "Any man who tries to deal with a hundred women at one time is insane."

"Be serious, Mom." Becky was pissed off. She heaved a big sigh. "You win. I'm going to bed."

April studied her daughter as she walked away -- erect, bone-thin shoulders pulled back, head held high, and eyes focused straight ahead. It was a dignified exit. She had acquitted herself well but she was thinking dangerous thoughts. The challenges were just beginning.

April forgot about her new phone until Tuesday morning. She had several voicemails and a couple of texts from Bridget. April's reply text said, *Sorry. Not used to Yvonne. It's a go. C U Friday nite.*

April waited until Friday to let Joe in on her plans. He had left the kids at the pool after swim practice and returned home to make some phone calls.

"I'm going to have to go out tonight," April said.

"To talk to somebody? Where are you going?"

"I've been in contact with a stripper. She is taking me to the club where she works so I can see what goes on and perhaps set up some other contacts." April looked down and shoved her hands in her hip pockets. Her right foot snuffed out an imaginary cigarette butt. "I'm not sure exactly where we are going. I completely forgot to ask where she works. I'll have my phone with me. I can call you if I run into any trouble." She raised her eyebrows and looked up like a puppy expecting to be scolded.

"Is this place in DC, Virginia, Maryland? Do you have any idea at all?"

"I'm pretty sure it's local."

"Did she say anything about an amateur night contest?" Joe sounded suspicious. He was staring at his wife.

April's cheeks flushed. "Yes. As a matter of fact, she did."

"Are you thinking about trying it?"

April could feel her cheeks redden. "The thought had crossed my mind but I don't think I would have the nerve."

"I would hope that you have better sense," Joe warned. "You are doing a story about prostitution. You don't have to become one."

"Joe, we have been together for 15 years. You know me better than that." She paused to study the floor. "No. Absolutely not. But I'm pretty sure that I'm going to have to push some boundaries to get what I need for this story." Then she added as an afterthought,

"At some point, I may get up on a stage and dance with no top."

Joe stormed off. He was too upset to continue the conversation. April wasn't surprised. That was how he reacted whenever she stepped out of bounds. She folded her arms across her chest and stared after him as he retreated to his man cave. She tapped her toe on the floor and mumbled, "Of course you know about the amateur night contests. You know all about those bars. You visited every one of them while you were down here without me. That was okay for you. I'll bet you even dated the women who got up there and strutted their stuff. But God forbid that your wife should put on a show for other men."

After dinner, she said goodbye to the kids and made them promise to go to bed on time. She knocked on the door to Joe's office and said, "I'm going. I'll see you when I get home." She walked out the front door and headed for her meeting at the mall.

12

BRIDGET HAD A car full of surprises. The rear door on the passenger side opened for April. As she got seated, Bridget swiveled in her seat so she could look back at April. "Yvonne, this is my friend, Ed, and his friend, Jeff."

A big, bulky man sat in the driver's seat. He seemed to have short, black hair and a dark complexion. April decided that was probably Ed.

A younger man with long hair tied back in a pony-tail was nestled in the back seat. That was probably Jeff. He extended his right hand. "Yvonne, I am pleased to meet you."

April shook his hand. "Likewise."

"Girls don't go to these things unaccompanied unless they're pros," Bridget said.

"I thought this was amateur night," Yvonne replied. She could feel the hairs on the back of her neck. Her skin was tingling.

"That's what it's called," Bridget said noncha-lantly. "But the regulars dance as well. Some pros claim to be amateurs so they can join the contest. It's an opportunity to pick up a little extra cash. The real amateurs get up there because their boyfriends get off on it."

Yvonne pushed aside thoughts of Joe and asked, "Are you going to dance tonight?"

"I don't think so." Bridget turned to the front and buckled her seatbelt.

The bar was called the Beaver Dam. It was nearly full when they arrived. Perhaps 20 women were sprinkled around. Some of them looked like they belonged. Others seemed to be attached to a young man. They were young and fresh-faced. One woman was up on the stage cavorting about in a G-String. She wore platform shoes with two-inch heels. When one of the men at the edge of the stage held up some money, she would sashay over, shake her butt in his face and bend down so he could stick the bill in the garter on her right leg. Yvonne grimaced. That wasn't what she had been expecting.

Bridget got them signed up for the contest. She advised the guy taking down the names that she did not want to dance but she was putting her name in just in case. The man, who obviously knew Bridget, told her he might need her. She shrugged.

Bridget took Yvonne back to the dressing room to change her outfit. Yvonne was wearing a bikini under a sporty blouse and a knee-length skirt. Bridget decided the blouse was okay but the bikini top had to go. After some discussion and a couple of practice runs, Yvonne agreed to hand the top over to Bridget for safe-keeping. They swapped Yvonne's skirt for a very short wrap around that Bridget had brought along.

"There is a big group of girls tonight," Bridget said. "Two of them are pros. They'll look good and wow the guys. Most of the others will be scared, awkward and praying for the music to finish so they can go hide. You'll fit right in."

The contest started at nine. Yvonne went last. She had downed three rum and Cokes by the time she had to get up on stage. A sea of gawkers surrounding the stage focused their undivided attention on her. It was terrifying. She was vaguely aware that the music had started and began to move her body. She felt clunky. Unbuttoning her blouse was an incredibly difficult task. She circled the stage once playing with her unbuttoned blouse to show and then hide her boobs. When she threw off her top, she could see that guys wanted to give her money but she couldn't figure out what to do about it. All that she could think about was how awkward and stupid she must look. Suddenly the music stopped. The emcee came on stage to thank her for the dance. The contest was over and the winner would be announced in 15 minutes.

Bridget met her at the bottom of the steps and shepherded her back to the dressing room. Yvonne was shaking.

"You did fine," Bridget assured her.

It took several minutes to get Yvonne back into her street clothes. They decided she should have one more drink to help her calm down before returning home.

When they pulled alongside April's car in the mall parking lot, Bridget got out to talk with her. "There's another one next week. Are you up for it?"

"I don't know. I felt horrible up there."

"Because you took your clothes off?"

"No. All those people were watching me and expecting me to perform but I couldn't."

"Being alone on stage is scary for everybody. You learn to deal with it by getting up there. Once the music starts, nothing else matters."

"I don't know."

"You want to write about women who fuck strangers. How are you going to do that if you can't even get up on a stage and perform for one song?"

"Alright. I will probably do it. I'll let you know."

As soon as she walked through the door of her house, Joe's face tightened into an angry mask. "You did it. Didn't you?"

"Yes"

"How was it?"

April was blushing. She could feel the heat in her cheeks. "Terrible."

"You can sleep on the couch tonight." Joe stalked off to the bedroom.

13

THE FIRST DANCE was horrific. Thinking about it the next morning made her sick but she couldn't stop thinking about it. She had strutted around half-naked in front of a roomful of men. Guilt and shame burned through her body and soul.

Joe had known immediately. He could probably see that she was drunk. It would have been easy for him to guess why. But the guilt trip that he laid on her had backfired. It was the antidote for her self-loathing. She raged against his anger. How could he pay women to take off their clothes for him and then get angry when she took her clothes off? He didn't think he was cheating when he did it. Why should it be cheating when she did it?

Joe had calmed down by Sunday morning. He did ask her if she had gone to confession as they were getting into the pew before Mass. She nodded. That was a lie - one more sin she would have to atone for.

April texted Bridget on Monday morning to say that she would be dancing Friday night. While Joe and the kids were at swim practice, she shopped at Walmart for the makings of a Daisy Duke costume, including thongs and a bra that would come off easily. Over the next four days, she practiced walking around the house in a thong and platform shoes while Joe and the kids were at swim practice.

Late Friday afternoon, she cornered Joe and informed him that she was going to another amateur night.

His eyes bored into her. The muscles in his jaw were clenched so tightly they twitched. "Are you going to dance?"

"Yes."

"You're a married woman. You shouldn't be doing that stuff." It was understated anger intended to let her know who was boss.

"I have to learn about that stuff." Her voice was quiet, reasonable but her jaw was set. She folded her arms across her chest and returned his stare. She wasn't backing down.

"There's nothing interesting to learn."

Her eyes narrowed. Her voice was cutting. "Which you know because you have spent a lot of time and money getting educated."

"That was before we were married."

"And while we were engaged to be married?" April sneered.

He looked at his feet. He said nothing. There was no point in getting into that again.

She burned with anger and resentment but she kept her voice calm. "Before we were married I stayed away from those places because I was a nice girl. The kind you wanted to marry. Now I need to know about the other kind of girl and I intend to find out."

"Be careful. There are lines that you don't want to cross," he said in a threatening voice.

"I love you. I do not want to jeopardize what we have. But this is something that I have to do. You have crossed every line in the book. Don't act so offended when I cross a few."

"You can trust me when I go out the door whether it's to work or on a trip around the world. I expect to be able to trust you."

"I have my job to do just like you have yours. I vowed to love you for better or worse in sickness and health until death do us part. That hasn't changed. You are the man I love." She paused as she studied her husband. She could feel the anger and frustration that he was holding in. "But right now my job is requiring me to do some things that we did not anticipate 15 years ago."

"That sounds like you are saying that I can't trust you," he growled.

"I am asking you to trust me just like I have trusted you over the last 15 years."

Joe closed his eyes, pressed his lips into a tight line, and shook his head. "You are obviously going to do whatever you want. Be careful. There are things that I will not put up with."

He turned and walked toward the garage to do some work while he cooled off. She called after him, "I'll see you later tonight."

He turned back. He nodded slightly as he studied her. "I'll be here making sure our kids are taken care of."

14

YVONNE WALKED FROM the mall across the parking lot to Ed's car and got in. She was wearing a fluffy sweater, a wrap-around maxi skirt, and pumps. Her Daisy Duke costume was in the large purse that she carried. As soon as she was settled, the car pulled off into the night. "I hope you don't mind if I change, Jeff," she said playfully

He grinned and shook his head. "No problem. Have at it."

She produced a pair of raggedy hot pants from her purse and made a little show of pulling them up over her hips before removing her skirt. She checked to make sure that Jeff was watching as she swapped shoes and dragged the fingers of her left hand up her thigh. The slit in her shorts went all the way up to her hip joint. Jeff nodded appreciatively.

She pulled her sweater off revealing a sleeveless denim top. She kept her eyes focused on Jeff while she methodically unbuttoned the top, rolled the waist halfway up her midriff and tied the ends into a knot.

"You've come a long way in just one week," he said. He took a dollar bill and folded it twice long ways. He hooked his left index finger into her bra and pulled to expose her cleavage. Then he stuck the dollar bill into the opening.

She recoiled when Jeff reached for her. She was shocked when he hooked her bra and pulled. But a thrill shot down her spine and into her crotch when he pushed the dollar bill into her chest. His hand casually slid up her chest and brushed against her cheek before he pulled back into his corner. She looked down and pressed her hands against her knees to regain her composure.

When she could look at him again, she asked, "Where do you work, Jeff?"

"Big Mike's Service Center. I am officially an auto mechanic but I do a little of everything."

"How long have you been working there?"

"A little over three years."

"And before that?"

Jeff did not answer. Yvonne said, "I'm sorry. I'm turning this into an interrogation. I just want to get to know you."

She could not see his face. It was too dark. His voice was thick with emotion when he spoke. "I assumed that Bee had filled you in. I went into the army right out of high school. I graduated in June 2001 three months before the attacks on the World Trade Center. A lot of guys got real patriotic and wanted payback. They signed up to fight. I happened to talk to a recruiter who knew me. He talked me into signing up for wheeled vehicle maintenance. He said that once the army hit the ground over there, they were going to need people to keep the vehicles running. He said guys with my skills would be crucial to winning the war. I got over to Afghanistan about a year later and I was still there when Bush re-deployed us to Iraq. I agreed to extend for a year in exchange for a promotion to staff sergeant. By the end of that year, I was tired of it. I came home and started looking for work. Big Mike's Service Center is where I ended up. You?"

Yvonne was stunned. He was a child. A man-child. But a child nonetheless. She couldn't tell him that she was married with children in 2001. She had to come up with something quick and hope it didn't contradict the story that Bridget had told them.

Yvonne focused her gaze on Jeff's face hidden in the darkness. She mustered all the sincerity she could find. "It's been a rough year. I spent most of last year going through a divorce. It was finalized in March. Then I was fired. I'm trying to put the past behind me and start over."

It was a decent sell job. Jeff said politely, "I'm sorry to hear that." There was nothing more to say. They rode the rest of the way in silence.

The conversation picked up again in the bar. Ed worked as a bouncer at the Tahiti. He had knocked around trying out different jobs for a couple of years after retiring from the Marines in 2003. He found a home at the Tahiti. He had met Jeff through a motor-cycle club for vets.

The two pros from last week's competition were back for this one. They came over to say hello to Bridget and her friends. One sat on Ed's lap. The other one sat on Jeff's lap and flirted with him. She asked him if his girlfriend was planning on turning pro.

Yvonne responded testily, "I haven't decided what I am going to do."

Yvonne nursed a couple of drinks while waiting for her turn to perform. When she got up on stage and started "dancing," she was able to focus on faces in the crowd instead of zoning out. One of the pros gave her a thumbs up. She spotted a man at the edge of the stage holding out a bill as soon as she bared her boobs. She worked her way over to him in bent down so he could stick his dollar bill in her garter. It was almost like genuflecting. His fingernail nicked her leg when he pulled on the garter. He let his fat, sweaty palm linger on her thigh after he had deposited the bill. She couldn't help but notice that he reeked of beer and cigarettes. Her internal breathalyzer said that he was in no condition to drive home.

As she straightened up, she lifted her bra straight up above her head. She twirled around as she circled the stage. More bills were being offered along the edge of the stage. She went from man to man collecting the offerings and suffering affronts with a smile.

When the music stopped, she blew kisses to the crowd, grabbed her clothes, and beat a retreat back to her friends. There was a little residual interest in Yvonne even though the next contestant was starting to perform. A waitress brought Yvonne a drink and pointed out a man sitting by himself a few tables away. He held up a twenty. She smiled and shook her head. She mouthed, "No. Thank you."

On the way back to the car, Ed asked if he could get a picture of Yvonne. She said fiercely, "I don't want my picture taken. I don't want it posted on the internet."

Ed recoiled as if he had been slapped. "I wouldn't post it," he apologized. "I was just thinking that we could use a waitress at the Tahiti. I would like to show my boss a picture of you in that outfit. He's always interested in good looking women who aren't afraid to show some skin."

"I...I'll need to think about it," Yvonne stammered.

Yvonne pulled on her sweater and skirt before climbing into the car and changing her shoes. When Ed pulled up beside her car in the mall parking lot, both she and Bridget got out.

"Did you really get fired?" Bridget asked.

The question caught Yvonne by surprise. She hesitated but answered nonchalantly, "Yes. When I asked for some time off to work on this story, they canned me."

"Ed's right. You could get a job at the Tahiti. Do you have any experience as a waitress?"

Yvonne tensed and scowled at Bridget. "Didn't Bill tell you?"

Bridget said nothing.

"I worked at Hooters a couple of summers."

Bridget took Yvonne's hand and squeezed gently. "Think about it. If you decide to apply, Ed and I will vouch for you."

"How is that going to work? All my identification is for April Walsh so I can't apply as Yvonne MacMahon."

"You can change the name on your social security card. Take the money you picked up tonight and get a bank account for Yvonne MacMahon. Apply for a credit card." Bridget paused to scan the sky. Then she continued in a conspiratorial voice, "Tell the Tahiti that you are applying under your maiden name because there are problems at home and you are worried about your husband finding out what you are doing. Most of the women down there are hiding from some sort of domestic situation. I can explain it to Ed. You will have to handle Jeff."

Yvonne had picked up about fifty dollars thanks to some generous men. That was hardly enough to open a bank account. "I'll let you know."

"This would be a good opportunity for you to get your foot in the door and start meeting the women you're interested in," Bridget urged.

"Thanks," Yvonne said absently. Her mind had already moved ahead to the confrontation waiting for her at home.

15

APRIL FELT HIS anger as soon as she walked into the house. He was sitting on the couch rigid and stone-faced. It brought back memories from long ago. They were not yet engaged. They had just started dating. She was a junior at Mount St. Mary's in Emmitsburg. He was a senior at Johns Hopkins in Baltimore about an hour away. He had shown up at her dorm unexpectedly and caught her messing around with another guy. Joe hadn't said a word. He had just turned and stalked out. Ever the pleaser, she raced after him. She got into the car seconds after he did. He sat in a silent rage. She tried to talk to him. He ignored her. She tried cuddling up to him and kissing him like a puppy dog. When she noticed he was getting hard, she reached down and stroked his cock. He relaxed a little. She unzipped his pants and gave him a blow job. That did the trick. He had taken her out to dinner and dancing. They screwed until the wee hours of the morning. She could do it again if she had to.

She kicked off her shoes, pulled off the sweater, and dropped her skirt. She walked over to him, shedding the sleeveless denim top as she went. He refused to acknowledge her. She knelt at his feet and put her head in his lap. She kissed his penis. Her hands slid up his chest, over his face, and into his hair. "I'm here for you, baby."

She crawled up on his lap straddling his legs. She kissed his neck and rubbed her cheek against his. With her boobs inches from his face, she removed her bra. She pressed her bare breast against his cheek. She rubbed her cheek against his and kissed his neck. She whispered in his ear, "I'm all yours, baby."

She reached down between her legs and unzipped his pants. His cock hardened as she caressed it. His face remained impassive but the rest of his body was responding.

She slid off his lap and pushed her hot pants and her thong to the floor. She pushed her pussy up against his stiffening cock and began to work up and down. She could feel herself getting wet. The musky scent of sex reached her nose. Joe moaned, "Oh Christ."

He locked her to his chest with his right arm. He stood up lifting her without any apparent effort and carried her up the stairs to their bedroom. He threw her onto the bed and piled on top of her.

16

THE ACTIVITIES AND the pace on Saturday morning were driven by the weekly swim meet. April was acutely aware of Joe. He was affectionate but silent. She was sure that their lovemaking had left him feeling pretty good. But he was still upset about the amateur night contests. He would have to work through it. She wasn't ready to stop. She was excited about the waitress job at the Tahiti. That might be better for everybody.

After the swim meet, he dragged her into the bedroom and made love to her. It was their best sex in a long time. She was just about to crawl on top of him for another round when the kids started fighting downstairs. Joe jumped up, sliding into his work pants on his way to the bedroom door. He yelled, "I'll be down in a minute. I just need to get my shoes on." He turned and looked at April. They both laughed.

They woke a little early on Sunday morning. He pulled her close for a kiss. As she lay with her head on his chest, her hand crept down and began caressing his cock. It stiffened. He stiffened. His breathing became shallow. His eyes closed as he focused on the sensations she was creating. At first, he squeezed her butt. Then he pushed on her head. She bent down to his cock and took it in her mouth. She worked it rhythmically until the cum exploded in her mouth. She gagged.

It took her several seconds to swallow it all. She worked her way up his body kissing his stomach and chest. When she got to his ear, she whispered, "Do I have to go to confession?"

He burst out laughing.

17

BY MONDAY MORNING, April had a plan. As soon as Joe took off with Becky and JJ for swim team practice, she went to work. First stop was the bank to open an account for Yvonne A. MacMahon. Second stop was the social security office to change the name on her account. The clerk advised her to apply online. The process was simple.

April still had time to look for a dance instructor. She found the one she wanted on the first try. Nailah Shafaq got right down to business. "How may I help you?" She had a husky Middle Eastern voice.

"I'm interested in pole dancing," April said. She began sketching a stage with a pole near the front.

"I have a class starting next week. You already know that because you visited my website to get this number. Why did you call instead of just signing up for the class?" Nailah sounded as if April's call was a bother.

"I'm in a hurry. I was hoping that I could arrange for private instruction." April sketched herself hanging from the pole by her left hand and knee.

"How big a hurry?"

"I would like to be ready to get on stage in about two weeks."

"You are going to be pole dancing on stage?"

"Not exactly. I don't think they have a pole on the stage." April put an 'X' over the bottom of her pole.

"So you are going to be stripping to entertain the men?"

"Yes." April sketched in a crowd of men near the front of the stage.

"I can help you. When can you come in?"

"Any morning between 9:30 and 11:30."

Nailah paused to check her calendar. "I am busy tomorrow morning. Can you come Wednesday at 10?"

"Yes."

"My rate is fifty dollars per hour."

"Okay." April wrote, *Wed 10 $50.*

"I will see you Wednesday morning," Nailah said and hung up.

The abrupt end to the call stunned April. She shook her head and shrugged.

The final step of the plan was coordination with Bridget. April called using Yvonne's phone. The call went directly to voicemail. April left a message saying that she was interested in the waitress job but she would have to put things off for a week because she had to celebrate July Fourth with her family.

Bridget replied immediately with a text. *Nd 2 Know ASAP can U interview W or Th*

Time? April shot back.

11

Thursday

Bridget texted a confirmation. *Tahiti Th @ 11*

April signed off. *Roger and out.*

18

THE SEXY LADY'S Dance Studio was a re-purposed store on Wilson Avenue in Arlington near the Rosslyn Metro Station. The reception area, which was fully visible from the street, was separated from the studio itself by a wall. The studio was a large open area with offices at the back. Curtains hanging from the ceiling could be used to divide the studio into smaller spaces to accommodate smaller classes or even private dance instruction.

Nailah Shafaq was very young when her parents brought her to America from Beirut in the sixties. Vestiges of her native accent and mannerisms stayed with her. She was warm, friendly, and no-nonsense. "Whether you succeed or not is up to you. I can show you some basics. You will have to master them. You should practice for one hour, twice each day. Practice the moves at least one hundred times every day."

"I don't know about 100 reps but I can put in a couple of hours each day."

"Good. Are you trying out for a position as a professional or is this just for your husband's birthday?"

April hesitated. "I'm trying to best a girlfriend in an amateur competition."

"Topless dancing at one of the clubs?" Nailah was familiar with the scene.

April nodded. "Yes."

"Have you tried it before?"

April held up two fingers. "Twice."

"How was it?"

"It went okay. As soon as I took my bra off, the guys started going nuts," April said. "But I felt awkward and clunky like I was walking around in cement shoes."

"Most of those men do not care what you do as long as you are naked. But for you and me, it is important to get it right. I was a professional dancer for several years. I gave it up when I got married but I believe that we should always be sexy. Dancing helps. Take off your shoes and your shorts. When the music starts, show me how you dance while you are taking off your top."

April slipped out of her shoes and dropped her shorts while Nailah started the music which sounded a little like Bolero. April tried to imagine a room full of men with the stage in the center. She began circling her imaginary stage as she unbuttoned her blouse and removed it.

She unhooked her bra and held it straight up over her head as she twirled around until Nailah said, "Stop. That is enough. Put your bra and your blouse back on."

Nailah restarted the music and donned a blouse while she walked over to join April. "You are very much a beginner. Do not be discouraged. In ten days you will be good, if not very good. You have the right spirit.

This time keep your bra on. I do not want anyone to accidentally see you and be shocked."

For the next ten minutes Nailah led April around the floor. They walked up and down and zig-zagged across while playing with their blouses. The music changed every couple of minutes. The rhythm of their movements changed with the music. April was breathing hard by the time they stopped to rest. After a short break, Nailah started basic belly dancing exercises. When the hour was up, Nailah said, "These exercises are very good for everything. Can you walk with a book balanced on your head?"

"I'm not sure. I could at one time."

"Practice that as well." Nailah smiled. "You can tell your lover that you are on a new exercise routine to spice up your love life. I would like you to come back on Monday at ten."

"I can do that."

"Can?"

"I will be back here Monday at ten. In the meantime, I will practice diligently."

"Do not be too serious. Have fun but make sure you practice."

19

ON THURSDAY MORNING, April had told Joe that she had an eleven o'clock meeting in DC with a contact to discuss the sex trade. She did not mention that she would be applying for a job at the Tahiti. April arrived at the establishment just as the lunch crowd was beginning to gather. Ed spotted her and took her back to Mr. Adrien Gautier's office. He was one of the business partners in DC Artists and Entertainment, Inc, the Tahiti's parent company.

April walked over to his desk and shook hands with him. "Mr. Gautier, I am Yvonne MacMahon."

"Ed and Bee have already told me a little about you. They think very highly of you. But I want to be up front with you. We have all of the full-time waitresses that we need at the moment. We do keep a stable of part-time wait staff on our books. If you should decide to join us on a part-time basis, I believe that we would be able to keep you busy but the hours would be unpredictable."

"I see. Well, I am open to that. I need to get back to work."

"Great." Adrien smiled and gestured for Yvonne to take a seat. "Can you tell me about yourself? Have you ever worked in a restaurant?"

She sat and leaned forward, clasping her hands on her thighs. "I worked at Hooters in the summers when I was in college. I have been a working mother for the last 10 years. Most recently, I was employed by the Smith Printing Company as a clerk doing data entry, typing, filing, and occasionally sitting in for the receptionist."

"Why did you leave your job with Smith Printing Company?"

"I was let go," Yvonne said. She kept her gaze focused on his eyes. "Work had slowed down and they were trimming staff starting with part-timers like me."

"This job would be a big change."

"I can handle it," Yvonne assured him.

"Does it matter to you whether you are working days or nights?"

"What's the difference?"

"The day shift goes from 9 to 6 with an hour off for lunch and breaks. The night shift goes from 5:30 to 2:30 with breaks when necessary and convenient. The tips are better at night."

"The day shift would probably work better but I can handle either one."

"Would you be able to come in next week? That would give us a chance to check each other out."

"I have a couple of appointments but nothing I can't work around."

"Tuesday, Wednesday, and Thursday are the slow days. I'll give you a call on Monday or Tuesday and let you know when we would like you to come in."

"I look forward to hearing from you."

"We also cater parties and get-togethers. We could probably use you from time to time to help with that."

"As a server?"

"Food preparation, setting up, serving, and cleanup."

"Sure. That sounds great." She wondered if that last bit was too 'over the top.'

"One last thing. How do you feel about adult entertainment?"

"I only know what I've heard. I'm okay with it as long as I am not expected to participate."

"This is a Gentlemen's Club with topless-bottomless dancers as well as a restaurant." His expression was serious. He was watching for her reaction. "We do not allow prostitution but the sex is explicit and occasionally borderline. Waitresses keep their clothes on just as they do at Hooters. I believe the work environment here is raunchier than the one at Hooters. Sometimes it is much raunchier. We would expect you to be able to tolerate some offensive behavior without overreacting."

"I see." April was disturbed. She knew that her voice betrayed her.

Adrien acknowledged her feelings. "Some women find this atmosphere too rough others enjoy it. We will need to see where you are on that scale before we actually hire you."

"But you will pay me if you call me in to work?"

"Of course," Adrien said. "We will set up a temp arrangement that allows us to pay you one shift at a time. If things work out for all parties, we will offer you a permanent position."

"Sounds fair."

Adrien walked over to her and reached out to shake her hand. "Is it okay if we just call you Eve?"

"Yes." She rose to leave. "I look forward to hearing from you."

"See you next week, Eve."

When April got home, she told Joe that the meeting had gone well. As a matter of fact, it had led to a job interview.

"What kind of job?" Joe asked.

"Waitress."

"I thought you needed time to work on this story."

"It's only part-time right now," April said. "DC Entertainment has a number of restaurants and a catering business. They need part-time waitresses to fill in for regulars all the time. They call me, and if I'm not too busy, I go to work. If I have something big, I tell them I can't make it."

"You're sure?"

April sat on her husband's lap. She put an arm around his neck and gave him a kiss. "Joe, we can't afford to pass up money right now. Besides, I am probably going to need a job after I submit this story. This gives me a foot in the door."

"But waiting tables?" Shock registered on his face.

"I've done it before. The tips can be pretty good."

"That was Hooters when you were in college," he objected.

She jumped up and stood over him with her hands on her hips. "What are you saying?"

"You have left those days in the dust," Joe said innocently.

"Meaning what?" She challenged.

"You're no spring chicken."

"I'm old and ugly?"

"You're one of the best-looking women on the planet," he blurted out. "But you're way past nineteen."

"Are you out there looking for a younger model?" She sounded upset.

"No," Joe said defensively. "Look, if you think this is the right way to go, I'm for it 100 percent."

"You better be and you better apologize if you expect me to make dinner tonight."

April turned away and marched off to her office.

20

APRIL'S FIRST ORDER of business was checking the messages on her cell phone. She had left it at home while she was playing Yvonne at the Tahiti. Pat Connolly had important news and needed to talk to her right away. Senator Andy Edwards, another family friend, wanted to discuss her article on prostitution as soon as possible.

She decided to deal with Senator Edwards first. He had probably heard rumors about her article. He certainly knew about Anna Muehlberg's plan to submit a bill legalizing prostitution.

When his receptionist answered, April said, "This is April Walsh returning the Senator's call. Is Andy available?"

"Please hold." That was followed by a minute of silence before a hearty male voice came on. "April, thank you so much for calling back. I know you must be busy."

She paused to take a deep breath while she considered her response. "Fortunately, I am busy but never too busy to chat with an old friend."

"I'll get right to the point, April. I have heard that you are working on a multi-part story on prostitution in this area."

"Yes. It should be coming out in the Times-Herald in September."

"And the gist of that story will be that prostitution should be legalized?"

"No. I am not writing a story that advocates legalizing prostitution. I plan on presenting an in-depth view of the sex industry that will feature some of the individuals involved," April said. "I believe the take away will be that these women are doing what they have to do to survive."

"You're not certain about what your story will say?" His tone was condescending. He wanted to provoke her.

"I have just begun my investigation," she replied calmly. "The story will be as much a revelation to me as it will be to the rest of the world."

"But Anna Muehlberg did request that the story be written and that you be the writer," the senator objected.

"I don't know how that worked. I wasn't there." April sketched a picture of the senator pounding his fist on his desk.

"I worked with your father to get rid of prostitution," Edwards reminded her. "It was a blight in this area. Fourteenth Street in DC was a notorious open sewer of sex and filth. We have cleaned up areas like that and we don't want them back."

"I agree with you," April assured him. She sketched a couple of hookers standing on a sidewalk. "Joe and I find that kind of stuff repulsive. We don't want Becky and JJ subjected to it every time they leave the house. We certainly don't want tourists thinking a red-light district represents our nation's capital."

"But it sounds like you believe that the prostitutes have a case."

"Apparently they do. You need to talk to Bill about that. He's the lawyer."

"Are you really going to overlook their whoring just because you feel sorry for them?" Edward asked in a tone of exaggerated disbelief. He was trying to get under her skin.

April closed her eyes and answered in a flat voice, "I believe that is a pretty good summary of the situation." She added fire and brimstone under his desk in her sketch.

"Then as a card-carrying liberal, you are going to ask the public to pitch in and rescue them."

"I have just started my investigation." Her voice was cold and hard. "I have talked to one woman who had to give up her nine to five job because she couldn't make enough to feed her family on her salary."

April added Bridget and her boys to the sketch. She continued, "You, as a card-carrying conservative, deeply committed to the sanctity of the family, should agree with me that any solution we come up with must provide her with the resources to take care of her family."

Edwards was unsympathetic. "She's trying to make it on a high school diploma. What happened to her husband?"

"I don't know. I gather that being around him was hazardous to her health." April sketched in the fugitive husband.

"He should still be paying child support." Edwards was smug.

"He should be but he isn't. You need to fix that problem before you go after the prostitutes," April retorted.

He ignored her. "She should go back to school and get a college degree so she can get a better job."

"She can't afford rent or food for her family. How is she going to pay for college?"

"That does not justify prostitution."

April sketched a face with eyes narrowed and teeth bared. She took a deep breath and sighed. "Andy, you're too intelligent to miss the point. These issues are all interrelated. You can't fix them one at a time. How many prostitute sweeps were conducted in the past year? Was it two or three?"

"Three."

Edwards had just served up a home run ball. April shook her head. She could not believe it. "What makes you think that the fourth one or the fifth one is going to solve the problem when the first three failed?"

"We can keep it up longer than they can," he said in a gruff voice.

"Prostitution was around when your ancestors were building Stonehenge. It will still be around when you and I are dead and buried." She added Stonehenge to her assemblage. "I get your point and you know that I am going to write my story the way I see it. Have a good afternoon. I have more phone calls to make."

She was furious. She paced around the room re-playing the conversation. Andy Edwards was simply refusing to engage in a meaningful dialogue.

April stopped pacing and folded her arms across her chest. She glared at the phone. "You know the situation, Andy. You could sit down and write this piece tonight. You just refuse to admit that this story has more than one side. You aren't going to let facts get in your way."

She studied the ceiling as if some answers might be written up there. She had defended Bridget without knowing the whole story. That bothered her. She wanted a drink - gin and tonic, rum and Coke, or maybe the bottle of Irish whiskey.

21

SHE CALLED PAT after she had calmed down. He answered in his exaggerated Irish brogue, "April, how are ye? Thanks for gettin' back t' me."

She closed her eyes and shook her head. "I have had better days."

"I'm thinkin' I can help wi' that."

"You've found a publisher for my book?" She was exuberant.

"Aye. He's quite excited about a report from within 'The Belly of the Beast.'"

"That's a very high bar," April cautioned. She sketched a leprechaun with horns and a pitchfork.

"But ya said ya were goin' t' walk in their shoes. Ya haf to make this story personal."

"I know," she sighed. "But I'm not sure how to do that without destroying myself."

"Are ye gettin' cold feet?"

"I'm being realistic. Jack Abbot spent his whole life in prison and when he got out, he was one fucked up individual. I've got about four more weeks and I hope to be normal when this is all over."

"Ya haf t' be committed, lass. Ya haf t' be willin' to get yer hands dirty. There are books by hookers and there are books by do-gooders who made friends with hookers. Ye promised a book by a woman who crossed the lines t' be one of 'em."

"I will get you a firsthand account. I will get as close as possible. I will be her friend. But I can't be her."

"If y're backin' out, best do it now." His voice was hard. She had never heard anything like that from him.

"Tell me, Pat, are you prepared to spend a night as a male stripper at the Hangar Club?"

"What does tha' haf t' do with it?" He complained.

"I've done it twice for this assignment already. I am going to do it again this Friday," April said. She was hot. She was going to make sure he understood what was going on. "I've landed a job at the Tahiti. I am moving in with the girls. By the time the clock strikes midnight, I will have my material. My stories about the whore life will be as compelling as Shakespeare's stories about a Roman emperor and a Scottish king."

"Well done, lass." He was backpedaling.

"I know what you want. I will give you something you will be happy with. Just don't expect me to use crack and get knocked up."

"Of course not. I just wanted to make sure ye'd be deliverin' somethin' authentic. The man has agreed to a fine advance. Ye'll be gettin' 50K right now."

"50K?"

"Fifty thousand dollars. Ye should be gettin' the check in a couple of days. Let me know one way or t'other by week's end."

"You're wonderful," she whooped. She wanted to jump up and down. "I can't talk now. Bye," she gushed and ended the call.

April flopped on the futon across from her desk. Her mind was a complete blank. Gradually she began to believe things might work out. This could be her office – the place where she made a living as a writer.

It would take her two years to make 50k at Smith's if she went full-time. With the advance, she could carry her family until Joe found a new job. She could certainly do it if she was working as a waitress at the Tahiti.

But Joe wouldn't be happy with that arrangement. He was already against her working as a waitress. If he found out she was working at the Tahiti, he would blow a gasket. Check that. When he finds out, he will blow a gasket.

If he knew about the advance, he would want her to stop altogether. Unfortunately, she was getting the advance because her agent and her publisher believed that she was going to go all the way.

She would have to keep the windfall a secret for the time being. She needed time to pry Bridget's story loose. She needed time to investigate the women at the Tahiti. Joe was going to have to go along with her working nights for at least a couple of weeks. And Tahiti management was going to have to find a slot for her on the night shift. One problem at a time. Right now, she could use some of that Irish whiskey.

22

INDEPENDENCE DAY, MEMORIAL Day, and Veterans Day were big days for the MacMahons and the Walshes. They were not quite as important as Christmas, Ash Wednesday, and Easter but they were close. April's father was a career Army Jag officer before he joined her mother's law practice and jumped into Virginia politics. April's grandfather had served under Eisenhower in World War II. Joe's father had been with the Marines in Da Nang in 68 and 69. Military service was a tradition for both the MacMahons and the Walshes going back at least to the Civil War. Family legends extended the military history back to ancient Ireland. Fabled Irish clans were represented here. Besides the MacMahons and the Walshes, April's mother, Gramma Becky was a Sullivan. April's mother-in-law was an O'Donnell. The ragtag remnant of once proud Celtic clans had come together to remember war and celebrate victory.

These gatherings were a problem for April. She felt like a failure. Everyone was nice to her and Joe because they were family. But, as they saw it, Joe was only a programmer. At the moment, he didn't even have a job. April herself had nothing to show for the 14 years since her graduation from college except for Becky and JJ.

Big brother Ted Jr was a colonel in the JAG service and would probably make general before he retired. His wife, Barb, didn't have a real job. She dedicated her life to charitable work. Ted and Barb had produced four children. The oldest, Ted III, was going into the US Military Academy in the fall.

Mary was 15 months younger than Ted Jr. She and her husband, Sam, had four children. She was a tenured professor at the school of law. "Dean" was often used in the same sentence as her name. "If they don't make her dean soon, some other school is going to snatch her up." Mary was not allowed to discuss law with Ted Jr at these gatherings because Gramma Becky was afraid that one of them would kill the other.

Sue was 20 months younger than Mary. She had limited herself to one child. Sue was a senior editor with a publishing firm. That caused some tension between her and April. Sue didn't think much of April's writing. Every time April tried to talk to her about writing and publishing, Sue quickly became defensive. She seemed to think that April was looking for help with a manuscript.

Liz was 20 months younger than Sue. She stood apart because she had little in common with the rest of the family. She was a fighter pilot with three confirmed kills. Neither the law nor literature interested her. She was divorced. She had no children. Her tubes were tied. Rumor had it that she and her husband went their separate ways because she was a lesbian. April doubted that. Liz certainly had an affinity for men. She was just not interested in long-term commitments. She was not going to settle down and raise kids. According to Ted Jr, Liz was currently involved with a general who was firmly committed to his wife and family.

April was 20 months younger than Liz. The two sisters had never had much of a relationship. April felt disconnected from her older siblings as if she and Bill were the second family. Ted Jr had started high school the same year that April entered the first grade. Mary was a year behind him and Sue was two years behind her. When Ted left for West Point, Mary was going into her senior year, Sue was going into her sophomore year, and April was going into the fifth grade. By the time April started high school, Ted had graduated from West Point. Mary and Sue were in college. Liz was in her senior year of high school but she attended St. John's College High School in DC so she could participate in JROTC. Liz entered the Air Force Academy the following year and never looked back.

Bill was 24 months younger than April. He read people so well that April was convinced he was psychic. He may have been as brilliant as Mary but he lacked her ambition. Bill was appalled by the way American leaders used the military to run roughshod over the rest of the world. A military career - even as a JAG officer - was out of the question. He and his wife, Carine, were content to live a quiet, unpretentious life out of the spotlight. Their two children, Will and Karen, were the youngest of the thirteen grandchildren.

The family gathered at Gramma Becky's house in the late morning. The grandkids made a break for the backyard while the adults mingled in the living room and caught up on each other's lives. Eventually, the adults moved outside for a family volleyball game or two. The main meal was a late lunch. That way those who were interested in the concert and fireworks at the National Mall would have time to get into DC.

Joe, April, Becky, and JJ were just getting settled on the South Lawn when Owen Stewart showed up. He was pleasant and sociable as always. After ten minutes of chit-chat, Becky announced that she was going to ride home with Owen.

Joe said, "You came with us, Young Lady. You can go home with us."

"Daaad," Becky objected.

"This is a family day, dear," April said. "You and Owen can get together tomorrow."

Becky shot an angry look at her mother. "Whatever."

A few minutes later, Becky took off to find a port-a-potty. Owen took off in another direction. The two were not seen again for the rest of the evening. Joe, April, and JJ arrived at their house just before midnight. It had taken over two hours to get on the Metro at Capitol South, ride to the Vienna Metro Station, pick up the car and drive home. Owen brought Becky to the door at midnight. She let herself in. She paused for a second at the bottom of the stairs to glare at her parents before she marched up to her room and slammed the door.

23

AT BREAKFAST THE next morning, Joe let his daughter know that he was unhappy. He and her mother were responsible for her well-being until she was self-supporting. That responsibility included making sure that she got safely home each night. The kind of thing that she did last night made his job impossible. Either she was going to conform to his rules or some other arrangement would have to be made.

It was a pretty good speech considering that he didn't have a leg to stand on. Becky probably agreed because of a deep affection for her parents. She could not imagine life without them.

Becky had considered striking out on her own and quickly decided against it. Taking off with Owen had been exhilarating but it wouldn't work in the long run. Becky said what was necessary to calm her parents down and assure them that she would behave in the future.

April waited until Sunday afternoon to have a talk with her daughter. Becky bristled. "I'm not having sex with Owen."

"Not yet," April said. "But you haven't graduated from high school let alone college and he is not the only boy in town."

"I have decided to keep my virginity until I get married," Becky huffed.

April smiled and caressed her daughter's cheek. "I'm glad to hear that but we need to think about the possibility that something will come up to change your mind." April studied her daughter while she waited for that thought to sink in. "I was actually impressed with your ability to make decisions and take risks the other night. But I have to worry what decisions you will make in the heat of passion."

Becky bristled. "I can take care of myself."

"No you can't," April said firmly. "You are human and eventually you will do what humans do." April regretted saying that as soon as the words were out of her mouth. She had just encouraged her daughter to go ahead and get laid.

"I have thought it through very carefully," Becky said. "I know what I am doing."

April clasped her hands in her lap and leaned toward her daughter. "Theoretically. But you have almost no practical experience."

"You worry too much."

"Not really. That sort of thing happens every day and teenage girls who should know better end up pregnant."

"I'm not going to get pregnant."

April's mouth fell open. Her eyes widened. "You've talked to somebody about the pill?"

Becky did not reply.

"Are you on the pill?" April demanded.

"No, Mom. I'm not on the pill." Becky sounded world-weary. "I'm keeping my virginity for my husband."

"You're going to have to do better than that. Even priests and nuns who take a solemn vow of chastity slip up sometimes."

"I won't," Becky insisted.

"Okay," April said. "But just in case, the pill will not protect you from STDs. Your partner will need to use a condom."

"I am not going to have sex with any man until I get married. I am certainly not going to have sex with somebody who has VD."

"How would you know if your partner was infected with gonorrhea or syphilis or herpes or AIDS?"

Becky was suddenly alert. The wheels were turning in her head but she said nothing.

"Has Owen ever slept with anybody?" April asked.

"I don't know. I haven't asked because it doesn't matter. I am not going to have sex with him."

"So, you wouldn't know if he has ever had sex with a prostitute."

"No, Mom. That isn't any of my business."

April leaned back and smiled. She reached out and took her daughter's hand. "The most important thing right now is that you can talk to me about anything."

"Have you ever given a man a blow job?" Becky asked.

April's head jerked back. Her voice was a little shaky. "Yes. Not my favorite thing to do but men seem to like it."

"Anal sex?"

"No and I don't plan to," April snarled.

"Did you and Dad have sex before you were married?"

April hesitated. "Yes."

"And that didn't spoil your wedding night?"

April shook her head. "No. Our marriage was a very special event in my life," she insisted. "The thing you have to hold on to is that marriage is about commitment. Marriage is about having a partner you can share everything with even the flu."

"Are you and Dad having problems?"

April smiled bravely. "We are dealing with some tough challenges. I believe that we can handle them."

Becky studied her mom for a long time without saying a word. Then she blurted out, "I love you both. I can't imagine life without you and I didn't mean to a be a problem Friday night."

"I know. You're a teenage girl struggling to be a woman. That's a big challenge," April assured her daughter. "But we can get through it."

Becky hugged her mom. "I love you."

April kissed her on the cheek. "I love you and I always will."

24

MONDAY MORNING ARRIVED much too soon. April had been too busy to practice her dance moves. The excuses didn't help. She would not be ready to face Nailah at ten. But she would give it her best shot. She hurried up to her office to get in some work while the rest of the family was eating breakfast.

She got a call from Adrien Gautier at 7:45. He wanted her to work two days during the week to get acquainted with the job and the staff. He guaranteed her $50 each day. She had to be ready to work by ten and stay until three. April suggested Tuesday and Thursday. Adrien agreed. She went back to her dance practice.

Nailah was working in an office space in a corner at the back left of the studio. She came out and greeted April with a grimace. "That outfit is neither sexy nor modest. Next time you come here wear a top that covers your breasts but shows them off. Your midriff should be fully visible. I will sell you a G-string for $20. You need to start wearing that."

She walked back to her office and emerged carrying a small box that she handed to April. "Put this on."

Nailah closed off a private space by positioning screens that hung from the ceiling. She put on some music. "Let me see how you are progressing."

April demonstrated her moves as Nailah called out the names. "You have not been practicing," Nailah observed. "You said you wanted to be ready for this Friday. I do not think that is possible. You need much more practice."

They went over the basics again. Sometimes it took several tries for April to execute them to Nailah's satisfaction. They began to put moves into sequences which were the beginning of routines. At the end of the session, Nailah said, "You are making progress but I do not believe that you can be ready for this Friday. Can you come back on Thursday?"

"I'm starting a new job and I have to report to work on Thursday. How about Wednesday?"

Nailah led the way back to her office and checked her calendar. "I can fit you in on Wednesday but that will mean one less day to practice."

"Can you fit me in a couple of days next week?"

Nailah eyed April suspiciously. "I thought Friday was your big competition."

"This Friday and next Friday and possibly the Friday after that."

"That might work. Will you get time to practice with this new job?"

"The job is only part-time. I will make time to practice."

"What is the job, if I may ask?"

"Waitress at the Tahiti."

"Dancers at the Tahiti make much more than waitresses," Nailah said.

"I'm not ready to go that far."

"Of course. But you might want to consider it."

25

APRIL HAD TO leave the house at 8 to get to the Tahiti by 9:30. The club's cool, dimly lit interior was a shocking contrast to the hot, muggy July day outside. Carla Russo, the head hostess on the day shift, greeted Eve almost as soon as she walked into the bar area. The two women sat down at an empty table so Carla could get to know Eve.

After Eve had told her story, Carla's face hardened. "You're lying."

Eve stammered, "What do you mean?"

"I called the company where you were supposed to have been working. They have no record of an Eve or Yvonne MacMahon."

Eve relaxed. "I thought that I had made the situation clear. My married name is April Walsh." Eve produced a driver's license for April Walsh. "That is the name I used at the last place I worked. They let me go because they were cutting back on part-time staff. Bridget said I could get a job here as a waitress," Eve explained. "I am having some problems at home and I am not sure how much longer my marriage is going to last. I decided to apply here using my maiden name. I have to protect myself in case my husband decides to divorce me."

Carla tilted her head and squinted. She produced a notepad from one pocket and a cell phone from another. She called a number and asked to speak to someone in personnel. When that person came on the line, Carla asked about April Walsh. Apparently, the answer was satisfactory. Carla put the phone and notepad back in their respective pockets. "How bad are things at home?"

"I don't know. My husband has been out of work since March. He says he's looking for work but I have no way of knowing what he's up to. His ass-hole days are starting to outnumber his prince charming days. He blew a gasket when he found out I had been fired. So far he hasn't beat up on me but he's a big, strong ex-football player. I am not going to stick around if he does get violent."

"I understand." Carla was warm and reassuring. "We have dealt with violent spouses and boyfriends before. You do a good job here and we will look out for you if things go south."

"Thanks. I haven't waited tables in a while but I used to be pretty good."

"Hooters right? I'm sure you'll do fine." Carla flipped from mother to manager without missing a beat. "I'm going to fix you up with a uniform. While you're putting that on, I will need to make a copy of that drivers' license for your personnel file."

The uniform consisted of three pieces. A nude-colored leotard with just enough material to cover the breasts and form a thong that snapped in the butt area, a black micro-mini skirt and a garter belt for collecting tips. The girls provided their own shoes. Most of them chose something that they could wear comfortably for an eight to ten hour shift.

Carla looked Eve over carefully and nodded approvingly. She handed the drivers' license back to Eve. "Put this away and we'll get started."

The center of the room was dominated by a stage. Tables were set up on all sides of the stage. They were arranged in a grid so they could be easily identified. Waitresses frequently had to hand off tables to other waitresses. Each waitress was assigned a zone. The size of the zones varied depending on the number of waitresses working a shift, and the expected volume of business. Eve's first task was to learn how to find any table from A1 to E10.

The dancers took turns on stage for one or two songs each. The energy level was low. The women were naked before the first number ended. At 11:30, that changed. Men were starting to fill up the tables and order lunch. The energy level picked up. Each dancer was on stage for three songs and she didn't get her clothes off until sometime in the second number. The dancers would come off of the stage and mingle with the men. Generous men got more attention.

Eve was stationed at the bar where she could observe the whole room. She had to deliver a few pitchers of beer and clear some tables. Towards one o'clock she was asked to deliver some orders for waitresses who were on a break. By two o'clock they were cleaning up. At three o'clock, Carla handed Eve fifty dollars and told her she could go home. "I'll expect you back here ready to go by ten on Thursday. You can't use our parking lot. I suggest you take the Metro. The DuPont Circle metro station is about a half-mile from here."

26

WEDNESDAY AND THURSDAY passed almost without incident. Nailah was happy with April's progress. She was convinced that April was finally putting in the practice time. Work at the Tahiti went off without a hitch. Taking the Metro was actually easier than driving. The walk was not as bad as April had expected. When she got home on Thursday night, she discovered that Owen Stewart had taken Becky and JJ to the pool. Becky was needed for a volleyball game. Her brother went along to see if he could find a tennis match. The kids were due back at six.

Joe jumped right in. "Are you going to amateur night again tomorrow?"

April looked up into Joe's eyes. She moistened her lips. "Yes."

Joe growled angrily. "How many of these things are you going to do?"

"I don't know." April cleared her throat. "Probably one more." She gazed out the picture window and took a deep breath. "My contact is starting to loosen up. I got some good information last time. I want to try to get the whole story from her."

Joe's eyes narrowed into an intense stare. "I get it. You think that you're not really doing anything." He turned and walked across the living room. He stopped at the doorway and turned back to face her. "You're just letting a bunch of guys ogle and drool over you." His voice was cutting. "That drives me crazy. It's hard for me to sit here thinking about you up there on a stage making a spectacle of yourself."

April through her arms up in the air. "Go out and do something to take your mind off it." She ran her hand through her hair. "I can get mom to take care of the kids. You can do whatever you want. Stay out as late as you want. No questions asked."

"That's very generous of you," Joe sneered.

April walked over to her husband. "I know this is difficult for you, honey, but this isn't my choice. It is the assignment that I was given." She smiled. "Look at it this way, I have had to sit around here and take care of things while you were on business trips. You never told me exactly what you did on those trips and I never asked."

Joe shook his head and waved her off. "Those were just business trips. I worked all day and spent my nights sitting around a hotel room. I would much rather have been here with you and the kids."

"That's exactly how I feel except that I'm working at night and sitting around all day."

Joe's eyes opened wide. He blurted out, "That was my job!"

"This is my job," April countered. "I hope that you understand that my job and my career are important too."

"I kept my clothes on."

April glared. Joe was being obstinate. She stepped towards him with her hands on her hips. Nose-to-nose with him, she said, "But you like women who take their clothes off. You enjoy *Dancing with the Stars*. You like to watch those practically naked women out there doing the tango or waltz or whatever with their male partners."

"They aren't naked."

"Right," she conceded. "They are wearing barely-there tops."

"But they aren't taking off those tops," Joe objected.

"Would you turn off the TV if they did?"

Joe's jaw tightened.

"Would you be acting like this if I was dancing half-naked on national TV?"

He stepped back, shoved his hands in his pockets, and studied the ceiling. "Alright we'll dump the kids on Gramma Becky and I'll go to the gym tomorrow night. Becky won't be happy about it."

"Would you rather she was here entertaining Owen?"

"No."

April walked over to the picture window and looked out. "I may have to start working nights so we are going to have to come up with a long-term solution."

"The waitress job?"

"Yes. It could end up being from four in the afternoon to six in the morning."

"What the hell are you talking about?"

"The night shift is from 5:30 to 2:30. The commute is at least an hour."

"Where are you working?"

April tried to find a nice way to say it but ended up blurting out, "The Tahiti."

Joe bellowed, "For Christ's sake, April!"

"I'm a waitress, Joe. The job gives me a great opportunity to get to know women who are working in the sex industry. That is my writing assignment."

"I hope you are not planning on making a career of it."

"I am planning on quitting as soon as I have what I need to complete my story."

He was suddenly concerned. "How are you going to get home? Metro doesn't run at that time of night?"

"I'll take a cab."

Joe pointed a finger at her and shook it. "This is bad, April. Really bad. This cannot go on."

"I promise you I will quit. I just need a month or two."

Joe walked away shaking his head.

27

ON FRIDAY NIGHT, April found herself sitting alone at home before she drove to the mall. Joe had taken the kids to Gramma Becky's and was headed for the gym. He would probably get a couple of beers before coming home. She was wearing her bulky sweater and wraparound maxi-skirt over her Daisy Duke costume even though she knew it was a pointless gesture.

April parked her car under a light in the mall parking lot. There were a couple of empty spaces on either side. Ed pulled up beside her. When she got into his car, she shed the sweater and skirt. Jeff tentatively took her hand. She did not pull back. They began recounting the adventures of the last two weeks. Eve's big news was that she had started working as a waitress at the Tahiti.

The evening passed quickly. Eve did not win but she was obviously a hit. Her garter belt was stuffed. As she left the stage the man who had offered her a drink two weeks ago caught her eye. He was holding up a twenty. Eve went over to sit with him. The waitress brought her a rum and coke. "That was pretty good," he began.

Eve blushed then smiled slightly and nodded. "Thank you."

"I like to come to these contests to watch the facial expressions and body language of the true amateurs. Most of them don't want to be up there. Almost none of them do it more than once."

"Do you come here every week?" Eve asked.

"No. I come in spurts. I've been binging lately and I've watched you go from a frightened girl to an old pro."

She smiled. "Thanks."

"Why are you doing it?" he asked.

She panicked but quickly recovered. "I was challenged. They said I couldn't do it. I said I could win."

"Have you ever thought of turning pro?"

She shook her head.

"What do you do?"

Her head jerked slightly. "I'm a waitress."

"Where?"

"That's a secret." She flashed a smile. "What do you do?"

He smiled self-consciously. "I'm an area sales manager."

"For whom? What do you sell?" Eve asked.

He chuckled and grinned broadly. "Do you have a name?"

"Eve."

"Eve? Is that it?"

She stood up to leave. She paused and looked down at him with a fiendish grin. "Sinful. Eve Sinful."

He laughed. "Eddy Martin." He held out the twenty and a business card.

She took them both. "Pleased to make your acquaintance, Eddy."

Eve turned and walked back to her table. She was riding an emotional high. She sat on Jeff's lap. "Well played," Bridget said. "What did you say that made him laugh?"

"He wanted to know my name."

"What did you tell him?" Bridget asked.

"Eve Sinful."

Bridget and Ed laughed. Jeff asked, "Are you sure you want to go there?"

Eve pointed to a spot on her garter, inches from her pussy. She pouted. "It's empty."

He rolled his eyes and pulled out a twenty. He pushed the bill into her garter making sure to brush his hand against her clit. "Much better," she said. She kissed him on the cheek and went back to her seat.

On the way home, Eve slid next to Jeff. He draped his arm over her shoulder and held her hand.

When they stopped next to her car, she pressed Jeff's hand to her lips. He pulled her close. They were nose to nose. They kissed. The first kiss was a light peck. The second was passionate. April pulled away and dashed straight to her car without looking back.

28

SATURDAY MORNING HAD a strange feel despite the routines. The family had breakfast and then took off for the weekly swim meet. Joe was in a great mood. He had run into Mike MacDermot at the gym and they had agreed to start playing racquetball a couple of times a week. When April said nothing, Joe asked if she remembered the MacDermots. She did. Amy Sheehan had been her best friend in college until Amy dropped out to marry Mike. April told the kids how she and Amy had spent a month on a vagabond tour of Europe after their sophomore year. She left out the part about working with Amy at Hooters after the two of them returned from their European adventure.

April's problem was Jeff. She was still in his embrace. She had gone upstairs and taken a shower after the kiss. She had crawled into bed with Joe. He had pulled her close, kissed her, and caressed her back. They had made love but he was much more into it than she was. Part of her felt like she had betrayed the man she loved. Part of her knew it was only a game - the dancing, the flirting and even the kiss. The part that knew it was a betrayal would not let her enjoy the morning with her family.

Later in the afternoon, April went up to her office to practice her dancing. She spotted Eve's phone and checked for messages. Carla Russo wanted Eve to cover the day shift on Tuesday, Wednesday, and Thursday. April returned the call and said she thought she could do it but needed to try to make some arrangements.

The outcome of the family discussion was that Becky and JJ would spend those days at the pool. Their dad or Gramma Becky would pick them up for dinner around 5. Joe was going to get together with Mike MacDermot on Wednesday evening to play racquetball. Becky and JJ would be on their own until April got home around 7. April warned her daughter that Owen had better not be anywhere near the house when she walked in the door.

On Monday morning, April told Nailah that she would not be taking any more dance lessons because she would be working at the Tahiti. Nailah insisted that if April was going to work at the Tahiti, she should be dancing. She closed off the workout area and made April spend an hour practicing striptease and dancing naked.

On Tuesday, April left the house at 7:30 along with Joe and the kids. She got back home at 7:30 that night. She was exhausted. That was the longest workday she had endured in a long time. Joe made a tuna sandwich and poured a glass of chardonnay for her dinner. She chatted casually but carefully about her day. She wanted to give the impression that she was working someplace like the Olive Garden or the Outback.

On Wednesday, April got home just before 7:30 p.m. She ordered a large pizza to be delivered to the house. Owen showed up at 8. He liked card games better than Scrabble so they settled on Gin Rummy. At the end of the first game, Owen suggested that they play some poker. Becky seconded the suggestion. April dug out the box of poker chips that had been gathering dust for over a decade. She explained 5 card draw for JJ's benefit and said each player would have to put $10 in the pot. The survivor would get the pot.

"You mean last man standing," Owen objected.

"'Survivor.' Two of us are women,'" April countered.

JJ was eliminated quickly. April was sure that he had made bad bets to get out of a game that he found boring. Becky didn't last much longer. As soon as Becky was eliminated April got serious. Owen wasn't nearly as good a player as he imagined. He had accumulated a good stake while JJ and Becky were being eliminated. April needed forty minutes to bankrupt him and send him home. Becky frowned. "Why does he have to go home?"

April folded her arms across her chest. "Because I have had a long day. I'm tired and I want to relax."

Becky escorted Owen to the porch. When she returned, she said, "You should have given him his money back."

"It was his idea to play poker." April was busy cleaning up the kitchen. "He gambled and lost. Never gamble with anything that you can't afford to lose."

Becky stood in the doorway with her hands on her hips. "It wasn't a fair game. You're like a pro compared to him."

"That's how I learned," April said. She did not even look at her daughter. "I've lost a lot more than ten dollars along the way. He got a pretty cheap lesson tonight."

April was sleeping in a chair in the living room when Joe got home. He woke her up. "How come you're not in bed?"

She got up and kissed him. "I need to take a shower."

"I need a shower too."

"I was hoping you would wash my back. I'll be happy to wash yours."

29

IT WAS FRIDAY night again. Joe had left early to take the kids to Gramma Becky's house. He was going to hang out at the library until it was time for him to get together with Mike MacDermot. April drove to her spot in the mall parking lot to wait for her friends. She sat in her darkened car alone with her thoughts. July was half gone. She had six weeks to finish her story. She was developing a friendship with Bridget but she was still waiting to hear the woman's story. She had a foot in the door at the Tahiti where she hoped to find the mother lode. That was it so far -- promising leads.

When Bridget and company arrived, Eve locked up and walked to their car. Jeff leaned over to kiss her as she got in. She gave him her cheek. She took his hand but sat on the opposite end of the rear seat. The conversation was forced. Jeff had sold a motorcycle that he had rescued and rehabilitated. Eve talked about waiting tables at the Tahiti. Bridget said that she and Ed would have to stop taking off on Friday nights because of pressure from the Tahiti management.

The club was packed. The crowd was noisy. Eve felt as if she was being swallowed up by a beast. The pros came by to tell Eve that they were pulling for her. Some of the amateurs were pretty good. Eve would have backed out if she thought she could. She forced herself on to the stage. Then the music started. She began to move and the thrill of performing took over. She had picked up some tips from the pros at the Tahiti. They told her that a thong was the hottest thing she could wear. It might even be hotter than not wearing anything. It was suggestive. So Eve shimmied out of her short hot pants and strutted around wearing nothing but her thong and her platform shoes. It was the winning performance that Eve had been striving for.

Eve and her friends stayed around for an extra hour. Strangers kept coming to their table to congratulate her. She drank too much. She was tipsy when they headed back to the car. Inside she crawled onto Jeff's lap. They began kissing. When she felt his cock pushing against her leg, she reached down and rubbed it through his jeans. He stroked her pussy. She got off his lap and knelt next to him so she could pull his cock out of his jeans and start sucking. He started moaning and then he came. Eve pulled her head up. Bridget put a hand over her mouth and said, "Swallow."

Jeff pushed Eve on her back and pulled her pants off. He licked her pussy until she came with a scream. If he had crawled on top of her and started fucking, she would have just laid there and let him have his way. But he pulled back and she put her pants on.

The house was dark and quiet when she got home. The alarm hadn't been set. Joe hadn't bothered with it. He didn't believe they needed an alarm. He tolerated it to avoid arguments.

April set the alarm and then stood in the darkened living room for several minutes debating her next move. She tip-toed up the stairs hoping to take a shower without waking the rest of the family. She rinsed with Scope three times to clear the taste from her mouth. Joe called out to her when she passed the bedroom door on her way to the futon in her office. As she crawled into bed with him, she said, "I thought you were asleep. I didn't want to wake you up."

"I was trying but I couldn't stop thinking about you." He kissed her and noticed the Scope breath.

"I won," she said. "I don't ever have to do that again. But there was a lot of celebrating. I drank too much and ate too much pizza. I couldn't stand the taste."

"Congratulations." He pulled her into his arms. Kisses and caresses led to love making. They fell asleep happy.

30

THE CALL CAME at 8:05 on Tuesday morning. One of the waitresses had failed to show. Could she get down to the Tahiti ASAP and take over the shift?

Eve was on the floor by 9:45. The wayward waitress wandered in shortly after 11. She was ready to work by 11:30 just as lunchtime activity was picking up. Carla pulled Eve aside and handed her $50. "We really appreciate your coming down here on such short notice,"

Eve smiled but said nothing. Carla continued, "I am not making any promises but I need to know if you would be available to work this shift the rest of the week."

Eve grinned. "Yes, of course. But I would like more notice."

Carla nodded. "Go on home. Someone will be in touch with you as soon as we have made a decision."

Eve went to Big Mike's Service Center instead. She found Jeff busy servicing the engine of a Dodge Caravan. He glanced up and immediately recognized her but he did not stop what he was doing. "I hope you're not here to get me to work on your car."

Eve felt a warm glow. She couldn't help smiling. "I was sent home early."

Now he looked up at her. She was wearing a Redskins sweatshirt with the sleeves cut off and tan slacks. He asked absently, "Home from what?"

"I was called into work first thing this morning. After I got there, they changed their minds and told me to go home."

"But here you are at Big Mike's."

She walked over to the minivans so she could inspect the engine. "I decided to come check you out at work."

"How am I doing?"

She leaned on the front to the Caravan and studied the engine. She knew just enough to figure out that he was replacing the spark plugs. She looked up at him and smiled. "You're well worth the price of admission."

"They charged you admission?" He sounded shocked.

"No."

"So, I'm worth it as long as the admission is free?"

She grinned. "Exactly."

He returned the wrench to his toolbox. "Want some lunch?"

"Sure," she giggled. She looked at Jeff. She blushed and giggled some more.

His only response was a quick glance out of the corner of his eye. He was busy cleaning his hands with a rag. "Do you have time for a picnic?"

"I have all afternoon."

Jeff put his rag down and walked over to close the hood. "There's a place in the mountains about an hour from here." He was smiling. Their faces were practically touching. "Scenic ride up there and a great view when you get there."

"Sounds exciting." Her voice was barely audible.

"I'm at a stopping point. Let me change and pick up a couple of beers from the fridge. We'll grab a sandwich from Subway and hit the road."

"What kind?"

"Footlong spicy Italian?"

Eve scrunched her nose. "With beer?"

"How about Black Forest Ham?"

She rocked her head back and forth. "Spicy Italian sounds better."

"Give me ten minutes."

The Naked Mountain Winery is an hour west of D.C. in Fauquier County at the edge of the Blue Ridge Mountains. For a novice like Eve, an hour on a motorcycle whizzing along 66 through scenic, rolling countryside was a thrill ride. Having a young stud like Jeff to hold onto was icing on the cake. They toured the winery and Eve picked up a bottle of Verdot to complement their spicy Italian sub before they settled down for a picnic lunch.

They were stretched out on the grass staring up into a cloudless sky on a hot July afternoon while their lunch settled.

Jeff asked, "Do you have any children?"

"My other life is going to be off limits at least for the time being," Eve said.

"I was just curious because I didn't see any stretch marks."

"I don't have any."

"Children?"

She gave him a sharp sideways look. "Stretch marks."

"You're sure?"

"Positive."

"It was dark in the car the other night. I would like to check again while we're out in the sunlight."

"That's not going to happen," Eve said firmly. "We are in a public picnic area. I am not going to take off my clothes."

"What's the big deal?"

"I know what will happen if I start taking off my clothes."

"That's your final answer?"

Eve said nothing. She had her own question. This was the time to ask but she wasn't sure she was ready for the answer. She raised up on her elbows. "What would you think of me working as a dancer at the Tahiti?"

Jeff clasped his hands behind his head. He turned to look at her. He turned back and closed his eyes. He took a deep breath. "I guess that I'd be okay with it, if that's what you want to do."

She turned to look at him. His rangy body was completely relaxed. "I'm not sure I want to do that," she said. She looked down at her toes and bit her lip. "But people keep telling me how much money I could make. That is a big consideration."

He sat up and turned to face her. He crossed his legs and rested his arms on his knees. "Money isn't everything."

Eve sat up and swiveled around to face him. She crossed her legs. "Don't you want to make a lot of money?"

"I want to make enough money to pay for an apartment, food, and clothes. What I really want and what I have is a job that I enjoy doing."

"That's heavy."

"Have you ever heard of Maslow's hierarchy?"

Eve was intrigued. "I can't say that I have."

"Back in the 1940s, a psychologist and philosopher named Abraham Maslow put out this theory that people are driven by needs. There are basic survival needs like food and shelter and there are psychological needs like friends and self-esteem. We have to take care of the basic survival needs before we can focus on the psychological needs. The highest need is to do something meaningful."

"Wow!"

"Dancers are mostly working on basic survival needs. They are doing whatever it takes to stay alive. They work at a place like the Tahiti because that gives them security. They also develop a network of friends. Some of them even get a measure of esteem. Bee, for instance, is at the top of the food chain. Not only is she a good dancer, she has a great personality and she's a leader. Everybody looks up to her." Jeff studied his hands. "But even Bee is falling short. She isn't doing it because that's what makes her happy."

"And she has to be careful to keep her profession a secret from normal society. Right?"

"Yes, that is a problem. You can be proud of almost anything you do except selling drugs or sex. That, of course, is another example of Christian hypocrisy. Coffee, alcohol, cigarettes, and other drugs are okay. It's okay to give sex away. But there are some behaviors that society wants to control. The best way to control them is by attaching a stigma to them. Sending people to prison doesn't work nearly as well as making them outcasts."

Eve leaned forward to rest her chin on her thumbs. "So, you personally don't have a problem with strippers or dancers?"

"No"

"Would you date one?"

"If I liked her."

"How about a long-term relationship?"

"I think so but I'm not good at long-term relationships."

"I'm sorry. Do you want one?"

"I do now," Jeff said.

Eve recoiled. Her face tightened. "Please don't go there. I like you a lot. I think you are one of the coolest men I have ever met but I am not ready to take on another relationship."

"Okay. But if I hang around long enough, that might change."

"I don't want you to put your life on hold just for me."

"I never put my life on hold. I always take it one day at a time."

Eve barely registered the ride back to Big Mike's. The scenery was wasted on her. Other vehicles on the road flew by like leaves in a windstorm. She was lost in thought about needs, about food, shelter, and security, about love and self-esteem. Things she had taken for granted all her life. Now she was entering a world where people had to struggle to get them. And the man in her arms was in love with her. She ached because she couldn't come clean. She already had a man and children who meant the world to her.

They stopped at the door of the garage and got off. He took his motorcycle inside to its spot. She followed carrying her helmet. Jeff took the helmet and placed it on the motorcycle.

He wrapped his arm around her waist and pulled her close. They kissed. Eve's mouth opened for his tongue. He slid his hands under her sweatshirt and pushed it up over her head. She pulled her arms free and wrapped them around his waist. He kissed her neck and chest removing her bra as he worked his way down. When he got to her right nipple, he suckled. She moaned softly as she felt heat spreading through her body.

She unbuttoned his shirt and pushed it open. She began kissing his chest and worked her way down to his belt. She opened his jeans and sank to her knees to suck his cock but he pulled her up to her feet. They held each other in a tight embrace - flesh against flesh. As they kissed he swung her around so her back was against the wall. He helped her out of her pants. She pushed his pants down to expose his cock. He lifted her up. She wrapped her legs around his waist. Her vagina pushed down against his cock. It slid into her wet, soft pussy. His rod drove up inside her. As the rhythm and intensity of his thrusts increased, she felt him swell and then release. That shouldn't have happened but she didn't care. Not at that moment.

He set her back on her feet. Their eyes locked. The enormity of what had just happened began to sink in.

She felt a desperate need to get away. She dressed and headed for the door. He grabbed her arm. "What's your hurry? It's too early to go home."

"I just need to be alone right now."

"Where are you going?"

"I don't know." She looked down. She pressed her hands against her head. She took a deep breath and sighed, "I guess I'll go back to the Tahiti and get a drink."

"Let me give you a lift."

She wanted to get away from him but she couldn't think of a better plan. A few minutes later Eve was inside the Tahiti, sitting at a table near the bar waiting for her whiskey - a double. Carla sat next to her, one arm across Eve's shoulders. "Are you okay?'

Eve smiled. "I will be."

"What happened?"

"I think I just had my first quickie."

Carla grinned. "I'll get you a pill just to be safe."

"Thanks."

When Eve had finished her drink, Carla said, "Go home. If anybody asks, I let you off early because business was slow. Come back tomorrow at the regular time. We want to use you the rest of the week. But be careful with this other guy. Getting involved like that before your divorce is finalized can be big trouble."

31

WEDNESDAY WENT OFF as expected. Eve was assigned a zone which meant that she served and kept the tips. There were still important things to learn like trading off tables to squeeze in a break. She made it through the lunchtime rush, the start of the evening rush, and the handover to the night crew. That left her running on adrenalin when she walked back to the Dupont Circle Metro station.

April dragged herself into the house at 7:17 and ordered a pizza. Owen showed up at 8. He said he would enjoy a game of scrabble. He played well. April held back so the game would be between Becky and Owen. Becky would have won but she was stuck with a 'Q' and an 'X' at the end of the game. April suggested that they could play a little blackjack if Owen and Becky had some money they wanted to lose. Becky got her wallet from her purse and produced $50 - her entire stash.

"Put some of that back. You will need it at the pool tomorrow and Friday," April said. "Owen, how much are you in for?"

He eyed April. "Are you playing?"

"I'll be the dealer."

Owen brightened up. "I'll put up whatever she's putting up."

"You should think about that. What's going to happen if you take all of her money?" April asked.

The teenagers agreed on $20 each. April decided that she would just watch the game. JJ took over as dealer. It was almost 11 when April called a halt to the game. JJ had most of the money. April confiscated his winnings and said she would hang on to them for another night. JJ was sent to bed while Becky escorted Owen to the door and April cleaned up.

On Thursday, Carla informed Eve that they had a full-time spot for her on the night shift. Eve wanted time to think about it but Carla needed her answer before the shift was over because they wanted Eve to start the next day.

Eve called Joe using her cell phone. "It's me, baby. I had to borrow a phone because I forgot to charge mine. They want me to start working nights. It's better money. They need to know right away."

"What's the alternative?"

"Find another job."

"Then find one."

Eve shook her head. "We have some big bills coming up."

"I'll be getting a job soon." Joe's voice was flat. He did not want to talk about it.

Eve closed her eyes and bowed her head. Her right foot started tapping. She straightened up. "I'll tell them that I am going to do it." She needed more time at the Tahiti. She wanted to be there at night when the real action was taking place. "When you have money coming in, we'll sit down and decide what to do about my job. Is that okay?"

There was a long pause before Joe answered. "I would like to continue my gym nights. The workouts are good for me."

Eve relaxed. "I'll call my mom. I'm sure she won't mind helping out." She was about to tell him she loved him when she thought of something else. "You should also talk it over with Becky and JJ."

"Talk what over?"

"Are you going to leave them with Gramma Becky all night on Monday, Wednesday, and Friday, or are you going to pick them up and bring them home? What are the rules for Becky and Owen? He's been over our house the last two Wednesdays. Make sure they understand that this is only a temporary arrangement. As a matter of fact, I'll be home on Monday nights so you are only talking about Wednesday and Friday."

"Okay. I'll see you when you get home."

She smiled. "Love you." She sent him a kiss and hung up.

The family was at peace when April got home. They talked about the day's events while she ate. Then they settled in the living room and watched "Vantage Point."

32

BRIDGET, A.K.A. BEE Sting, did not wait long to start pushing for Eve to dance. She told Eve to go for it as soon as possible so she could make her deadline. Bee also pressed management. She touted Eve's win in the amateur night contests. On Saturday night, the demand for escorts was unusually high. By midnight, only a few women were still around to perform on stage. The process was to announce each dancer's name and let the audience know that she would be available for a private dance when her stage performance ended. When one of the men arranged with the night manager for a private dance, he would be led to a back area where he would be seated next to a stage that was blocked off on three sides by a curtain. The dancer would get on the stage and shed her clothes. She would sit close enough to rub noses with the customer. He could touch her legs, arms, or back but not her face, breasts, or butt. They would commune in this fashion for the duration of the next three dance set on the main stage. When the time was up, the woman in charge of the dancers would show up and talk to the customer. During the conversation, she would suggest another set or, even better a little private time with the dancer away from the Tahiti. If the customer was interested in the escort service, he paid $100 for two hours with his "date." The night manager would strongly suggest that a generous tip would help the time with the woman go much better. The escort and her customer were free to negotiate additional arrangements once they had left the Tahiti. It was generally expected that an escort would not be returning after she left the building.

The night manager, Anna Stroom, was a tall, thin, graceful blonde. She had been doing this job for the last 20 years. She was good at it. But this Saturday, the demand for escorts had consumed her regulars and most of her stand-ins. Renting out the spares was good business but it reduced the number of dancers that Anna had available in-house. Those dancers provided the entertainment that drove the sale of liquor and food, which generated most of the club's revenue. Anna was forced to stretch her resources. She could put the remaining dancers up on stage more often or she could get a few waitresses to take a turn dancing. Some of the waitresses were willing to get up on the stage and dance in a pinch. Anna cornered Eve who was taking a quick breather. "Bee says that you are interested in working as a dancer."

Eve gulped and stammered, "I have been considering it but I'm not sure I can do it."

"If you're thinking about dancing, this is about the best opportunity you are going to get."

Eve opened her mouth to answer then closed it. She squinted at Anna and tapped a finger against her lips. Anna read her perfectly. "Dolly P is up next. You can go up with her so it's not so overwhelming the first time. What do you say?"

"Alright. I'll give it a try."

"Good. Go back in the dressing room and find Dolly. Tell her that I said you are going on with her. She should help you get ready. You have 5 minutes."

When they got up on the stage, Dolly had Eve wait at the edge while she sashayed to the center.

She held up her hands asking for silence. "Gentlemen and the rest of you bums out there, it is mah pleasure to introduce a very bad woman. Ah want y'all to make her feel welcome. Ah want y'all to let her know that y'all want her up on this stage dancin' for y'all."

Dolly led Eve to the center of the stage. "Ah present t' y'all Eve Sinful."

Whoops, whistles, and cheers burst from the crowd as Eve walked forward.

Eve did her best to follow Dolly's lead. She tried to remember what she had done at the amateur night competition but this was bigger. The atmosphere closed in on her and threatened to crush her. Their clothes were off early in the second number. Dolly took Eve's hand for a jitterbug. They danced around the edge of the stage picking up tips. The third number was the Viennese Waltz. Dolly pulled Eve close and waltzed around the stage with her. The crowd went wild. The women would stop to let the men slide bills up under their garters and then go back to their waltz.

When the music stopped, Eve held Dolly's hand and gazed into her eyes. Dolly was on fire. Her breasts and nipples were fully erect. Eve's breasts were swollen and hard. Her pussy was dripping wet. Her whole body was trembling. She needed release. She almost kissed the younger woman but she did not dare cross that line.

Dolly pulled free and started dressing as if nothing had happened. While they were putting their clothes on, Dolly said, "Some men want t' talk t' y'all. Ah'll introduce y'all and leave. Be nice t'them. Take their money and get back t'the dressin' room. Y'all should be back there before Double-Oh-Seven has her clothes off."

"Got it."

Eve did three solo sets that night. In between, she circulated around the room visiting with any man who indicated an interest in her company.

At the end of the shift, Anna said, "You've got the job if you want it."

"I want it," Eve gushed

"Tomorrow night you will start off as a waitress as you did tonight. Later in the shift, I will get you up on stage. Starting Tuesday, you will be a dancer. I won't ask you to wait tables unless I am really desperate."

Eve had a silly smile on her face. Her cheeks were flushed and her eyes gleamed.

"Are you okay?" Anna asked.

"Yeah. I just can't get that waltz out of my head."

"I can't either. That was brilliant." Anna grinned.

33

ON SUNDAY EVENING, Eve filled out papers which specified what she would and would not do as an entertainer at the Tahiti. She opted not to work as an escort. It took Bridget less than an hour to find out about that decision. She pulled Eve to an isolated table in the back to lay down the law. "They said you told them you wouldn't be an escort. You can't do that. Being an escort is part of our bargain."

Eve looked at her feet and shook her head. "I can't do it, Bridget."

"Why not? How many men have you had sex with? One dozen or two?" Her voice was cutting.

"That was before I married Joe." She held an index finger up. "I have only been with one man in the last 15 years."

"Two at least. You had sex with Jeff."

Eve blushed. "That was a mistake. I was drunk and so pumped up I didn't know what I was doing."

"You sure looked like you knew what you were doing. And the week before that, you gave him a very hot kiss."

Eve buried her face in her hands. "I was drunk. I went overboard."

"Drunk is okay - within limits."

Eve looked Bridget in the eye. "I just can't imagine myself hopping in bed with strangers - drunk or sober."

Bridget's eyes narrowed. She tilted her head to the side. "Have you ever done it with multiple men in one night?"

"Maybe. A long time ago."

"Did you plan on doing that or did it just happen?"

Eve looked off toward the stage. She could feel herself tensing up. She turned back to Bridget and swallowed. "I went to a party with a pretty good idea that it could turn out that way."

"Okay, so you leave the Tahiti as an escort with some guy. You have a pretty good idea what is going to happen." Bridget shrugged. "A few years from now you won't even think about it."

"I had a tough enough time convincing Joe that it was okay for me to dance," Eve objected. "I will never get him to agree to me having sex with another man."

"Did you tell him about Jeff?"

"Of course not." She would never tell her husband something like that.

"Then you don't need to tell him about the other men."

"I couldn't do that to Joe."

"Guys do it all the time. Joe would do it if the opportunity presented itself."

Eve shook her head. "No, he wouldn't. He's really committed to his family."

"Half the guys I escort are committed husbands. They figure it's okay as long as wifey doesn't find out. Joe has probably tried it a few times."

Eve glared but said nothing. Bee continued, "What if I can prove to you that Joe will fuck the first woman who lets him know that she's available?"

"It won't happen."

"But if it does, you'll agree to work as an escort?"

Eve looked down and shook her head. She took a deep breath and sighed, "I don't know."

"You can use Jeff as an icebreaker. You sign up to be an escort and arrange for him to be your first customer."

"He doesn't pay for sex."

"He would help you out. He really likes you."

Eve closed her eyes and shook her head. "I don't know."

"If Joe cheats on you, then you work as an escort," Bridget said. "That's the only way that you will get what you need for your story."

"Alright," she said softly. It was a bad deal and she knew it. She looked up at Bridget. "How are we going to know what Joe is up to?"

"I'll introduce you to my friend when she gets here."

After Eve's last set, Bridget introduced her to a slight woman in a stylish pantsuit. "Eve, this is Nickey Arnold. She has agreed to meet with Joe."

"Hello, Nickey." Eve shuddered involuntarily. "So you're the woman who is going to seduce my husband."

"I don't actually seduce men. I just make myself available and let them do the rest."

"I don't think you will be the first," Bridget said to Nickey. Then she turned to Eve. "Didn't Joe have a thing for your roommate in college when you two were about to get married?"

Eve glared. She was furious with her brother for talking so much.

"Can you tell me something about his habits?" Nickey asked.

Eve walked away to regain her composure. She stared up at the ceiling, hands on her hips and counted to ten. She had to play the game. She didn't have to like it. She walked back and stood glaring at Nickey, feet planted in a broad stance, arms folded across her chest. "He's looking for work. He takes the kids to swim practice every weekday morning. Then he goes downtown either for a job interview or to research potential employers." She cleared her throat and added, "Right now he plays racquetball with an old friend on Monday, Wednesday, and Friday evening. Is that enough?"

"I think so," Nickey said. Her voice was calm. "Do you have a number where I can reach you?"

Eve gave Nickey her cell phone number and walked away.

34

APRIL SPENT A tense week waiting for Nickey's call. The longer she waited the more certain she became that the news would be bad. At least her work kept her busy. She got home around 4:30 in the morning. She slept on the couch for a couple of hours. Her cell phone alarm woke her up at 6:30 for breakfast with Joe and the kids. After they left for swim practice, she went back to sleep for a few more hours. She got up and ate. Then she worked on her writing until it was time to leave for the Tahiti.

Joe came home and found April asleep twice. He woke her up with a kiss and told her that he was going to an interview.

On Sunday afternoon, her cell phone vibrated letting her know that she had a message. She went upstairs to her office to return the call. It was from Nickey. "What's up? Are you screwing my husband already?"

"Not yet. Soon." Her tone was businesslike. "I have found out some things you should know about."

"What exactly is it that you do?" April pulled out a notepad and sketched Nickey with horns and a pitchfork.

"I'm a private investigator. I work for your brother and other lawyers on a contract basis. Usually I'm looking for dirt."

April added a sketch of Bill. "So what is the dirt that I need to know about?" April drew a line connecting Bill and Nickey

"The good news is that Joe is about ready to sign with a temp agency. But I guess he has already told you that."

April sketched Joe in and completed the triangle. "No. We've talked about it but I thought he was holding off. How did you find out?"

"I had lunch with him twice last week. I told him that my name was Natalie and that I was a systems analyst. He seems to enjoy my company."

April said, "I'll bet." She scribbled, *2 interviews and 2 lunches???* Then she asked, "What's the bad news?"

"Joe is playing racquetball with Mike MacDermot and two women. One of them is Mrs. MacDermot. The other one is a Lee Bell," Nickey said. "I don't know how she fits in but she is staying with the MacDermots. I sent you a text message with a picture."

April pulled up the text message to look at the picture. "That's Amy's sister, Aileen. I met her at Mike and Amy's wedding. I honestly don't see a problem."

"The nights are getting longer," Nickey said. "They went for pizza and dancing on both Wednesday and Friday. Joe didn't pick up your kids until 11 and I am pretty sure your mother wasn't happy."

April rolled her eyes. "How would you know that?"

"I followed him of course. I found a spot where I could work out and watch the racquetball game. Then

I changed at the same time the women did. Lee is a very attractive woman."

"So is Amy. A lot of women are." April closed her eyes and shook her head.

"I drive by your house from time to time just to see if anything is going on."

"And…"

"Thursday night, Mrs. MacDermot's car was parked outside your house. Lee came out of your house around 2:30 and drove back to the MacDermot's."

April cringed. "Do you have any idea when she got there? Do you think the kids were up?"

"Very hard to tell without bugging your house. But Friday night, I was following Joe. He picked up the kids just before 11. The pattern of lights in your house suggested that the kids went straight to bed when they got home. Lee showed up in Mrs. MacDermot's car around midnight."

April was folding into a ball. Her arm was pulled tight against her stomach. "And stayed until 2:30?"

"Yes."

April straightened. "I guess I asked for this." She could feel tears welling up. "What are your plans?" She sketched Lee Bell with one hand touching Joe.

"Nothing specific." Nickey was detached and professional. "I believe that I will have an opportunity to put Joe's loyalties to the test next week. I might even be able to find out what is going on between him and Lee."

April drew several circles around the Joe-Lee-Nickey triangle. "I really didn't want to know all of this."

"Just remember the truth will set you free even if it hurts."

"I need to get back to my family." April terminated the call.

She wiped the tears away with her hands. She pulled a compact from her purse to see how bad it was. Her eyes were a little red and puffy. She smiled. The face in the mirror smiled back. It wasn't great but it would have to do.

35

BY MONDAY MORNING, April had come to terms with the truth. She and Joe had been navigating under society's rules for married couples for 14 years. Sticking to those rules had enabled them to develop a successful partnership. They had produced two great kids and acquired a comfortable suburban domain that included a large house and two cars. They had always enjoyed their sex. They had experimented liberally in the good old days. The rules had forced them to change. Now she had tried to skirt those rules. Instead, she had knocked them to the floor. They lay there shattered like shards of fine china.

Her fling with Jeff had proven that she had not really changed. She didn't know what was going on with Joe and Lee but it was hard not to assume. Put a good-looking man in a room with a good-looking woman in the middle of the night and things move pretty fast. There was almost no chance that Joe would say no to Nickey. Poof! Fourteen years of marriage wiped out in the blink of an eye.

She couldn't go back. No do-over. She had broken into the asylum. She only had three more weeks to get her story. Tomorrow would be critical. She would crash through the last safety net and land in the mud.

On Tuesday morning, April announced to her family that she had a busy schedule. She was going to meet with some people to get information for her story and would be out until sometime in the afternoon. Becky and JJ were to stay at the pool after swim practice. Either she or their father would pick them up at 5 for dinner. As soon as they had left for swim practice, April got ready. Her outfit was designed for action. A white, sleeveless pullover, no bra, mini-skirt, and sandals. She drove to the Vienna metro station and rode to DuPont Circle. She walked to the Tahiti. April kept telling herself not to go through with it. There had to be a way to get her story and save her marriage. But it was Eve who walked into the Tahiti. "I've changed my mind about working as an escort," she said as soon as she found Carla Russo. "Can we take care of the paperwork as soon as possible? I have to get to another meeting."

She took a cab from the Tahiti to Big Mike's garage. Jeff was working on an engine. He didn't say anything but he was clearly thinking, "*What the fuck?*"

"What's the matter?" she asked.

He held up his greasy paws. "You're wearing white."

"If I was worried about a little bit of grease, I wouldn't be here."

"Okay. But you don't want to spend the rest of the day walking around with greasy hand prints on that nice white sweater. Come with me."

He led her to the back of the shop where he found an old shirt she could wear. Then he led her into the bathroom and locked it. She stood behind him as he cleaned up his hands. "To what do I owe the pleasure of this visit?"

"I want to ask a favor."

He turned to face her. She was leaning against the door. They were only inches apart in the tiny room. "Big or small?"

"Enormous"

"What are you offering in return?"

She pulled off her thong and put it in his hand. "Nothing. I have nothing left to bargain with but I need your help."

Jeff pulled back. He cocked his head and stared down at her out of the corner of his eye. "What's going on?"

She took a breath and exhaled through her pursed lips. "I'm going to start working as an escort."

"I told you that is out of my hands. I am not going to judge you." His voice had a hard edge. "But I am not sure what that means for us down the road."

She looked down and shrugged. "I can't explain myself right now. I hope that things will be better down the road." She looked straight into his eyes. "In the meantime, my life is falling apart and I know that there are people who will judge me for this decision. That has nothing to do with what I want from you."

"What is it that you want?"

She was trembling. "I start tonight. I want you to come to the Tahiti and be my first customer. Tell them you want me to give you a private dance and then hire me as an escort."

He shook his head. "It's against my principles to pay for sex."

"I know so I'm going to pay." She wiped her sweaty palms on her skirt. She pulled four 50 dollar bills out of her clutch and held them out.

Jeff stood for a long time studying Eve with a concerned look on his face. "I'm only doing this as a favor to you."

He took the money and put it in his pocket. "Okay. Tonight."

He grabbed her right wrist and put her thong in her hand. He stared at her and shook his head. He pushed past her to get out of the room and back to his engine. She put her thong on and put the shirt back. She paused to look at him on her way out. He ignored her.

The rest of the afternoon was pure torture. April felt weak and sick. Her family was worried. She told them that the interviews had been emotionally wrenching but that she would be okay once she was busy waiting tables.

At the Tahiti that evening, Anna Stroom asked her if she was sure she wanted to be an escort. Eve nodded. But she wanted her friend, Jeff, to be her first customer. Anna objected. Eve insisted. She was prepared to risk her friendship with Jeff to be with somebody familiar the first time out.

Jeff showed up at the Tahiti around nine. Ed notified Anna. She was in no hurry. She kept Eve in the dance rotation until after 10. Finally, Jeff approached her and said that he would like a private dance with Eve.

Eve smiled when she saw Jeff. He was all dressed up. His jeans looked new. He was wearing a midnight blue shirt with a white collar and cuffs. He wore tan boots that looked dressy. He was dazzling. But the private dance dragged on interminably. The last time Eve had given a private dance, she had been able to pass the time with small talk. She and Jeff were talked out. They stared at each other while 15 minutes of adult entertainment, that neither of them wanted, played out. They rushed through the formalities of setting up the date before running out of the building. Eve reached the parking lot with Jeff before it occurred to her that riding on the back of his motorcycle was going to be a problem. Jeff laughed. He led her to a Ford Fusion that he had borrowed for the night.

36

THEY DROVE IN silence back to Jeff's apartment. Eve stopped just inside the door to survey the place. On her right was a dining area. She could see an oak table with four chairs. A computer desk sat in one corner. The living room was carpeted. It was furnished with a sofa, a lounge chair, a coffee table, and a large screen TV. She was struck by the neatness of the place. It seemed obsessive.

A large panoramic photo hung over his sofa. It was an aerial photo of downtown DC - Independence Avenue crammed with motorcyclists like an endless march of ants. He followed her gaze. "Rolling Thunder, July 4th, 2005. That was the first time for me. I got back from Iraq at the end of 2004."

He led her back to the bedroom. She noted that the bathroom door was across the hall from the bedroom door. The bedroom itself was clearly a dual-use space. His Murphy bed was down and ready for the night's activities. In one corner, his weights and bench were neatly stowed. A chin-up bar was mounted on the wall a few feet away. A weapons cabinet sat near the other corner. As far as she could tell, it held a shotgun, a high-powered rifle with a scope, a couple of pistols, some knives and a bow with a quiver of arrows. The bow was nearly as tall as she was. "Do you hunt?"

He grinned. "That's how I get most of my meat. I bag a deer and get it butchered every year. I try to get a wild boar, too. That gives me at least a couple of pounds of meat every week, which is plenty for me. If I get any more, I sell it."

She looked up at him with pleading puppy dog eyes. Her hands clasped in front of her chest. "I don't know how to get this started."

A grin spread across his face. "My first time, too."

She unbuttoned his shirt. "Do you want me to take off your clothes or do you want to do that?"

"I liked what you did at the club." He gave her an encouraging smile. "Why don't you strip for me and then you can take my clothes off."

She stepped away from him unzipping her dress and kicking off her shoes. She turned back to him and slithered out of the dress. She walked back and removed his shirt. It had a soft cottony feel. She pressed up against his chest and wriggled out of her bra. His hands slid lovingly down her back. He held her butt and bent to kiss her. She pushed his jeans down. He kissed her neck while she caressed his cock. She pushed him onto the bed and knelt to pull his boots off. The leather was surprisingly soft. The odor was intoxicating. He wasn't wearing socks. His jeans were more of a challenge but she got them off. She stood and climbed out of her thong.

He grabbed her butt and pulled her onto the bed. He began fingering her pussy. She smiled. She stroked his face and ran her fingers through his hair. His hand slid to her butt crack. His middle finger began to work into her asshole. She grimaced and buried her face in his neck. She had never let Joe get away with that but now she had to give her customers what they wanted. When she couldn't stand it any longer, she pulled his hand away and whispered, "Not yet."

He rolled her over and lifted her legs off the bed. He drove his cock deep inside her. She grabbed his forearms and held tight while he humped until he came.

They lay together in silence for awhile. She rested her head on his chest and listened to the beating of his heart . At first, his arm was wrapped around her with his hand resting on her hip. Gradually, he began to gently rub her back and butt. His cock started getting hard again. His hand worked its way to her rear end. He began to worry at her asshole. She gently massaged his cock until it was rock hard. She climbed on top of him and started kissing his neck and chest. She worked her pussy down onto his cock and rode him. She rode him hard. They both came.

She collapsed on the bed beside him. He pulled her close for a passionate kiss. He explored her body with his kisses. But he was not giving up on her ass. He rolled her over and wrapped his arms around her chest. She put her hands on his hands. As he pushed up against her from behind she maneuvered her vagina onto his rod. He began pumping her. The rhythm and intensity built until he came. He lay there holding her. His chest pressed against her back. His nose against her neck.

After a while, he went to the bathroom. When he returned, he took her hand. She got to her feet. Suddenly he pushed her face first into the wall. He pinned her against the wall with his left forearm while he pushed his cock into her asshole with his right hand. He forced his way in and humped. It took everything she had to keep from screaming or fighting back. When he had finished and let up, she went over to the bed completely spent. She sat on the edge of the bed with her face buried in her hands. She forced herself to take deep slow breaths until she was able to look at him again. She spoke in a low, husky voice. "I don't feel well. I need to go home."

"I thought you were going to stay for a while."

She checked the clock on the chest of drawers next to his bed. It was after one in the morning. "My two hours are up. I want to leave."

She got up and started dressing. He tried to put an arm around her. She pushed him away. "Not now."

He started pulling on his clothes. "I'll give you a ride."

"No. I'll call one of my cabbie friends. I'll be fine. I just need to get to my own bed."

She was almost out of the bedroom when he grabbed her arm. He stuffed a wad of bills into her bra. "This is for you. I want you to have it."

She nodded and left the apartment. She couldn't think of any cabbies to call so she called a cab company that was on her contact list. She gave them the address and said she would be waiting outside.

37

THE CABBIE WHO pulled up minutes later was a woman in her twenties. "You look terrible. Are you okay?" She had a lyrical, contralto voice with a drawl that suggested the Deep South - Louisiana or Texas.

"Yeah. I'm fine."

"Eve. Vienna Metro station. Right?"

Eve tensed. "How did you know?"

"I gave you a ride from the Tahiti last week."

"Oh. Sorry I didn't recognize you." Eve tried to retreat into her shell.

"I guess you weren't working as a waitress tonight."

"No."

"Permanent change?"

Eve shot a look at the driver - eyes wide, nostrils flared, teeth bared. She spoke in a barely audible growl. "Yes."

"You sure you don't want to go back to being a waitress?"

"No!" Eve snapped. Then without thinking she added, "I'm doing what I have to do."

"Nobody has to do anything. There is always an alternative."

"How did you end up driving a cab on the grave-yard shift?" Eve sneered.

"I'm working toward my MBA." The driver was imperturbable. "Driving a cab is one of the things I do to pay the bills."

"And you couldn't come up with anything better?" Eve challenged.

"I could wait tables at some place like the Tahiti," the driver replied in her soft, lyrical southern drawl. "I like to drive. I like driving much better than waiting tables."

"What are the other things you do to pay the bills?"

"I'm a professional party girl. I do everything from being a clown at kids parties to being a stripper at bachelor parties. I'm a magician and a part-time martial arts instructor."

"When do you find time to work on your degree?"

"Anytime I want. I'm enrolled in the University of Phoenix. You should look into it."

"Why?" Eve was cold. She had a real degree from a real university.

"You need to plan for the future and you're obviously too smart to think that you can do this for 30 or 40 years and retire."

"I plan to be a writer. I get to write during the day."

"It might help to take some courses on writing."

"I've taken some courses on writing," Eve retorted. "What I learned is that you learn to write by writing."

"Have you published anything?"

Eve shrugged and shook her head.

"Do you have a blog?"

"I haven't really thought about it."

"That's a good way to practice writing and you can easily get one for free."

"Not tonight," Eve said. She closed her eyes and shook her head. *Would you please just shut up and drive.*

The conversation ended abruptly as if the driver had read Eve's mind. They rode in silence for a while. Eve could feel the fury building. She wanted to take a bat and beat the shit out of Jeff.

"I'm a mind reader," the driver announced. "Would you like a demonstration?"

"Do I have a choice?" Eve much preferred staying in her shell where she could savor her fury.

"You were raped. The guy got on your back and butt fucked you. Right?"

"He pinned me against the wall and rammed his cock up my ass. You were close. Does that make you happy?"

"How did he pin you against the wall?"

"He pressed his arm across the middle of my back."

"Left arm?"

"Yes. Could we not discuss this?"

"The main force was on your left because his weight was concentrated in his shoulder and elbow," the driver continued. "You could have escaped by moving to your right."

"He is a very strong man."

"But he is a man and that means he had no way of preventing you from moving to the right away from his weight," the driver said. But even as she spoke, she realized more would be needed in this situation. "Also, a kick would at least distract him and get him off balance. All you had to do was swing your right leg back and hit him. His groin would be the ideal target but even a good shot to the knee would get his attention."

"I'll try to remember that next time."

"Also, you want to plant your kicking leg back between his legs with your foot behind his, if possible. Then you push your butt into his center. That disrupts his balance which compromises his power. If you can get his butt moving backwards, you can knock him to the floor very easily."

"I'll keep that in mind." Eve kept hoping the woman in front would take a hint and drop the subject.

The driver handed a business card to Eve. "I'm Hattie. I teach at the Sun Tang Woo Martial Arts Studio in Arlington. We teach some good self-defense courses for women. Once or twice a month we teach a weekend course. It's four hours on Saturday and four hours on Sunday. It would be a good investment of your time and money."

When they got to the Vienna Metro station, Eve pulled Jeff's tip money out and peeled off 60 dollars. She guessed that was close to half of what he had given her. When Eve handed it to the driver, the woman caught her hand. "Can we talk?"

Eve hesitated but pulled her hand free and walked away.

Hattie got out of her cab. "Please. I just want to talk to you for a minute."

Eve stopped and turned back to look at the woman. "You have been talking to me for the last half hour."

Hattie walked up to her. "I know but that was so impersonal. You were hiding in the back seat and I was trying to be a good driver."

Eve could feel the hairs standing up on the nape of her neck. "You want to get personal? Are you a lesbian?"

Hattie smiled sweetly. She opened her arms to offer a hug. "I just want to say a few more things to you before we part company. I am really sorry about what happened to you tonight. I want to let you know that I care about you."

Eve folded her arms across her chest and tapped her right foot.

Hattie asked, "What would your mother say if she was here right now?"

Eve's voice was low and threatening. "It doesn't matter. She's not here and she is never going to hear about what happened."

"But you need to talk to somebody."

"Like you?" Eve snapped.

"Why not?" Hattie pressed. "I'm a woman with some experience. I don't have any axes to grind."

"What makes you think I want to talk to you?"

"You haven't walked back to your car yet." Hattie's soft, lyrical drawl was soothing.

"I notice you parked far enough away that I couldn't just get out of your cab and jump into my car."

"Good point." Hattie laughed. "Can I give you a hug?" She raised her eyebrows and extended her arms forward.

Eve eyed her suspiciously. "Are you a lesbian?"

"Bi-sexual."

Eve shrugged. Hattie embraced her. She smelled of sweat and honeysuckle perfume. "I would like you to close your eyes," Hattie said as she gently squeezed Eve to her chest. "Think about the last time your mother held you and made you feel warm and safe."

Eve thought about her mother. She remembered being held and comforted. She sighed. Hattie had a way about her. But her mother preferred scents like lilac.

Hattie went on, "This is a tough love talk." She stuck another business card into what remained of Jeff's roll of bills. "My full name is Hattie Stewart. I want you to call the number on that card any time you need a ride. It doesn't matter what time of day or night. I may be in a situation that will make it difficult for me to get right to you. But I will find you and make sure you are safe."

"How much is this going to cost me?" Eve sulked.

"I don't know. Fifteen dollars an hour." Hattie sounded exasperated.

"I only make ten."

"But you get tips."

"Twelve fifty."

"Okay but 25 dollars minimum."

"Done." Eve smiled in spite of everything.

Hattie grimaced and resumed her lecture. "Life is a contact sport. You are going to get beat up pretty badly as often as not. Get used to it. If you want to get ahead, you need to be tough enough to take your lumps and keep going. I tried boxing for a while. The big thing about boxing is getting up and answering the bell every round no matter what. I have been hit so hard that I couldn't make it back to my corner under my own power. But I had to get up and go back out there when the bell rang to start the next round."

"But you weren't raped."

"He was going to butt fuck you and you were going to let him no matter what. He just came on strong because he needed to let you know he was the boss. It's a man thing. The big difference between a right cross landing on your jaw and a cock being jammed up your ass is that the right cross can kill you. The cock in your ass might cause hemorrhoids."

"What's your point?"

"I decided pretty quickly that I didn't want to be a human punching bag. I quit boxing. You need to decide if you want to keep putting up with the sexual assaults and rapes. If not, go back to waiting tables."

38

JOE GAVE APRIL a kiss and asked how her night had gone when she climbed into bed. She said it was a rough night. The restaurant had been busy and one of her customers kept giving her a hard time. He put his arms around her and went back to sleep. She couldn't stop thinking about what had happened.

April woke with a start at eight. Joe and the kids had already gone to the pool for swim team practice. Good thing he was available to take care of them. What were they going to do when he started working?

She dressed and ate breakfast. She made notes on yesterday's events in her diary. That opened the wounds again. She struggled with her anger. Eventually she decided that a survey of the other women would give her essential insights for her story. She could ask about first date, worst date, and best date. Dolly P would be at the top of her list. Eve's phone rang. It was Bridget. "How'd it go last night?"

"It was a nightmare. He raped me."

"Jeff raped you?" Genuine shock registered in Bridget's voice. "What happened?"

Eve had started sketching a picture of Jeff. She paused. "Everything was fine. Then he got me on my feet. I thought he wanted to do it standing up against the wall. We've done that before. Instead he slammed me face-first into the wall and held me there while he rammed his cock into my ass." Eve had to pause. She was choking up and couldn't speak. When she regained control, she continued, "It hurt like hell. When he stopped, I just sat on the bed trying to pull myself together. I told him our time was up and I was going home."

"That was pretty bad but I am not really surprised."

Eve was adding horns and a goatee to her sketch of Jeff. She stopped abruptly and screamed into the phone, "You knew about this and didn't say anything?"

"I've never been in that situation with him," Bridget said in a calm, reasonable voice. "I have never had sex with him. He picks up women easily. They date him for a while and then they just stop. It's a pattern that indicates he has some unresolved issues. I didn't mention it because I didn't expect you to be dating him."

Jeff's face now had a malevolent leer. "But you did suggest that I should get him to be my first date."

"I wasn't thinking about Jeff. I was worried about you trying to get some stranger in bed on your first outing," Bridget sputtered. She paused. She was back in control when she spoke again. "You guys seemed to do alright in the car the other night."

"We did. Then he took me on an afternoon outing to Naked Mountain and we had sex in the garage when we got back. He was a real gentleman the whole afternoon," Eve said. She pressed so hard on her pen that it snapped in two. "I can't imagine what he was thinking last night. But he was much rougher than I expected."

"You're not going to report him are you?"

Eve frowned. "Strange question. No. I couldn't prove anything." She started crying and had to pause to regain her composure. "I don't want him to get into any trouble. I don't know what to do."

Bridget started, "He's a great guy..."

Eve jumped in. "A great guy who takes his dates home and rapes them."

Bridget's stammered, "I'm sorry. I am really sorry about last night. But that is not the Jeff that I know. Clearly something is going on. It reminds me of Dirty Harry."

"Dirty Harry? The Clint Eastwood character?"

"Dirty Harry, my ex who idolized the movie character. They were roughnecks in high school who went straight into the Army. Jeff spent a couple of years in a combat zone. That probably toughened him up. But he may have developed some psychological issues. I'm sure Harry had problems with depression. He may even have been bipolar. Who knows what Jeff is dealing with when we're not around."

Eve closed her eyes and shook her head. "Has he ever seen a doctor about his problems?"

"I don't know. Do you want me to talk to him?"

"Please don't. There is no place in my life for him. I already have one broken relationship. Joe is probably going to want a divorce before this is all over." Eve sketched Joe above and to the right of Jeff.

"I guess Nickey told you what's going on."

"Yes." Eve added a halo above Joe's head and then crossed it out with an 'X.'

"I'm sorry."

"I'm sorry too but I don't know what I could have done differently."

"You could have ignored me and found yourself some talkative prostitutes to tell you their stories."

"Too late for that. Isn't it?" Eve's voice was resigned. She sketched herself plunging headfirst toward the bottom of the page.

"If it's any comfort, dancing was difficult for me at first. I had to get drunk the first time I stripped naked on stage. After that, I drank too much and experimented with crack. And then I escorted a guy to a hotel room. That was about the scariest night of my life."

Eve sketched a flaming cauldron at the bottom of the page. "How do you get started when you get in the room? I got in Jeff's apartment and realized I had no idea what to do."

"The first thing is to get the guy to shell out some money. You must be careful and make it clear that it's only a tip but a big tip is important for getting you in the right mood. You don't want him to claim that he paid you for sex. Then you want to be in charge. You take off your clothes and approach him. If he gets the idea that you are weak or scared or both, he could give you a lot of trouble."

"I guess Carla and Anna did tell me some of that stuff. I just couldn't think when I got in the apartment with Jeff."

"You'll do better next time. Or did Jeff scare you out of it?"

"I'm not ready to quit yet," Eve said. "Can I ask you a question?"

"I guess you've earned one."

"You have a son?"

"Two sons – Bill who is 8 and Alex 5 going on 6."

Eve sketched two boys with eager, smiling faces. "How do you manage? Joe takes care of our two in the morning but I will have to take over when he goes back to work."

"I get a lot of help from my parents. Sometimes the mornings are a challenge especially if I have been up most of the night entertaining. The boys know that I need my sleep in the afternoon. Usually their grandmother can keep them for me so I get a few hours of uninterrupted sleep."

"Do your parents know what you do?" Eve wrote down two questions: *Bridget's parents and her maiden name.*

"Yes. We've had that discussion several times."

"And they just accept it?"

"Not really. I am on probation of sorts. The boys and I get to live in their house as long as I am going to college and saving money for the future."

"You go to college?" Eve sketched Bridget in a cap and gown.

"I'm enrolled in an online program through Strayer University."

"What are you studying?"

"I don't want to talk about that right now. I will tell you that we reached a breaking point four years ago. My parents told me I could move in with them and get my life straightened out or they would file for custody of the kids and I could go to hell."

"Wow!"

"Yeah. Wow."

"What happened?"

"I'll tell you that story another time. See you tonight?"

"See you tonight."

39

ANNA GRABBED EVE for a debrief as soon as she showed up for work. Bridget had already told Anna about the problems with Jeff. Now Anna wanted details from Eve. It took a while but Anna eventually got a blow by blow of the date with Jeff.

"I told you that dating a friend as an escort is not a good idea. Besides, I didn't like him from the time I first laid eyes on him. He looked angry and aggressive," Anna complained.

"He was always respectful of me before last night."

"Before last night, you were his girlfriend. Last night you were his whore. Acceptable treatment for whores is quite different from acceptable treatment for girlfriends." Anna had the air of a mother scolding her daughter. "The men who come here are looking for something that is missing from their everyday life. Many of them want to do things that their wife or girlfriend won't allow. They want a blow job or they want a butt diddle. The wife or girlfriend won't go along with it so they come here. Our women are expected to provide whatever their date is looking for. Sometimes that can be dangerous. I do what I can to avoid putting our women in dangerous situations. But, as you found out last night, that is not always possible."

Anna's face softened. She said in a solicitous tone, "At least he let you leave without a fight. I guess that you are still sore. Do you want me to keep you off the market tonight?"

"Yes. I would like a night to heal." Eve brightened. The tongue lashing was over.

Anna went over the rules and protocols again. She explained what Eve was supposed to do when she got to the room with her date. She emphasized that Eve must make it clear that she is not being paid for sex or lascivious acts but that she expected a tip for her escort services just as waiters expect a tip for serving meals.

Dolly P made a point of sitting down for a chat with Eve when they were alone in the dressing room. "Ah hear y'all had a rough nawt."

"I guess everybody knows about it by now."

"We worry about each other so we're curious about the dates," Dolly explained.

Eve took a fresh look at the young woman sitting next to her. "How did your night go?"

"So-so. He was married and had to git home early. Not much of a tip. Married guys don't have much money t' throw around."

Eve moved on to her survey. "What was your first date like?"

"Ah was an old pro by the time Ah stahted workin' at the Tawhiti. Ah went from bein' an easy lay in high school t' bein' a gal who would put out for some help with food an' a place t' sleep t' bein' a hooker." Dolly made it sound so ordinary and unremarkable.

"So there was no big, traumatic moment when you lost your virginity?"

"There was one. The first time mah old man screwed me. Ah was thirteen."

"Oh shit. You were abused. Did you run away from home?"

"Nah. It went on for years. Mah old man had me convinced that Ah was helpin' him hold the family together. We had t' keep it secret from maw. Ah found out later that she knew all along. She was keepin' him aroun' t'pay the bills."

"So what happened?"

"Mah brother saw a TV special about parents abusin' children. He recorded it so Ah could see it. Stupid me. Ah went to the police and reported mah old man. He was arrested and sent to jail. Maw had to git a job cleanin' hotel rooms. She tole me Ah would have to fend for mahself. Ah hung around for a while moochin' off friends an' turnin' a few tricks. But the police wouldn't leave me alone so Ah decided to git outta town. Ah ended up in DC. A pimp took me under his wing. Ah left him when Ah turned 18 and got a job at the Tawhiti."

"What was it like working for the pimp?"

"Terrible. Adrien, Carla, Anna, and Ed rescued me. Ah came in here the day after Ah turned 18 and said Ah would do anythin' but Ah had to git off the street. They decided to help me out even though Ah was a mess. Ed talked t' the pimp to make him understand that he had t' keep his hands off me. If they hadn't done that, Ah would be layin' in some alley stoned outta mah mind raht now."

"I don't know what to say."

"Don't say anythin'. Ah don't want to talk about it. Ah really just came in here to see if y'all was okay." Dolly gave Eve a sympathetic look. "Are y'all sore?"

"I'll live."

Dolly walked over to her stuff and pulled out a tube. "This here ointment will heal the tissue and make y'all feel better. It has a painkiller."

Eve reached for the tube. "Thank you."

Dolly pulled the tube away and shook her head. "Y'all cain't just squirt it in there. Y'all have t' work it around inside."

"How do I do that?"

Dolly produced a dildo. "This. And it will help y'all git used t' having things shoved up yer butt."

"That doesn't sound good."

"It's one of the main things guys want when they take us to a room." Dolly put a hand on Eve's shoulder and smiled. "Ah'll be gentle and you'll thank me when it's over. Now git down on your hands and knees."

Eve was not happy but she complied. Dolly pulled Eve's pants off of her butt and squeezed some of the ointment on her asshole then worked it in with a finger before easing the dildo in. Eve started taking short panting breaths like she had learned in Lamaze. "Huh Phew. Huh Phew." Eve managed to say, "You're enjoying this, aren't you?"

Dolly laughed. "Yeah. How about you?"

"Huh Phew. Huh Phew."

The procedure wasn't that bad. It was about the same as a visit to the proctologist. But Eve was relieved to get the dildo out of her ass. She could tell that the pain level was lower. Not gone altogether but not as bad as it was. Eve pulled up her pants and sat waiting for the sensations to subside. "Are you originally from the Ozarks?"

"Knoxville, Tennessee. Ah guess the twang gives me away."

"I had relatives in Tennessee for a while."

"Where?"

"Green, Tennessee. Fred Mayberry married Priscilla Yoakum there back in 1792."

"Are y'all serious?"

"I am. They were on their way from Virginia to Illinois."

"Cum'awn. How would y'all know somethin' like that?"

"I looked it up online."

"Y'all can look stuff like that up on line? How do y'all even know what to look for?"

"You start with your parents and grandparents and work backward."

Dolly let out a disgusted sigh and shook her head. What a perfectly ridiculous waste of time. "Shouldn't y'all be gittin' ready for yer next dance."

Eve nodded. "Yeah." She started putting on some clothes that she could take off as soon as she got on stage. *There goes the bell. Time for the next round.*

40

AT 10:05, ANNA caught Eve leaving the stage after a dance set and led her to a table where a man in a business suit sat alone. His name was Jerrod and he very much wanted a private dance by Eve Sinful. Eve's head jerked back slightly. "Now?"

"Yes." Jerrod flashed a broad smile. "Now would be great." He was a small man with a large, forceful personality.

Eve offered him her arm and escorted him back to the curtained off dance space. After the dance, he wanted her to escort him back to his hotel room. She was going to object but Anna was standing behind him, vigorously nodding her head, "Do it."

He was in one of the most expensive rooms in one of the swankiest hotels in DC. Negotiations were easy. She explained the rules. He put a hundred dollar bill on the dresser for later. She was disappointed but that was the target tip. It was more than she might get at a Marriott or a Howard Johnson's. She removed her clothes and went over to help him with his. They had sex. He came a couple of times then they lay in bed and cuddled. He talked about his business and his travels.

He was on the road at least six months out of the year. He sounded like he had grown up in New England.

She asked if he was married. He had been. The marriage had lasted less than a year. Since then, he'd had steady girlfriends. They didn't want marriage and they weren't possessive. It was very casual. He had developed a list of women he could hook up with in various cities during his travels. He hadn't been in DC for a while and did not know who to get in touch with. His cab driver from the airport to the hotel had suggested that he try the Tahiti. So here they were lounging in a big bed after some great sex.

When he rolled her over and started stroking her butt, she said, "We're going to have to use a different condom."

He stopped in mid-stroke as if he had been slapped. Eve said, "It's alright. I've had some rough experiences and I have to take precautions."

"Oh. Spoils the spontaneity doesn't it?"

"I'm sorry but these condoms have special lubricants that will make it better. You can do that for me, can't you?"

"Yes. Of course."

She got out of bed and sashayed over to her purse for one of the condoms that Dolly had given her. While her legs transported her across the room her head engaged in conversation with a disembodied Hattie Stewart. Hattie drawled, *"I told you. No matter what he's going to butt fuck you and you are going to let him."*

"At least he's being gentle."

"But you are still answering the bell."

"And he's going to use a lubricated condom." Eve turned and showed the condom to Jerrod. She gave him a happy grin.

Hattie's voice asked, *"What about when you get home? Is Joe going to want some nookie?"*

"His little bimbo is probably taking care of that right now. When I get home, he'll kiss me and tell me he's glad I'm home. Then he'll roll over and go right back to sleep, if he wakes up at all."

When she got back to the bed, she took Jerrod's cock in her hand and gave it a little special treatment before pulling the condom down over it. She kissed him on the chest and then on the mouth. Then she rolled over on her side and presented her butt to him. He picked up where he had left off but was quickly knocking on the door. He went in and humped her. It was easier than last night. She kept making squealing sounds that might have indicated pleasure but in fact were reactions to the pain. He held her in his arms for a while after he had finished. She kept her eye on the clock. At two she said, "Last call. I'm off duty in half an hour."

"I thought we could negotiate how the night went. I would like you to stay here. I'll get you home in the morning."

"I have to leave. I can't stay. There is nothing to negotiate."

Jerrod frowned. "Why not?"

"It's a personal matter. But look, you got a great deal. You paid for two hours and you got three."

Jerrod's mouth turned down in disappointment. "How about one more blow job?"

When she had finished, she jumped out of the bed and raced to the bathroom to rinse out her mouth. She found her cell phone and texted her location to Hattie. "What was that?" Jerrod asked.

"My ride."

She walked over to him and kissed him. "I enjoyed tonight. You are a great guy."

"Can I see you again?"

"You know where I work," Eve said curtly. She was pulling on her clothes.

"No. I mean can I get your contact information so I can skip the Tahiti BS?"

Eve closed her eyes and shook her head. "I'm not going to freelance. It's too complicated."

"What if you're not there next time I get back?" He demanded.

She slid into her dress and slipped on her shoes. She studied him for a moment. "I like all of the women at the Tahiti. I'm sure anyone of them would be happy to take care of you."

Jerrod stared intently at Eve, his jaw set. "I want to see you again."

Eve shrugged. "If I am available next time you're in town, pick me up at the Tahiti." Her tone was matter of fact. "I would love to do this with you again. Now I have to go."

She checked her cell phone. Hattie was on the way. Jerrod got out of the bed and walked to his pants. Eve was at the door when Jerrod said, "Wait a minute."

He pulled out his wallet. He walked over to her and handed her four more hundred dollar bills. "This is partly to let you know that you have really made this a special night and partly to keep you thinking about me until I can get back to town."

She kissed him and walked out of the room.

41

HATTIE SIGNALED FOR Eve to get in front with her. She called in that she was taking a break and flipped on the "Off Duty" sign. As she pulled away from the curb, she asked, "How'd it go?"

"Much better. But I was trying to have sex with this guy and all I could think about was you telling me he was going to butt fuck me and I was going to let him."

"I was right. Wasn't I?" she said in that sweet, Deep South voice of hers.

"Yes. But I didn't need you in my head."

"I'm right about something else," Hattie said. She reached over with her left hand and pulled Eve's head around. They were inches apart looking into each other's eyes. "You need to learn how to protect yourself. We are going to have a self-defense course this weekend. Look into it."

Eve gently removed Hattie's hand. "I will as soon as I can get myself out of bed." She laid her head back against the seat. "Maybe I'll get dressed and have some breakfast. But I promise I'll look into it this morning. Will you put on some music and let me close my eyes for a little while?"

Eve felt someone shaking her. She opened her eyes and looked around. She was in a car parked next to her car at the metro station. She looked over at Hattie and said in a sleepy voice, "Thanks."

"I can drive you home if you want."

"No. I'll need my car when I wake up. Besides I need some time to adjust to being April."

Hattie's head jerked around. "Who is April?"

"A few weeks ago, I would have said that I was April, now April seems to be the woman who lives with my family and takes care of things around the house."

"Eve's alter ego?"

"The idea was for Eve to be April's alter ego." There was a bitter edge to her voice. "Either way please don't let on that you know."

"Your secret is safe with me," Hattie assured her.

Eve looked at her watch. "Less than two hours. I owe you twenty-five dollars."

"Correct."

"But I got a good tip so you get a good tip." She peeled off one of Jerrod's hundred dollar bills and handed it to Hattie. "Keep the change."

When she got home, April poured herself two fingers of Jameson Signature Reserve and took it up to bed with her. As predicted, Joe kissed her on the cheek and said he was glad she was home then rolled over and went back to sleep. She sipped her whiskey and considered the situation. She was almost out of the swamp but she had no idea what waited on the other side. It was going to be different. That was the only guarantee. She snuggled up to Joe's back and put her arm around him.

42

JOE AND THE kids were still eating breakfast when April made her appearance in the kitchen. After they had left for swim practice, she cleaned up the kitchen and poured a second cup of coffee. She felt a lightness that made her think of the song. *"I could have danced all night. I could have spread my wings and done a thousand things I've never done before."* She felt like dancing. It made no sense, but that was how she felt.

She called the Sun Tang Woo Martial Arts Studio. When Ernie Williams answered, she asked about the self-defense course scheduled for Saturday and Sunday. Ernie said they still had some slots but she should come in and register now because it would probably fill up by this time tomorrow.

April found the studio in Arlington. The main area was a 400-square foot open space. Most of the floor was covered with heavy mats to prevent injury from falls. An L shaped walkway led from the front door to the back where there was an office for Williams and his staff, and dressing rooms for the students. The wall opposite the front door was covered with mirrors. A stretching bar, punching bags, and kicking targets, were set up along one wall.

Williams explained the history of the studio and the various programs ranging from training for kids to adult classes to full combat training. Williams had become interested in oriental martial arts while stationed in Japan and Korea as a sergeant in the army. After he left the army, he spent five years in Taiwan mastering the Sun Tang Woo style and returned to the US as a certified instructor authorized to bill himself as a Sun Tang Woo master or Sifu.

April said that she was interested in the course because Hattie Stewart had told her about it. She was going to register and would be here for the classes this weekend. She also wanted to register her daughter. Williams said her daughter was a little too young for this course, but he promised to make an exception, if there was room. He really hoped that April's daughter would sign up for classes designed for teenagers.

April walked the three blocks from the martial arts studio to the Sweet Nothings Adult Inclinations Shoppe. The store windows were decorated with sexy bedroom clothes for both women and men. Inside, the store featured more clothes as well as paraphernalia, books, videos, and bawdy games. April stared at the clerk in disbelief. She looked like she should still be in high school. She wore her straight cut hair down to her shoulders. The clerk displayed body piercings in her ears and nose. What April couldn't see were the decorations on her breasts, navel, and clit. April couldn't bring herself to discuss dildos and ass cream with this child.

The young woman appeared strong and confident. She smiled as she approached April. "Can I help you?"

The clerk read April's look of dismay and assured her, "Don't worry. I'm familiar with everything in here and we can talk about anything."

April pressed her lips together and cleared her throat. "I'm looking for some condoms."

"Anything in particular?"

"I'm looking for ones that are lubricated."

"You mean the ones they recommend for butt fucking?" The young woman led April across the room to a condom display. She pointed out three different kinds.

April frowned and bit her lip. "Can you recommend one of them?"

The clerk pointed to the Trojan brand. "I use these."

"A friend of mine said that I should get some kind of cream that has a mild anesthetic for my rectum." April paused before adding sheepishly, "My boyfriend was a little overzealous the other night."

The clerk produced a tube of the cream that Dolly P had used. "Do you want a dildo?"

"My friend suggested that I should get one."

"What size?"

"I have no idea."

The clerk produced a sleeve that had 6 dildos from small to very large. "You should probably buy this. It isn't expensive and you can experiment with different ones."

She noticed April staring at the largest one. "I know. I tried that one once. Never again. But it's great in your vagina."

April paid and thanked the clerk for her help. She walked back to her car and drove home wondering what Becky knew about things like that.

43

AS THURSDAY EVENING wore on, Eve grew tense and restless. She fretted about Joe and Nickey. Joe's relationship with Lee ate away at her. Around 10:30 she focused on a nerdy, mid-level professional guy. Either an accountant or an engineer. She pulled up a chair next to him and asked how he liked the show. "Pretty good," he said.

"Have you seen me dance?"

"Yeah. You're hot."

Eve lit up. "Thanks." She focused her gaze on his eyes. "Maybe you would like a private dance."

He pulled back - eyes wide with shock. Eve leaned forward to give him a good view. His eyes locked on her boobs.

"Or maybe you would just like to go someplace where you and I could have a quiet conversation by ourselves."

He frowned and bit his lip. "I don't think I could do that."

Eve put a hand on his arm. She was sympathetic. "Worried about your wife?"

He said nothing but she had clearly hit a nerve.

"There's no need for you to worry," Eve assured him. "We're not going to do anything that will get her upset."

He shook his head. "I could get in trouble."

Her eyes were captivating, her perfume intoxicating. She oozed sex - cried out to be fondled. "How could you get in trouble? You're here and that's okay. Why wouldn't it be okay for us to go someplace quiet for a private conversation?"

He tried to look away. "How much would that cost?"

She stroked his arm. "It's just a hundred dollars for two hours."

He shook his head. "I don't have that kind of money with me."

"You could use a credit card."

"My wife would spot a charge like that and want to know what it was all about."

Eve brightened up. "Where are you staying?"

"The Marriott."

"Okay. They have an ATM machine in the lobby, don't they?"

"I think so."

"They do. I've been there before." Eve looked off toward the stage and wet her lips. "You could take out some money and say that you needed it to cover meals and things."

He took a swig of his drink. He shook his head. "I don't know."

"I'll tell you what. I really like you." She squeezed his hands. "I'll cover the escort fee. When we get to your hotel, you can take out some cash and pay me back."

He blushed. A smile crept across his face. Eve signaled for Anna to come over to the table. "What's your name?" Eve asked.

"John Smith."

"John Smith? Is that really your name?"

"Yes. That is really my name."

Anna came over to the table. Eve said, "John Smith wants me to go back to his room with him."

"Okay. I'll take care of the paperwork while you change."

Eve looked up at Anna. "But he doesn't have the money with him." She smiled at Smith. "I told him I would cover it and he could give me the money when we get to his hotel."

Anna frowned. Smith asked, "What paperwork?"

Eve pulled his hands to her lips and kissed his fingers. "It's nothing, just some information in case I end up dead in your room. That's not going to happen, is it?"

His mouth dropped open. He wasn't a murderer. He would never do anything to hurt this woman. He shook his head.

Eve said, "By this time tomorrow night those papers will be shredded and in the dumpster with a ton of other stuff."

Smith looked dubious. Eve brushed her breasts against him as she rose and leaned in to give him a kiss on the cheek. "Don't worry. We are going to have a great time and it will be our secret."

Anna was still frowning. Eve winked at her.

Anna took Smith's hand. "Come on, John. This will only take a couple of minutes then you and Eve can get going."

Smith was stiff and uncomfortable when they got to his room. They had a tense discussion about the tip. Eve told him to put out a twenty. If at the end of the night, he didn't think she was worth the money, he could keep it. But if he was happy with the way things went, she would appreciate him adding a couple of more twenties. Then there was a lot of foreplay before he would relax and have sex with her. She kept her eye on the time. At one o'clock, she informed him that their time was up and she had to get back to work. While she was getting dressed, he got up and produced a couple of more twenties. He handed her the sixty dollars. "I had a great time."

"Me too," she said and gave him a kiss before escaping from the room.

Eve called Hattie and told her to make it quick. "I want you to take me by my house. I want to surprise Joe."

44

THEY REACHED THE house a little after two. Hattie found a parking spot across the street where they could observe without being seen. Eve pointed to one of the cars in the driveway, "That one must be hers."

"Whose?"

Eve's lip curled into a sneer. "My husband's girlfriend."

"You're kidding."

Eve shook her head. "I've been told that she hangs around until two thirty and then takes off." She looked back at the house. "That's when I get off work. Joe figures that I can't get home before three. They give themselves a little safety margin."

"What are you going to do?"

Eve pulled out her cell phone. "Take some pictures."

At 2:25 Eve got out of the cab and took a position where she had a good view of the front door. She took a couple of practice shots. The front door opened just after two thirty. Eve switched the camera to movie mode. Joe stepped out on the porch. He was followed by an attractive woman who looked to be in her late twenties or early thirties. The couple embraced and kissed for a while. Then the woman strolled to her car and drove off.

Eve got back in the cab and asked Hattie to drive her back to the metro station so she could retrieve her car. "Was that her?" Hattie asked.

"I haven't seen her for almost twenty years but I'm sure it was."

"You know her?"

Eve's jaw tightened. Her voice was bitter. "She's an old friend's younger sister."

A Lexus drove by and blinked its lights twice before they could get going. Hattie asked, "Do you know her?"

"Nickey. It's complicated. Let's get going."

Joe jumped when April climbed into bed with him. "You're home early."

"It was a slow night." She kissed him on the cheek. "I kept thinking about you so I decided to take off early and come on home."

He rolled over on his back and propped himself up with his elbows. No hug. No kiss. "I've been meaning to tell you something but I haven't had a good opportunity."

April went cold. Her heart started racing. Joe said, "I'm going back to work on Monday. You are going to have to start taking care of Becky and JJ in the mornings."

April relaxed. "This is sudden."

"I told you before that if I couldn't find a permanent job, I was going to have to sign up for temp work." He turned to get her reaction. "We have some big bills coming up and I need to start bringing in some money. One of the agencies that I have been talking to called me on Tuesday and said that they had a spot for me with Verizon but I had to start immediately. I went in on Wednesday and filled out the paperwork. Yesterday, Verizon agreed to take me on."

"That's great, honey." April smiled. "About those big bills," she began, "I guess that I forgot to tell you about the advance for my book."

"You got an advance?"

She nodded. "It came in a week or so ago." She put her hand on his arm. "I've been pretty busy and didn't get around to depositing the check until this week."

"How much?"

She squeezed his arm. She giggled, "Fifty K."

Joe stared at his wife in disbelief.

She was suddenly serious. "I told you, baby, my life has been really hectic." She stroked his arm. "Pat told me I was going to get the advance but I didn't know what it was when it showed up in the mail. After that, I guess it just slipped my mind." April was as sweet and sincere as she could be under the circumstances.

He grunted and said, "It sounds like we're in pretty good shape all of a sudden."

She closed her eyes and pressed her lips together. He hadn't said anything about her job at the Tahiti. That was a worrisome sign.

She perked up. "How about I get us a drink to celebrate?"

April went downstairs to pour two whiskeys. She took her time. The whiskeys weren't needed. Joe had rolled over and gone back to sleep. She went back downstairs and sipped good Irish whiskey with her feet curled up under her on the couch. Thoughts about her husband and the other woman kept her company.

45

EVE WAS IN a good mood by the time she left for work Friday night. She had worked on her story, gotten in a workout, and started a romance/adventure novel about an Irish girl who comes to the United States in the nineteenth century. Jeff was waiting for her near the entrance to the Tahiti when she arrived. He blocked her path a few yards from the door. "Why are you accusing me of rape?" he hissed.

She stopped and looked up wide-eyed. "What are you talking about?"

"You're telling people that I raped you."

"No," Eve said emphatically. She looked Jeff straight in the eyes. "I am not telling people any such thing."

"Bee said you told her that I raped you," Jeff insisted. "You were the one who wanted to go to my apartment. Our sex was consensual. Why did you tell her that I raped you?"

Eve closed her eyes and looked up to the heavens. "Ah. I see." She frowned at Jeff. "That was a private conversation with a friend and I specifically asked her not to talk to you about it."

Jeff leaned closer. Their faces were almost touching. His eyes were wild with anger. "Why did you tell her that I raped you?"

Eve met him with a cold stare. "Because you did and I needed to talk to somebody about it."

"I didn't rape you." Jeff was getting angrier and louder.

Eve crossed her arms. "Actually you did." She gritted her teeth. "What you did was wrong and you know it."

"You were there of your own free will and our sex was consensual."

"It was consensual until you slammed me into the wall and pinned me there while you forced your way into my butt."

Jeff pulled back in shock. He stared, unable to speak for a long time. "Why didn't you tell me to stop?" he asked almost inaudibly.

"You forced yourself on me. That is rape," Eve shot back. "It doesn't matter that I came into your room and took my clothes off so we could have sex. It doesn't matter that I let you have your way." She paused to glare at him. Her face contorted into an angry snarl. "You forced yourself on me and that is rape."

Ed came up and grabbed Eve's arm. "You two can't stand outside and have this conversation." He pulled Eve toward the club. "Get inside and get ready for work."

She pushed past Jeff and continued toward the entrance to the Tahiti. The sounds of Ed dressing-down Jeff followed her. "Stay away from her. She's trouble." The ass-chewing continued but Eve shut it out.

Later in the evening, Ed came up to Eve. "Are you okay?"

"I'll be fine."

"If he bothers you again, let me know."

"I hope it doesn't come to that. I like him but I should not have gotten involved with him."

"I have never seen him react to a woman the way he reacts to you. He's just obsessed with you."

"I know he wants to have a relationship with me. I can't handle that right now. I tried to tell him that before."

"I told him to stay away from you. I hope he listens."

"I don't know what you heard but it's a private matter between him and me," Eve said.

"I'm not sure that's true. There may be a bigger problem. You may be the first and only woman to tell him to his face but I don't think you are the only woman who wanted to tell him off. I told him that he needed to listen to you."

She told Anna that she would dance but could not go out with anybody that night. She also asked for a night off on Saturday.

On the way back to her car, she told Hattie about the run-in with Jeff. Hattie said she needed to get a gun. Eve rolled her eyes. Jeff wouldn't hurt her and she couldn't shoot him. But the stakes would change in less than 24 hours. An armed man would confront and shoot an escort - his former lover - and her date in the Tahiti parking lot. The escort, Lena Johnson, would be critically wounded. That would change everyone's calculations.

46

BECKY LEFT HER Saturday morning swim meet an hour early so she could attend the self-defense course with her mom. She rode in silence for a while before asking, "What's going on with you and Dad?"

April turned to look at Becky. "I think all of the stress that we have been dealing with is starting to get to us." She turned back to the road. "Your dad has been out of work for almost six months. That hasn't happened since he started working. And that was before you were born. I had to take this night job as a waitress after I was fired from my other job. That has put a real crimp in our family life."

"Dad says he's going back to work. Does that mean you can quit your job?"

"Yes and no. Your dad won't be getting paid for a few weeks. In the meantime, we have bills to pay. I will quit but I don't know when exactly."

Becky eyed her mother suspiciously. "Dad seems pretty upset with you."

April smiled. "Dad has always been the breadwinner. He isn't happy about me taking over that role."

"Why is that woman visiting dad at night?"

April's head jerked toward Becky. "What woman?"

Becky studied her mother's face. "I don't know for sure. She just shows up after dad has put us to bed. They talk in real soft voices so we won't hear them."

April drove in silence trying to figure out the best way to answer. "I think we are just going to have to let that one ride for the time being." April turned and smiled at Becky. "I'll talk to your father about it when I get a chance."

They reached the studio well before the class began. Hattie came over to greet them. "April, I'm glad you could make it. Is this your daughter?"

"Yes. Becky, this is Hattie Stewart. She makes sure I get back home safely after work."

Becky shook hands with Hattie. "It's nice to meet you, Mrs. Stewart."

"I'm not married. Just call me Hattie."

"Mom, I thought you took the metro," Becky said.

"I take the metro when I go to work but the trains stop running for the night before I get off." April nodded toward Hattie. "She picks me up after work and drives me back to my car."

After the class, April asked Becky if she remembered them talking about the MacDermots. She did.

"They live pretty close. I would like to see if we could drop in for a short visit on the way home."

"Okay."

The MacDermotts were relaxing in the living room when April and Becky rang their doorbell. Amy pulled April into the house for a big hug. "It's been so long." She looked April up and down and nodded approvingly. "I see you are taking good care of yourself." She hugged Becky. "It is so good to finally meet you. You look just like your mother." Becky blushed. "It is very nice to meet you, Mrs. MacDermot."

The adults caught up on events of the last seventeen years and reminisced about the good old days. Amy was an executive assistant to a senior VP. April said she was back to waiting tables and trying to launch her writing career. Becky listened patiently for a while. The tales from her mother's past were educational but only mildly interesting. She fell head over heels for some guy in Rome and was ready to marry him until she found out he was already married. She skipped class to attend a rally for women's rights. Nothing earthshaking. Becky roamed the living room inspecting photos. One of them stopped her in her tracks. She blurted out, "Who is this?"

"That's my little sister," Amy said.

"She's beautiful. Is she a model?"

"Nothing so glamorous. She's a receptionist."

"How is Aileen doing?" April asked.

Amy shook her head. "Not so great. She went through a divorce last year and was laid off in June." Amy studied her hands. "We invited her out for a visit to give her a chance to figure things out."

"Is she here now?" April asked.

"No. She had to fly back home to take care of mom." Amy clasped her hands between her knees. "Mom had a stroke yesterday. The doctors think it's an aneurysm that started bleeding out." Amy looked up at April. Her eyes were moist. "Lee agreed to go back and see what she could do."

"That's too bad. If it was an aneurysm the prognosis isn't too good," April said sympathetically

"No. It isn't. I'll fly out there sometime in the next couple of days to see what I can do to help."

April closed her eyes and bit her lip. Then she turned to Amy's husband. "Mike, I'm thrilled that Joe bumped into you. The racquetball seems to agree with him."

"It's been good for me too. Keeps the legs and heart in shape."

She leaned forward and rested her arms on her knees. "You know, I met Joe at your wedding but for the life of me, I can't remember whose friend he was."

Mike laughed. "Both. Joe, Amy, and I were part of a rat pack in high school. Joe and I went to college together but the whole gang stayed close for a long time."

They continued chatting until April looked at her watch and said that she had to get home to make dinner. As April and Becky walked back to their car, Becky pointed toward the driveway. "She drives that car."

April stopped short. She looked at her daughter and then at the car. "Who drives that car?"

"Mrs. MacDermot's sister. She drives that car when she comes over to visit Dad."

April forced a smile. "Well, if she's back in Ohio, she won't be coming over for visits. Please try not to worry about it. I will talk to your father."

Nothing was said about the visits during dinner. Later when April and Joe were alone, she said, "We stopped by the MacDermots on the way home this afternoon."

"I guess that's why you were so late getting back." Joe did not bother to look up from the newspaper he was reading.

"Mrs. Sheehan had a stroke yesterday. Lee had to fly back to Ohio this morning to look after her mother."

"Oh?" Joe jerked his head around to catch April's expression. She was sure that Lee's departure was the upsetting part.

"Becky told me that Lee has been using Amy's car to drive over here and visit you at night."

Joe started to deny everything but thought better of it. April continued in a cold hard tone, "In the future have some consideration for your daughter. Take your slut to a hotel room. Keep her away from our home and our children."

April and Joe were living in separate universes even though they were sitting in the same room watching the same TV. The eleven o'clock news opened with a breaking story about a woman being shot outside a bar in DC. The name of the victim had not been released. A suspect was in custody. More details would be provided as they became available.

April said, "Shit!"

She stormed upstairs to her office and shut herself in for the night. She didn't need any more details. It was the Tahiti. The woman was an escort and the suspect was no doubt her ex. Those details would be available tomorrow. For tonight, one of her friends was in the hospital with a life-threatening injury inflicted by someone who used to love her.

47

MASS WAS A strange experience. April felt like a hypocrite attending the service with Joe as husband and wife while their marriage was falling apart. They were still together physically but the spiritual separation was palpable. She had not felt wrong about Mass last Sunday after spending a night entertaining men at the Tahiti. She didn't feel a need to confess her nightly liaisons. April was completely detached from the goings on in Eve's life. She remembered every conversation and every act but they meant nothing to her. She was not the least bit contrite. That bothered her. Celebrating love and community with Joe when their love was being destroyed felt terribly wrong.

April took Becky back to the Sun Tang Woo studio for the second part of the self-defense course. Hattie caught April and Becky as they were leaving the studio. "You heard about the shooting last night?"

"I saw it on the news," April said.

"It was one of the dancers from the Tahiti, Lena Johnson. She was shot by an ex-boyfriend. They haven't determined a motive. But you have to get a gun before somebody shoots you."

April mouthed, "Watch what you're saying."

Becky either didn't notice or chose to ignore the exchange. She asked Hattie, "Do you carry a gun?"

Hattie leaned over to pick up a piece of paper. When she straightened up, she had a pistol in her hand. "Yes."

Becky's eyes widened in shocked surprise. "You wear it on your ankle. Right?"

"Very good," Hattie said.

"Have you ever had to use it?"

"Once. One of my passengers stuck his gun to my head as soon as he got in. He told me to drive to an ATM and get some cash. When we got to the bank parking lot, I pulled my gun as I was getting out. Then I hesitated after I stood up. When he stuck his head between my seat and the door frame to tell me to hurry up, I shot him."

"What happened then?"

"I called the police. They confirmed that it was self-defense. They shipped the body to the morgue and took my cab to their headquarters. I had to get a lawyer to get them to give my cab back so it still cost me."

"Can I see it?"

Hattie handed her gun to the girl. "I'll tell you what. If we can get permission from your mom, I'll take you to a range where you can practice shooting."

"Isn't she too young?" April objected.

"Where I grew up," Hattie said condescendingly. "Everybody started learning to use a gun almost as soon as they could walk." She fixed a hard stare on April. "You're off tomorrow. Do you want to pick out a gun and take care of the paperwork?"

"I suppose," April mumbled. "Right now I have to get home and get ready for work."

Hattie softened. "I'll meet you at your house and drive you over. That will save you some time and energy."

48

HATTIE INSISTED THAT April close her eyes and try to get some sleep on the way to the Tahiti. Eve had a message from Nickey to deal with first. Nickey answered right away. "Hi, Eve. How are you doing?'

"I'm on my way to work. I don't have much time. Do you have anything important?"

"Lee Bell went back to Ohio."

"Her mother is in bad shape. Lee had to go back to take care of her. I talked to Amy MacDermot yesterday. Anything else?"

"Joe is going back to work."

"He starts first thing tomorrow morning. He told me."

"Did he tell you that we celebrated by doing it in a stall in the men's room?"

"No." Eve rolled her eyes and shook her head. "At least he knows better than to tell me something like that. I don't want to hear any more about you and Joe. Is that clear?"

"Yes. Have a good evening."

The atmosphere at the Tahiti was somber. The police had shut the place down for most of the day while they conducted their investigation. From the Tahiti's point of view, nothing came of the it. There was no evidence that the man had been a customer. He was hiding in the parking lot waiting to ambush his ex-girlfriend when she came out. He may have been out there one or more times previously to plan his attack. The lack of security in the parking lot was an issue but it didn't amount to criminal negligence. Ed was responsible for keeping an eye on the parking lot but he was busy with other duties at the time of the attack. He heard the shots and rushed out to see what was going on. It was over by the time Ed reached the scene. The escort and her date were lying in the parking lot bleeding. The shooter was standing over them in shock. He offered no resistance.

The crowd that showed up Sunday night included gawkers who were suddenly interested in what was happening at the Tahiti. The security presence in the Tahiti parking lot was noticeably beefed up. For her part, Eve wanted the night over as soon as possible. The high she got from performing on stage improved her mood. She did a few private dances. Acting like she enjoyed it helped her feel better. Eve went to a motel with one man early in the evening but told him that she had to get back as soon as their time was up. She called a cab from the lobby of the motel because she didn't want to bother Hattie.

Vickie Szabo, who used the stage name Vixen, wanted to go downtown to check on Marge Bechmann, a friend who was working the streets. She had not heard from the woman in over a week, which was unusual. The shooting in a relatively safe place like the Tahiti parking lot made Vickie think about what might be happening to her friend. Dolly P said she would go along. Eve couldn't pass on the opportunity. It would give her a chance to check out another aspect of the business. She sent a message to Hattie to let her know the plan.

At 2:35, Vickie sent out a *Where RU* ping to Marge. The response was *FrnklnSq*.

Franklin Square was a public park on 13th Street NE in DC. At 2:50 the three women headed out to the parking lot where Hattie was waiting to give them a ride. Vickie texted Marge, *CU n 15*.

They found Marge with some friends occupying two benches near the center of the park, enjoying a dumpster dinner. The food had been snagged before it reached a dumpster. Marge had traded a blow job for a couple of mostly full bottles of Merlot and a partially eaten birthday cake. The main course consisted of two pizzas which were supposedly purchased at the kitchen door for a buck apiece.

Vickie had gotten married right after high school. She went from an abusive father to an abusive husband. The marriage lasted less than a year. Vickie supported herself by working as a waitress and keeping a couple of boyfriends happy. One night, Marge showed up at the kitchen door of the restaurant where Vickie worked. She desperately needed something to eat. The two women struck up a friendship and Vickie invited Marge to crash at her apartment. They operated a successful brothel for a short time before the apartment management got wise and had them evicted. Marge then schooled Vickie in street survival. Vickie found out about the Tahiti during a chance encounter with one of her old boyfriends. She applied for work and was offered a job as a dancer. Marge didn't make it because she needed her crack. The Tahiti management wanted nothing to do with addicts.

The two women kept in touch. While Marge occasionally stayed with Vickie for short periods, Vickie wouldn't allow any business in her apartment. She could not afford another eviction.

The other women in the group all had tales of abuse. They were runaways. They were homeless. They did whatever was necessary to survive. They would screw, suck, steal, and beg to get what they needed. The hard part for Eve was that three of them were underage girls. One of them was almost exactly the same age as her daughter.

Talk turned from hard luck stories to politics. Obama was going to win the election. No question about it. The Republicans had a grumpy old curmudgeon and his ditzy, glamour girl running mate. The Democrats had a suave, good-looking young stud. The contest was over except for counting the votes. Marge said she hoped Obama would get them out of Iraq. Her younger brother was on his third tour and it was destroying him. A youngAfrican American girl called Serena went into a comic riff. She carried on a three-way conversation: President Bush and Vice-President Cheney trying to explain the importance of the Iraq War to an incredulous Laura Bush. It was hysterical. It was also heartbreaking. Here was one of the most talented comediennes that Eve had ever seen sitting in a public park eating food from a dumpster after a night of turning tricks.

Hattie tugged on Eve's arm. "It's five. We've got to get going."

April had several urgent messages from Joe. He was concerned because he hadn't heard from her. She called and told him that she was in a cab on the way home. She explained that the opportunity to meet some street prostitutes was too good to pass up.

49

HATTIE PULLED UP in front of April's house at a quarter to six. "Lousy timing. We're too early to wake people up and too late to go to bed," April observed. "I want to sit here in the car and close my eyes for half an hour."

They entered the house at 6:20. Joe was dozing in a recliner with his phone in his lap. He was dressed except for his sport coat. April nudged him gently and said, "Hey, baby, I'm sorry I'm so late. Do you want a quick cup of coffee before you leave?"

Joe opened his eyes and studied her. "Are you okay? What happened?"

"It was a rough night. Everybody was upset about the shooting. One of the girls decided that she had to go check on her friend in DC. I went along to see if I could get a different slant on the business. Hattie went along to make sure I got home in time."

"Was it worth it?"

"It was for me but I guess you didn't get much sleep."

"I got enough. I woke up around four and realized you weren't home. After that, I couldn't sleep. You've been up all night. What are you going to do?"

"I'll be okay. I'll get the kids to the pool and take a nap while they're at practice. Then Hattie is going to take me shopping for a gun. Becky will probably go with us so JJ will either be at the pool or with Gramma Becky. By the way, Joe, this is Hattie. And, Hattie, this is Joe. I'm going to make some coffee and get the kids moving."

April was singing softly as she walked away, "Too-ra-loo-ra-loo-ral, Too-ra-loo-ra-li. Hush now don't you cry…"

Hattie and April dropped the kids off a half hour before swim practice and went directly back home for a nap. Hattie drove while April rode shotgun. Back at the house, April grabbed the couch. Hattie stretched out on the floor. She was asleep in two minutes and her internal clock was perfect. She woke up seconds before the alarm on April's cell phone chimed. The women had fifteen minutes to get to the pool and pick up Becky. It took less than an hour to get to the Smith and Wesson Gun Emporium. The emporium was owned and operated by Frank Smith and his wife, Olivia (Wesson) Smith, who was a descendant of Daniel B. Wesson a co-founder of Smith and Wesson Firearms. The Gun Emporium carried a very complete selection of firearms. It had indoor and outdoor shooting ranges. It also had rooms for providing instruction to customers. The Gun Emporium was one of many establishments in the area certified by the Utah Bureau of Criminal Identification to train customers and issue a concealed carry permit. The Smith's daughter, Jade, managed most of the day to day operations.

Hattie found Jade and introduced her to April and Becky. Jade said, "I assume that we are trying to get you outfitted today, April."

"Yes," April replied.

"And you have no idea what you are looking for because you have never wanted to be anywhere near a gun."

"That's about it."

"We'll rent you a gun and a lane for an hour. During that hour, I will give you some basic instructions then we will have you practice with four or five guns. When you have settled on one of them, we'll get the paperwork started. You should be able to come in and pick up your gun next Monday."

"That fast?" April asked sarcastically.

Jade smiled condescendingly. "Actually that is fast. I am assuming that you will want a concealed carry permit that is good in Virginia, Maryland, and DC. The district is the hang-up. You will have to take your paperwork to police headquarters to be processed. If you're lucky, they will mail your license out late Friday and you will get it on Monday. But it could be closer to a week from Friday. We have to complete a background check, which doesn't take long but there is also a mandatory waiting period. You will be able to pick up your gun next Monday and play with it even if you haven't received your DC license."

April nodded. Jade turned to Becky. "What can I do for you today, young lady? You are too young to get a license but you are certainly old enough to start getting used to the idea that you have a right to protect yourself."

"I'd like to try some guns and find out what it's like to shoot them."

"I'll give you the same deal that I gave your mom. Hattie can show you what to do."

Hattie took Becky off for a tour of the emporium and its gun collection.

Jade asked April, "Why are you interested in carrying a gun all of a sudden?"

"I work night shift at the Tahiti. One of our women was shot a couple of days ago so now I have to carry a gun for protection."

"You don't sound convinced."

"She was ambushed by an armed assailant. Would she have fared better if she had been carrying a gun?"

"I'm sorry about what happened to your friend. But she might have been able to shoot her attacker before he shot her, if…" Jade paused. "If she had had a gun and was prepared to use it."

April looked at the floor and crushed out an imaginary cigarette.

"Remember he was drunk and inexperienced. He probably made some mistakes that would have allowed her to reach for her gun and shoot."

"She was a stripper on her way to a hotel room with a date," April snapped. "Where was she going to be carrying this gun?"

"Is that your situation?"

"Between you and me, yes."

"We have some nice purses with pockets for carrying your weapon. You just casually reach inside, pull the weapon out, and start shooting."

"And if he starts shooting while I'm reaching into the purse?"

"You're no worse off than you would be if you didn't have the gun. A professional hit man is going to kill you if that's what he wants to do. A drunken boyfriend, who is venting, probably won't realize what you are up to until it's too late. There's a good chance that you will find the gun useful when the situation arises."

April folded her arms across her chest and looked across the room. "How much will this gun cost me?" She didn't want a gun.

"I would really like you to try the guns out and get a feel for them before we start talking price."

"You would like me to fall in love with something expensive so I'll buy it whether I need it or not."

"You have never fired a pistol before. Get the feel of the weapons and then worry about price," Jade said patiently. "The guns that I have in mind are moderately priced and good value. You can buy whichever one you like."

Jade set April and Becky up with 5 guns: a Glock, a Beretta, a Sig, a Smith and Wesson and a 1911. She gave April and Becky a brief lecture on use of the weapons, gun safety, and range protocol. April teamed up with Jade and fired two clips with each weapon. Becky teamed up with Hattie and performed the same exercise.

Jade told them the 1911 was just for the experience. It wasn't something that April would actually carry. "Do you like it?" Becky asked.

"I do. But I use it in competition," Jade said. "It isn't a practical gun anymore."

"You use it in competition?" Becky's face lit up. Another chance to compete.

"That and other guns. The NRA sponsors competitions. I am also an active member of the IDPA and the USPSA which focus on self-defense situations, equipment, and training." Jade was fascinated by Becky's eagerness. She added the kicker. "And I am hoping to win a spot on the US Biathlon team in the 2010 Olympics."

"What gun do you think my mom should get?"

"Whichever one she wants. Any of the guns you tried would do the job. Which one did you like?"

"The Sig P238," Becky gushed.

"Excellent choice. It is one the best on the market."

"Which one is the cheapest?" April asked. If any of them would do the job, why pay extra?

"I can sell you the Smith and Wesson Shield for under $400. The Beretta Nano is slightly more expensive. I would like you to think about the Glock 26 because it fits your hand better but it goes for $500."

"I'll take the Shield," April said.

The next couple of hours were spent filling out forms and taking the training course required for the Utah-sponsored concealed carry permit.

They dropped Becky off at Gramma Becky's and went to the DC Police headquarters to file the paperwork for April's license to carry a concealed weapon in the District of Columbia.

Hattie refused an invitation to dinner. She had to get some rest and go to work.

50

IT WAS STILL Tuesday when Eve was introduced to a man who wanted to hire her as an escort. The man gave Eve the chills; she was surprised that Anna had agreed. He had a flat nasal voice that seemed incapable of expressing emotion. The skin on his face and arms was hard and leathery from long exposure to the elements. His dry, rough palm irritated her when they shook hands. He had an iron grip. Eve wanted to say no but she agreed like a good trooper. She told herself that Vickie and Dolly would have taken the man in stride. He was no different from many other men they had known in the past.

He was difficult to work with. He didn't respond to her overtures. He had little to say. Their most significant exchange was about the difference between paying Eve for sex and tipping her for being a good companion who might engage in sex. In the end, he put a folded stack of bills on the table as a tip which she could claim at the end of the night. The top bill was a twenty. The whole wad was worth a hundred if she was lucky.

She began undressing, trying to coax a reaction out of him. He wouldn't kiss her on the mouth. He kissed her cheek, neck, and shoulders. He ran his rough, irritating hands over her naked body. But there was no sense of foreplay.

He insisted on removing his own clothes. She lay on her back on the bed with her legs slightly apart and watched as he stood beside the bed and took off his clothes. When he was naked, he crawled onto the bed and straddled her. He started jacking off. She decided he planned to spray her. She wondered if he was going to make a point of coming in her face. He didn't go that far. He was getting close when he stopped, raised his right arm, and punched her so hard she saw stars.

She instinctively pulled her arms up to protect her head. They absorbed enough of the next blow that she was able to recover. She found herself staring up into the twisted, angry face of a monster. She realized with sudden clarity that it was now or never. She reached up with both hands and grabbed the back of his head. She pulled with all of her strength. He didn't move. She did. As their faces came together, she rammed her forehead into the bridge of his nose. He recoiled and let out a bellow.

She needed to unseat him but there was nothing to grab. Except his ear. She grabbed his left ear and shoved her left hand into his jaw. Her fingernails dug into his cheek. She tried to pull him to the right and nearly tore off a piece of his ear. When he pulled back in the other direction, she went with him - yanking on the handful of right cheek, pushing on his left ear, bucking and twisting her hips. He lost his balance. The two of them tumbled off the bed into the middle of the room. She jumped to her feet. He was up almost as quickly as she was. His foot drove into her gut knocking her backward a couple of steps. She maintained her fighting posture. He came forward to land another kick. This time she stepped back and caught his foot, lifted it and pushed. He stumbled backward but managed to stay upright. He charged at her throwing punches as he moved forward. She pivoted back to her right and threw up her right hand to push him away. His momentum carried him past her.

He whirled and came at her again. This time he grabbed her and turned her to face the wall and drove her toward it for a body slam. At the last instant, she pulled her knees up and jammed her feet against the wall. He kept driving her into a ball. She took the impact with her feet and forearms. Suddenly all of the slack was gone. Her body was like a rock. He crashed into it unexpectedly and came to an abrupt halt.

She pushed back with her butt and shoulders. He had no chance to react. As she uncoiled, his shoulders and then his butt were forced past the tipping point. He went over backward like an unsupported plank. He landed flat on his back. His head slammed into the floor with concussive force. Her butt landed on his midsection forcing all of the air out of his lungs in a loud "ooomph"

She rolled off of him. Her hand landed on a sock. She grabbed it and tied it around his left wrist. She rolled him over on his stomach and used the sock to tie his left wrist to his right wrist.

She grabbed his shirt and used one sleeve to secure his ankles. Then she dragged him under the small dining table and used the shirt to tie his feet to a table leg.

He began to struggle and shout obscenities. She picked up his other sock. When he opened his mouth, she stuffed the sock in. She took his belt from his pants and wrapped it around his neck. She tightened the noose and hissed into his ear, "If you want to leave this room alive, you will be good and lie still until someone comes to rescue you." He stopped struggling.

She called Ed and told him what had happened. She wanted to call the police but he ordered her to wait. He would get the police and be there in ten minutes.

Eve sat on the edge of the bed staring absently at her clothes. She was going to dress as soon as her head cleared. But she was still sitting there when someone banged on the door and a female voice yelled, "Police. Open up."

Eve forced herself to shuffle through what seemed like a dense fog to reach the door and open it. Both police officers opened their mouths as if to say, "What the hell?" But no words came out. They just stood in the hall adjusting to the sight of a naked woman holding the door and inviting them into the room. Ed gave a gentle nudge to the male officer. He recovered and strode past Eve into the room. He stopped as he reached the edge of the bed and turned to Eve. "What happened to him?"

Eve said, "He hurt me."

Ed was recording the scene with his cell phone. The male officer untied the man and asked him if he was okay. "'Hayell no. Thet fuckin' whore biet me 'n' clawed me half t' death." He showed the right side of his face with deep gouges from Eve's fingernails.

"What's your name?" the officer asked.

"Amos Goethels. I wan' thet bitch throwed in jail for 'tackin' me."

The female officer said, "She's got a pretty nasty bruise on the left side of her face. Can you tell us how that happened, Mr. Goethels?"

"Ah dun know, Mahta hit 'er."

"Was that before or after she grabbed your cheek?" the female officer asked.

"We'll need to get a complete statement from each of them," the male officer interjected.

"Eve has a concussion," Ed said. "Can we get them dressed and over to the hospital for evaluation? You can take their statements over there."

The police transported Goethels in their cruiser while Ed drove Eve to the hospital. The police were able to get them rushed in for examination. They were done in an hour. Eve gave them a partial statement but she had only a vague memory of the fight. She insisted that he was on top of her on the bed when he punched her without warning. They struggled. Somehow he fell backward and hit his head. She was able to tie him up while he was unconscious. Then she called Ed. Then they showed up at the hotel room door. Eve asked Ed to take her back to the Tahiti. She had a friend who would see that she got home okay.

Goethels insisted that Eve had started the fight and he was just defending himself. His description of what happened was vague. The police advised him that the two of them had been alone in the room so there wasn't enough evidence to charge either one of them. Ed confronted Goethels like a Marine sergeant dressing down a private. He told Goethels bluntly that the best thing he could do would be to go home and forget about what happened.

The night was almost over by the time Eve got back to the Tahiti. She was in no condition to perform but she didn't want to go home either. She sat in the dressing room with a cold compress on her eye until closing. Then she called Hattie for a ride back to her car at the Vienna Metro station.

51

HATTIE JUMPED OUT of her cab and ran to Eve as soon as she saw her bruised face. The eye wasn't black and blue yet but it was swollen shut. Hattie wrapped her arms around her friend and pulled her close. "What happened to you?"

"Bad date," Eve mumbled.

Hattie stepped back to look Eve in the eyes. "How bad? What did he do to you?" Her voice was a decibel or two below a scream.

"He hit me - right cross, I think." Eve tried to joke but it didn't come out right.

"Then what?"

"We wrestled. He fell and hit his head. I tied him up and called Ed."

"Why didn't you call the police?" Hattie demanded. "Why didn't you call me sooner?"

"Ed brought the police. They took a report." Eve struggled to get free and walk to the cab. All she wanted was a ride back to her car. "I had a terrific headache so I took some pain meds and waited for them to kick in."

Hattie lifted Eve's chin for a better look at her face. "Did anybody check you for a concussion?"

"Yes. I was examined at the hospital and released." Eve sounded exasperated. She wouldn't look at Hattie. "I have a concussion but I'm fine."

She took a step toward the cab. Hattie pulled her back. "You are not fine."

"I made it this far under my own power," Eve snapped. "I was able to call you for a ride." She took a deep breath. Her voice was calmer. "I'm a little shaky but I can drive home if you will just get me back to my car."

Hattie kissed her on the cheek. "Damn you."

Eve leaned her head against Hattie and hugged her hard. "I'm glad you quit boxing."

Hattie squeezed Eve to her chest. "I'll be glad when you stop escorting ass holes."

Hattie got Eve into the back seat. "Close your eyes and try to rest. I'll let you know when we get there."

When they reached the Vienna Metro Station, Eve got out and walked around to Hattie's window. She handed her friend five twenties. "That's too much," Hattie objected. Eve put her arm around Hattie's neck and kissed her on the mouth. "Thank you."

"For what?"

"For everything."

Hattie reached up and pulled Eve in for a more prolonged kiss. She brushed her hand over Eve's swollen eye. Eve winced and pulled back. "Just so you know," Hattie said, "I am going to follow you home. If you have any problems, pull over."

Eve smiled and walked to her car.

52

EVE'S EYE WAS still discolored on Wednesday night. Dolly and Vickie tried to cover up the bruise with makeup. Anna wasn't satisfied with the result. She sent Eve home for the night. Bridget spotted Eve leaving and stopped her to find out what was going on. She took one look at Eve's eye and said, "Let me buy you a drink."

Eve gave Bridget a blow by blow account of the outing that led to the black eye while they sipped Irish whiskey. Bridget said, "Anna tries to prevent situations like that but she can't keep everyone safe all of the time. This is a risky business."

"Anna set this one up," Eve said bitterly. "Can I ask you a question?"

"Yes. I have had some terrible experiences," Bridget said. "How bad do you think this guy was?"

"I really thought that he was going to kill me."

Bridget looked sympathetic and shook her head slowly.

Eve signaled for another round of drinks. She turned back to Bridget. A hint of a smile played across her face. "What did you do after your parents threatened to take your kids?"

"I was scared and angry. I was determined that I wasn't going to let that happen." Bridget paused to study Eve. "I needed a lawyer so I went to the only one I knew."

"My brother?"

"Yes. I told Bill what was going on and I demanded that he put a stop to it." Bridget looked down and forced air through her nostrils. "He said my parents had a good case. I had no visible means of supporting a family and I had a record of arrests for drug possession and prostitution. I told him that I now had a job as a dancer and that I expected to be bringing in enough to support myself and the kids." She looked over at the bar and collected her thoughts. "He said that the courts would still favor my parents because the job I had would lead me back into prostitution and drugs. Besides, I would have to show that I had someone to take care of the children while I was at work."

The waitress delivered their whiskey. Eve took a sip. "Of course, Bill had an answer."

"He told me to negotiate with my parents. He said they didn't really want to take my kids. They wanted me to get my life straightened out. Otherwise, they wouldn't have asked me to move in with them rent free. They would have just sued for custody." Bridget studied her drink. "Bill, Carine and I came up with the idea that I would sign up for a degree program so I could get an acceptable job in four or five years and I would put aside money for myself and for the kids every month." She took a swig. "They would have to agree that I could continue to work as a dancer while I was earning my degree."

"How did that work?"

"It was a tough sell but the only changes they made to the plan were that I would have to agree to drug testing and to part-time work in their real estate business." Bridget chuckled. "That was smart. As far as people in Virginia are concerned, I've had to move back in with my parents because my husband abandoned me but I'm working as a real estate agent and earning a college degree. I'm legitimate."

Eve sipped her drink. "I'm guessing that they didn't know your job included working as an escort."

"I hadn't started at the Tahiti at that time. When I did, we had to go through the whole negotiation again." Bridget sighed. "They weren't about to buy the idea that an escort was different from a prostitute. I was getting good grades in my college courses and I was putting away money on a regular basis. I was a good daughter. I pitched in and helped out any way I could. If I couldn't do something myself, I generally had a friend who was willing and able to take care of it." She smiled at Eve. "I think that is the secret. As long as I'm good and generous, they can overlook some things. They don't expect me to be perfect."

Eve nodded. "How is college coming?"

"I'll tell you about that the next time. But I do want to tell you something about Carine. She took me on as a pro bono client until I started making too much money." Bridget played with her drink. "She came up with the idea that I was an entertainer. She also helped my parents accept what I was doing. She told them that prostitution is legal in France and that she had known many women who were either working as prostitutes or who had worked as prostitutes and then went on to other careers." Bridget pursed her lips. "Carine told my parents that as my financial planner, she preferred escorting over just dancing."

Eve put her elbows on the table and clasped her hands. "How much money do you make?"

"Last year, I took home 250 k. I am on track to top that this year."

Eve stared wide-eyed. "You made a quarter of a mil in tips at the Tahiti?"

Bridget had made a mistake. She played with her whiskey while she considered her response. "This is not my only job."

Eve waited. Bridget struggled. "I belong to a mental health organization."

"You're joking."

"I'm a licensed counselor. I work with an organization that arranges afternoon sessions for men with serious issues and deep pockets."

"Afternoon delights?"

"Something like that. I average three to four sessions per week. Each session goes for one hour."

"How does that work? How are the sessions arranged?"

"That information is best kept out of our discussions."

"You're told where to meet. You show up and take care of business and walk out with a wad of cash?"

"Yes and no. The arrangements can be handled in a number of ways. I do not accept any money from them. Money shows up in a PayPal account."

"Who handles the money?"

"Out of scope. Does the name Jeane Palfrey mean anything to you?"

"The D.C. Madam? Didn't she hang herself a few months ago?"

"Maybe. The point is: the less you know about things like that, the better off you are."

Bridget drained her glass. She was finished talking about that subject. Eve went back to something more comfortable. "How close are you to achieving your goals?"

"We'll talk about that next time. What did you tell Joe about your eye?"

"I said that I accidentally collided head-on with a customer."

"Okay. I've got to get back to work. Go home. And remember: you don't have to be perfect just loveable and loving."

53

APRIL CALLED JOE to let him know that she would be home early and she would pick up the kids from Gramma Becky's house. Joe sounded disappointed. He said that he might have a couple of beers with Mike since she was there to take care of the kids.

"Okay. Enjoy yourself. I won't wait up for you."

Gramma Becky was shocked when her daughter walked into the living room at 7:30. "What happened to your eye?"

"Collision with a customer. The aisles are narrow and neither one of us was paying attention. Just a stupid accident."

"Is that why you're not working tonight?"

"It's not as bad as it looks. They don't want me running around the place looking like I had been beaten up, so they sent me home."

"You shouldn't be working there in the first place."

"It's only for a little while. I'm almost done with the article and Joe is back at work. I'll quit in a couple of weeks. A month at most."

"Then what will you do?" her mom fretted.

"I've got a book deal. I'll write the book and look for another job."

Her mother looked skeptical "Why are you getting a gun?"

"Just so everyone will stop worrying." April waved it away. "I haven't needed one for the past 35 years and I can't imagine that I will need one over the next 35 years."

"A woman was shot in the parking lot, wasn't she?"

"She was ambushed by an ex-boyfriend. No one is going to do that to me."

"Are you sure?" her mother asked.

"You know what? I would like a glass of wine." April grabbed her mother's elbow. "Would you like us to stay for a while? We could have some popcorn and watch a movie."

"Of course, I would love for you to stay. Stay all night, if you want."

"Don't go there, Mom," April warned. She turned to Becky. "Can you and JJ find a movie without getting into a big fight?"

April escorted her mother out to the kitchen for the wine and popcorn. "Joe and I are having our problems. But they are our problems." She spoke in a hoarse whisper. "We get to solve them the best way we can. In the meantime, I do not want to be discussing issues in front of Becky and JJ."

Her mother said, "They already know something is going on."

"I'm sure they do. But I want to work things out with Joe first."

Gramma Becky was skeptical. "Exactly what are you doing to work things out with him?"

"I'm letting him figure out how he wants to handle the situation," April sulked.

"What about you?"

"I love Joe and I love our family. I've got a job to do and I am going to do it. Joe has gone off for weeks at a time and left us to fend for ourselves when his job demanded it. I don't see that anyone has any right to complain about what I'm doing."

"He wasn't with other women," Gramma Becky countered.

April's eyebrows arched. "Are you sure?"

"Do you think Joe has been running around on you?"

"I don't know. I haven't asked and he hasn't said."

"But you think he might have?"

"He has had plenty of opportunities. Did you ever wonder about Dad?"

"The thought crossed my mind sometimes."

"But you kept believing that you had a good marriage. Now you have six wonderful kids and a great bunch of grandkids to prove you were right."

"That doesn't prove I was right."

"It proves that you were right to keep the crap out of our family life."

When the popcorn was ready, April and her mother moved into the living room with the kids to watch "Nim's Island."

54

JOE MUST HAVE slept on the couch. He came up the stairs as April was going down the hall to wake Becky and JJ. They passed without speaking. She thought she caught a whiff of Nickey's perfume as he walked by. She got the kids going and went downstairs to start breakfast so Joe could get dressed in peace.

There was still some discoloration around her eye. She decided to take another night off. She worked on her writing and spent a couple of hours at the gym. She was feeling pretty good when she brought the kids home from the pool. However, the tension was palpable after Joe returned home from work. He stayed away from the family as much as possible. Becky and JJ stayed in their rooms. The family ate dinner in silence.

Getting back to work would be a relief. Eve's life seemed so much more straightforward than April's. The stage performances and the private dances gave her a lift. She could deal with the quirky, rough-edged men who took her to hotel rooms for sex. She had come to accept the impersonal sex. She missed the intimate companionship of a real love life. This was just a phase, a temporary situation. She held tightly to the hope that she would emerge from this tunnel into a bright new day very soon.

Eve returned to work on Friday night. Her date that night, Jerry, presented himself as a red-neck, country boy. She guessed that there was some truth behind the image but she was certain that he was exaggerating. He was easy going. He had no problem shelling out 200 dollars when they got to the hotel room. His sexual interests were normal. He didn't need a blow job and he didn't even attempt to get into her butt. He did come three times. She was on top the last time.

After the sex, he held her in his arms and started talking. "We're headed for disaster."

"Really? What's going to happen?"

"Something." He held up his right hand and counted off. "The economic situation could bring the government down. We'll find ourselves in the middle of a civil war. The North Koreans or the Iranians could use their nuclear weapons to attack us. The illegal immigrants are just waiting to start a war." He held up his left index finger. "The supervolcano under Yellowstone is overdue."

"And, of course, there's global warming," Eve added.

Jerry looked at her in disbelief. "Those climate change idiots are just trying to scare us with a bunch of made up numbers. Nothing is going on." He rolled over on his side to face her and propped his head on his hand. "If you pick the right data you can make a good argument that the world is going to come to an end by 2050. People have been saying things like that for thousands of years and we're still here."

Eve arched her eyebrows. "So there's no global warming?"

"Nah. All that nonsense has been debunked over and over again. There's nothing to worry about."

"Nothing at all?"

"There's plenty. We're facing threats from natural disasters, economic disasters, and political crises. But global warming is a hoax. I'm worried about the next four years." He sat up and put his hands in his lap. "One of the best presidents of our lifetime, if not one of the best ever, is about to retire and it looks like we're going to replace him with a loser - either a nigger or a crazy old coot." He turned to Eve. "Either way, the situation is going to get a lot worse before it gets better and this country is ready to blow at any time."

"You mean like a civil war?"

"I'm not going to stand by and watch it happen. I won't allow it. And I'm not alone."

"What can you do about it?"

"Me and my buddies are building a fortress in the mountains just across the West Virginia line. We're stocking it up with food and ammunition so we can hold out for a year or two. By then we should be able to decide how we can do the most good."

"I guess that would work no matter what the disaster is."

"Everything but a direct hit by an asteroid, which is so unlikely that you don't even consider it."

"How about your families?"

"We're planning for them. Some of the guys are married. Some aren't but they'll likely have their pick of women when the time comes."

"You've got a wedding ring."

"I used to be married."

"What happened?"

He lay back down and clasped his hands behind his head. He studied the ceiling in silence for a couple of minutes. "I don't know. My wife was replaced by somebody I can't stand. I don't even recognize her. It might be an alien plot. You know they grab a bunch of good-looking women and make clones to use as bait when they get ready to take over the world."

"Your wife has been replaced by a stranger? Like one day she left on an errand and some stranger came home in her place?"

"Something like that." He looked over at Eve. "All I know for sure is that I woke up one morning and realized that the woman in bed with me was not my wife."

"What do you mean?"

He studied the ceiling and chewed his lip. "I started going with my wife in high school. She was a hot, sexy woman who could do anything. She was great in bed. She loved to go out and do things. She cooked, cleaned, did the wash. She was perfect." He ran his hand through his hair. "All of a sudden, I'm living with a fat, dumpy, lazy bitch. The house is a mess. All she does is bitch and nag. She fights with the neighbors. She fights with the people at her job. That's all she wants to talk about." He stopped and looked at Eve. "Thank God she isn't interested in sex because I can't stand the thought of making love to her."

"So you started picking up women like me to satisfy your needs?"

"Not all the time but you were really hot and I decided I was due for something special."

"Well thank you."

"Could I get a phone number so I can call you?"

"I'll have to think about that. What kind of gun do you have?"

"I have several. Why?"

"You said you were stockpiling ammunition. I just bought a gun. I would like to know what kind of gun you use."

"I have an AK-47, a 12 gauge shotgun, a thirty-aught-six with a telescopic sight. I have a 1911 and a magnum 44 revolver. The revolver is for reliability. I also have a Beretta." He frowned at Eve. "How come you just bought a gun? You have to be crazy to walk into a situation like this without a gun."

"I was naive but I know better now. I have to be able to protect myself."

"What did you buy?"

"A Smith and Wesson M&P Shield."

"Not a great choice. Glock and Sig make better sidearms."

"I hope I don't have to use it. My big problem is the permits."

"Yeah. You have to deal with several different jurisdictions. It's ridiculous. We shouldn't have to jump through all those hoops just to carry a gun for self-defense. It's our constitutional right."

"I'm getting that Idaho Concealed Carry permit."

"I've got one of those. Somebody at least is looking out for us."

"Can I see it?"

Jerry got up and retrieved his wallet. He produced a handful of permits for his guns in various jurisdictions. Eve memorized his home address.

She checked the clock to make sure she wasn't cheating him. "Our time is up. I have to go. I have some personal business that I need to take care of." She gave him a kiss. "You've been a great date."

He was disappointed but chivalrous. She dressed and kissed him goodbye before walking out of the room without looking back. Minutes later Hattie was driving her to the Vienna Metro Station.

55

APRIL SLEPT FOR a few short hours before she had to get up to take care of her family. She jotted notes in her diary while the rest of the family was getting ready for the weekly swim meet. She wrote: *Jerry Tompkins: wife but no children. He was obsessed with conspiracy theories and the looming calamity that would end life as we know it. He and his friends were dedicated to preparing for survival after the doomsday event. His other obsession was his unnamed wife. They had married as soon as she graduated. Everything was great for a while. Then poof. She wouldn't talk to him let alone sleep with him.*

April couldn't get the woman out of her head. Jerry's wife was part of the prostitution story. April had to cover that aspect as well. She decided to pay a visit to the woman under the guise of conducting a survey on attitudes towards sexual mores and the advisability of legalizing prostitution. April called Nickey with two questions: What was the name of Jerry's wife? Was Jerry working this Saturday morning?

April needed answers in the next half hour to forty-five minutes so she could get out of the swim meet.

Nickey called back forty minutes later while the family was finishing breakfast. The wife's name was Lydia. The man would be at work until noon.

April thanked Nickey. She told her family that she had just found out that she had an opportunity to talk to someone she had been trying to pin down for weeks. She would have to miss the swim meet. The announcement was greeted with silence and long faces as if she had just committed treason. Once again, she was putting her job ahead of her family. But there was nothing to be done about it. Joe, Becky, and JJ finished breakfast, packed, and left for the meet.

April threw together some questions and looked up directions on Google. She parked at the house across the street from the Tompkins. She started there to make it look more like a neighborhood survey.

Cynthia Jones was in her seventies, sophisticated and open. She wasn't a prude. Her children had been encouraged to experiment when they were in high school. Some of her grandchildren had had more than one sexual partner. That was okay as long as precautions were taken. But legalizing prostitution was a bad idea. Nothing good could come of it. She pointed out that legalizing the use of alcohol had not protected society from the evil, sometimes deadly, consequences of drinking. The interview had gone well and they parted on friendly terms.

As April started up the walk to the Tompkins residence, she realized that she had made a big mistake. Cynthia Jones was watching her and drawing conclusions. Lydia Tompkins was probably watching as well. If Jerry was right about her disposition, she would be hostile. Any woman would be suspicious under the circumstances.

Lydia Tompkins was not suspicious when she opened the door. She was ready for a fight. She sniffed the air a couple of times. "You're the woman he was with last night."

April stared at the frumpy, angry woman in her bathrobe and slippers. "I'm sorry. What did you just say?"

The woman's face was taut with anger. "You're the whore he was with last night. I smelled you when he came home. Your smell was all over his clothes that I just threw in the wash."

April stepped back. "Ma'am, I am a reporter for the Times-Herald. I am here to conduct a survey."

The woman sneered, "And you just happened to start with Cynthia across the street and then come straight to my house?"

"Yes."

"It has nothing to do with the fact that you slept with my husband last night?"

April was stuck. She looked down and crushed out an imaginary cigarette butt with her foot. She straightened and looked directly into Lydia's eyes. "I came here to talk to you. I am a reporter for the Times-Herald and I am working on a story about prostitution in this area. I am working undercover to get insights that would not be otherwise available. Your husband solicited my services last night and I spent a couple of hours with him."

Lydia pulled back. "What do you want from me?"

"I need your perspective. If I only have the story from the perspective of the women and the men who use their services, my story is going to have to conclude that we should legalize prostitution. Mrs. Jones gave me another angle with some good arguments. I want to hear what you have to say."

"Why me?"

"Jerry talked quite a bit about you and your marriage. I believe what he told me but I also believe that your side of the story is important. So I decided to come and interview you while Jerry was out of the house."

Lydia glowered. She was not happy.

"Would you please let me in so that we can sit down and talk?"

Lydia's jaw muscles rippled as she debated whether to invite the reporter in or tell the whore to go straight to hell. She opened the door and invited April in with a wave of her hand.

She stood by the door. Arms folded across her chest. Eyes locked on April. "What did he say about me? Did he tell you what a cold bitch I am?"

April took a seat on the couch. "It's what he didn't say that interests me. He did say that you had let yourself go and that you were always angry. He said it was impossible to please you." She paused to gauge Lydia's reaction. "What I want to figure out is why a bright, likable, good old boy would marry a cruel witch in the first place. That doesn't make sense."

Lydia closed her eyes and looked up at the ceiling. She shook her head. "He is bright and charming when he's with someone new. With me, he is sullen, morose, uncommunicative, and sometimes pretty mean. The smallest problem can make him blow up."

"Was he always like that?"

Lydia looked like she had been slapped. "Of course not. I'm not stupid or hard up. I wouldn't have married a man like that."

"So you got along pretty well when you were in high school?"

"We were a couple of teenagers in love. He was a great guy. He was smart. He was good with his hands. He liked things more than people but he could be sociable when he wanted to."

"Did either of you consider college?"

"He didn't. He hated school. He wanted to go to work and buy his own house. He didn't see any need for college. He has gone to school to get certified as a mechanic and an air conditioning tech. But studying things like English and History is never going to happen."

"How about you?"

"At first, I didn't care about college. I didn't see any value in a college degree. I was happy being a housewife. I was looking forward to having children."

"But now?"

"I need a degree. I'm management material but I'm never going to get a shot without that degree."

April understood that feeling. She was never going to be a real writer until she published a bestseller. She was never going to publish a bestseller without a publisher who believed in her. She wanted to help this woman but she felt helpless. Her thoughts must have shown on her face. Lydia said, "What?"

"You should go for it."

"What do you mean?"

April looked up at Lydia. "If you believe you have a shot, you should go for it."

Lydia threw her hands up. "How am I supposed to do that?"

"Start taking courses at George Mason or one of the community colleges. Build from there."

"We can't afford it."

"You can if you want to. Your company probably has a college tuition program. There are plenty of resources to help women get started." April looked down at the floor and chewed her lip. She looked back up at Lydia. "You have equity in your home. You can borrow against that." She stood and started toward Lydia. "Money isn't the problem. All you have to do is decide that you're worth it."

"Jerry will never agree to anything like that."

"Don't give him a choice."

"That would just lead to another knock down drag out fight. And in the end, he would get his way."

April shrugged. "Divorce him."

"I don't want that."

"He doesn't either." A smile crept across April's face. "Just threatening to divorce him would put him in a bind. If you get a divorce, you can force him to sell the house or buy you out. So you get your share of the equity. Then he would have to pay you alimony since he's the primary breadwinner." April walked over to Lydia and put a hand on her shoulder. "It shouldn't be hard for him to figure out that paying for your college education is a lot better than going through a divorce."

Lydia looked like she was going to cry. "God, you're awful," she said in a husky voice. "I'd hate to have you for an enemy."

April grinned. "Thanks. Sometimes I surprise myself."

Lydia wiped away her tears. "Do you think I could make it as a stripper?"

"If you clean up your act. You would need to lose ten pounds or so and start projecting a positive image. But it's not something that I recommend."

"You're doing it."

"Like I said, I wouldn't recommend it."

"I was just wondering what Jerry would do if he saw me up on stage dancing for a room full of guys."

"That can be arranged, if you really, truly want to find out."

"How?"

"If you were in the Tahiti, when I was up on stage, you could join me."

"Seriously?"

"You would have to make some changes before I would actually want you up there with me. But you could do it." April pointed to a photo on the wall. "That woman will always drive men crazy."

"Seriously?"

April pulled a business card from her purse. "Don't share this with Jerry. Give me a call, if you decide that's what you want to do. I need to get going. I have another appointment this afternoon."

Lydia gave her a hug. "Thank you for coming over."

"What should I do if Jerry wants another date?"

"Do your job. I'll take care of him."

56

HE WAS SITTING alone at a table in a corner of the room. The waitress assigned to his table would bring him a drink every so often. He had shown no interest in any of the women. No one had spoken to him. No one had even approached him except the waitress whose job it was to bring him drinks. But he stood out. He was the only African American in the building. He looked like someone you would expect to see being interviewed in a locker room after some big football game. He would be the team's star player -- the quarterback, maybe. His broad forehead framed intense eyes and brooding lips. He was a cop. Eve was sure of that. He was cataloging everyone in the room. Was he planning a raid? Tahiti management had jumped through all the hoops to make sure that their operation was strictly legal and they had nurtured friendships high and low to make sure they didn't get any unwanted attention.

Eve casually walked up to the table and took a seat. The waitress came over and asked what she wanted to drink. Eve ordered a daiquiri.

The man said, "No!" There was unexpected force in his deep, strong voice.

"You're not going to buy her a drink?" The waitress was offended by the breach of protocol.

"No. I am not buying her a drink. I did not invite her and I do not want her company." Every word, every syllable was pronounced slowly and distinctly.

"Put it on my tab," Eve said to the waitress. Then she asked the man, "Do you mind if I sit here and relax for a few minutes?"

He shrugged.

"Are you enjoying the show?"

He shrugged again.

"I guess all those boobs and butts can get pretty boring," she observed.

He turned to look directly at her. She was getting under his skin. "Yes. Now that you mention it." His voice was deep and powerful even when he spoke softly.

"Present company excluded, of course."

"You flatter yourself."

"So you're interested in the men?"

"I'm interested in people in general. This is a good place to watch misfits in action."

"Anybody in particular?'

"Three tables over to my left is a guy who is actually wearing a suit. He's a generous tipper. He gives every girl who stops by a twenty."

"You're kidding." Eve sounded hurt. "I didn't get one."

"Yes you did. I saw him give it to you."

She grinned. "Wow, you really are taking everything in."

"Which makes me wonder why you're here trying to strike up a conversation with a man who won't even buy you a drink."

"Curiosity."

"Curious about a black man in a white strip joint?"

"That and I've never had a chance to sit down and get to know a cop."

"You think I'm a cop?"

She chuckled. "Do you think I'm a stripper?"

He said nothing.

She tilted her head and pursed her lips. "You've had your fill of naked broads and I could use a change of pace. Why don't we go somewhere quiet so we can have a real conversation?"

"Are you trying to pick me up?"

"Yes. I would like you to hire me as an escort for the next couple of hours."

"Are you propositioning me?"

"I would be happy if we could just have a civil conversation."

"That's all you have in mind? A conversation?"

"A conversation would be fine. Anything else would be icing on the cake."

He toyed with the idea for a while before agreeing. When they got settled in the hotel room, he took out a handful of bills from his wallet. He held them up for her to see. "First, you need to clear some things up for me."

"Of course. You're a cop. You get off on interrogating people. How about we play the informant game? You put some money on the table and ask a question. If you like my answer, I get to keep the money."

"I've got a better idea. You explain yourself and if I'm happy with the explanation, I will consider putting some of this money on the table."

"In that case, we need to go back to the Tahiti because this is not going to work."

"What are you hiding?"

"Everything. That's a requirement for this job. Nobody wants to deal with the truth."

"Well, I need to know the truth."

"Really? Nobody ever lies to you?" When he didn't answer, she continued, "I will be truthful but I don't promise to tell you everything. Put a twenty on the table and ask a question."

He put a twenty on the table. "What's your name?"

"Eve"

"Eve what?"

"Eve Sinful"

"Bullshit. You promised to be truthful and right off the bat you give me that bullshit made up name."

"That is my name. You can ask anybody at the Tahiti."

"That's a stage name."

"Nevertheless, it is my name."

He bore down on her with his intense, black eyes. "It's fake. Your parents didn't name you Eve."

"Did your parents name you Jack?"

"John. But I've always been called Jack."

"Yvonne. A lot of people call me Eve."

"What is your surname?"

She tapped a finger on the table. "What else do you want to know?"

He put another twenty on the table. "What are you really up to?"

"I'm earning money to pay my bills."

He shook his head. "That's not it. You don't go after the money. You pick up a cop who's not tipping anybody." He held up his stack of bills. "You could have made this and more if you had stayed back there working the crowd."

She tapped her finger on the table. "That answer is more expensive."

He put another twenty on the table. She tapped her finger again.

"What's the problem?" he demanded.

"That is an answer that I have kept from all but my closest friends and allies. I am not sure I want to give it to you."

"You could have just said you wouldn't discuss it. But you didn't"

"You won't take no for an answer."

"You don't care about the money. What do you want?"

"I want some assurance that will not use my answer against me."

Jack rolled his eyes. "Are you engaged in some criminal activity?"

"If you were in my shoes, would you take the risk?"

"What's at stake?" Jack demanded.

Eve fixed him with a stern look. "My life and your soul."

He waved his hand in disgust. "Get serious."

"That's the deal. Do you still want to know the answer?"

He nodded. "Let's have it."

"I'm working undercover."

"You're a cop?" He shook his head. "No way."

"I'm a reporter."

"What are you working on?"

She tapped the table. "Just put the rest of your money in the pot."

He lowered his hand with the remaining bills and pulled it back three times. She held her finger on the table and eyed him. He put the money on the pile but held it down with his thumb.

"I'm doing an undercover investigation of the sex industry. My report is supposed to encourage support for legalizing prostitution."

He sneered, "I hope nobody buys your crap."

"Why is that, officer?"

"Prostitution is a dirty, nasty, crime infested business. We need to get rid of it."

"Prostitution is like public peeing. It may not be nice but it is often necessary."

"Just for the sake of our discussion, what you're doing is prostitution," Jack said. "It is the nicest, most innocuous variety available. Using that version as an argument for legalizing prostitution is essentially bait and switch." He paused to lean in. His face only inches from hers. "Once you legalize prostitution for those sweet ladies in the Tahiti, you will open the door for a bunch of worthless, drug addicted, criminals to come in and take over. The women I know are dangerous bitches who would just as soon cheat or steal and maybe even kill as give a john what he paid for."

"I don't know the women that you have dealt with." Eve stared into his eyes. "You don't know my friends at the Tahiti. Many of them have worked the streets in DC." She nodded. "They have done bad things in their young lives." She wagged an index finger for emphasis. "They don't do that kind of stuff now because they don't want to be kicked out on their asses."

Eve looked down and bit her lip. "Most cops are good guys trying to make the world a better place. But there are bad cops. Some of the good cops have done bad things. Let's not single out prostitutes."

"Apples and oranges. Being a cop is legal. Prostitution is illegal. A successful prostitute has to have a criminal mind." He jabbed his finger in her face. "If you make it legal, you will be promoting criminal behavior."

A mischievous grin spread across Eve's face. "But it would be apples and apples if we made it legal. Wouldn't it?"

He grunted and said in disgust, "Bullshit."

"People turn to prostitution in a desperate battle for survival. Criminalizing it only makes that battle more difficult." Eve paused and closed her eyes. She could feel the anger, the frustration boiling up inside, and fought for control. She sighed. Looking Jack straight in the eye, she said, "Maybe your crack addicted prostitutes need to use illegal drugs so they can deal with a lifetime of bad days."

"Maybe and maybe they are just pathetic losers."

"Come on, Jack. You can do better than that. Or has spending day after day dealing with criminals ruined your mind?"

"I'm telling you exactly how it is. You do not want to open up the suburbs of Virginia to those bitches."

"For the sake of our discussion, I am a prostitute. A successful prostitute. I pull in the same weekly salary as a mid-level engineer. Do you think I am a nasty criminal?"

"You scammed me out of two hundred dollars."

She turned on him. "If you think I'm cheating you, take your fucking money and go home."

He walked away from her. He punched his palm. He turned back. "I apologize. I do not think of you as a criminal."

"You and I see things differently." Eve softened. "It can't be helped. You uphold the law, whether the law is right or wrong. I challenge the law even though it may serve an important purpose." She looked across the room. "I would never fault you for doing your job." She turned back to face him. "But I have to try to change the attitude that some worthless crack addict who supports her habit by spreading her legs for anybody with a few bucks is representative of all prostitutes."

"The women at the Tahiti are not representative prostitutes either."

"I know that," Eve said. "Do you remember the Vixen?"

"Yeah. Tall, beanpole. Doesn't have much up top so she flaunts her pussy."

"Do you have any idea what is missing from that picture?"

"She's a brunette with big dark eyes."

"She's a divorcee whose husband abandoned her. She used to be a good waitress. Could probably make a good politician." Eve cleared her throat. "She and a friend ran a successful brothel for a couple of months. They could have made a go of it but prostitution is illegal."

He threw up his hands and shook his head.

"What about Dolly P?" Eve asked.

"Nice tits. Great smile. She has one of those happy personalities that makes people like her."

"Her father abused her. Her mother kicked her out of the house when she reported the abuse to the police. She dropped out of high school and came to DC. She worked on the streets for a year before she landed a job at the Tahiti." Eve was choking up. She paused to regain her composure. "She should be in medicine. An RN at least. But she could be a doctor. She's the best proctologist I know."

He shook his head. "Okay. Some of the women at the Tahiti have had their problems."

"So have some of the women in your corner of the world."

"Probably."

"The Vixen took us downtown to check on her friend. We had breakfast with six women. Three of them were minors. Girls who should be in high school."

"That happens, unfortunately."

"That happens? That's the best you can do? Did you ever arrest one of those girls?"

"I have had to do that in the past."

"Did you arrest the john who fucked her?" Eve's lip curled up into a snarl. Tears were welling up in her eyes. "Did you charge him with statutory rape or don't you believe you need to enforce that law?"

His hand slid to the back of his head. He looked up at the ceiling. "No. I don't arrest the johns. There is no point in trying to prosecute them."

"Then don't you ever try telling me that your job is to uphold the law."

"I'm sorry. Those are the realities."

"And they will be the realities until people change the way they look at the situation."

"Legalizing it won't work."

Eve closed her eyes. "There is just one other thing."

"What's that?"

She put her elbows on the table and clasped her hands. "If you prosecute the johns, you will put those girls out of business. They won't be able to buy food. That will be very bad unless we come up with some other way to take care of them."

They just looked at each other. When Eve spoke, her voice was husky. "We have to stop talking about this. Could you pour me a drink? Maybe you could make it a double?"

He glared at her.

"I just need to get off of this jag. I'm not going to get drunk," she said. "You brought me here for a good time and I intend to see that you get one."

He looked in the liquor cabinet. "Two bottles of Jack Daniels."

"Do you mind if I get both of them?"

"Coming up."

He poured the whiskey into a plastic cup for her. He poured vodka for himself. He sat down in a large cushioned chair. She came over and sat on his lap. She pulled her knees up and rested her head against his shoulder. He put his hand on her thigh. She kissed him on the cheek. They sipped their drinks for a while.

"I could get used to this," Eve said.

Jack grunted. He moved his hand between her legs. She pulled it down to her pussy and held it there while he stroked her with his finger. She sighed and pulled his head down for a kiss. She brought his hand up to her lips.

She got up, walked a few feet toward the bed, and turned to face him. She pulled her dress up over her head slowly revealing herself.

"That is one ugly bra," he said.

Eve grinned. "Not for show. Easy off. Easy on when I'm ready to make my getaway."

She pulled the bra up over her head and dropped it next to the dress. She played with her breasts. "It really feels good to get that thing off."

She turned around so he could watch her butt as she slowly worked her thong down to the floor. She turned to face him again and lifted her arms above her head. "Voila!"

He smiled faintly.

"You could act a little excited," Eve said. "I have reason to believe that I am a very good lay."

She took his hands and pulled him to his feet. He waited patiently while she undressed him. After she removed his pants and shoes, she began to suck his cock. He pulled her to her feet. "I don't want that now."

"Whatever you want. It's okay."

"I feel a little strange. I have never been with a white woman."

"I'm pretty sure it's almost exactly like being with a black woman. Your cock is big but it will fit okay."

"You are nasty."

"Once you get on top of me in that bed, everything will be fine."

She rubbed her hand gently down his erection. "There is just one little thing we have to take care of first."

She reached in her mouth and pulled out a condom. She worked it onto his cock. "It's a tad small."

In a few minutes, he was thrusting up inside her. The rhythm and intensity gradually built until she felt him explode. They lay wrapped in each other's arms for a brief eternity.

She coaxed his erection back and slid another condom in place. This time she crawled on top and began riding him. They both came. She buried her head in his neck. "That was awesome."

She lay there. Head on his chest. Fingers exploring his body. Until she could no longer stand the tension. "I've got to get dressed and get out of here."

"What's the matter?"

She got up. "Personal business. I'll turn into a pumpkin if I stay much longer."

"What's going on?" Jack asked suspiciously.

She quickly pulled on her clothes and then sat next to him. She kissed him and stroked his cheek. "Look at me. I am not lying. I want to stay more than anything. But there are things that I have to take care of."

"Such as?"

She hesitated. Her lips pressed into a thin line. "Children."

"And a husband?"

She scrunched her nose while she held her right hand up and rocked it back and forth. "I can't discuss that. I'm going but I'm taking a part of you with me."

"You really know how to mess with a man's mind."

"You insisted on the truth," Eve said. "There it is. I'm screwed up. My life is a mess. I apologize for dragging you into it but you were too good to pass up."

"I just fucked a momma with a husband and kids," he retorted angrily.

"You gave a woman what she wanted. You made her happy. If it's any consolation, I'm planning on joining the atheists so I don't have to worry about Christian morals. You're welcome to come with me."

He laughed. It was a deep, rolling musical sound. "Wait a second," he said.

He went over to his pants and took out his wallet. He took the remainder of his cash out and a business card. "Call me if there is anything that I can do for you."

She took the business card but refused the money. "A deal is a deal. Hasta la vista."

She turned back just before she closed the door. "Yvonne MacMahon a.k.a. April Walsh."

She texted Hattie as she made her way down the hall. She was on her way back to the Vienna Metro Station and April's world.

57

APRIL GOT UP in a good mood on Thursday morning. Not even Joe could spoil it. She basked in the giddy afterglow from a hot night of sex. She found it frustrating that her partner was Jack and not Joe. But he was barely speaking to her. She had taken to sleeping on the futon in her office rather than confront his stony anger in the bedroom.

She dropped Becky and JJ off for swimming practice and drove to Smith and Wesson's Gun Emporium for a shooting session. She got back in time to check with the kids when swim practice ended. They wanted to stay at the pool. All of their friends were there and there was nothing to do at home.

April's DC gun permits were waiting for her in the mail when she returned home. She studied them, signed them, and stuck them in her purse. Her S&W Shield went into the purse's holster along with an ammo clip. Not that she was ever going to need that stuff.

She went back to work on her story. It was coming nicely. So nicely that she could quit the Tahiti if she had to. But she was still picking up bits and pieces of information that helped her flesh out the article. A six-part series is a huge space to fill with words. A whole book, which she would have to produce next, was gigantic. She estimated that the book would be ten times as large as the series. It would require all the material she could get her hands on.

She had decided that next week would be her last. She had even considered quitting after next Thursday's shift so she could have Memorial Day Weekend off. Either way, she would be back with her family for Memorial Day. She would stick her story in a drawer to age - marinate - for a week. Then she would take a fresh look and make a final rewrite. She would hand the package over to Craig Robertson by close of business on Friday, September 12. That date could be moved forward a day or two if he insisted on an earlier delivery.

On Friday night, the crowd at the Tahiti was lively and generous. Eve was enjoying a great night. After her set at eleven, she was requested for a private dance. The guy called himself Bill. He was a thirty-something government weenie. He wasn't rich but he wasn't broke. He gave her a decent tip after the dance. Anna talked him into a date with Eve. They left the building and headed into the parking lot around 11:45. As they were crossing the parking lot, they heard a group engaged in a loud argument. Somebody in the group was shouting profanities. A woman screamed, "Charlie, don't!"

Eve looked over and saw that a man in the group had a gun. The woman, a dancer who called herself Rhonda, was trying to calm the gunman down. She made another terrified plea, "Charlie, put the gun away. Let's go somewhere and talk."

Bill froze. Eve could feel his panic. She told him to go inside and tell the men to get out to the parking lot ASAP. He looked toward the Tahiti and then turned back to Eve. "What are you going to do?" he stammered.

She reached into her purse and casually pulled out her gun. "I'm going to convince Charlie to put his gun down before somebody gets hurt."

Bill did not need to be told twice. He took off for the entrance of the building. Eve released her safety and chambered a round. Charlie reacted slowly. He stopped yelling and turned as if to check out the noises behind him. He froze when he saw Eve walking toward him with her gun drawn. "Give it up, Charlie. You don't stand a chance."

"What are you going to do, bitch?"

Charlie had positioned himself so that he could confront Eve while keeping one eye on Rhonda and her date. He was using a two-handed grip. His left arm was shielding his torso. Eve focused on a six-inch square just below his elbow. She was sure she could put a round in there. She hoped it wouldn't take more than one. "Shoot you, if you don't put that gun down immediately."

"Charlie, put the gun down. She means it," Rhonda screamed. She was certain that one of them was about to die.

Charlie stared at Eve. He couldn't figure out what to do so he did nothing. Eve continued to walk calmly toward him. She had closed the gap to fifteen feet. Ed came running across the parking lot shouting, "Eve, put the gun down."

Rhonda stepped toward Charlie and put her hand gently on his. "Please, Charlie. Put the gun down."

She guided his hand to the ground and kissed him on the cheek. He released his grip on the gun. Rhonda straightened him up and put her arms around him. Eve engaged the safety and returned the Shield to her purse.

As Ed walked towards Eve, he said, "I hope you've got a license for that thing."

"Of course I do. I'm not stupid."

"That was a pretty stupid thing to do. You're a dancer, not a security guard."

"I wasn't about to let him shoot Rhonda."

The police arrived to take over. Eve had to give her version of the story and produce her brand new carry permits. The police agreed that her quick action had probably prevented another shooting incident.

By the time the police had finished with her, Eve was trembling. She sat at the bar and ordered a whiskey. Paddy, the bartender, pulled out a pint of Jameson Black Reserve. "I hear this is your poison." He was grinning from ear to ear.

"Aye, laddie. That will get you to a woman's heart every time."

She emptied the tumbler and pulled out her phone. Her hands were still shaking but she was able to get a text off to Hattie: *Tahiti ASAP*

A second round and 10 minutes later, her phone chimed. Hattie's text read *Outside.*

Eve pulled out a handful of bills and laid them on the bar. She was putting the bottle of Black Reserve in her purse when Paddy pushed the money back to her. "It's yours. You earned it, lass."

She grabbed him by the back of the head and pulled him close. She kissed him on the cheek. "There's more where that came from, laddie."

She climbed into the back of the cab. Hattie said, "C'mon up front."

"I've got an open bottle of whiskey."

"Okay. Where to?"

"Someplace desolate."

Hattie found a parking spot along the Potomac at Haine's Point across the river from Ronald Reagan International Airport. "Good spot for watching submarine races," she said.

They stood beside the cab in the moonlight. Eve took a couple of swigs of her whiskey. "I almost shot a guy tonight."

"Almost?" Hattie said skeptically.

"He had a gun. He was threatening one of the girls and her date. I had a gun, so I pulled it out and confronted him."

"That doesn't sound like 'almost' to me."

"He asked me what I was going to do and I said, 'shoot you.'"

Eve took another swig from her bottle. "I think I was ready to pull the trigger at that moment."

"But you didn't." Hattie smiled and winked. "You did exactly what you were supposed to do."

Eve looked down at her feet. "I guess."

Hattie leaned over and kissed Eve on the lips. It was a light kiss. But it was on the lips. Eve took another swig of whiskey and pulled Hattie in for a longer, more passionate kiss. One thing led to another. Hattie put an arm around Eve and pulled her close. Their cheeks rubbed. They kissed. When Hattie's tongue pushed against Eve's lips, they opened. Their tongues touched and Eve lost her grip. The whiskey bottle fell to the ground. It shattered throwing glass splinters against Eve's bare calf. She jerked back. She pushed her friend away. "I think you better take me to my car."

"Are you upset with me?" Hattie fretted.

"No. I wanted it. I want you. But it's just not my night. Can you take me back to my car?"

"You're in no condition to drive."

"It's a short drive. I'll be okay."

"Get in the back and close your eyes."

58

THE WALSHES WERE on their way to the Saturday morning swim meet, when they heard a news report about a shooting at the Tahiti. Joe shot an angry look at April, "Did you know about this?"

"Of course, but it wasn't anything like that." April looked over at him. "One of the girls ran into her boyfriend in the parking lot. They got into a loud argument. Another girl was out there on a smoke break. She notified our security chief. He went out and broke it up."

"Mom, they said somebody was shot," Becky objected.

"That's an exaggeration." April turned to look at Becky. "I don't think there were any guns involved. It was just a shouting match."

"So you weren't in any danger?" Joe asked.

"None whatsoever." April shook her head. "I work inside. The whole thing took place in the parking lot."

"But the police were called in?" Joe asked.

"An overabundance of caution. One of our dancers was shot a couple of weeks ago. They didn't want to take any chances this time."

They rode in silence the rest of the way to the pool. Attention turned to the swim meet by the time they had parked the car. April was relieved but she could not be sure that she had put the issue to bed. The meet was exciting and routine. On the one hand, everybody took the competition seriously. On the other, parents were busy getting kids ready for the events, timing the swimmers, and watching for infractions that might DQ a swimmer.

They were back home still putting stuff away when the doorbell rang. Joe opened the door to an attractive woman in her late twenties or early thirties. She was 5'7" with red hair and penetrating gray-green eyes. Her blue dress was decorated with carnations. She smelled of jasmine and musk. "May I speak to April?" she asked with a hint of a southern drawl.

"About what?" Joe asked.

She smiled pleasantly. "I was in the neighborhood and thought I would drop by."

Joe had a bad feeling about the woman. She was connected to the Tahiti and he didn't like it. He wanted to ask but Becky and April were already descending the stairs.

"Bridget, come in," April called as soon as she spotted her friend. When April reached the bottom of the stairs, she hugged Bridget. "Joe, this is Bridget Allen. Bridget, this is my husband, Joe. And the young lady on the third step is our daughter, Becky."

Joe shook hands with her. April led her to a seat. Joe could not take his eyes off Bridget. He was mesmerized. She did not seem to notice.

Bridget said, "I can't stay. Besides, you're busy. But this is about the most wonderful day of my life." She smiled and squeezed her arms into her body. "I simply had to get out and do something. I know it sounds crazy but I just ended up in this neighborhood, and I decided I should stop by to say hello."

Bridget held up a business envelope. "I have been accepted into George Washington University School of Law."

April looked stunned. "I didn't realize that you were that far along. Law school? Wow. I had no idea."

"Bill insisted that we keep it quiet until I got my acceptance. A lot of things could have gone wrong." Bridget grinned. "He said there would be plenty of time for celebrating after I got the official notice."

"Did Bill talk you into law school?"

"He suggested it. But I would probably have ended up there anyway." Bridget held up the envelope. "This means I'm free. I can walk away from the Tahiti and not look back."

"Are you the woman who has been helping April get information on prostitutes?" Joe demanded angrily.

"Yes." Bridget was suddenly sober. She had said the wrong thing. She knew it.

Joe leaned forward, his face taut. "And you got her started on the topless dancing?"

"Yes. I am really sorry for any trouble I may have caused."

"Get out." Joe stood up and took a threatening step toward Bridget. "I want you out of my house. I never want to see you or hear of you again." His fists were clenched. The veins in his neck stood out.

Bridget stood up and glared at Joe. She straightened. Her body relaxed. She was calm and commanding. "Peace. I'm leaving."

Joe continued to glare at her. Bridget calmly walked over to him. "Y'all should watch yourself." The drawl was exaggerated. "Yer daughter is sittin' right over theya."

She put her arm around Joe's neck and raised up to kiss him on the cheek. "Y'all take care," she said in a soft, sweet voice. "We know what's goin' on."

That was another blunder. She was angry with Joe but she should have left well enough alone. Eve would eventually come to see that taunt as the dagger strike that doomed April Walsh's struggle for survival.

Bridget strolled toward the door. As she came to the steps, Becky asked, "Is it Miss or Mrs. Allen?"

"Allen is my married name. So 'Mrs.' But you just call me Bridget or Bee. That's what my friends call me."

"Do you have any children?"

"Two boys."

"Do they know what you do?"

Bridget's head jerked back. "No." She squinted down at Becky. "Someday they will but for the time being they don't need to be bothered with such stuff."

"Because you're ashamed."

"No," Bridget shook her head. "I am afraid of what people would do to them if others knew about my work."

"So you believe that what you do is okay?"

"Neither more nor less okay than other occupations."

When Becky did not say anything, Bridget asked, "Did I answer your question?"

"I think so."

Bridget clasped her hands. She smiled as she studied Becky. "You are growing up quite fast. You need to watch yourself around young men. Don't be in a rush."

"I won't," she mumbled.

Bridget said in a soft maternal voice, "Good. I made that mistake when I was a teenager and I have paid dearly for it."

Bridget continued to the door and let herself out.

Joe turned to April and said, "I don't want that woman in my house or near my children. Is that clear?"

April crossed her arms. "This is my house, too. They are my children as well. She is my friend, whether you like it or not."

"Dad, what did she mean? What's going on?" Becky asked.

"I have no idea," Joe snapped. "Ask your mother."

He walked to the door, stopped and turned back to April. "I need to get some fresh air. Don't hold up dinner for me." He slammed the door as he walked out.

"Mom, what's going on?" Becky asked. She sounded panicky.

April shook her head. "I don't know."

"What did Mrs. Allen mean?"

"I don't know. I'm sorry but I just don't have the answers."

59

SUNDAY MORNING WAS tricky. Joe was up before April. He had gotten a short nap on the couch after he got home from wherever he had gone. He avoided her while they were getting ready for church. Mass was another tense, mortifying experience. At the Kiss of Peace, Joe stared straight ahead while everyone else in the church greeted the people around them with, "Peace be with you." April kissed him on the cheek. He ignored her. April hugged Becky and JJ. Joe ignored them.

The tension continued through breakfast. After breakfast, Joe suggested that he and Becky and JJ go for a bike ride on a nearby trail. Becky demanded to know why her mom was not invited. April said, "I've got a lot of work to do. I promise I will go with you next week."

When the house was empty, April broke down in tears. She was interrupted by a phone call. It was Nickey. Instead of her usual cheery greeting, she asked, "What's wrong?"

"I've had a rough morning." April wiped the tears away. "I don't know how much more of this I can take."

"Maybe I should call back later."

"No." April shook her head. "But it had better be important."

"I wouldn't have called you, if it wasn't."

April sighed. "What's the matter?"

"Mrs. Sheehan has died. Her funeral was last Wednesday."

April shut her eyes trying to focus. "Okay."

"Your friend, Amy MacDermot, flew out there," Nickey continued. "Lee came back with her on Thursday. The first thing they did was find an apartment for Lee."

"And you know all of this how?" April felt like she was struggling through a dense fog. None of this made sense.

"I had a friend in Cleveland monitoring Mrs. Sheehan and her daughter. Nothing serious but he did spot the obituary."

April took a sip of her coffee. She was still struggling to see the point. "So you checked to see what flight Amy would take?"

"Yes. Her return flight booking was changed so that Lee could fly back with her."

April panicked. "You haven't been stalking either Amy or Lee. Have you?"

"No. Of course not. I just did a little checking out of curiosity. Lee signed a lease on an apartment on Friday."

"And?"

"She's been calling Joe every day."

April closed her eyes. She took a long breath forcing the air out through her nostrils. "How would you know that?"

"I checked his cell phone when he came by yesterday to talk to me about Bee."

"He went to see you yesterday afternoon?"

"He was distraught. He wanted to know if I knew Bridget Allen. Apparently something she said rattled him. I told him I wasn't familiar with the name."

"And while you were showering him with TLC, you filched his cell phone and checked the call log."

"Actually, she called while he was with me. He told her he was in the middle of a meeting and would call her back later. After that, I filched his cell phone so I could get her number."

"How did you know it was her?"

"His voice. He was talking to a woman and it wasn't you."

April shook her head. "Shit."

"I don't suppose that you want to hear any more."

"No." April forced air through her nostrils. "But I guess that I should thank you for giving me a heads up."

"I'm sorry."

"Not as sorry as I am." April took another sip of her coffee. "I have to get some work done."

"Bye, sweetie."

April received two more messages that afternoon. Both Bridget and Ed sent texts urging her to contact Jeff. She called him. The conversation was stiff. April reluctantly agreed to meet him for lunch the next day at Clyde's of Georgetown. She told him to make reservations for sometime after 11:30 and text the details.

60

APRIL DROVE INTO Georgetown after making sure that Becky and JJ were set for the afternoon. Jeff had said that he had good news but he wanted to tell her face to face. The rendezvous put her in unfamiliar territory. She was only going to be Eve for a couple of hours instead of a whole shift. Normally, April had the stage during the day. Eve took over at night. This outing was going to require a couple of rapid transitions. On the way to the meeting, Eve was driving April's car. That was a first. On the way back to get the kids, April would be driving and she couldn't let Eve's issues interfere.

She was escorted to Jeff's table. He was wearing a suit and tie. It was a remarkable transformation. "You look great. You should be president of something," she said as she took her seat opposite him.

"Thanks, I wanted to impress you. But it's just a costume. I'm still a grease monkey."

"It's nice to see this side of you." A faint smile played across Eve's face. "Are you going to tell me the secret or keep me waiting until the food arrives?"

"Why don't we order our drinks and our meal. Then we can talk."

After the waitress took their orders, Jeff plunged in. "I want to apologize for the way I treated you."

Eve grimaced and replied politely, "There's no need, Jeff."

"I needed to say that to you." His expression was dead earnest. His eyes were focused on hers. "I care about you and I am ashamed of how I behaved. What I did ruined our relationship. I want to fix that."

"It's more complicated than that. I am in no position to get into a serious relationship with you or anybody else."

Jeff put his elbows on the table and clasped his hands. "I also want you to know that I thought long and hard about what you and Ed said to me that night." He looked down and bit his lip. "I have started going to counseling. I have a long way to go but I want you to know that I am committed to getting my life straightened out."

Her expression was blank. "I'm glad, Jeff." Her voice was flat. "That makes the trip down here worthwhile."

"Can you tell me what's going on with you? Is there any way that I can help?"

"No and no. But I appreciate your asking."

They sat in silence for several minutes. Jeff couldn't stand it so he started telling her about a motorcycle tour he was planning. He wanted to spend a month or two touring wilderness areas in upstate New York, Massachusetts, Maine, and Canada. He might go for a whole year if he liked riding around like that. The conversation carried them through the lunch.

"Do you know what was wrong with the Iraq war?" Eve asked without warning.

"It was a stupid idea?"

"In retrospect, it was." She looked off to the side. She spoke with profound sadness. "The planning was inadequate. The goals were poorly stated. There was no exit strategy." She turned back to look at Jeff. "It seemed like we expected to just walk in and turn a bad situation into a great one and everybody would be happy." She moistened her lips. "We could think that way because we didn't understand the situation or the people we were dealing with."

"Which is a fancy way of saying that it was a stupid idea."

She took a sip of her wine. "I'm working on a project. It is probably just as stupid. My planning was non-existent so I am caught up in a bad situation with no clear exit strategy."

He rubbed his index finger against his lips while he studied her. "What's the project?"

"I'm supposed to be getting fresh insights into prostitutes and prostitution."

"By turning yourself into a prostitute?"

"Yes."

He took a sip of his wine and sat back. "So you are going to have to do what Obama is promising to do. Admit it was a bad idea and walk away from it."

She nodded. "That will stop the carnage." She buried her head in her hands. "But it will not rebuild the world I've lost nor will it heal the wounds."

"I can't help you there. But I am sure that in time the wounds will heal and the lost world will be replaced." He reached across and lifted her chin. "All you have to do is accept that you are not really in charge and let the universe right itself."

Tears glistened in her eyes but she smiled. "That actually makes sense."

"So when you are ready to take the big step, let me know. I'll fix you up with a bike and take you on a grand tour of our wonderful continent."

She took his hands in hers and squeezed. "I'll have to think about that. Thank you for lunch, Jeff."

Eve got up and walked out of Clyde's of Georgetown so April could return to her family.

61

APRIL SWUNG BY the pool to check in with Becky and JJ before heading home. JJ was on the tennis courts engaged in a round-robin tennis tournament. He waived and shouted, "Hi, Mom."

Becky was nowhere to be seen. April found a couple of her friends. They said Becky had been with Owen most of the day. One of them thought the pair had gone over to the high school to work out on the track. April drove over to the high school. Owen's car was sitting in the shade of a tree at a far corner of the parking lot near the edge of the track. It appeared to be unoccupied. As she got closer, she noticed movement in the back seat. The back door on the driver's side was open. She pulled to a stop behind Owen's car. Something was going on and it was not a track workout. April got out of her car and walked to the side of Owen's car. Bare feet were sticking out of the door.

She banged on the trunk of the car and ordered, "Break it up."

Owen jumped backward onto the pavement. April looked up at the sky and shook her head. "Pull your pants up."

"How could you?" Becky demanded. April briefly regretted not letting the couple finish. "What happened to your vow of chastity?"

"You said I wouldn't be able to keep it and you were right," Becky said in a measured, sarcastic tone.

"Get dressed and get into my car," April ordered. She turned her attention to the young man. He was tanned, lean, and long-limbed. He had a broad forehead and an eagle beak nose. No wonder Becky couldn't get enough of him. She said sternly, "Where's your condom?"

"I'm not fertile, Mom," Becky yelled.

April turned to look at her. "How would you know that?"

"I just had my period last week."

April returned to Owen. "Where is your condom? Don't tell me you had your period last week."

Owen looked like a puppy being scolded for pooping on the carpet. "It isn't what you think."

"I know exactly what it is. I've been doing it for 20 years." April glared at him. "You will always use a condom unless you want your partner pregnant."

"Mom!"

"He needs to get into the habit of protecting himself from STDs." April turned to look at Becky. "And he needs to protect his playmates from everything."

"Grow up, Mom"

She turned back to Owen. "You have one hour to bring two boxes of condoms to our house. Becky, get in the car, we're going home."

Thirty minutes later, Owen showed up at the Walsh's front door. He had a bag with two boxes of condoms. April brought him into the kitchen and called Becky down. When everyone was in the room, April said, "Owen, give Becky her box of condoms."

"Becky, take out one of the condoms. Owen, let's see your finger." He just looked at her. He didn't seem to understand what she wanted. She showed him the middle finger of her right hand. He hesitated but produced his finger.

"Becky, show me that you can put a condom on that finger."

Becky looked horrified. She recovered and put the condom on Owen's finger as if she had been doing it all her life.

"Okay. You know what to do. I expect you to do it."

After he left, Becky asked, "You were fifteen when you did it the first time?"

April pursed her lips and cocked her head to the side. "I was about a year older than you."

62

APRIL'S PHONE RANG. She was getting ready for a power nap before starting her evening chores and heading to work. It was Lydia Tompkins. She had started working as a waitress at the Tahiti. She wanted to know if April was still going to help her teach Jerry a lesson.

April visualized the frumpy woman that she had talked to ten days earlier. She wanted to say no but she couldn't. Lydia had gone to the trouble of getting a job at the Tahiti. April said she was sorry but this was going to be her final week. She would not be returning after Labor Day.

Lydia suggested that they could do it before the end of this week. Jerry and his pals always ended up there on Thursday nights. April pointed out that Lydia was on day shift so they would have to find a way to slip her into the club at night without making Anna Stroom suspicious. If Lydia did get inside and onto the stage, they would both be fired.

Lydia said, "You're going to quit anyway. I don't care if they fire me. I can find another job but I am not going to get another chance like this."

April sketched Lydia on the Tahiti stage in her bath-robe. "I might be able to get someone to switch with you this Thursday. But that could get her in trouble."

"Why can't I just hang around after I get off work?"

April closed her eyes and shook her head, "There's no place to hide. Anna monitors the tables and checks the dressing room."

"I'll find a place to hide until Jerry shows up and you are ready to go on stage."

April drew furious circles around Lydia. "Alright. I need to get some rest. I will get to the Tahiti a little early on Thursday and work out the details with you."

Eve spotted Jerrod Johnson sitting at a table by himself a little after nine that evening. He raised his glass when he saw her looking his way. She made her way over to him. "What are you doing here?"

"Looking for you." He grinned up at her.

"You found me. Should I sit down or did you have something else in mind?"

"I would like to invite you to breakfast."

She pulled up a seat. "That's a very nice offer. But I'm going to have to decline."

"I'm a big tipper. I'll make it worth your while."

Eve smiled. "Some things are more important than money. We can leave now and have four or five hours. Or you can pick up somebody else. There are a lot of women here who would jump at that offer."

"I was looking forward to spending time with you."

Eve bowed to Jerrod. "I'm flattered. I would really like to spend the next few hours with you. But that is all that I can give you." She tilted her head and arched her eyebrows. "Do you want to work things out with Anna while I change?"

He sipped his drink and considered his options. "Okay. Let's get her over here."

Inside the hotel room, Jerrod stood watching and waiting for the tip speech. Instead, Eve walked up to him, put her arms around his neck, and gave him a hungry kiss. "You know the situation. I don't need to explain it to you. You can handle the money any way you want. Put it out there now. Stick it in my bra when I'm ready to leave. Or play me for a fool and send me home empty-handed."

He slid the dress off of her shoulders and down to the floor. But he was baffled by her bra. She guided his hands under the bottom to her breasts. "Push up. It comes off quick and easy."

She stopped him from removing her thong until she had removed his clothes. While she was down on her knees removing his shoes, socks, and pants, she began sucking his cock. She kept it up until he came in her mouth.

He lifted her to her feet and pushed her thong to the floor. He turned her around and began pushing at her butt. She pulled away and retrieved a condom from her purse. "How do you want me?" He led her to the wall. She leaned her hands against the wall and offered her butt to him. He worked his way inside and humped until he came. She was surprised that the experience was almost pleasurable.

She grabbed a box of condoms from her purse and led him to the bed. They continued their lovemaking for over an hour. "What do you really want to do?" Jerrod asked.

Eve stared at him wide-eyed trying to make sense of the question. "I'm sorry. What are you asking?"

"I'm asking what you are going to do next," Jerrod said evenly. "You can't be enjoying this life. What would you like to be doing?"

Eve panicked. This was too personal. It had to be off limits. She got out of the bed and walked across the room. She turned to face him. "I don't think this is the time to be discussing my career."

"I want to know and you are here to entertain me." Jerrod's eyes narrowed to a squint. His voice was threatening. "So please humor me with an answer to my question."

"I like to write," Eve stammered. "I think that I could be a successful writer one of these days."

Jerrod nodded and smiled approvingly. "Suppose that I gave you an opportunity to do that."

Eve ran her hand through her hair. "What's the catch?"

"No catch," Jerrod said. "You come to work for me. I make sure that you have food, a place to live, and time to work on your career." Jerrod raised his arms in an expansive gesture. "In our spare time, we enjoy evenings like this."

Eve covered her mouth to suppress a laugh. "You are offering me a job as your mistress?"

Jerrod growled, "Yes."

"I don't know. That's a big commitment. What if we discovered that we were only compatible in the bedroom?"

"We would be fine together," he assured her. He was as firm and confident as ever. "Besides, I stay busy with my job and you would have your writing."

"That sounds good on paper," Eve said. "But you do realize that I am paid to be nice on one night stands. You have no idea what I'm like the rest of the time." She paused and then added, "For all I know, you're a homicidal maniac who only takes me out on his good nights or while he's working up the courage to strangle me."

"If you believed that you wouldn't be here right now."

Eve shook her head. "That's a pretty small gamble compared to a marriage of sorts." She looked down and crushed out an imaginary cigarette butt. She looked straight into Jerrod's eyes. "And you still know nothing about me."

He pursed his lips and studied the ceiling. He looked at Eve. "I'll bet that I can put you at the mother lode for a great writing project. If I'm right, then you should give my proposal serious consideration."

"You don't know what my writing interests are."

"That's the fun part. I'm guessing that there is one thing you would really like to write about," he said gleefully. "If I'm right, then I do know something about you."

Eve looked over to the window. When she looked back at Jerrod, she prompted, "Well?"

"You tell me what you think you would like to work on and I will tell you what I have in mind," Jerrod proposed. "If we are close enough, I want you to quit the Tahiti and join me."

"I can't. I have personal commitments that I can't just walk away from." Eve leaned back against the dresser. "Besides, I get my ideas when I'm walking around doing nothing." She smirked. "I can't do it while I'm lying in bed with a hot date."

"Start with an idea that you have thought about already," Jerrod insisted.

She looked down. She looked out the window then back at Jerrod. "This is a terrible idea." She cleared her throat. "I would like to write about the Kennedy Assassination and what it meant."

"Why is that terrible?"

"The topic has been written to death. There are hundreds of books covering every aspect of the Kennedy-Johnson era. Everything that can be said has been said."

"And yet you are not satisfied," Jerrod pointed out. "None of those hundreds of books fully addresses your issues." Eve nodded. Jerrod continued, "There have to be thousands of people in the same boat who would love to hear what you have to say."

Eve shrugged. "Your turn. What did you have in mind?"

"First, I think that you need to address one critical question," Jerrod said. "What is your fresh approach?"

"I don't know." She studied the ceiling. "Maybe somebody thwarts Jack Ruby and Oswald goes to trial. Or maybe, Kennedy doesn't win the nomination. Say his meds are discovered and the Democrats decide to give the nomination to Johnson."

"Great ideas. I can put you near both the Johnson Library and the Kennedy Library so you can research to your heart's content."

"That's a tempting offer but I would be your mistress. My primary job would be to make sure you're happy."

Jerrod shrugged. "I'm sure that we can work that out. Supposing we look at a ninety-day trial. You will make more in those ninety days working with me than you would be able to make at the Tahiti - guaranteed."

"And my undisclosed personal commitments?"

"We can work through them."

"What exactly are you proposing?" Eve demanded.

"I have to tour our operations in the Far East. I would like you to come with me."

"I can't commit to that right now."

"I can put the tour off for a month."

"Please don't do that. I am not at all sure that I will be any closer to resolving my issues in one month or even in two months. Why don't you get one of your other concubines to help you out?"

"They are highly successful women with commitments and responsibilities. I could get one of them to go with me on a Far East vacation. But if you come with me, I could kill two birds with one stone. I would get you out of this wretched situation and I would get to spend some extended time with you."

"I'm touched, but I can't even consider a proposal like that at the moment."

"Think about it. Let me know definitely in two weeks."

"I am not going to make any promises." Eve looked down at her clothes then back at Jerrod. "Can we cut this short so I can go home and think about your offer?"

"Okay."

While she dressed, he got up and counted out ten $100 bills. He stuffed them in her bra and pulled her close for a kiss. "I'm not like any other man you know. Life with me is not like any other life available to you." He cupped her head in his hands and kissed her again. "I have good taste in women. My friends are all successful and happy. I see you as belonging in that group."

She kissed him. "Thank you."

She walked out of the room without looking back.

63

EVE ARRIVED AT the Tahiti a half hour early on Thursday night. She passed a note to Lydia Tompkins telling her to meet on a side of the building that was not routinely watched. The woman who rounded the corner was a revelation. Her black dress hugged incredible curves. She looked like 38-28-38 D-Cup. Black curls framed a taut, well-defined face. The woman knew how to use makeup. But it was the eyes that got Eve. This new version of Lydia was direct, forceful, unyielding. Eve stood smiling and shaking her head. Lydia walked up and hugged her. "Thank you."

"You look great." Eve kissed her on the cheek. "What's your plan?"

"I don't really have one."

"What are you going to wear on stage?"

Lydia indicated the clothes she had on - a simple dress that buttoned down the front and platform shoes. "What kind of underwear are you wearing?"

"A bra - clasp in the front and a thong."

"That'll do. What time do you expect Jerry and his crowd?"

"I don't know. I've never asked him about it. I thought you would know what time he usually shows up."

Eve shook her head. "I haven't been paying attention to him." She looked across the street and blew air through her lips. "Let's plan on sometime before eleven." She cocked her head to one side. "That gives us five or six hours. But you can't hang around waiting for him."

Lydia said, "I know. I've been checking it out after work the last two nights. I can wait at the Burger King up the street."

"You're overdressed."

"I can handle it. Jerry and I used to run with a pretty rough crowd."

"How are you going to get back inside?"

"The girls prop the back door open when they go out for a smoke."

"So come back here around ten thirty. Find a seat near the steps to the stage. If we're lucky, Jerry will be in the audience when I go up. You can join me as soon as I start my routine."

Lydia nodded.

Eve continued, "Anna won't interrupt a performance. But she will want to grab us as soon as we leave the stage. You will have to get off the stage as far from her as possible. Go straight to Jerry's table."

Lydia looked a little lost. Eve grabbed her shoulders and gave a shake. "If you have any doubts, say so before we get started. Once you get up on that stage, we can't turn back. We can't even hesitate."

"I can do it," Lydia said.

She sounded unsure. Eve let it go. Everyone gets nervous at the thought of getting on stage and performing. Eve handed Lydia a piece of paper. "If you lose your nerve, call this number. It's for a cabbie named Hattie. Tell her that you are my friend and that you need a ride. She will take care of you."

Lydia took off towards the Burger King. Eve went into the Tahiti to get ready for work. One situation worried her. If she was hired as an escort, she might have to leave Lydia stranded. Eve was hired for a couple of private dances but she managed to avoid being sent to a hotel with a date.

The timing of the caper was not predictable. There were too many variables. Shortly after ten, Eve made her way from the dressing room to the stage. Lydia was seated alone at a table near the stage. The two women made eye contact. Eve gave Lydia a thumbs up when she spotted Jerry and his group. Lydia nodded and flashed a smile. Eve had a queasy feeling in her stomach as she mounted the stage.

She began with a tease that took her around the perimeter of the stage. Lydia slipped quietly onto the stage. Eve led her to the middle. The two jitterbugged as they started exposing flesh. They were down to thongs, garters, and platform shoes by the end of the second piece. The thongs were gone as soon as the music for the third piece started. They played to the men crowding the edge of the stage and waving bills to get their attention.

As predicted, Anna watched the performance without interfering. She did position herself at the steps so she could intercept the women as they left the stage. Just before the music ended, Eve told Lydia to grab her dress and get off the stage at the far corner. Two men lifted Lydia from the stage to the floor and helped her with her dress. When Eve reached the bottom of the steps, an irate Anna demanded, "What the hell was that?"

"She just wanted to dance for her husband one time."

"That is not the business we are in."

Eve wanted to say that Lydia had put on a good show. She wanted to point out that Lydia was a crowd-pleaser. But she limited herself to, "Yes, ma'am."

"If you ever pull a stunt like that again, I will fire you on the spot. Is that clear?"

"Yes, ma'am."

Anna headed straight for Lydia with Eve following at a safe distance. Lydia was seated on Jerry Tompkins' lap. She smiled at Anna and said, "This gentleman wants to hire me as an escort." She gave him a kiss.

Anna waved her over for a private conference. "I don't appreciate what you just did one bit. You are not one of our escorts so I can't hire you out."

Lydia was poker-faced. "He's my husband. He comes here all the time to ogle the women on that stage. He has hired at least one of your escorts."

"That's how it works," Anna responded coolly.

Lydia ignored her. "He has seen what I can do on the stage. Now he is going to pay to take me home."

Anna glared. Lydia stared back poker-faced. Anna snorted, "You are not an escort. I cannot hire you out."

"You work it out any way you want. Donate the money to charity or stick it up your ass. I don't leave here until he pays you for my company."

Anna had to avoid a scene. She growled, "Go get the rest of your clothes while I talk to the gentleman. You are not to step foot in the Tahiti ever again. I will inform Adrien and Carla that you have been fired."

"Deal," Lydia said. She chuckled as she walked off to retrieve her clothes.

When Lydia returned, she put her arms around Jerry's neck. "Did you pay the woman, sweetie?"

Jerry nodded.

"Good. Let's go have some fun."

64

IT WAS NOT yet ten on Friday evening when Anna introduced Eve to a man named Grif. He wanted a private dance. The vibes were bad from the start. The twenty minutes they spent together in the private dance area seemed like hours. He showed almost no interest in her. She was naked and there to be touched, stroked. He made little effort to take advantage of the opportunities. They were so close that she could see the stubble on his cheeks and chin in detail. She noticed an old scar by his right eye. She was sure that he was dying his hair to hide the gray. A normal man would have bumped against her breasts at some point. A normal man would have let his hand slide down her back to her butt and made her reach back to move it away. This man was cold and detached. When he touched her, it seemed like a move calculated to show that he was aroused.

She was glad when the music ended. She wanted to get back to the roomful of normal nuts. But Grif quickly took Anna up on the suggestion that he hire Eve as an escort. As Eve prepared to leave with Grif, she made sure her pistol was loaded and ready to go.

All she had to do was grab it, release the safety, and pull the trigger. When they checked into the hotel, she discreetly sent a text to Hattie, *Marriott dupont 533 x me 1hr.*

Inside the hotel room, Grif was too easy. He let her ramble on about the tip. When she had finished, he pulled out his wallet and put two $100 bills on the table. He pulled a chair around so that he could sit facing Eve who was standing near the foot of the bed.

She asked, "What would you like to do?"

He took forever to come up with something. "How about if you strip for me like you did on the stage?"

Eve forced herself into a striptease. Once she got moving, her body went through the routine on its own. It was a good performance. When she was completely naked, he wiggled his finger to call her over. He grabbed her butt and forced her to sit astride his thighs, her face inches from his. She felt detached as she examined that face again – the stubble, the scar, the hair dyed black. Now she noticed the tobacco smell and a faint odor of beer. He probably ordered a couple of beers and played with them because the Tahiti had a two-drink minimum. His hands slid from her butt up her back to her breasts. He sucked on her left nipple and rubbed his stubbly cheek against the soft, ivory skin on her breasts and neck. "Can we go over to the bed?" he asked.

Eve stood up. Grif held her arms and guided her back to the bed. He gently pushed her onto her back and pulled her feet up on the edge of the bed. She lay with her legs spread wide while he ran his hands down her thighs and up her abdomen. He fondled her breasts and kissed them. Then he stepped back and studied her for a moment before heading toward the door.

He stopped and turned when he reached the door. "Your husband hired me to find out what kind of work you do at the Tahiti. He will be most interested in the video I made of your activities. It's probably a good thing that you didn't try to use your piece. I would have enjoyed blowing your brains out but your husband would have been upset with me."

Grif walked out. Eve lay on the bed too stunned to move. An urgent knock on the door brought her back to the moment. Hattie banged on the door again and yelled, "Eve, are you okay?"

Eve yelled back, "Coming."

She walked over and opened the door. Hattie rushed in, pistol in hand. She surveyed the room. When she saw the blank expression on her friend's face, she asked tenderly, "Are you okay?"

"Yes. But it's all over. By this time tomorrow night, I will have been destroyed."

Hattie put her arms around Eve. "That guy I passed in the hall?"

"He's a private investigator hired by my husband. He got a video of me dancing, stripping, and submitting to foreplay." Eve pulled free from Hattie's embrace and walked across the room. "That should be enough to get Joe whatever he wants when he files for divorce."

Hattie shook her head sadly. She walked over to Eve and put her arms around her. She kissed her on the cheek. Eve wrapped her arms around Hattie and squeezed. They were cheek to cheek. Eve began to yield to stirrings in her body. She kissed Hattie. First on the cheek and neck. When she kissed her full on the mouth, Hattie responded. The kissing became more passionate until Eve's tongue pushed into Hattie's mouth. Hattie pulled back. "Not tonight. I'll want you in a good mood for that."

"I am in a good mood," Eve bristled.

"I want us in a nice bed in a nice room with a 'Do Not Disturb' sign on the door."

Eve pointed at the door. "I'm sure we hung out the sign when we came into the room."

Hattie shook her head. "That doesn't count." She hugged herself and shuddered. "He's still here."

"Grif is gone."

"No. He's still here. I can feel him watching us. Besides I have to get you home so April can take care of her family."

"Are you saying my children are a problem?"

"No. Nothing like that. Becky is the little sister I always wanted but never got. JJ is a great little guy." Hattie was rushing her words. She sounded panicked. "But you worry about them. If you are worrying about them, I have to worry about them."

Eve screamed, "What am I supposed to do?"

"I don't know." Hattie's voice cracked. "I don't want to take you away from them. I just want you for a little while. I want to close the door and make love to you until the sun comes up and then hold you in my arms until it sets again." She took Eve's face in her hands and kissed her. "That's all I want. After that, you can go back to Becky and JJ and to Joe if that's what you want. I will be satisfied with whatever is left over."

Eve studied her friend for a long time before putting her arms around her again. She kissed Hattie on the cheek and whispered, "Someday."

Then she put on her clothes and said, "Let's go."

They stopped for a drink at a bar in Georgetown but Eve wanted to get home and hide under the covers in her bed. When Hattie dropped her off at the Vienna Metro station, she said, "I'm going to my mother's house."

She gave Hattie half of Grif's money as she got out of the cab. The cab followed her as she left the Metro station.

65

APRIL WAS BUSY fending off questions from her mom when Joe called. "Where the hell are you?"

"I'm with my mother."

"What are you doing over there? I need you here."

April looked over at her mother. She was serenely eating and scanning the paper.

She said, "I didn't think it would be safe to come home after your PI threatened me."

"I have no idea what you are talking about." Joe was exasperated.

"Grif," April barked in a loud, forceful voice. Then more conversationally, "You know. The guy you paid to check up on me."

"Ok. Grif came by the Tahiti last night. So what?" Joe did not seem to be getting it. He was probably distracted by his duties as Mr. Mom.

"We went to the Marriott for fun and games. After capturing it all on video, he left," April said. "On his way out the door, he told me that he was sorry I hadn't given him an excuse to blow my brains out."

"What are you talking about?"

April was pacing about the kitchen. "Come off it, Joe. You wouldn't have sent a PI if you thought I was waiting tables."

"Alright, so what happened?" He was finally on board.

"Nothing really. I was naked a lot of the time but he went home before anything happened."

"You were naked in a hotel room with a man you had never met before?"

"Yes, Joe. And he caught it all with his hidden camera." April closed her eyes and shook her head. "You'll be able to look at it as much as you want. Of course, it's nothing you haven't seen before."

"You fucking bitch," Joe growled.

April ran her hand through her hair. "I hope Becky and JJ are out of earshot."

"They're in the kitchen eating breakfast." His voice was still angry. "They've got a swim meet. You need to get your butt over here."

She stopped pacing. A vision of him - tall, muscular, rigid, domineering popped into her mind. She would die before she would submit. "You don't actually need me. Just make up some story. You're good at that."

"You are their mother. Your place is here with your family."

She rolled her eyes. It was a command - straight from the head of the house. "I think we are at the point where we need to talk about that. When you're ready to talk about our situation, give me a call."

"There's nothing to discuss." Joe was dismissive. He was the boss.

"Really? Are you going to call a divorce lawyer?" she asked sarcastically. "Or have you already lined one up?"

"I'm not planning on divorcing you." His tone was still dismissive.

She could hear him take in a deep breath and let it out slowly. He switched to soft and conciliatory. "Just come on home."

She shook her head. "Not right now. You get the kids to their meet. We can talk later or maybe tomorrow." She hung up.

April's mother looked up at her. "What was that all about?"

"I was doing research for my newspaper assignment. I went too far."

"Then you need to go back home and get things straightened out with your husband."

"It's not that simple," April said wistfully. "Joe is having an affair with a divorcee. He sent a PI to the Tahiti to get dirt on me so he can divorce me and marry her."

"Are you sure? You didn't mention an affair when you were talking to him." April's mother was unflappable. She had been dealing with family messes for forty years.

"Neither did he." April scowled. "He has been careful not to mention his girlfriend in any way. But that's what is going on."

"You're overreacting, my dear."

April pulled out Eve's cell phone and found the video of Joe kissing Lee on the front porch. She showed it to her mother. "That was at two in the morning.

They thought I wouldn't be home until three. I have a witness to back me up."

"Why haven't you said anything?"

"I have to quit my job before I confront Joe."

"When are you planning to do that?"

"Sunday night will be my last night."

"Why not call them now and tell them you're quitting effective immediately?"

April rolled her eyes. Another command disguised as a suggestion.

"I probably should," April conceded. "But I don't think that will help my marriage and I don't want to burn any more bridges."

"Do it your way." Her mother shrugged. "But trust me. Your family is much more important than your standing at the Tahiti."

They finished their breakfast in silence.

April left for the Tahiti at her usual time. She had not heard from Joe or the kids. When she got to the Tahiti, Ed grabbed her and escorted her to the office. Adrien Gautier was waiting for her. He was calm but he was not happy.

He sat with his arms folded across his chest and stared at her for several seconds before he said, "I will make this brief, Eve. You are fired. You have violated our trust in you. You lied about your situation when you applied for a job.. Carla will take you back to the dressing room where you will gather any personal items. You will leave the premises immediately. Please do not return here for any reason."

"May I ask what I did to deserve this?"

"A Mr. Griffin Boothe, a private eye has been investigating you. He informs us that the real reason that you sought work here was to write an expose of the Tahiti for the Washington Post."

"I am not writing for the Post, and I am certainly not writing an expose of the Tahiti. I have been treated well here. I have great respect for the way you do business."

"Please go with Carla. Get your belongings and leave."

Carla took Eve's arm and led her away.

66

APRIL CALLED A cab. Riding with Hattie in her condition was out of the question. The driver stopped and waited at a liquor store so she could pick up her own whiskey and not have to depend on her mother's stock. Jameson Black Reserve was expensive but it sounded like it fit her mood.

When her mother called her for Mass on Sunday morning, she said that she would look online for a late mass and go later. She didn't bother. It seemed hypocritical and Jesus didn't like hypocrites.

Becky called in the afternoon to see if she was okay. "Yes, sweetheart. I'm working on my story for the Times-Herald."

"Why don't you come home and work in your office?"

"Things are tense between your dad and me. I think it's best if we let the situation settle down."

"Are you going to get a divorce?"

"Not if I can help it."

"Is that yes or no?"

"It's I don't know because it's not up to me."

"Why not?"

"Both parties have to commit to a marriage. Either one of us can decide to end the marriage but both of us have to agree to work on our issues if we are going to stay married."

"So it's up to Dad?"

"I think that is something we still have to figure out. Can you leave it at that for the time being?"

"I love you, Mom. I don't want you and Dad to divorce."

"I know that, sweetheart. We can talk some more later. I love you very much." April ended the call and poured some more Black Reserve so she could get back to work.

67

JOE CALLED ON Monday afternoon to ask April to come stay at the house. He had not been able to find anybody to take care of the kids while he was at work. He had found a place to stay temporarily so he would move out of the house until things got settled. April agreed as long as there would be no shouting matches in front of the children.

Becky and JJ were happy to see their mother back in the house. Then they found out that their dad was moving out.

"Why does Dad have to leave?" Becky demanded.

April studied Joe while she waited for his answer. He took his time. Finally, he said, "We need some space right now. This is just a temporary arrangement to give us a chance to work through some issues."

"But there's plenty of space here," Becky objected. "Dad, you're going to be at work most of the time. Mom spends a lot of time in her office. We could work out a schedule so you guys didn't have to sit down and talk to each other or even look at each other."

"I could make myself scarce. I don't mind that," April volunteered.

"I've already arranged for a place to stay and I'm packed. I'm going to give this a try. Besides, it will cost me as much to pull out of the deal as it will to go through with it," Joe insisted.

"How much is it going to cost, Joe? I'll reimburse you," April said.

"That's alright. Like I said, I'm already committed."

April's second phone rang. She pulled the pink flip phone from her purse. "Hi."

"Eve, it's Jack Edwards."

April turned away from her family. "Jack, I'm in the middle of something right now."

"We need to talk. You have been identified as a potential witness in a case we're working."

She shook her head. "You must be mistaken. I haven't witnessed anything."

"You know Amos Goethels?"

She looked up at the ceiling. "The name sounds familiar."

"He just put a woman in the hospital." April shuddered. Jack continued, "When we went through related case files, we came across a report that he attacked you in a hotel room."

April looked at the floor and crushed out an imaginary cigarette butt. "I declined to press charges because there were no witnesses. It was going to be a waste of time."

"I'm asking you to reconsider. This guy is dangerous. We have to get him off of the street. The only way to do that is to establish a pattern. That means we need you and a couple of other women to take the stand against him."

April closed her eyes and shook her head. "That sounds like a terrible idea. His attorney will crucify the women to protect his client. Goethels will get off and the DA will look like a jackass."

"I need a statement from you. I'm asking you as a friend. If that doesn't work, I'll have to send my officers out to get your statement."

April sighed. "Tomorrow. I will come down tomorrow morning and meet with you and your officers."

"Thanks. I knew I could count on you." He hung up.

April put the phone away and turned back to her family. Three faces stared at her in open-mouthed disbelief. "It's nothing. I had a run-in with a man. The police got involved but nothing came of it. Now, he has put a woman in the hospital and the police want more details about what happened between us."

"What did happen?" Joe demanded.

"I'm not really sure. He slugged me and everything after that is a blur. He fell backward and hit his head. I called the police. They came and took our statements. Then they took us to the hospital. We were examined and released."

"So that's how you got the black eye?" There was anger and hurt in Joe's voice.

"Yes. I didn't tell you about it at the time because I figured it was all over with. I didn't want you to worry needlessly."

Joe pressed his lips together and shook his head. "Apparently, we had good reason to be worried."

"Of course there was some risk, Joe. But I felt I could take care of myself and I was right."

"Who is Jack?" Joe asked suspiciously. "Sounds like you're pretty good friends."

"He's a police officer that I interviewed to get a beat cop's perspective on prostitution. Can we get back to the issue?" April studied Joe. Her eyes pleaded. "Joe, put your stuff away and stay with us. I will do my best to be invisible."

"I think that phone call underscored the problems we have to address before I am willing to share a home with you."

Joe hugged Becky and JJ. "Sorry, kids. You have my phone number. Call me if you need anything."

He picked up his suitcase and walked out to his car.

It was a miserable evening. The kids had to make sure they had everything ready for school. For the first time, they would be going to different schools with different schedules. April said that she would be going to talk to the police between ten and eleven. She expected to be back in plenty of time to pick them up. Otherwise, Gramma Becky would pick them up.

Amos Goethels made the news that night. Becky asked if that was the man. "Yes, he's the one," April said.

"He looks scary," Becky said.

"He is. When you meet him, you can tell he's not quite right. You don't realize how dangerous he is until he attacks you."

"He hit you first?" Becky asked.

"Yes."

"How did you get away?"

"I don't really remember. We were sort of wrestling and somehow he lost his balance. He fell back and hit his head. He wasn't moving. So I called the police."

"You were lucky," JJ said.

"Very lucky. Now get to bed."

As soon as the house was quiet, April called Bill to tell him what was going on. She asked him to meet her at the police station and to represent her as things moved forward.

"How bad is it?"

"I'm not sure. I haven't done anything but his lawyer will almost certainly portray me as a prostitute." April could feel herself falling apart. "When that makes the news, my life will be pretty much over."

Bill's voice was confident and reassuring. "It'll be rough but other women have made it through. You'll be okay. See you in the morning."

68

APRIL AND BILL were shown to Sergeant Jack Edward's office at 10:54 on Tuesday morning. Sergeant Edwards handed them off to a pair of his detectives who led them to an interrogation room. They introduced themselves as detectives Bill Andrews and Elizabeth Smith.

Andrews began, "I see you brought your lawyer along."

"Of course," April replied.

"You know that we just wanted to clear up a few things." Andrews said.

"I'm not sure what needs to be cleared up but my lawyer can hear anything that we have to say."

"It just seems a little strange that you would feel the need to have a lawyer present for a friendly conversation."

"So far this meeting is anything but friendly."

"What makes you say that?" Andrews sounded offended.

April smiled but said nothing.

Andrews got tired of waiting for a reply. "What is your name?"

"Yvonne MacMahon."

"It's not April Walsh?" Andrews pressed.

"No. Why would you think that?"

"Because that's the name you used for years."

"Ah. You've been investigating me."

"Is your name April Walsh or Yvonne MacMahon?"

"My name is Yvonne April MacMahon. Walsh is my husband's name. I used it until very recently."

"What was the purpose of the name change?"

April looked over at Bill but said nothing. "Can you help us out here, detective. What are you looking for?" Bill asked.

"Your client gave her name as Eve MacMahon at the time of her encounter with Mr. Goethels. We could not find any record of Eve MacMahon but we were able to determine that April Walsh was the woman who talked to the police that night."

Bill nodded to April. She reached into her purse and produced a driver's license and Social Security card issued to Yvonne A. MacMahon. "I recently read that professional women do better when they use their given name. That sounded like a good idea so I changed my name. People prefer Eve to Yvonne. I answer to any or all of those names."

"When you started working at the Tahiti?" Smith smirked.

"When I got an advance for the book I am working on." April glared at Smith. "I considered that a major step in establishing myself as a professional writer."

"So you think of yourself as a professional writer?" Andrews asked.

"Yes"

"But you were working as a secretary until you got fired in June," Smith said. "Then you went to work as a call girl for the Tahiti."

"Writing is a tough business. Thousands of books go on the market every month. Millions of words are written for publication every day. People like me who are trying to get established have a tough time. We take whatever work we can get to pay the bills." April hissed. "And for the record, I was never a call girl. I worked as a waitress at the Tahiti before I started dancing and working as an escort."

Andrews said, "You were working as an escort when you met Mr. Goethels, took him to a hotel room, and offered to have sex with him for 200 dollars."

"I did not offer to have sex with Mr. Goethels."

"What was the 200 dollars for?"

"Mr. Goethels offered me a tip for my services as an escort. I never found out how big the tip was."

"He claims that he gave you 200 dollars for sex."

"The money was a tip. As I explained to Mr. Goethels, I got only a small part of what he paid for my services as an escort. The Tahiti expected me to make my money from tips."

"According to Mr. Goethels, when you got in the room, you offered to have sex with him but he had to give you 200 dollars."

"That is incorrect."

"Why should we believe you?"

"Why should you believe Mr. Goethels?" April retorted. She looked at Andrews and then at Smith to gauge their reactions. She leaned back in her chair.

"I had strict instructions on how I was supposed to proceed. I followed them."

"Did those instructions include stripping naked and removing your client's clothing?"

"No"

"But you were naked when you opened the door for the police detectives and Mr. Goethels was naked on the floor with his hands and feet tied and a sock stuffed in his mouth."

"Sounds like pretty kinky sex." Smith grinned.

"Mr. Goethels removed his own clothes. We did not engage in sex." April closed her eyes and shook her head. "He was not interested in that."

"What was he interested in?"

"I don't know. My guess is, he wanted to find out what it would feel like to kill me."

"Maybe he wanted you to tie him up and work him over," Andrews suggested.

April did not respond. Bill said, "Mr. Goethels assaulted my client. She tied him up to keep him quiet until the police could arrive."

"Can you prove that?" Smith asked.

"It is up to you to prove that something else happened," Bill answered.

"Why don't you give us your version of what happened?" Andrews said.

April looked at Bill and he nodded his assent. "I am not entirely clear about everything that happened that night. I sustained a concussion so some of the stuff is blurry. I was introduced to Goethels by Anna Stroom. She's the night floor manager. She told me that he wanted to hire me as an escort. We went to the hotel room and I gave him the spiel about the tip. He took some money out of his wallet and put it on the dining table. It might have been 200 dollars. It might have been a hundred or even less. I didn't touch the money. I don't know what happened to it. As best I can tell I went home without it." April cleared her throat. "The start of the session was awkward. I asked him what he wanted to do. He had me take off my clothes and lay on the bed. I watched while he removed his clothes. Then he climbed on top of me." She paused. Her lip curled up in disgust.

"What did he do?" Andrews demanded.

"He started masturbating."

"Then what?"

"I could tell he was getting ready to come. I remember wondering what he was going to do with it. I figured I was going to get a face full. Then he hit me on the side of my head. It hurt like hell. My head was ringing. All I could see was stars. He hit me again but it wasn't as bad. When I could see, I was looking up into the face of a monster. I thought he was going to kill me. I grabbed his head and pulled hard. I was able to land a headbutt. Then we wrestled and ended up rolling off of the bed. The next thing I remember clearly is being pushed into the wall. I was able to get my feet up against the wall. He kept crushing me into a ball. Then we went backward. I heard his head hit the floor about the time I landed on top of him. He just went limp. I wanted to call for help but I was afraid he would come after me again. So I tied him up."

"How did you do that?"

"I grabbed a sock and tied his hands together. It wasn't great but I figured it would hold him until I could get help. I grabbed his shirt and tied his feet together."

"What about the sock in his mouth?"

"I don't remember that. I remember him shouting. I wanted him to shut up."

"Did you threaten to kill him?"

"I don't remember."

"Do you remember calling the police?"

"No. I called Ed Rockmeier. He's the head of security. I wanted to ask him what I should do. He told me to just sit tight. He would bring the police with him. I sat on the bed. I don't know how long it took. I was sitting there with a splitting headache. All of a sudden the police were banging on the door and yelling. So I let them in."

"At what point did you threaten Mr. Goethels with your gun?" Andrews asked.

"I didn't have a gun."

"You own a gun. Don't you?" Smith challenged.

"I had just picked out the gun the day before. There was a waiting period before I could take possession. Plus, I had to wait for my DC carry permit."

"So you had just gotten your gun and a permit to carry when you went out and attacked one of the customers in the parking lot?" Andrews asked.

"Is that what you call it when you confront an armed assailant?"

"How did you know he was armed? What if you had shot and killed an unarmed man?"

April shot back angrily, "He was armed and I didn't shoot anybody."

Andrews studied his notes. He looked at his partner. She nodded.

"You can go for now," Andrews said. "We may have additional questions after we have a chance to check your story."

Bill grabbed her arm and pulled her toward the door before she could say anything else. Jack wasn't in his office when they passed. April wondered if he had watched the interrogation.

69

APRIL WAS REQUIRED to shuttle between two worlds. Sometimes the ordinary, everyday world was successful in its efforts to keep her trapped in its dungeons. Tuesday was such a day. It started with mom duties - getting Becky and JJ out of the house and off to their principal activity - school. Then she had to go to the police station where she endured two hours of rudeness by people who had nothing better to do than harass people like her. The verbal assault had been so trying that she was unable to function when she got back home. She went to the community college gymnasium. She worked with the weights, swam, and soaked in the Jacuzzi. The rest of the afternoon and most of the evening were devoted to making her children feel loved.

Jack called around nine. He apologized for the way that she had been interrogated. He was sure that everything was going to be okay. The DA was working with Goethels lawyer on some sort of plea deal. She thanked him and said that she didn't want any interruptions for a while. She had to take care of her children and focus on her writing.

Wednesday started off badly. Detectives Andrews and Smith were waiting for her when she returned home after taking Becky and JJ to school. They wanted to check her weapon. She led them upstairs to her office. She unlocked a file drawer on the right side of her desk and took out a lockbox. She unlocked the box and slid it over to the detectives so that they could inspect her S&W Shield.

Smith put on latex gloves before inspecting the weapon. "Nice piece. Have you ever fired it?"

"At the firing range," April said.

"Where do you keep your ammo?" Andrews asked.

April unlocked another drawer that contained a partially empty box of 9mm rounds and two fully loaded clips for the Shield. "How often do you take it out?"

"Right now, I don't. I'm a stay at home mom and a writer who's trying to get her assignments completed."

"When was the last time you carried?" Smith asked.

"Last Saturday."

"That was the night you were fired?" Andrews asked.

"Yes."

"And you came straight home and locked it up after you left the Tahiti?" Andrews prompted.

"No. I went to my mom's house. I came home Monday afternoon and put the gun away when I got around to unpacking."

"So Monday was the last time that you carried."

"I don't think of that as carrying. The gun was with me because it was in my purse. I wasn't thinking about it. It was just there."

"Why didn't you go home?" Andrews asked.

"I was pissed at Joe and I didn't want to be any-where near him."

"So you went somewhere where you wouldn't be tempted to shoot him?" Andrews suggested.

April glared at him. "Don't be ridiculous. I just didn't want to be around him. I think most of all I did not want to get into a big fight about what was going on."

"What was going on?"

"I was working as an escort at the Tahiti. It was driving him crazy."

"Why didn't you quit?" Smith asked.

"I was about to. Mom told me to call them Saturday and tell them that I was through. I wanted to leave on good terms so I went in Saturday planning to tell them that Sunday would be my last night. They fired me before I got the chance."

"Just like that? Out of the blue, they fired you?"

"It was personal. Joe's PI told them that I had lied when I applied for a job with them. He also convinced them that I was planning to write an expose on the Tahiti for the Washington Post. That got Mr. Gautier so mad that he had to can me on principle."

"Are you writing an expose on the Tahiti?"

"No. I am writing a six-part series on the sex indus-try and sex workers. The Tahiti was just a convenient base of operations."

"So you decided to work as a prostitute to get your story?" Andrews asked.

"No. I just ended up working as an escort. I started out working as a waitress. I think Joe could have lived with that. He might even have let me get away with dancing. But being an escort was too much for him."

"So your husband knew what was going on?"

"I told him about the job as a waitress. I tried to keep the rest of it a secret. He's too smart for that. Besides he has spent enough time in those clubs. He knows what goes on. He hired a PI to find out exactly what I was doing."

"Who are you angrier with? Your husband or his PI?" Andrews asked.

"I'm not angry with either one of them." April scowled at Andrews. "I think we need to end this little session. You came to inspect my gun. You've inspected it. I want to have a lawyer present before we go any further."

"Just one more thing," Smith said. "Sergeant Edwards mentioned a woman. I am pretty sure that she was a reporter investigating the sex industry. Was that you?"

"You need to leave, detective. I am not answering any more questions without my lawyer present."

April needed some time to calm down after the detectives left. She was able to finish up the last part of the six-part series before she had to pick up her children. Her plan was to spend the next day working on the book and make a last sweep of the series for the Times-Herald on Friday so she could send it in before work on Monday morning. Her problem was that she couldn't stop thinking about the visit from the detectives. They were fishing for something. She didn't know what kind of game Jack was playing but his detectives acted as if they were still investigating her.

70

THURSDAY STARTED WELL. April got Becky and JJ off to school without a hitch. She went directly up to her office to work on her book. The plan was to focus on the women she had worked with at the Tahiti. But it would go deeper into their lives than the Times-Herald articles had allowed. Dolly's story was a real winner but pieces were missing. The mother's side of the story should be included. Nickey had agreed to do some much needed investigating.

April wanted to talk about other issues such as domestic abuse and wives who wouldn't leave abusive husbands. She wanted to investigate the internet as a sex marketplace. There was plenty of porn out there. Some women were marketing themselves through casual meet up sites. Prostitution on the internet was changing the game. It was going to put traditional venues like the Tahiti, street walking, and red light districts out of business.

Eve's cell phone interrupted the reverie. She answered without checking the caller ID. It was Nickey. "Hi, sweetie, how are you?"

April managed, "Oh, Nickey. What's up?"

"I just called to see how you were doing?"

"I'll bet."

"Seriously, Bill and I have been talking about you. He was unhappy about the way you were treated at the police station the other day."

April relaxed. She let herself believe that this was a friendly call. "Any idea what's going on?"

"That crowd has an intense dislike for whores, which includes you as far as they are concerned. It'll blow over."

April sighed. "I hope so."

"I'm told the police and hospital reports back your version of the Goethels incident. His attorney has decided to look for a way out. Goethels is going in for a psych eval to determine if he is competent to stand trial."

April scribbled *Amos Goethels* on her notepad. "Why are they still investigating me?"

"What do you mean?"

April slashed through the name with a violent stroke of her pen. "Detectives Andrews and Smith came over to check out my gun. Then they started questioning me about my marriage and about getting fired from the Tahiti. It almost sounded like Joe had been threatened and they wanted to blame me."

"I haven't heard anything. Where are you keeping your gun?"

April sketched the Shield on her notepad. "In a locked drawer in my desk."

"I think you should get a storage locker at whatever shooting range you use. Let them take care of the gun for you. Go back at least once and check the gun out so you can go through your regular practice routine.

Make a note of what they do to record when the gun was checked out and when it was checked back in."

"Why?" April added a discharge flash and a bullet coming out of the barrel of her gun.

"PI's get death threats all the time. Some of them are serious. The guy that Joe hired, Griffin Boothe, has a reputation. Something could happen to him at any time. It will be harder to make a case against you if you can prove that your gun was in secure storage when the crime was committed."

April wrote *Grif Boothe* on her notepad. "Cheery thought."

"Did they ask you about him yesterday?"

April added *John Wilkes* under *Grif*. "Sort of. They asked if I was angrier at Joe or his PI."

Nickey's train of thought jumped the track without warning. "By the way, do you know where Joe is staying?"

April wrote *Real issue: Joe*. "No. He walked out and I haven't heard from him since."

"He's staying with Lee Sheehan."

"Sheehan?" April echoed the name. "So Aileen has reverted to her maiden name? And my husband has moved in with her? How do you know this?"

"I followed Joe after he left work. Then I asked around. He's well known there."

"I hope you are not stalking Joe."

"Your mother called Bill to find out what was going on. He asked me to look into it. Joe has rented an efficiency but doesn't stay there. He checks the mailbox but no one remembers seeing him entering or leaving the apartment."

April sketched Joe in on her notepad. "It's only been two days."

"Actually, it's been over a week. Joe rented the apartment the Monday after Bridget showed up at your house. He hired Griffin Boothe the same day." Nickey paused for a breath before exhaling noisily. "He's been seen visiting Lee. Her neighbors believe that he moved in with her on Labor Day. Bill wants you to get a divorce lawyer."

"I'm not planning on divorcing Joe." April sketched herself in next to Joe. She encircled the couple with a heart.

"He's getting ready to dump you. His lawyer is the kind who will take your recent employment and turn it into an argument for giving Joe sole custody of your children."

April gasped, "Oh, God."

Nickey exhaled noisily and pushed on. "You need to get started on your defense. I'll text you contact information on a couple of lawyers that we recommend."

April pulled into a ball. Tears welled up in her eyes. "Why isn't Bill telling me this himself?"

"We thought it would be easier coming from me. You can call Bill. He'll tell you the same thing."

"When?"

"Probably in the next week to ten days."

"This is crazy. Who is going to take care of Becky and JJ?"

"That has to be worked out. Joe wants sole custody but he will have to convince the judge that he can handle it."

After the call, April poured herself a double shot of the good Irish whiskey and considered her situation. She wouldn't mention the divorce to Becky and JJ until she received the papers. She contacted the first of Bill's recommended lawyers, Eleanora Bailey. Ms Bailey's receptionist took a message and said the lawyer would get back to her as soon as possible.

The receptionist at Smith and Wesson told April to come by any time during business hours. She could take the Shield to the shooting range after she dropped the children off at school. But that would mean putting off her work for another morning at least.

71

ON FRIDAY, APRIL dropped the kids off at school and drove to the Smith and Wesson Gun Emporium to put her Shield in storage. She drove from there to Eleonora Bailey's office for a late morning appointment. April was still reluctant to take the divorce seriously. She had to fill out some forms before she actually got in to meet Eleonora. Ms Bailey asked the obvious questions and took notes. When she asked if April was still a prostitute, April said, "We need to stay away from that term. I worked as an escort, which is legal. I never engaged in prostitution."

"You did have sex with men other than your husband as part of your work as an escort," Eleonora countered.

"Yes. But it is important to maintain the distinction between what I did and prostitution as it is legally defined," April insisted. "I know this won't help my position in the divorce proceedings but it will minimize the chances that I will be charged with a crime I didn't commit."

Ms Bailey scribbled some more notes and studied the papers on her desk. She looked up at April. "Okay.

So you were a sex worker who provided entertainment to adult males and sometimes during the course of that entertainment you engaged in various sexual acts with said males. But that was incidental. Those acts were not what you were paid to do."

That sounded terrible. April nodded but said nothing.

Eleonora continued. "What are you looking for? How do you want this to come out?"

"I would like to reconcile with my husband but that is not going to happen. So I want to be the primary parent for our children and I want a fair settlement on the property."

Eleonora jotted some more notes. She looked up at April and asked, "Why do you say that you won't be able to reconcile with your husband? You are out of the sex business, aren't you?"

"Yes," April nodded. "But he wants to divorce me so he can marry his girlfriend."

Eleonora pulled back. "What makes you say that?"

April laughed. "I'm a woman. I've been married to the man for 14 years. I can see what is going on."

"Do you have any evidence to support this womanly intuition?"

"She was visiting him at night while I was working. Last Monday, he moved out of our house and into her apartment. My brother and his investigator found out about the living arrangements and told me."

Eleonora called Bill and conferenced Nickey in. She confirmed the information about Joe. April threw in that she had confronted Joe after their daughter Becky complained about the late night visits.

Eleonora said ruefully, "The judge may decide that neither one of you is a fit parent."

The meeting left April in a funk. She stood staring out the picture window. Her mind was blank. Slowly a plan of action took shape. She called Joe to ask him to take Becky and JJ for a couple of hours on Saturday.

"Why?" Joe asked suspiciously.

She was pacing around the living room. "They are your children and they haven't seen or heard from you in almost a week."

"I have to work this Saturday."

She stopped pacing. "How about Sunday?"

"That's my one day to rest. I don't think they would have much fun hanging around with me."

"That was easy. Are you sure you don't have something else going on?"

"What the hell is that supposed to mean?"

April retorted angrily, "It means that if you were really interested in your children, you would spend some time with them."

"I work for a living. I have to pay the bills. It's exhausting. I need a little relaxation."

She could feel the urge to punch him. She started back toward the kitchen. Her voice was low and threatening. She pronounced every syllable slowly and distinctly. "I work for a living too. I have been paying the bills for quite a while."

"My work doesn't involve cheating on you," he said sarcastically.

"I hope not because if you are cheating, you will be caught. That is a guarantee."

"You should talk."

"And you know how that worked out. So you had better hope that you don't get caught with your pants down."

She wanted a drink but that would have to wait. It was almost time to collect her children. She wondered if they would be interested in dinner and a movie for a change. She was going to have to work most of the weekend to finish the articles for the Times-Herald.

72

AT BREAKFAST ON Saturday morning, April announced that she was going for some target practice. JJ made arrangements to spend the day with a friend. Becky wanted to go along so she could practice shooting too. The session took about an hour including checking out weapons, shooting, cleaning the weapons, and checking them back in.

April took Becky for a visit to Doorways for Women on the way home. Such visits were not the norm for the women's shelter. Volunteers were expected to apply online and go through an established process. April talked her way in by explaining that she was writing a book on women's issues. She promised that she would join the volunteer force before the year was over.

"Could you end up there?" Becky asked as they drove home.

"No. The MacMahons take care of their own. No matter what happens, my family will make sure you, JJ, and I are taken care of. Besides your dad is a good man. We'll work things out so that everybody is okay."

"So you two are getting a divorce?"

"I don't know, honey. Your dad is upset. I'm waiting for him to figure it out and tell me what he wants to do."

Becky glared at her mother. "It's your fault, isn't it?" Her tone was cutting. "He's mad because of what you have been doing."

"Yes, it's mostly my fault." April looked over at her daughter. "I could have chosen to do things differently. But there were no good choices. I was going to lose something no matter what I chose."

"Was it worth losing your family?"

"No. And if I had realized that I was going to be having this conversation with you, I might very well have chosen differently."

"But you might have gone ahead and done it anyway?"

April considered the question carefully before she said softly, "Yes, I might have."

They rode the rest of the way home in silence. When they got to the house, Becky marched up to her room and shut her door. April had to turn around and get to the post office before it closed. Two pieces of certified mail were awaiting her signature. One contained the divorce filing from Joe's lawyer. The other was a summons to appear for a preliminary hearing on Wednesday. She called Ms Bailey to inform her that the papers and the summons had arrived. She would have to talk to her children about the situation later.

73

APRIL HAD PREPARED a Shepherd's pie with mashed potatoes, hamburger, carrots, and green beans for dinner. She was about ready to serve when her phone rang. "What the hell is going on?" Joe demanded.

"I'm making dinner."

"Why is your daughter calling me at my friend's house?" Joe insisted.

"I have no idea what you are talking about. I am making dinner. Becky has barely spoken to me today." April forced her breath out through her lips. "She is your daughter too. You need to own up to that fact."

"I was sitting here having a quiet conversation with my friend when her phone rang. It was Becky. Then I get a call from JJ. When my friend tried to politely tell Becky that I wasn't there, Becky said she knew I was because she could hear me on the phone with JJ. So I think you owe me an explanation for that little stunt."

"The explanation is simple. They are your children and they want to know what is going on." April looked at the ceiling and shook her head. "If you had taken them to dinner instead of hanging out with your girlfriend, they wouldn't have had to call you."

"Who said it was my girlfriend?"

"You did. You said that she was your friend. Hence, you are having dinner with your girlfriend. And it is pretty hard to miss the implication. I think any court in the land would come to the same conclusion I did."

"How did they get her number?"

April sat down. This conversation could go on for a while. "I have no idea, Joe. I certainly don't know her phone number. Becky didn't let me in on her plans. She isn't speaking to me."

"It had better not happen again."

"Wow. I would love to kick that one around with you." Her jaw tightened. "Wake up. Becky is an adult. She is an intelligent, hard-driving woman. If you don't start treating her like you understand that, you are in for a lot of trouble."

Joe was furious. "She's a child and she needs to start showing respect to her elders."

April hung up and muttered, "You better send Grif back to finish the job if you want custody of my children."

She was trembling as they sat down to dinner. She felt like she was going to explode but she let the meal start in silence. "I understand you called your dad. How did that go?"

Neither of the kids looked at their mother. Becky replied casually as she continued to eat, "He wasn't happy about it."

April forced a nonchalant, "So I heard. How did you know the other number?"

Becky continued to focus on her meal. "Nickey gave it to me."

"How did you happen to be talking to her?"

Becky looked directly into her mother's eyes. "I called her and asked how to get in touch with my dad."

"But you've never met Nickey and I doubt that anyone gave you her number."

Becky shrugged. "It was on Eve's phone - the pink one in your purse."

"The one that is password protected?"

Becky was exasperated. "It wasn't much of a password, Mom."

"She got 'Dancer' right away," JJ said brightly. "I had to tell her it was 'Dancer0' because you had zero clothes on when you were dancing."

April almost choked. She took a sip of water. "So you broke into my phone and picked Nickey's number off of the contact list. Then what happened?"

Becky smirked. "She said, 'Hi, Eve. What's up?' and I said 'This is Becky.' She said, 'Oh' as in 'Oh shit.'" Becky shrugged. "I told her that I wanted to know where my dad was and how to get in touch with him. She gave me his cell phone number." Becky took a bite of her pie and chewed while she studied her mother. "I told her I wanted the other number. She made me give her my cell phone number. She called me back and gave me Lee's number."

"So you set up a trap," April said. "You called Lee while JJ called your dad. How did you know it was Lee?"

"I recognized her voice. She tried to tell me I had made a mistake." Becky sneered, "I told her she had made the mistake. She hung up." Becky was triumphant.

"Nickey will be proud of you when she hears about this."

"Who is Nickey?" JJ asked.

April paused for a bite of her dinner. "She's a private investigator who works for your Uncle Bill."

"Who is Eve?" Becky asked but it was more of an accusation.

"I am. A couple of months ago, I decided that it would be more professional to use my birth name. So I filed the paperwork to legally change my name. People still don't like Yvonne so they call me Eve."

"Have you told Dad?" Another accusatory question.

"I have been April as long as your dad has known me. I don't expect that to change." April folded her hands and rested her chin on her thumbs. "I am getting ready to publish a book and I want to announce myself to the world as a professional woman."

"Can we call you Eve?" JJ wanted to know.

She smiled. Her son knew how to brighten up a conversation. "When you graduate from high school. Until then I'm mom or mother."

"Why did you need a separate phone?" Becky demanded.

April gave her daughter a stern look. "A business decision. Right now we have to decide what to do with the rest of the evening."

74

THE MEETING CONVENED on Monday after-
noon at three sharp in Craig Robertson's conference
room. The Times-Herald was represented by Craig
and four assistants. Senator Muehlberg showed up
with one assistant, Rose Thornton. The purpose of
the meeting was to decide the fate of April's six-part
series. Robertson was clearly disappointed. The women
he had expected to emerge were not there. "I don't see
why anyone would do that stuff."

"I believe the articles make it very clear that these
women are driven by one thing: the need to survive,"
Rose said.

"Do you think these people are representative?"
Robertson asked.

"I could match her story-for-story from people
that I know," Rose said. "The DP woman breaks my
heart. She could be my sister. I graduated before my
mother kicked me out. I was more of a rebel. But I
believe that she and I are very much alike."

A couple of the newspaper staff challenged the
accuracy of the story. It did not seem possible that
this sort of thing was going on without any challenge

from the police. April pointed out that not everyone sees prostitution as a crime. As long as it is kept under wraps, most people don't care about it. Legal action against prostitutes doesn't do much good. Police find it practically impossible to get a john convicted. As a result, policing is sporadic. A de facto truce allows players on both sides to get on with their lives.

April surveyed the room. Five newspaper people were ready to scratch her story. The state senator wanted it run. She was the one who counted. The editor could overrule the senator. It was his paper but he didn't want to renege on a deal. He just needed an excuse to agree to run the series.

April said, "Mr. Robertson, you were right. You said that some women would look at the problems and decide the money wasn't worth it. Other women would look at the money and decide they could put up with the shit. What I found is that individual perceptions of the problems drive the decisions. A single woman making twenty to thirty thousand dollars in this area has problems. A single mother in the same pay range has almost insurmountable problems. But prostitution is unthinkable in her situation. She gets a second job and drives herself to the limit trying to care for her family while working insane hours. A single woman with no job can decide to put up with the shit because it can't possibly be any worse than the shit she is already dealing with. I know that the women in my story don't match the women you have met over the years but they are consistent with the findings of every study on prostitution conducted in the United States. These women are my sisters. I owe it to them to tell their story. You owe it to your readers to tell them the truth even if it isn't the truth you wanted to hear. I ask you to publish this story as is for my sisters and for your readers."

Senator Muehlberg said, "I think it is a great series. It has limitations. That is always true of the written word. The report does make a powerful argument for rethinking our attitudes toward prostitution. I believe it provides a springboard for efforts to change ineffective laws. I hope that you will run Ms Walsh's work without substantial changes, Craig."

Robertson grimaced. The senator would get her way. There was no point in arguing. "Some editing will be required but I think we can keep it intact." He turned to his staff. "Okay. Back to work. I want this story ready to run this Sunday. Mrs. Walsh gets the proofs by COB Wednesday. We get her okay by COB Thursday."

He stood abruptly and left the room. As the others filed out, Rose approached April and gave her a hug.

Rose said. "Is there anything we can do to help?"

"I don't think so. My husband is divorcing me and he wants custody of the children. It might not be so bad if he wasn't such an ignorant ass. I don't think either he or his new girlfriend is capable of coping with my daughter let alone guiding her through her high school years."

Rose hugged her again. "Keep us posted. Contact me at any time. We can probably help you in ways that you would not even think of."

75

WEDNESDAY ROLLED AROUND too quickly. The hearing was supposed to be preliminary. It was intended to formalize the separation and start a process of counseling and reconciliation. But Joe's attorney, Dante Hopkins, charged that Mrs. Walsh's behavior had been so outrageous that there was no hope of reconciliation. She was a prostitute and a serial adulteress. Hopkins introduced a motion that Mrs. Walsh be barred from further contact with the children for their protection.

Judge Roy Smith said that the divorce proceedings could not move forward without a report from a marriage counselor. The judge did agree that Mrs. Walsh's behavior was flagrant. He said he would consider barring Mrs. Walsh from further contact with the children but he needed to know what arrangements would be made for their care. Hopkins stated that his client had hired a live-in nanny. He was requesting that Mrs. Walsh vacate his house and home immediately so that he could move back in and establish a living pattern for the family.

April's attorney objected to the use of the term prostitute. She argued that her client was never a prostitute. Use of the term was inappropriate and would make it difficult for her to obtain a fair hearing.

Judge Smith said, "I have seen the video of her work."

Eleonora Bailey responded, "It is shocking but it is not prostitution. There is no suggestion that my client would perform sexual intercourse of any kind in exchange for money. It does not appear that the person who made the video removed his clothing at any point. So what you have is my client providing entertainment in a natural state."

Hopkins jumped to his feet. "What was natural about that?"

"Humans were around on this earth long before clothes. In the beginning, Adam and Eve didn't even know what clothes were. So nakedness is natural. Walking around clothed in an air-conditioned environment is unnatural," Bailey responded.

"Nonetheless," Judge Smith said. "Mrs. Walsh will vacate the premises so that Mr. Walsh can move back in and take control of it."

"Shouldn't you find out something about this nanny?" Bailey demanded. "Ten days ago Mr. Walsh asked my client to move back into the house and take care of the children because he was unable to do so himself. Today he is ready to kick her out. His big plan is to turn the care of his children over to an unnamed person that no one at this hearing has ever even met."

"Mr. Walsh, have you interviewed this nanny?" Judge Smith asked.

"No, Your Honor. I arranged for her services through Reliable Guardians which has a five-star rating online."

Judge Smith excused himself and left the room. When he returned, he announced that he had an opening at four on the following day. Mr. Walsh was to arrange to have the nanny show up at that time with credentials and references. If she was acceptable, she could start work. Otherwise, Mr. Walsh would have to find someone who met with the court's approval. No nanny was to be introduced to the children until Judge Smith had given his consent. In the meantime, Mrs. Walsh was to move out of the house immediately. Mr. Walsh was to take over parenting responsibilities.

"This is extremely burdensome for my client," Hopkins objected.

"Mrs. Walsh is being barred from further contact with the children. Your client must take over care of those children. That's what sole custody means. If that is too burdensome for your client, the court will make its own arrangements," Judge Smith retorted.

After a brief consultation, Hopkins said, "I apologize, Your Honor. I misspoke. My client will move back into his house and assume responsibility for the children as soon as he leaves this hearing."

"Where will this nanny be sleeping?' Ms. Bailey asked.

"In the room at the far end of the hall from the master bedroom," Joe said.

"That is currently my client's office. She will need twenty-four hours to move her stuff out."

"Everything in the house is community property," Hopkins objected. "Mrs. Walsh should not be allowed to remove anything from the house."

"The clothes that Mr. Walsh wears are considered his. The room that Mr. Walsh uses for his workspace along with its contents are considered his. He alone uses them. The room under discussion and the items in it have been used exclusively by my client. She also has clothing in the master bedroom that she alone wears. Those things are hers in the same sense that his things are his," Ms. Bailey pointed out.

Judge Smith banged his gavel. "Mrs. Walsh will have until two tomorrow afternoon to remove her clothing and her personal items from the room that she has been using as an office. Anything left after that will be considered part of the household goods and disposition will be determined at a later date." He turned his gaze on April. "I want you out of the house before the children return from school and I expect you to move your things out tomorrow while they are in school."

"Your Honor, this is an extremely cruel way to treat the children who have had no say whatsoever in any of this," April objected. "I request that you allow me to explain the situation and to say goodbye to them."

"You are the problem here," Judge Smith said. "I don't trust you with them and I don't want you anywhere near them."

"Up until a few minutes ago, I was the only person who could be relied upon to look after those children. Now I can't even say goodbye to them? How does that make sense?"

"I didn't see that video until yesterday."

"That video was made two weeks ago." April's voice was firm and measured. "I stayed away from my husband, our house, and our children for two and a half days voluntarily." She turned her gaze on Joe. "My husband was fully aware of the video and its contents when he called me on the third day to say that I had to come home because he was incapable of taking care of our children." She brushed her hand through her hair. "His daughter requested an in-home separation arrangement. My husband would get the master bedroom. I would move into my office. I would take care of the children as needed and I would stay out of the way when he was home. I agreed to cooperate with the arrangement. Her father, my husband, refused. He walked out."

April turned back to address Judge Smith. "My husband abandoned his children. Since that time I have been the sole caregiver. No one has suggested that I harmed them in any way and no one has suggested that they have been harmed while in my care. There is no reason to believe that giving me an opportunity to meet with them and help them through this transition will cause them any harm."

"Nevertheless, I cannot in good conscience allow you an unsupervised visit," Judge Smith said.

"Fine. I will have them brought here. You or someone you appoint can supervise, and Joe can take them home when we are done."

"How will you arrange for them to be brought to the court?"

"My mother will pick them up and bring them here. She is our emergency backup."

"Mr. Walsh?"

"I can agree to that," Joe said.

"How soon can you get them here?"

"I suggest four o'clock so that I do not have to pull them out of school," April said.

"I will arrange for a room and someone to supervise the visit," Judge Smith said.

"There is one other issue," Bailey said.

"What is that?" Judge Smith asked impatiently.

"We need you to order Mr. Walsh to cease and desist using my client's money to pay for his lifestyle."

"Please explain."

"Mr. Walsh is charging all of his expenses including the apartment that he is supposedly living in, gas and maintenance for his car, and even Mr. Hopkins' retainer on a credit card that is tied to the joint checking account."

"Money in a joint checking account belongs to both parties," Judge Smith retorted.

"As long as both parties are putting their income into the account, both parties should be able to access the money. Mr. Walsh is sequestering his income. My client is the only one who has put money into that account for some time. Mr. Walsh is using his wife's income from the Tahiti to provide himself with a lavish lifestyle. If he truly objected to the work my client did to support the family while he was unemployed, he should use his own money."

"What do you mean?"

"He has been back at work for over a month. There is no sign of a paycheck. He hasn't deposited any money in the joint account that he is using to pay his bills."

"Mr. Walsh?"

"I decided to open a separate checking account so that she could not take off with my money. I kept using the old credit card out of habit. It was an honest mistake," Joe explained.

"I will need financial records from each of you by four this afternoon. I will issue a decision on how the money is to be divided up tomorrow."

April jumped in. "Your Honor, this has not been an ordinary month. I have had to pay the real estate taxes and the homeowner's insurance. Furthermore, I have been fired from my job at my husband's behest. I supported him while he was out of work. I expect him to support me in this situation."

"You should be glad he got you out of there," Judge Smith retorted. "The work you were doing was demeaning and despicable."

"And yet my husband has no problem enriching himself with the money that I earned."

"The money from your husband's account will be added to the money in the joint account. The total will be divided between the two of you. That is final."

"Please check the legal documentation. He is joint-owner of the property. In all fairness, he must compensate me for his share of the real estate taxes and the insurance before the money is divided up."

"You couldn't have made that much money as a prostitute," Judge Smith said.

"Again Your Honor, I must insist that you refrain from using the word prostitute. I was a dancer and an escort, both of which are legal occupations. In answer to your question, most of that money came from the advance on my book."

"You're writing a book? Let me guess it's about prostitution," Judge Smith said sarcastically.

"In part, yes."

"Which is why you went to work as a dancer and escort?"

"Yes, Your Honor."

"I will not change my rulings today. But I will take that into consideration as we move forward."

76

WHEN APRIL CALLED her mother to ask if she could pick up Becky and JJ from school, she managed a brief semi-private conversation. April's mother had known Judge Smith since his law school days. They were on good terms. Her mother felt sure that she could get custody of the children for a couple of days while Joe tried to get his nanny approved. She also suggested that April move into Joe's apartment, to comply with Judge Smith's ruling. That would give her a place to work without having to go through the hassle of arranging temporary quarters.

April liked the idea that her children would be with her mother for the next few days. The proofs from her article would be in her email inbox. She had to return them by COB tomorrow. She would have to review and pass on all the editorial corrections that night. Tomorrow would be too busy. She wanted the by-line changed from April Walsh to either Eve McMann or YA MacMahon. Robertson could make the final decision on that. But from this day forward, she would be Eve MacMahon. April Walsh was history.

Judge Smith had given Eve over four hours to pull together her financial records. She had already taken care of that and given a copy to Ms Bailey as part of their trial prep. Those records contained no evidence of Eve MacMahon's slush fund in an account owned by Bridget Allen.

Eve used the time to buy a new laptop and set it up. She transferred the files from her desktop to the laptop and cleansed any questionable files from the desktop memory. She scrubbed the hard drive. All her work files and all of her secrets were already stored on a CD. She shoved the CD into her purse, packed a suitcase, and loaded her car. She was ready to work out of the apartment that she was taking over from Joe.

Her office furniture sat impassively as if it had decided not to move. Eve looked around the room but could not come up with a workable plan. She was tempted to call Jeff but she didn't want to be indebted to him. She considered calling Bill but she knew how busy he was. She was saved by a call from Lydia, who had been trying to reach her. The call lasted only a few minutes. During the conversation, Eve mentioned that she had to vacate her house the next day. Lydia said she would get Jerry and his truck over to help with the move. The two women agreed on a follow-up call to work out the details.

At 3:57 p.m., Rebecca MacMahon entered the court meeting room with her grandchildren Becky and JJ in tow. She wore a black skirt suit which showed off her full figure. Her dark hair was sculpted back over her ears and trimmed half-way down her neck. Her icy blue eyes took in everything. She moved with the dominant air of a seasoned defense attorney. When Judge Smith saw her, his face brightened and then took on a panicked look. He finally put on a gracious smile.

Bailey whispered to her client, "I think he has just realized why your name is so familiar."

Eve nodded.

Rebecca MacMahon extended her hand as she approached the judge, "Leroy, it is good to see you again."

"Yes, it's been a long time, Mrs. MacMahon. I am sorry it has to be under such circumstances."

"I'm sure it will all work out. They are upset now but after they have had a chance to cool off, they will realize how important they are to each other."

"I hope so," Judge Smith said unconvincingly.

"Leroy, I know you are going to do a good job but there is one thing I must ask of you."

"What's that?"

"No more talk of putting my grandchildren into foster care. If there is a problem, the first option should be to place them with relatives. Now that you know I am available, I assume that you will consider me your first option. Of course, my son, Bill, and his wife would also be more than happy to take these two into their home. There are lots of good options. Let's not have any more talk about foster care."

"Of course not," Judge Smith stammered. "I didn't actually mean that I would put them into foster care. I just meant that neither of the parents should be taking care of these children."

"That is a very harsh judgment. Once you get to know the children, you will realize that they were raised by good parents. Joe and April have done a good job up to this point. I see no reason why they shouldn't be allowed to continue once they have ironed out their differences."

"And until they do, I have to worry about making sure these children are properly cared for."

"That brings up the second point that I wanted to discuss with you. I would like to have the children stay with me tonight and tomorrow night. That would give Joe more time to get himself organized. I think he is still struggling to arrange for child care."

"Mr. Walsh has promised to provide a nanny by tomorrow."

"Has anyone met this nanny? Is anyone sure that she will be an adequate replacement for my daughter?"

Judge Smith almost said anyone would be an improvement over that whore. Instead, he said as politely as possible, "I will make sure that the nanny is fully qualified to care for your grandchildren."

"What will happen if Joe is unable to find a nanny or if the one he finds is not qualified?"

"I see what you mean. The children can stay with you until Mr. Walsh has an approved nanny. That will work out best. But where will your daughter be staying?"

"She can take over the apartment that Joe is renting. He won't be needing it since he is moving back to the house."

Judge Smith turned to Joe and his attorney. "Mr. Walsh?"

Joe nodded. Hopkins said, "My client agrees to those arrangements."

Judge Smith then turned to Eve and her attorney. Eve nodded and Bailey said, "My client agrees to those arrangements."

"You may have a few minutes with your children, Mrs. Walsh," Judge Smith said.

When Eve got close, Becky demanded, "What the hell is going on?"

"I told you everything is going to work out okay and it will. But it may get worse before it gets better. Right now you are being put in your father's custody. I have been ordered not to have any contact with you."

"Why can't we stay with you?"

"Gramma Becky will explain it to you when you get to her house. You are going to be staying with her for a couple of days while your dad makes arrangements. Right now this is what I need. You must do your best to cooperate with your dad. Listen to what he tells you and focus on school. We need some time to work through our issues. Five or ten years from now this will all be nothing more than a childhood memory."

Becky growled, "I am not going to stay in the same house as that bitch."

"She should never be in the house except possibly as a dinner guest. If she is there for any other reason, call Gramma Becky or Uncle Bill. One of them should be able to take care of it. In the meantime, it might not hurt you to get to know her. She is not a bad person. She just feels the same way about your dad that you feel about Owen."

"What about Hattie and Nickey?"

"They're your friends. I don't see any reason why you can't talk to them."

Eve hugged JJ. "There you are, being a tough guy just like your father. I know a lot is going on in your head. Don't be afraid to talk to Gramma Becky. She raised two sons who turned out to be pretty good men. You can talk to her about anything. Just keep believing that I am going to work this out."

"Time's up, Mrs. Walsh. I would like you to vacate the premises now," Judge Smith announced.

Eve kissed each of her children on the cheek. She gave her mother a hug and whispered, "Call me later. I have a long night ahead of me but call me anyway."

77

EVE AND LYDIA agreed to meet at the Walsh residence at noon so the move could be completed over a long lunch break. When Eve pulled up, two pickups were sitting in front of her house. Joe was sitting in a car parked across the street. Three muscular young men and a woman emerged from the trucks to greet Eve. The men mauled her and begged her to come back to the Tahiti. Lydia ended the love fest by announcing, "The guys are going to move everything out of your office. You and I will bring down the clothes. Eve, you take them upstairs and show them what you want done. I'll be up as soon as I set up the wardrobe boxes for the clothes."

Eve led the men to her office and showed them around. There was not a lot to move but things like the futon and her desk were big enough to justify having a couple of men to do the work. Eve left them and grabbed an armful of clothes from the master bedroom. When she emerged from the front door, she saw Lydia engaged in a heated discussion with Joe. "I see you two have met," Eve said as she approached the pair.

"Not formally," Lydia snapped.

"This woman says that you have changed your name," Joe charged.

Eve proceeded calmly with the formal introduction. "Joe, this is my friend, Lydia Tompkins."

"Have you changed your name?" Joe demanded.

"When I married you, I changed my name from MacMahon to Walsh. A couple of months ago, I decided to go back to my given name, Yvonne April MacMahon."

"When were you going to tell me?"

"I hadn't thought about it. It didn't seem that important. I've been April as long as you have known me. There is no need for that to change. Sometimes I'm April. Sometimes I'm Eve. What difference does it make?"

"If it wasn't that important, why did you do it?"

"First of all, professional women have found it advantageous to use their given name instead of their husband's name. 'Mrs. April Walsh' implies that I am your property and we both know that isn't true. 'Ms Eve MacMahon' implies that I am my own person, which is what I want to be." She folded her arms across her chest. "Secondly, I'm getting tired of April. She's a grown-up child. She's always bright and cheerful and does exactly what she's told. Eve seems more of a doer. She has an agenda and she knows how to get things done."

"What's your agenda, Eve?" Joe asked sarcastically.

"I am working to become a successful writer. I'm busy writing a book. It's going to be published and I am going to work to make it a best seller."

"Is that a good enough reason for destroying your family?"

Eve looked at the ground and shook her head. "You're the one filing for a divorce so you can marry your girlfriend."

"I'm filing for divorce because I can't stand living with a whore who'll sleep with any man who has twenty bucks."

"Bullshit. You decided to marry her before you knew I was working as an escort. You may have even decided while I was still working as a waitress."

"You're crazy," Joe shot back angrily.

Eve cocked her head and studied Joe. "You know your friend, Natalie?"

"Sorry doesn't ring a bell."

"You know. The woman you screwed in the men's room to celebrate landing your new job. The woman you ran to for comfort after Bridget's visit. You must remember her."

Joe's jaw dropped. The color drained from his face.

"She lied to you. Her name isn't Natalie and she's not a systems analyst. She's a private investigator. She specializes in getting men into compromising situations." Eve swallowed. "She was supposed to seduce you to pressure me into working as an escort."

Eve looked at her feet and crushed out an imaginary cigarette butt. "It was a bet. I bet on you. I was sure that you were too grown up and that you cared too much about your family to do something like that. Lee Bell proved me wrong. Natalie found out about the two of you while she was setting you up. That's how I found out that I have nothing."

"That bitch."

They looked at each other for a long moment. Lydia was horrified. She looked like she wanted to escape but couldn't.

Eve continued. "Your daughter hates your girl-friend. She hates her because she came over to spend time with you while I was at work. You thought you got away with it but Becky knew and Natalie found out. They told me. Hattie and I checked it out. I've got a video if you want to see it." Eve closed her eyes and shook her head. She seemed to be on the verge of tears. "Becky hates her because you were with her instead of your family last Saturday night."

Eve paused to let that tirade sink in. "The last thing you want to do is put those two women together in the same house let alone in the same room. You can have Lee or you can have Becky. If you try to have them both, Becky will drive Lee out of your life, and it won't be pretty."

Eve paused for his response. "Were you her first? Is that why it was so easy?"

Joe was caught by surprise. He looked puzzled. Eve said, "Mike told me about your high school rat pack. You were a big-time hunk back then. I bet lots of girls flopped for you. Was Aileen Sheehan one of them?"

Joe turned and stalked off shaking his head. Eve called after him, "You're not winning, Joe. You're making this worse than it needs to be. If you want to marry Lee, go ahead. I won't fight it. But I get custody. You should agree for Lee's sake. She won't last a week with Becky around."

Lydia pulled Eve into a hug. "I'm sorry. I'm so sorry."

"Don't be. We did this to ourselves. This blow up was coming sooner or later. It's probably best that you were here to keep things from getting out of control."

Lydia held Eve as she sobbed on her shoulder. When the sobbing had stopped, Lydia said, "I guess we should finish moving your stuff. Where are the guys?"

Eve looked around. Tears were glistening on her cheek but she was grinning. "Inside. Waiting for the storm to blow over."

78

THE TIMES-HERALD BEGAN running a series on prostitution in the Sunday morning edition. It was attributed to Eve McMann.

Becky and JJ went back home with their father on Sunday afternoon. The nanny, Maria Hernandes, was waiting for them. She had set up shop in the room that used to be their mother's office. She spoke English with a thick Hispanic accent. It was all very strange.

Joe had picked up a car for her. They drove the route that Maria would use to drop the children off at school in the morning and pick them up again in the afternoon. The woman's driving skills left something to be desired. She could cook. They had a nice Mexican dinner.

Gramma Becky heard about it during a phone conversation with her granddaughter. Eve got the information while chatting with her mother. She asked Nickey to check on the woman.

Eve was pleased with her series on prostitution and with the public's reaction. Readers responded strongly. Some agreed. A lot of them were opposed and took the time to say so. Friends like Bridget, Lydia, and Hattie congratulated her.

Eve MacMahon was suddenly a real person. People who had known April Walsh could still call her that. But as far as she was concerned, April was a relic, a reminder of what had been.

On Monday afternoon, Eve was at Big Mike's Service Center discussing a motorcycle that Jeff had picked up for her. He was saying that he would need a few days to fix it up and she should take some lessons so she would be ready to ride by the weekend. His phone rang. As he listened, he started smiling and then laughed. "She's right here." He passed the phone to Eve.

"Mom, I have to talk to you," Becky said.

"Okay. What's the matter?"

"That stupid woman never came to pick us up from school."

"You told the school administrators, didn't you?"

"Yes. They had to call Dad to pick us up. He must have stopped by the house because Maria was driving. I don't like her. I think she has something going on."

"Give your dad a chance to work things out. This is all brand new. There are bound to be some hiccups."

"Aren't you going to do something?"

"I'm working on it. For the time-being, we should give your dad a chance." Eve looked over at Jeff and grinned. "By the way, how did you get this number?"

"Gramma said you were with Jeff but she didn't have the number so I called Nickey. Is he one of your boyfriends?"

"I've decided I want to ride a motorcycle. He's helping me get started."

"Because he likes you. Right?"

"Don't push your luck. This is strictly about motorcycles. How are you coming with your homework?"

"Not much to do. I'll get it done. I'll let you get back to your boyfriend but dad had better get this straightened out pronto."

"So that's your daughter," Jeff said as he put his cell phone away.

"That's my daughter."

"I can't wait to meet her in person."

"You'll have to. I'm not ready to introduce you to my family."

Eve met Adrien Gautier at the Tahiti for lunch on Wednesday. He asked her to come back to work at the club. She told him that if her situation became desperate, she might be interested in working as a waitress but she would never escort another nut case to a hotel room.

On Thursday, Eve showed up at Big Mike's just before noon. Jeff took the afternoon off. They went out for a motorcycle ride that included a late lunch on Naked Mountain. When Eve got back and checked her cell phone, she discovered that her children had gone missing. They had disappeared as soon as school let out. No one had been able to find them. Eve checked with her mom. Gramma Becky was aware of the situation but had no idea where the children had gone. She suspected that Becky had arranged to disappear because she was unhappy with the nanny situation. Nickey didn't know what was going on with the kids.

However, the Hernandes woman should be fired. She was turning tricks while the kids were in school.

Hattie did know where the kids were. She had taken them to the Sun Tang Woo Martial Arts Center for after-school activities. She had been told by Becky that Joe thought it was a good idea and had signed the permission forms. Eve said, "Well, unfortunately, Joe doesn't understand that. He thinks his children have been kidnapped. The police are looking for them. You had better make Becky call her father and her grandmother immediately. You should be okay but Joe and his nanny are going to be in major trouble."

Eve was about to ride away from Big Mike's. She turned her motorcycle off and walked over to Jeff. She took his hands and looked up at him. Her expression was so sad that he panicked. "Jeff, you are a wonderful friend. I never want to lose your friendship but I have to be honest. It will never be anything more than that. We can't have the relationship that you want."

"Are you still upset with me about that stupid night in my apartment?"

"No. We both made mistakes. You have promised that you will never do anything like that again, and I believe you."

"Then what?"

"We have different needs. I want a stable relationship with a man who will be there for the next ten, twenty, or fifty years. You're a gypsy -- a wanderer. I'll be lucky if you are still here next year."

"I've been here for almost five years. I don't plan to go anywhere."

"Jeff," she scolded. "You are planning a tour of the continent that might last six months or a year or the rest of your life."

"Oh God, Eve. Don't hold that against me."

"I am not holding it against you. When you told me about it, I was excited. I wanted to go with you at that moment. But I can't walk out on my family. That's not me."

"I don't have to go," Jeff snapped.

"Yes, you do. I couldn't be happy if you dropped your plans just because of me." Her voice was choked. Her eyes pleaded almost to the point of tears.

"What the hell am I doing wrong?"

"Jeff, you're too smart for that. What happened to all that wonderful philosophy you laid on me?" She pulled his head down and gave him a kiss. "I will not be part of chaining you to a stake in the ground. It has been my privilege to be friends with you. I will be happy, if once in a while you show up on my doorstep to let me know that you are okay. Now I have to say goodbye and get back to the real world."

She walked back to her motorcycle and rode off without looking back.

79

BY TEN ON Friday morning, Eve wished she had a receptionist. Her lawyer and Judge Smith's administrative assistant had called to tell her that she needed to attend an emergency meeting with Joe, the lawyers, and Judge Smith in his chambers.

Then Detective Andrews had called. He wanted to know where she was now and where she had been all night. Griffin Boothe's body had been found in a vacant lot in Southeast earlier in the morning. Eve had told him she was sorry to hear that but she had more important issues to deal with at the moment. She was still getting dressed when Jerrod Johnson called. He wanted to talk to her about his job offer. She had told him she would have to get back to him later.

"Nice of you to join us," Judge Smith said as Eve entered his chambers.

"And it was nice of you to give me a generous heads up so I could get dressed and drive over here."

"You had two hours. That would have been sufficient for a responsible adult."

"And it would have been plenty for me if Joe's PI hadn't gotten himself killed last night."

"What does that have to do with your showing up late?"

"Apparently I am the prime suspect in the murder. I had to convince the detective that I had nothing to do with the man's death even though I don't have an alibi. As it turns out there is no way to verify that I spent last night all alone in a strange apartment."

Judge Smith rolled his eyes. "Are you the author of the series on prostitution in the Times-Herald?"

"Yes, Your Honor."

"They misspelled your name."

"I am trying to maintain a firewall between my family and my work. Many people are upset by the article. They don't like the methods that I used to get the story."

"With good reason," Judge Smith observed dourly. He shook his head and took a deep breath before proceeding. "Mr. Walsh, can you explain to me what is going on?"

"Ms Hernandes, the nanny that I hired has been a disappointment. She does not seem to be able to pick up the kids from school as scheduled. I don't know what the problem is but I am in the process of replacing her."

"Your Honor," Eve said. "I am the only person who is qualified to take care of those children."

"You will wait your turn, young lady." He leaned forward and looked Eve directly in the eyes. "There is no way that I am going to grant you custody of those children."

"Why is that?" Eve demanded.

"I will not entrust them to a prostitute," Judge Smith shot back angrily.

"You just did."

"What did you say?"

"The nanny that my husband hired and that you approved is a known prostitute. She could not be bothered to pick my children up from school because she was busy turning tricks."

"Those are serious charges. You had better be able to back them up."

"I can, Your Honor. I had my investigator check her out." Eve turned to Joe. A sly smile crept across her face. "She can come in here and provide a detailed report if you believe that is necessary."

"That isn't going to change my mind about granting you custody."

Eve turned back to Judge Smith. She was suddenly serious and professional. "It is out of your hands. My daughter is insisting on exercising her legal right to choose which parent she lives with. She has already retained a lawyer."

Judge Smith glared at Eve. She pressed on, "There is zero probability that you will find anyone who is capable of taking care of those children as well as I can. Stop confusing the work I did for a couple of months with my performance as a mother." She looked at her husband lovingly. "Joe is a great engineer. He is a good father. But he is a disaster as a mother. Those children need a mother and I am about the best there is."

Judge Smith continued to glower in silence. Eve consulted with her lawyer. "Joe, you can withdraw your divorce filing. We can sit down and work this out by ourselves."

She walked over to where he was sitting and guided his hands down to the table. Her hands rested on his. Her face was inches from his. The smell of lilacs filled the air around them. "You can have your divorce. The only issue is custody. I want it. You don't," she said in her soft, throaty, Eve Sinful voice. "Let's go to mediation and get a solution that works for you, me, Becky and JJ. Can we do that?"

Joe consulted with his lawyer. Hopkins said, "Your Honor, we respectfully withdraw our filing for divorce."

Dante Hopkins grabbed his client by the arm. "Let's go." The two men rose and walked out of the judge's chambers. Eleonora Bailey and her client followed them.

80

AS SOON AS they reached the sidewalk, Bailey pulled everyone together for an impromptu meeting. "This process could take weeks or even months. The children need a stable situation so they know what to expect from day-to-day."

She insisted that Joe and his lawyer sit down with her and Eve to hammer out ground rules for the immediate future.

The group found a booth at the Erin Go Bragh tavern in Fairfax and ordered lunch. They reached quick agreement that Gramma Becky's was the best place for the children to stay until a final settlement was reached. Getting Joe to agree that Eve should move back to her mother's house took more effort but they finally concluded that the old lady would need some help and Eve looked like the best option if not the only one.

Eve pushed for a commitment from Joe that he would spend some time with the children every weekend. He was reluctant. Eve suspected that Lee was the problem. She was sure Joe wanted to spend Saturdays with his girlfriend. That left Sunday. Eve didn't want to take the children to Mass because she felt like a hypocrite when she was in church. The final agreement was that Joe would pick up Eve and the kids for Mass on Sunday morning. They would attend as a family. After Mass, Joe would drop Eve at her mother's house and keep the kids for the afternoon. "Joe, do you and Lee have any plans for getting married?" Eve asked.

He scowled but said nothing.

Hopkins said, "I don't see why you have to bring that topic into this discussion."

"So you admit there's an issue," Bailey said.

Eve's gaze was fixed on her husband. "Joe, I don't really care whether or not you two are planning to get married, but you need to let your children know what is going on."

He continued to eat in silence.

"She's right," Bailey interjected. "They already know something is going on. You need to discuss the situation with them."

"We aren't going to make any definite plans until the divorce is final," Joe said grudgingly.

"It sounds like you have already made some plans," Bailey countered.

Joe returned Eve's stare while he took a drink of beer and set his glass down on the table. He turned to Bailey. "We care for each other. We want to get married. That's it."

Eve said, "Joe, I am not trying to pressure you. That's between you and Lee. But I don't believe that it's fair to ask Lee to commit to marriage without at least introducing her to your children."

She took a bite of salad while she waited for his response. When none came, she continued, "Becky has issues with Lee. If you don't deal with that, leaving the kids with the two of you is going to be a serious problem."

"So now we get to the real issue," Joe shot back. "You want to be able to dump them on me when you have better things to do."

"You were suing for sole custody," Eve responded evenly. "What did you think was going to happen, if you won?"

"I would have worked it out."

"Okay. Let's start working it out. I want custody. I want it on my shoulders." Eve took Joe's hands in hers. "I also want them to have a dad in their lives. I believe that we should all be able to at least tolerate one another. And yes, I may have to travel as part of my work so I would like to believe that I can depend on you to help out occasionally."

Joe finished his French fries. He wiped his mouth and set his napkin on his plate. "I'll talk to Lee."

Bailey asked for the check. Joe and his lawyer got up and walked out. "You could have let Hopkins help pay for that," Eve chided.

"We can afford to be generous," the lawyer replied with a grin. "We have the core agreements that will make the rest of the negotiations smoother and faster. The only big issue remaining is your house. If you try to get rid of it right now, you will lose money. Possibly, big money. Let Joe buy you out."

"I'll bet I end up paying for this lunch," Eve complained.

Eleanora smiled. Eve said, "Thank you for everything."

"I am going to get you and your children a good deal. Do you have the name of their lawyer?"

"I'll get it to you this afternoon."

The two women hugged and went their separate ways.

81

IT WAS AFTER two when Eve got back to her apartment. That was eleven in California. Eve guessed that she had thirty or forty minutes to call Jerrod Johnson before he went to lunch. She filled a coffee cup halfway from her bottle of Jameson Black Reserve and sat down to recover from the day's exertions.

She still had April's cell phone. It had a lot of useful information. Most people would use that number to contact her. Eve's cell phone number was a carefully guarded secret. She had only shared it with people who would need to contact Eve. Both cell phones had been busy that morning. Eve had gotten up around six to work on her book. April's cell phone rang just before eight. Eleonora Bailey wanted to make sure that her client had been invited to the emergency meeting in Judge Smith's chambers. When Eve said she had not heard about anything, Bailey told her to plan on attending because it was important.

Eve was finishing her breakfast and scanning through the local news when April's phone rang again. It was Judge Smith's assistant telling Eve to come to a meeting in the Judge's chambers at ten. Eve finished her breakfast and showered.

Detective Andrews called while Eve was in the shower. She picked up on the fifth or sixth ring. He was outside her house and no one was there. Where was she hiding out? Eve explained that she was in an apartment in Rosslyn because she had been evicted from her house. He wanted to know where she had been between 10 p.m. and 6 a.m. She said she had been alone at the apartment all night. He demanded that she come down to the station to answer some questions. Grif Boothe's body had been discovered earlier. Eve was a person of interest. She told him that was ridiculous. What was her motive? Did he have any evidence placing her at the scene of the crime?

Andrews countered that she had a beef with Boothe and a gun. That made her a person of interest. Eve told him to check his notes. She did not have a beef with Griffin Boothe. Her Shield was locked up at the Smith and Wesson Gun Emporium. Jade Smith would confirm that. She hung up and turned off the phone.

Jerrod Johnson called on April's phone to congratulate Eve on the article. He renewed his offer of a job. Eve cut him off in mid-sentence. She told him she was late for a meeting and would have to call him back later. She shut down April's phone. No more calls until after the meeting.

Eve had emerged victorious. Joe had agreed to withdraw the divorce filing and go to mediation. The whole mess was out of Judge Smith's hands. Eve and her lawyer had been able to get Joe and his lawyer to agree that Eve should be the principal guardian.

By 2:30, she was getting antsy. She turned April's phone on and checked for messages. Jerrod had left several. He was persistent.

"How did you get this number?" Eve demanded when Jerrod answered his phone.

"When I saw the articles, I had this intuition that you wrote them. I checked with my contacts at the paper. They were able to get the number for me." He was proud of himself. She could hear it in his voice.

"Well, whoever did that violated a contractual agreement. I don't want strangers intruding on my life. My contact information is not to be given out without my explicit approval." She took a sip of her whiskey.

"I'm not exactly a stranger."

She rolled her eyes. "You're not on my list of approved contacts either."

"But we have some outstanding business."

She shook her head. "I don't believe that we do."

"I offered you a job as my personal assistant on my next tour of operations in the Far East. You said you would think about it and get back to me."

"You made that offer to Eve Sinful. She is history. I am not an escort. I am an author."

"I would like you to join me, whatever your name is," Jerrod insisted.

"Is there a real job offer?" Eve pressed her lips closed and shut her eyes. Big mistake.

"Of course."

"What is the salary? What are the duties? What are the qualifications?" Eve looked up at the ceiling and shook her head. She should have just said that she wasn't interested.

"If you know anything about real jobs, you know that all of that stuff is negotiable. The main thing is that I like you and I can see that you are talented. You belong on my team."

She ran her hand through her hair. "So when I get to the part of the Visa application where it asks purpose of travel, should I put down 'suck my boss's cock whenever he's in the mood'?"

Jerrod didn't answer. She took another sip of whiskey.

He seemed flustered when he asked, "Can I put you on hold for a couple of minutes?"

"I don't know, Jerrod. I'm trying to write."

"Please, I want to give you a good answer to your question."

"Alright. But if you're not back in three minutes, I'm going to hang up and turn the phone off."

A Mozart sonata came on the line to keep her entertained.

When Jerrod returned, he said, "My assistant VP for communications has agreed to hire you. She likes your series. The starting salary would be $65k. She'll get out an offer with a job title and responsibilities this afternoon. Where should she send it?"

"She can address it to Eve McMann care of the Times-Herald. She can attach a PDF to a text message sent to this phone. Either way, I'll get it. I will give her an answer within 10 days."

"How do you spell McMann?"

"Just like it's spelled in the newspaper."

"Why can't you give me your name and address?"

"I want to know what you're offering before I get too excited. Send me your offer and I will consider it. I've got to get back to work. You have a nice day." Eve terminated the call and turned April's phone off.

She surveyed the apartment and smiled. Moving out was going to be a piece of cake. Lydia and her crew had moved the furniture from the Walsh residence to her mother's place because her apartment was so small. Everything she had with her would fit into the trunk of her car. At the moment picking up JJ was the top priority. No arrangements had been made for picking up the kids. Joe would assume that was her responsibility. She sent a text to Becky letting her know that her mom would be picking her up.

82

EVE ATTENDED MASS on Sunday with Joe and the kids. A police car was waiting for them when they reached Gramma Becky's house. Joe and Eve got out of their car and hurried to the house. Gramma Becky came out to meet them. A strapping, black police officer was with her. "What's the matter? What's going on?" Eve yelled.

"It's nothing to be concerned about," the cop assured them. "I just want to talk to the two of you."

Joe stopped arm's length from the cop. "What's the problem, Officer?"

He said, "I need to clear up some details about the murder of Griffin Boothe,"

"We had nothing to do with that." Joe was hostile.

"I know that," the officer assured him. "His killer is in custody."

"So you don't need us."

"I would like to get a statement from you that would provide us with as much detail as possible about your interactions with Boothe - phone conversations, meetings, things like that."

"I haven't spoken to him for two weeks," Joe snapped. "He handed over his report on my wife's activities along with the video he made. I paid him. That ended our relationship."

"I want a copy of the report and the video. I need details about your dealings with him. They could help us in our investigation."

"Why? He was killed and you have the killer in custody."

"There have been several attempts on Mr. Boothe's life. I want to know if those previous attempts have anything to do with his death. I can't explain why he was in Southeast DC. I can't figure out what happened to the gun she used. No guns have been found. I have to clear all of that up."

"She?" A chill ran through Eve's body.

"A prostitute named Serena Wilson."

"Jack, you can't be serious. She's a child. She's not a murderer."

Jack said, "You know her. Good,"

Joe looked at his wife then at the cop. He looked at his wife again. "Jack? This is your cop friend, Jack?"

"This is Sergeant Jack Edwards. He is the cop that I interviewed to get his views on prostitution," she said evenly.

"How did you find us here?" Joe demanded.

"We went by your wife's apartment and found that she was no longer staying there. We went to her home address. A young woman, Miss Lee Sheehan told us this would be the best place to look for you."

"Is that the royal 'we'?" Joe asked sarcastically.

"I sent my detectives home," Jack said. "They aren't on the best of terms with your wife and I need her help."

"What do you need, Sergeant?" Eve asked.

"Ms Wilson is not cooperating. She told us that she shot him. When we tried to get more details, she said, 'What difference does it make? He's dead. I shot him.'"

"You want me to talk to her?" Eve asked.

"Yes. Detective Andrews suggested that she might relate to you better than she does to us."

"Where does she live?" Joe asked.

Jack said, "We think that she's homeless. Why?"

"Winter in DC is pretty rough for the homeless. I worked on a prison mission when I was in high school. Every winter, especially in December, vagrants would get themselves jailed so they could get off the streets. Maybe she's just looking for a ticket off the streets."

"She would be going to jail for more than a winter," Jack said.

"She's a juvenile. She would get out with a clean record when she turned 21," Joe said. "That could be a good deal if she played her cards right."

Eve looked at her husband in absolute shock. This was a revelation. This was a new side to the man that she thought she knew like the back of her hand. She turned to Jack and said, "I'll talk to her. But I want Bill with me. Even if Joe is right, she needs a lawyer."

Jack nodded. "Can you come down today?"

"I'm sure that I can but I will have to talk to Bill," Eve said. "I'll give you a call after I work things out with him."

Eve became aware of Becky and JJ standing a few feet away. They had no doubt heard the entire conversation. Becky was staring a hole through her mother. "I met her about a month ago when I went downtown with some friends to check on a group of street prostitutes. We had breakfast and talked," Eve explained. "A couple of them, including Serena, were teenagers. Serena is a tiny thirteen-year-old. She is obviously very bright but there she was eating, talking and telling jokes after a night of turning tricks. It broke my heart." She was choking up. Joe stood there staring at his wife and shaking his head. When he noticed the look of horror on the kid's faces, he walked over and gave them a hug.

He asked, "You kids still up for that bike ride?"

Becky and JJ nodded solemnly. "Good. I think we need it. We're gonna take off, honey. Call me later and let me know how it worked out."

Eve stood in the driveway feeling terribly alone as she watched her family drive away. She mumbled, "There goes the bell. Time for the next round."

83

EVE AND HER brother spent twenty minutes talking with Serena Wilson. They emerged with some additional details and a coherent story. Serena had accompanied a pimp named, MacB, on a drug sale. The pimp got spooked. He produced a gun and ordered Serena to frisk the buyer. She found a 1911 in a holster strapped to the man's back and a snub-nosed revolver strapped to his ankle. The two men started arguing. MacB cursed the man and accused him of being a cop. The buyer said he had the money and produced an envelope. MacB walked over for a look. He kept his gun pointed at the man's chest.

When MacB went for the envelope, the guy grabbed MacB's gun and knocked him to the ground. Then he started beating MacB. Serena thought he might kill her pimp so she hit him on the back of the head with his 1911. He swung around and knocked her on her butt. She pointed the gun at him and told him to beat it. He charged at her. She panicked and started shooting. The guy dropped to his knees and then fell face first onto the pavement. Serena looked around and saw a dead man, a pimp who wasn't moving, cash and drugs. She dropped her gun and ran for it.

The next day she heard that the police had found the dead body. It looked like a robbery gone bad. Serena knew the pimp had managed to get away and take everything with him including the murder weapon with her fingerprints on it. She decided that her best bet was to turn herself in and tell her side of the story. But a friend talked her into pleading guilty to manslaughter so she wouldn't have to testify against MacB.

Bill convinced Serena to engage him as her lawyer. He wanted her released into his custody. Jack said she was a flight risk. He insisted on keeping Serena locked up until he could bring the pimp in for questioning. Serena was put in a holding cell with a motherly, middle-aged woman who was awaiting trial for embezzlement.

The pimp did have a police record although he had never been convicted of anything more serious than traffic violations. He had been arrested for drug dealing and pandering but the evidence was insufficient, and no one was willing to testify against him. He managed to stay below the radar for the most part. He was a ghost, or perhaps more accurately, a poltergeist. He dealt in drugs, sex, and fear. But he had another life. He was Bryce MacBean, formerly in Army Intelligence, a veteran of Desert Storm, with an MBA from George Washington University and a CPA. That made him a legitimate business consultant with ties to several venture capitalists.

Eve agreed to work with detectives Andrews and Smith to start looking for him. She called Joe to let him know what was going on. She said she probably wouldn't get home until late. They agreed that he would keep the kids with him for the night and she would pick them up in the morning for school. He asked her to send him a text when she arrived home. She wanted to say, "I love you." But nothing came out. They just said goodbye and hung up.

Eve told the detectives that all her contacts were dancers at the Tahiti. She was sure that Vickie had talked about working for MacB. Smith would go with Eve to the Tahiti and get Vickie to help them find the pimp. Andrews would go in a separate car and make the arrest once they had located him.

Anna Stroom came over as soon as Eve and Liz Smith had taken a seat at the Tahiti. "How are you, Eve?"

"I'm doing well, Anna. I see business is booming without me."

"Better than ever." There was a bit of frostiness in Anna's voice. She wasn't ready to forgive the betrayal.

Anna looked at Liz suspiciously. "We would like to talk to the Vixen," Eve explained.

Anna didn't budge. Eve put a hundred dollars on the table. "Can I get a private dance?"

"I'll get her," Anna said reluctantly. There were no rules against a woman getting a private dance. If Anna refused, she would have to deal with Adrien Gautier who was a fan of Eve's at the moment. "Could she sit and have a drink with us first?" Eve asked.

Vickie showed up moments later. She gave Eve a hug and a kiss. Drinks were ordered. They chatted while they waited for the drinks. When Eve's series in the Times-Herald came up, Vickie suddenly became taciturn. "Did I say something wrong?" Eve asked.

"Not really. You were real careful, but people who know what's going on could figure out who you were talking about."

"Are you worried about your pimp? Wasn't his name MacB?" Eve asked.

Vickie didn't answer but the look on her face said that Eve had hit a bull's-eye. "Do you remember Serena Wilson?" Eve asked.

Vickie nodded. Eve said, "She's in jail. She shot a man and has confessed to manslaughter."

"I'm sorry to hear that. I liked her," Vickie said.

Eve continued, "It was a drug transaction gone bad. MacB was going to sell drugs to an undercover agent. There was a fight and Serena jumped in to protect MacB."

"What do you want?" Vickie asked warily.

"We want to get MacB and bring him down," Liz said.

Vickie looked down at her hands resting on the table. When she spoke, she was resigned to a bad situation. "She shoulda put a bullet in him while she had the chance. Now you best forget about MacB. Let her serve her time."

"It won't be that easy," Eve countered. "Serena gave the police enough information for warrants to arrest MacB and search his home. They will get DNA samples that will match blood and tissue found at the scene. We want to arrest him tonight before he has a chance to run."

"What do you want from me?"

"You put Ed in contact with him once. Can you help us?" Eve said.

"I arranged a meeting. It took a couple of days. He wouldn't fall for that again." Vickie was looking down at her hands. Her voice was empty. She knew this was hopeless.

"Could you tell us where to look?" Liz asked.

"He moves around. Nobody knows where he's going to be unless he tells you to meet him someplace," Vickie said.

"Can you ride around with us and show us where to look. If we find him, Liz and her partner will arrest him. If not we thank you for your help and forget that we ever talked to you. Either way, we will bring you back here safe and sound," Eve said.

"I'll do it for you," Vickie said. "But I don't go anywhere near him. He can't even see me."

Eve told her to go get changed while she took care of things with Anna. As soon as Vickie was out of earshot, Liz said, "I don't like paying her for this."

"She's an escort. This is her livelihood. I'm going to see that she gets paid. You don't have to mention it in your report." There was a hint of anger in Eve's voice.

Liz drove. They would go to a spot that Vickie suggested and Liz would check for anyone matching the description Vickie had given her. The third spot was a pool hall and bar. Liz came out with video on her cell phone. MacB was playing pool at one of the tables. Liz and Bill Andrews went back inside and made the arrest without much difficulty. Vickie laid down on the back seat so that she could not possibly be seen when MacB emerged from the pool hall. The two detectives waited out on the street for a few minutes until a squad car showed up to take MacB down to police headquarters.

"Eve, can you just hold me for a couple of minutes? I'm shaking all over," Vickie said.

The two women got out of the car and embraced. Eve felt her breasts harden. She could feel a tingle in her pussy. Vickie kneaded her back and kissed her on the neck. "We have some more time. Do you want to get a room?" Vickie asked.

They kissed. It was a long, wet kiss that ended with their tongues connecting. Eve could feel sensations shooting through her body. She longed for someone lying on top of her and pushing up inside her. She shut it off. "No. Not tonight. I have to get back to my children."

Eve kissed Vickie on the cheek and pushed her into the back of the car. Liz drove them back to the Tahiti.

On the way back to the police station, Liz asked, "Why did you turn her down?"

"What do you mean?"

"She was ready to do you right there on the sidewalk. Why did you push her back into the car?"

"I have to get home to my children."

"Was that it? Or were you just afraid of what would happen, if you said yes?"

"Have you ever done it?"

"With a woman? Sure. I've done just about everything," Liz said nonchalantly.

"Would you have gone to a room with her?"

"You bet. She was on fire."

"I wish I had known that. You could have had her. I would have called a cab."

"Oh no. I would have insisted that you join us. I've never tried it with two women at the same time."

The drive back to her mother's house was very long. She texted Joe: *Safe & Sound. CU 6:30.*

Sleep did not come easily.

84

EVE DRAGGED HERSELF out of bed closer to 6:00 than 5:30. As she rushed over to her house to pick up Becky and JJ, it dawned on her that it wasn't her house anymore. "*My name is on the mortgage. I still have a key. But it will never be MY house again.*"

She let herself in and made coffee while the kids were getting ready for school. Her mind was running in overdrive. "*They're going to have to have clothes at both houses. How are they going to figure out which house to call home?*" She managed to get the kids to school on time and put in a couple of good hours on her book before Jeff called. "It's gorgeous out there. Want to take the bikes out?"

"I'm sorry. My days are booked. I'm a single parent working on a best seller."

"What about this weekend? Saturday? Sunday?" He pressed.

"This is a bad time, Jeff," she hedged. "We are still trying to figure out how to make this work." Eve could not bring herself to say what was on her mind. "*It's over, Jeff. We are not getting back together.*" Instead she ended with, "I've got to get back to my writing."

Eve put her phone down and gazed at her laptop. She was empty. Her body would not move. The call had ruined her momentum. Getting out for a ride on a sunny afternoon while the kids were in school sounded like a good way to get back in the mood. So that's what she did.

A police car was sitting in front of her mother's house when she got back with Becky and JJ. Jack Edwards stepped out of the car and walked up to them as they were going inside. He said, "Eve, there is something I want to discuss with you."

"Am I in trouble?"

"No." He grinned. "I thought you might be interested in how the case is going."

"Why don't you come inside before we scandalize the neighbors?"

Jack began, "We have enough evidence to put Mr. MacBean in jail for a few years."

"That's good. Right?"

"We want more. We want to add pimping and anything else we've got so he stays put away for a long time."

"I suppose the women are refusing to testify against him." Eve was sympathetic.

"I'm still trying to identify the women," Jack said. He looked straight into Eve's eyes. "I have Serena and possibly Vickie Szabo. I haven't brought her in for questioning yet."

"You can get a conviction on the drug charges. Can't you?"

"We threatened him with a murder charge. We told him that we had been able to identify him as Griffin

Boothe's assailant by matching DNA from blood and tissue found at the scene to his DNA." Jack shook his head. "He wanted to know how we had found him and how we managed to get his DNA. We told him that he'd been under surveillance. He said Boothe knocked him out. When he woke up, Boothe was dead and his partner was gone. He agreed to plead guilty to possession with intent." Jack took a deep breath and exhaled through his nose. "His lawyer is trying to work a plea deal. I'm pushing the DA to hold off until we can go through Booth's stuff and figure out what he was doing the night he was killed."

Eve walked over to the picture window. "How do I fit into all of this?"

"I would like you to talk to Serena and Vickie. We need names to turn over to Vice so they can build a case against MacB."

"I'm not sure they'll cooperate. They would have to betray their friends."

"You told me that we would be on opposite sides sometimes. But you also said that you would never fault me for doing my job. Getting MacB off the streets is my job," Jack said. "I don't want to hand Vickie over to Vice but I will do whatever it takes to get that bastard."

"Could she get into a witness protection program?"

"I don't know. I'll look into it."

She looked up at him. The eyes got her. An animal magnetism emanated from the man. It filled up the room and swept her into his arms. She put her arms around him. He pulled her close and pressed her into his chest.

"Did I ever tell you that I could get used to this?" Eve asked.

"I believe you told me that once before."

"Mooommm," Becky called from somewhere in the distance. "Is this another one of your boyfriends?"

Jack laughed. It was a deep rolling belly laugh. He let go of Eve and turned to face the daughter. She was halfway down the staircase. Her eyes were almost at the same level as his. He said, "You must be Becky."

"And that woman you are pawing is my mother."

"I see we have gotten off on the wrong foot," Jack said apologetically. "Can I start over?"

Becky crossed her arms and scowled.

"I'm Sergeant Jack Edwards. I'm here to discuss a criminal case with your mother."

"Do you always grope women when you are talking to them about crimes?"

"Almost never."

"I believe 'never' is the only correct answer to that question."

Jack smiled appreciatively. "Jade was right. You are special."

"Jade? Jade Smith? What did she have to say?"

"She told me how good you are with a gun. She also said you are very smart."

"When did you talk to her?"

"A little while ago. I was doing some background investigation on your mother and her gun. Your name came up and Jade had some very good things to say about you."

Becky stared at Jack and waited.

"Have you ever considered a career in law enforcement?" Jack asked.

Becky pursed her lips and shook her head.

"I would like you to come with me on a ride-a-long. I'll show you what cops really do and we can talk."

"Seriously?" Becky was incredulous. "Like I would go riding around alone with you after you just got through buttering me up with that line about how smart I am."

"If I don't behave myself, you can get me fired for sexual harassment."

She waved her hand dismissively. "My word against yours - I lose."

"I promise to behave myself. Why don't you talk it over with your mother?"

Becky shot a suspicious glance in Eve's direction.

Eve smiled self-consciously. "I have one more thing to discuss with Sergeant Edwards." .

Becky shrugged and walked back up the stairs.

Eve turned to Jack. "Leave Joe out of this. You don't need anything from him now. You don't need that report or the video."

Jack rolled his eyes.

"Come on, Jack. That stuff is no longer relevant." She put her hands on his biceps. "I don't want you reading the report or looking at that video."

"Why not?"

"Because I don't want you to see me like that," she snapped. She walked back to the window and folded her arms. "It's humiliating. The thought of that video and people looking at me - particularly people I care about. It's killing me."

He shook his head and breathed out noisily.

She turned back to look at him. Panic was written on her face. "What's the matter?"

"Boothe had several copies of the video. I've seen it. I don't know who else has seen it but it has been posted on at least one porn site."

"Oh God, Jack. JJ is going to see that. What am I going to do?"

"Forget about it. It stinks. It's getting the lowest porn quality rating in history. They're only giving it one star."

"That's not funny," she growled.

"Yes it is. Look. I've seen the video and I'm still here. Joe seems to have gotten past it. There is so much good porn out there that your video will be forgotten in no time."

"What about JJ and Becky?"

"I don't know. I'm not a parent. I guess if it gets bad enough we can put them in witness protection."

Eve smiled. She almost laughed.

Jack turned serious. "I've got to get back. Are you going to help us?"

She nodded and gave him another hug before he walked out the door.

85

EVE CALLED ROSE Thornton after Jack left. She left a message saying that she had a problem and could use some help. Rose returned the call an hour later and Eve explained the situation. "They're such bastards," Rose said.

"What am I supposed to do?"

"You'll have to tell her what's going on and get her to cooperate. They'll beat it out of her if they have to."

Eve sketched Vickie strapped into a chair. "Can you help?"

"I'll put out some feelers. I am sure I can find her another job." Rose paused. "Do you think she would be willing to relocate?" She sounded concerned.

Eve sketched a gun pointed at Vickie's head. "Does she have a choice?"

Rose must have counted to ten before she said, "I'll call you back tomorrow. I'll try to get back in the morning but it may take longer. Are you going to be around?"

"I'm holed up at my mom's house slaving away on my book."

"Okay. Say some prayers. Wish me luck. Whatever."

Rose called back just before noon on Tuesday. She felt sure she could place Vickie at a car dealership but it was outside of Roanoke. The owner was an anti-prostitution activist. She would go out of her way to hire an ex-prostitute to help her get a fresh start. She would not hire anybody with drug problems, and she wouldn't tolerate a poor work ethic. Eve would have to vouch for Vickie until they could talk to her.

"Does Adrien have a problem with her?"

"Adrien Gautier? Why?" Eve was shocked by the question.

"I want him to write a letter of recommendation."

Eve sketched Adrien. She smiled. He really was a sweet man. "I never heard anything negative. As far as I know, she was a model employee. But I don't know how he will feel about one of his girls quitting."

"He was supportive when I did it," Rose said.

"Did you know Vickie?"

"She probably started after I left."

"Do you know Bridget Allen?"

"Yes. Can we stick to the subject?"

"She knows Vickie better than I do. I can call her if you want."

"Do that," Rose commanded. "Ask her about drug use and any negatives during her time at the Tahiti. If she knows of anything, call me immediately."

"What's next?"

"We've got to break the news to Vickie. Tomorrow morning after she's gotten some rest will be the best time. I'll get a lawyer to represent her."

Eve asked, "Do you want to meet at Vickie's apartment at ten thirty tomorrow?"

"I don't know for sure. I need to talk to the woman at the dealership again and get a lawyer on board. Can I call you back tonight?"

"Eight or nine?"

"Okay. Talk to Bridget and let me know if there's a problem."

Eve went down to the kitchen for a snack. Cheese and crackers and some grapes. She was thinking about Vickie. Two things were certain: Vickie was not going to be happy, and Vickie was going to blame her for the situation. Jack had not contacted Vickie yet. That meant they were getting ready to corner her and pressure her into cooperating. Eve couldn't allow that.

She called Bridget to fill her in on the situation and ask about Vickie's reputation. Bridget gave her a positive report. She also said that she wanted to be part of the meeting with Vickie.

Eve waited until after one to call Jack even though she suspected the cops ate lunch at their desks. Jack handed her off to Liz. She said she had collected enough evidence to make an arrest. She was about ready to make a move.

"From two years ago?" Eve couldn't believe it.

Liz said, "It wasn't that hard."

"Can you hold off until the end of the week?"

"Why?"

"It looks like we can relocate her out of the area to protect her from retribution."

"We want her here to testify against MacB."

Eve shook her head. "She won't cooperate."

"She will if she wants to stay out of jail."

Eve got up and started pacing. "What if she would rather go to jail than turn on MacB and her friends?"

"I'll deal with that when I get her into interrogation."

Eve ran her hand through her hair. "Are you going to offer her a deal?"

"If she helps us, we'll help her."

"Why not offer her a clean slate and a fresh start with a new home and a good job?"

"I can't."

"I believe I can. It looks good right now, but we can't close the deal just yet."

"I'm ready to move."

"Give me twenty-four hours. She helped you find MacB. You owe her that much."

"If I don't hear from you by one tomorrow, I do it my way."

Eve called Rose to let her know the situation. The call went straight to voicemail. When Rose called back, she said, "That's a load of crap. I could get those charges dropped. Your detective can't connect Vickie to the pimp so she wants to pressure her into providing the link."

"Which she won't do because she's terrified."

"I detest the man and I only know him by reputation."

Eve sketched MacB. She hadn't gotten that good a look at him - it was dark and he was standing across the street. But his face was now as clear to her as if she had been standing next to him. She shuddered. "So you want to bring him down?"

"Yeah. We have to work with your detective. We also need to protect Vickie."

"Shouldn't we be talking to her?"

"Tomorrow morning. She can have the job if we can get her to agree to the arrangements. I'm waiting for a lawyer to call me back. She'll be on board in time for our meeting."

The meeting in Vickie's apartment was tense. She didn't want to testify against MacB and she did not want to give up her life. Rose and Bridget convinced her that her only real choice was whether to cooperate voluntarily or suffer the consequences. Vickie finally agreed to check out the situation in Roanoke. It was just after noon. The lawyer, Cele Masson, called Detective Liz Smith and convinced her to give Vickie another day to get things in order.

Joe called on Wednesday evening. He didn't seem to have any special reason. He chatted with Eve for a few minutes then he asked to talk to JJ. They talked about school and the start of soccer season. Becky got on the phone and chatted for a few minutes about school and tennis then she took the phone into her room and shut the door. The conversation went on for an hour.

When Becky returned to the living room, she looked at her mother and her brother. "We talked about a lot of things. It was a good conversation."

Eve got in a couple of productive hours on her book after the kids went to bed.

86

ON THURSDAY AFTERNOON, Eve and Rose showed up at police headquarters to support Vickie. She was led into an interrogation room with Detectives Andrews and Smith and an assistant DA. They handed her a contract with her plea agreement. It guaranteed her immunity from prosecution. She signed it. Her lawyer, Cele Masson, gave them a prepared statement. They read it and asked questions for the next hour.

Vickie paused briefly to glare at Eve and Rose on her way out of the building. Rose got up and intercepted her. Vickie stared angrily at Rose. Her jaw was tense. Her eyes flashed with anger. Rose said, "This is a good deal. Don't blow it." Her was voice was soft and kind.

"It's a good deal for everybody but me."

"It's a chance to get your life back."

"I have my life. I have friends. I have a job and my own apartment. There is nothing for me down there."

"You'll have an apartment. The job is better. It's time for you to make some new friends." Rose sounded like she was getting pissed off.

"Why?"

"If you were on the Titanic and somebody offered you a seat on a lifeboat, would you turn it down so you could stay on the ship and drown with your friends?"

Vickie's lip curled into a sneer.

Rose smiled sympathetically. "You can't do anything about the situation. You need to accept it and move on."

"This is about MacB. Nobody gives a shit about me."

Rose pointed at Eve, who was standing a few feet away looking devastated. "She doesn't give a rat's ass about MacB. She's been fighting for you."

Vickie glared at Eve.

Rose said, "I've been through this. You can make it. Trust me. Talking a guy into buying a car is no harder than getting him to put some money on the dresser for you."

"I won't be selling anything. I'm a goddamn entry-level clerk."

"For now. Show them that hiring you was a good decision and you will get your shot at sales soon enough."

Rose took Vickie's hand and placed a business card on her palm. She pushed Vickie's fingers closed on the card. "You're right. I hate MacB enough to do just about anything to bring him down. But that doesn't mean I don't care about you. Call me anytime."

She hugged Vickie and kissed her. "Try me. Call me in the middle of the night and see what kind of response you get."

Vickie pulled away. She nodded to Cele. The two of them walked toward the elevators.

87

JOE CALLED ON Thursday afternoon. He wanted to know if the kids would be interested in a movie that night. He and Lee had decided to see "A Good Year" starring Russell Crowe. Both Becky and JJ agreed immediately even though they thought the movie sounded dorky. Eve told Joe that she wanted the kids home by eleven. He said, "We are already too late to make the five o'clock show. The next show starts at 7:30. We won't get out until 9:30. I promise to have them home by 11:30 or midnight at the latest."

"That's awfully late for a school night."

"They can handle it. I need some slack on this. I worked very hard to get Lee and Becky to agree. I don't want to give them a chance to change their minds."

"Alright. No later than midnight and try to plan these things for the weekend in the future."

"That's the other thing," Joe said. "If this works out okay, I want the four of us to ride part of the C&O Canal on Saturday. It's a fifty miler so it would be an all-day outing. I would like to pick them up for dinner Friday and keep them the whole weekend."

"Wow," Eve gasped. She walked across the room. "Are you serious?"

"Very."

She took a deep breath and let it out slowly. "What if I didn't go to Mass with you?"

"That could be awkward. I don't want to have to explain why you're not with me."

"Go to St. Matthews or the Shrine. Nobody knows you there."

"I'll have to think about it. We can talk some more tomorrow."

"Alright, I'll have the kids ready by six."

Joe called during his lunch on Friday. He said the movie night had gone smoothly. The kids liked his plans for the weekend. They worked out the details while they were eating ice cream after the movie.

"Is Lee sleeping over?"

"Yes. She has moved in with me."

"Do you think the kids are going to have a problem with that?"

"I'm not going to tiptoe around it. That's the way things are."

"I don't want you to. I'm just worried."

"If we act like it's normal, they will accept it. By the way, Becky and Lee discovered that they both love tennis. That went a long way to smoothing out their relationship."

"I hope you're right."

"Are you okay with it?"

"I have to be. Like you said, that's the way it is."

"It didn't have to be."

"Joe, we can't go back and do it over. We're here and we are going forward."

"I'll pick the kids up on my way home from work if that's okay."

"5:30?"

"I should be pretty close to that but it might be six, depending on traffic."

"Okay. We'll be waiting for you."

Eve pulled her cell phone out of her purse. "Hattie, it's me, Eve," she said when the woman answered. "I have a sudden urge to spend a weekend in Vegas do you think you could give me a ride to the airport?"

"Are you interested in some company?"

Eve giggled. That was the point of the call. "I think a weekend with you in Vegas would be perfect. I'll call you back around seven so we can make final plans."

Eve switched to April's phone. She was on a roll. Time to take care of Jerrod. The job offer had been prepared and sent by Donna Wang, Assistant Vice President for Corporate Communications and Public Affairs. Ms Wang agreed to talk to Eve using Skype so they could see each other while they were talking. Eve began, "I want to thank you for the very generous offer."

"Do you have any questions?" Wang asked.

"No. I have spent some time considering the offer. It is very appealing but I am going to have to decline."

"Jerrod said you were between jobs." Wang sounded upset. She probably expected Eve to try negotiating the salary or start date.

"I am fully employed. Jerrod may be confused because I was fired from the position that I held when we met."

"That is disappointing. I could increase the salary if that would help."

"Thank you. Money is not the issue. I like what I am doing and I am comfortable with my current situation."

"I see."

"I will send a formal response to your job offer shortly, but I wanted to speak to you face-to-face to let you know how much I appreciate the offer."

"Thank you. If you should change your mind, please contact me directly. You seem to be the type of person that we could find a spot for at any time."

"There is one thing that you could do for me."

"What is that?"

Eve held up a business card. "Do you know what this is?"

"It's Jerrod's business card."

"I have had it for about a month. I did not call Mr. Johnson about his informal proposal for a reason."

"What was that?"

"I am not interested in working with Mr. Johnson. I am most certainly not interested in becoming one of his concubines. Would you please let Mr. Johnson know that although I like him, I do not want him to contact me ever again. I do not want a fight but if he ever contacts me again, I will consider it harassment and I will take whatever steps are necessary to make sure that it ends. Could you give him that message for me?"

"Yes. I will let Jerrod know how you feel."

"Thank you. Have a good day." Eve terminated the call.

She studied flights and hotels for a weekend in Las Vegas. If she and Hattie flew out Saturday morning, they would only have 24 hours from the time they checked into the hotel until they had to check out. She could go as soon as Joe picked up Becky and JJ. Hattie might have to work. Eve called Hattie and told her the options. Hattie wanted to leave for Dulles before 5:30. They agreed on 4:30. Eve scheduled a flight and a hotel then she called Joe and told him that she had just found out about a book show in Las Vegas. She would have to leave the kids with their grandmother so that she could get to the airport in time for her flight. He wasn't happy but he agreed that she needed to get out and promote her book.

88

EVE CALLED JOE from the Las Vegas airport just before noon on Sunday and told him that she would pick up the kids a little later than anticipated. Joe told her not to worry about it. He and Lee were having a good time with Becky and JJ. They could keep the kids for dinner. She could drop by later to pick them up. By the time Eve and Hattie got back to Gramma Becky's shortly after five, the plans had changed. Gramma Becky had invited Joe, Lee, and the kids to come over for dinner. They made room at the table for Eve. Hattie begged off because she had to get ready for work.

Gramma Becky was proving to be quite adaptable. The meal featured foods that she would normally have served if she had had all day to prepare. But they were store bought. Joe had run to the grocery store for a spiral sliced ham and a bucket of potato salad along with pie and ice cream. The biscuits were baked but they had come packaged and ready to go. Lee had prepared the biscuits and set the table while she chatted with Joe's mother-in-law. The two women quickly developed a cozy relationship.

Lee took Eve's hand as she and Joe were leaving. "It was so nice to finally meet you, April."

"Actually, we met at your sister's wedding."

"That was a long time ago. I do remember saying hello to you but not much else."

"We should get together for lunch so we can get re-acquainted."

Lee considered the idea and then asked, "Any suggestions?"

"There are a lot of good places in Fairfax and Centerville. Clyde's of Georgetown is nice." Eve pursed her lips. "We could try the Inn at Kelly's Ford - that would give me a chance to show you my bike."

Lee smiled and said sweetly, "What about the Tahiti?"

Eve nodded. "We could do that." She scowled at Joe.

Lee said, "Sorry, my bad." She smiled condescendingly at Eve. "You've been banned. Haven't you?"

Eve waved the suggestion away. "That's all patched up. I just assumed that you wouldn't want to be having lunch with a bunch of cheaters." She smirked. "But on second thought, you would be right at home."

Lee glared and balled up a fist but said nothing. Eve smiled and said sweetly, "I think the Tahiti would be perfect. The meals are good and I could set you up with a job interview."

Joe grabbed Lee's arm and hurried her to the car.

Eve and her mother cleaned up after dinner. As Gramma Becky stacked dishes into the dishwasher, she asked, "What are you going to do?"

"About what?"

"About your life. What else?"

"Joe and I are going to negotiate a divorce settlement, and then, after I finish my book, I will think about rebuilding."

"I believe that Joe's young woman thinks that she can push you right out of the picture."

"Raising a family takes more than one big weekend."

"But one weekend can be a good place to start."

"She played varsity tennis in high school and college but she only has a two-year degree in business." Eve put the leftover potato salad in the refrigerator. She packed leftover ham into baggies for future meals. "After college, she married an asshole. She got a job as a peon in a small office – a combination receptionist, typist, file clerk, and bookkeeper. A high school dropout could have handled the job. She struggled with the situation until she realized there was no hope for the guy and divorced him. Then she was fired without much warning."

Eve turned to her mother and shrugged. "Now she's on the rebound. She has found herself a good man who has learned to be a pretty good father and husband even though he can be overbearing."

She poured herself another glass of wine. "Lee hasn't begun to prove that she can make this new relationship work. Now she's going to follow-up on the leads you gave her this afternoon. She will land the best, most demanding job she has ever had. Suddenly her life will be so full she won't know which way is up."

"So you don't think that she will be able to keep up the charm offensive?"

Eve frowned at her mother and shook her head. "How long were you a professional woman with a husband and children?"

She sipped her wine and began to grin as she considered the situation. "Lee will be 32 in a month. If she wants children of her own, she and Joe are going to have to get busy."

89

JACK CALLED AFTER eleven. "Is this a good time?"

Eve was sitting on her bed in a chemise. She was working through a book of puzzles that she had picked up at the airport. "That is an interesting question. I'm the only one still up and I'm not that busy. But I don't know what you want."

"I'm sitting here drinking by myself and I keep thinking about you."

The clue was "roll with a hole" - five letters. Bagel.

Eve stopped long enough to ask, "Which is worse?"

"Maybe we shouldn't be drinking alone."

"I'm not drinking. I'm psyching myself up for a jump back into the real world."

"I could drive over there if you would like to have a drink."

"Not tonight. My kids and my mom are in bed asleep."

Jack did not say anything. Eve paused over "California Valley" - four letters. Two possibilities but the word coming down was "Hari" as in "Mata ___." The valley in question was "Napa." Eve put the puzzle aside. She leaned back against the pillows and closed her eyes. "Why were you in the Tahiti that night?"

Jack took a drink, swallowed and said, "I think I was looking for a fight. It was probably the worst night of my life. My divorce was just sinking in."

"What happened?"

"We drifted apart. We spent all our time working or fighting. She got tired of it and walked out."

"What's she like?"

"She's smart. Very smart. Tall. Good looking. She's good at everything she tries."

"Except being married to you," Eve said.

"It wasn't her fault. Our careers were worlds apart and the more successful we became, the more difficult it was for us to connect in our personal lives."

"It wasn't your fault either. You were doing the best you could with the hand you were dealt."

"Is that experience speaking?"

Eve picked up the puzzle and spotted the clue "Temptress." Jezebel jumped to mind but the puzzle was looking for a three-letter word.

"What's her name? What kind of work does she do?"

"Virginia. She's a branch manager for Bank of America."

"So you both came home at night stressed to the max and there was no way to defuse the situation."

"When I made it home."

"Work-related, I hope." She tensed. He had every right to hit her hard for that one.

He played it straight. "Double shifts, stakeouts, raids. Some of it humdrum. Some of it dangerous."

Eve could feel the wheels turning in Jack's head. She waited. She thought he took another swig. He said, "I think what got her the most was not knowing what condition I would be in when I got home if I made it home at all."

She pictured Joe waiting for her to come home. "I never thought of that."

"Whenever a cop was shot or even injured in a routine traffic stop, our life would be rough for days."

"Is that why she left?" Eve asked in a hoarse whisper.

"I think so. The counselor had some good suggestions for dealing with the stress. He couldn't help with the uncertainty about whether or not I would be alive at the end of the day." He took another drink. "Then one of our friends found out about his wife's death on the evening news."

"Wow. That sucks."

"I'm pretty sure that was the day our marriage died."

"I'm sorry, Jack. I really am."

He didn't say anything.

Eve said, "Drinking like this isn't the answer."

"It's the only thing I can count on."

"We need to find ways to spend time together."

"I could drive over there," Jack offered.

"Not now. Maybe for dinner on Saturday or Sunday. That would be a place to start."

"Is that an invitation?"

"I need some time to work on that. If you want somebody to keep you company on a ride-along, why don't you ask me?"

"When can you go?"

"Any time you want. My mom and my daughter can hold down the fort for one night."

"This week or next week?"

"Both. If we can put up with each other all night in a car, we might have a chance of making a go of it."

"Probably Thursday or Friday. I'll give you a call when I have it scheduled."

She got up and walked to the window. She gazed out on the street below. "Jack, if you're sober enough and you want to come over, there is a diner not far from my house. I could go for a piece of pie and some coffee."

There was another pause. Another swig of whatever he was drinking. "Would forty minutes be okay?"

"See you then."

AFTERWORD

MY "RESEARCH" ON the subject of prostitution goes back over fifty years. As a young man in the sixties, I read two books that formed my basic understanding of the institution. They are "A House Is Not a Home" by Polly Adler and "The High Cost Of Loving" by an author whose name I have forgotten. I was unable to find copies of these books when I started my research for "The Walshes."

My search was not a complete loss. I discovered "The High Cost Of Loving" by Lewis J. Baker, Ph.D. This book provides a 40-page history of prostitution and is, in my opinion, one of the best sociological studies of prostitution available.

Rachel Moran's "Paid For: My Journey Through Prostitution" had the strongest impact on "The Walshes."

The internet provided a wealth of information on the subject.

None of the characters or incidents in this book is real. Many of the characters are inspired by real people. Dolly P is loosely based on Rachel Moran. I will note that Ms Moran states that her parents were not abusive. They certainly were not from Tennessee. Bridget Allen and the Tahiti were inspired by a situation that I found myself in one night. Bridget's effort to get herself out the business by attending college is based on one of the women who worked in Polly Adler's brothel. She was a college student who used her spare time to study. "The Vixen" Vickie Szabo is inspired in part by Polly Adler herself. She fell into her role as America's Madam when she rented out her apartment to a friend for her trysts. Ms. Moran also ran a home brothel for a while and then helped out a friend who was operating a home brothel.

Senator Anna Muehlberg and Rose Thornton represent a small army of women, including Rachel Moran, who are working to end prostitution or at least help those who want to escape the life. Senator Muehlberg's story about her family in Europe in the 1920's is a reference to Bernard Wasserstein's book "On the Eve" which describes the life of Jews in Europe between the end of WWI and the beginning of WWII.

Craig Roberts, the editor, knows about Vietnam, cyclo girls and house girls because I was stationed in Vietnam as a member of the US Army, Vietnam (USARV) from December 1967 through May 1969.

April's brother Bill was created to introduce her to a prostitute who could help her get her story. He became a lawyer because one of my neighbors told me that she is a public defender and some of her clients are prostitutes. Bill has a much bigger role as a lawyer than was originally planned.

Joe Walsh is an engineer as I was before I retired. He is smarter, better looking and more athletic than

I ever was. But I was unemployed and searching for work in crowded markets at several points in my career. In December 1994, the start-up that I was working for folded. I had to turn out the lights on Christmas Eve. I worked as an independent consultant and as a temp until a company that I was supporting landed a big contract in July 1999. My spare time was spent job hunting at fairs and on interviews during that out-of-work period. I was fortunate enough to have a good job throughout the economic meltdown of 2007 – 2008. Many engineers, like Joe, were left scrambling for anything they could get.

I was a single parent with two daughters for 18 months before Anita and I got married. She had a daughter and a son whom she was raising on her own after her first husband died.

A well-meaning friend introduced me to the woman who was the inspiration for Lee Bell (Aileen Sheehan).

April is completely fictitious. She shares my passion for writing. She probably embodies my worldview better than any of the other characters. Her ancestors, Fred Mayberry and Priscilla Yoakum, are my ancestors. They are also the ancestors of half dozen or so cousins that I have met through my genealogical research.

Jeff is fictitious. I do have a friend who is an elevator maintenance engineer, a biker, and a hunter. I also have a daughter and son-in-law who are career Army and who have served several tours in Iraq and Afghanistan. I know about PTSD both through personal experience and through reading about the trials of our combat veterans.

Jeff's assault on Eve in his apartment is included because of incidents in Rachel Moran's memoir. I have not made a serious study of rape or sexual assault. According to Department of Justice statistics available online, 16% of women and 3% of men experience rape or attempted rape. Sixty percent of sexual assaults are never reported. The numbers appear to be higher on college campuses. I have also read that approximately one in three women and one in five men will experience rape at some time in their life. No matter which numbers are used, sexual assault is a serious problem in modern society. I do not mean to trivialize it.

Victims, especially prostitutes, have limited recourse after an assault. Even if the attacker is identified and arrested, going to trial can be worse than the original humiliating attack.

Eve's reactions immediately after the assault and her subsequent forgiveness of Jeff have drawn more comment than any other aspect of this book. I understand the concerns. But I can point to numerous stories in real life and in literature that support my description of Eve's behavior.

Jeff is a force of nature. He exerts a powerful influence on Eve. At the beginning of the story, April considers faithfulness to her marriage vows one of her most import moral obligations. Cheating on Joe would be one of the worst sins that she could commit. But she does exactly that when she is with Jeff. I do not believe it is unrealistic to depict her as having mixed feelings about Jeff after the sexual assault and humiliating violation of the relationship that both of them were working towards.

Bonus Material

Nickey Arnold teams up with Jack Edwards

to end a crime spree

when businessman Adan Jackson

goes off the deep end

Demented

A thriller by Joe Clark

1

THEY GATHERED AT the same table in the Il Mediterreano on Connecticut Avenue in DC every Friday night. They called themselves The Gal Friday Group. Most of them had mid-level jobs as administrative assistants, accountants or lawyers. Cindy Foster had been promoted to manager recently, but the group decided she could stay because she was one of the founding members. Ellen Magee was a partner in a law firm, but it was a small firm, so that didn't count. There were twelve women in the group, but there were always a few no-shows. Six women were seated at the table on Friday, the first of May, 2009. Cindy sat facing the door. Ellen sat across from her. Their table was next to the restaurant's main aisle.

The Il Mediterreano is a medium sized restaurant that can seat a hundred patrons comfortably. More seating is available outside in front of the restaurant. Inside the tables are laid out in a matrix that provides a comfortable space between parties. They are arranged to give the feeling of a warm, casual dining experience.

The restaurant was full that night. Having a conversation with anyone more than a couple of feet away was difficult. The Gal Friday Group had split in two. Cindy was engaged in a discussion about balancing home and career with June Wilson and Ashley Maddox. June was an accountant in payroll with two children and an ex-husband. Ashley was an executive assistant who held the front office together. She had a wonderful husband and a bright, high-strung daughter. Cindy managed the Tax Services department at the DC office of America First Financial Services. Her husband Eric was the manager of computer systems. They had married a year ago and bought a house in Bowie, Maryland. They were working on starting a family.

Ellen Magee was a woman's lawyer. She took on divorce cases, discrimination suits, domestic violence, and sexual harassment cases. She was always the warrior fighting for the woman or women in those cases. Anne Michaels was another lawyer who was cutting her teeth on women's issues. Betty Saunders, a public affairs specialist, was on Ellen's left. She sat facing Anne. Betty was married to an accountant. They had a teenage daughter and two preteen sons.

Cindy suddenly jerked her head up. Her eyes widened in shocked disbelief. She stared transfixed toward the entrance. Ellen turned to look. Two men had entered the restaurant and were walking toward their table. They were overdressed for this setting. Both wore expensive suits and flashy ties. The man in front was middle-aged, medium height, balding and bespectacled. The second man was a 6 foot tall, 220-pound athlete. He had sharp Teutonic features with blonde hair and blue eyes. His gaze was fixed on Cindy as he made his way into the restaurant. Blue Eyes touched his companion on the shoulder and directed him to a small table off to the left. It was about 20 feet from where the group was sitting. Blue eyes took a seat that gave him a direct line of sight to Cindy.

The two men ordered and fell into conversation. The shorter man was animated. The taller man seemed bored. He would occasionally look over at Cindy. She picked at her food and tried to follow the conversation, but the attention bothered her. She did her best to hide her discomfort. When she made eye contact with Ellen, she could tell that she wasn't succeeding. Ellen was struggling to stay engaged with Anne and Betty. She would look at Cindy and then over at the intruders. She would go back to the conversation briefly. Then she would be drawn back to Cindy. Her eyes darted back and forth between her distressed friend and the men at the other table.

Shortly after eight, Cindy called for her check. Almost immediately, Blue eyes tapped his companion on the arm and pointed to Cindy. Baldy turned to look at her, pursed his lips, and nodded. The two men rose and ambled across the room toward the Gal Friday Group. Ellen threw her napkin down on the table and pushed her chair back. There was fire in her eyes. Cindy shook her head and mouthed, "No." Ellen froze. With a slight nod of her head, she signaled, "What gives?" Cindy grimaced in response. She recognized the men. Blue eyes was Adan Jackson, a senior account manager at AFFS. This would have to be handled diplomatically.

Ellen relaxed a little and waited. Her hands rested on the edge of the table, ready to push off and spring into action at the slightest hint of trouble. She tracked the approaching men with a fierce stare.

An elderly man sitting behind Cindy had pushed back from his table so that his chair was almost touching Cindy's chair. He was reading the Washington Post. He paused to look at Adan Jackson and his companion as they walked in his direction. The glance was so subtle that Cindy missed it, and Adan ignored it.

Adan halted next to Cindy. He looked down with a faint smile and said, "Cindy, this is Ron Goldsmith, CFO of HamNX. Ron, this is Cindy Foster, the manager of our tax section. She is going to be handling your account."

Goldsmith extended his hand. "It is a pleasure to meet you, Ms. Foster. I look forward to working with you."

Cindy shook his large, fleshy, sweaty hand. His limp grip offended her. She smiled. "We spoke on the phone on Monday. It's a pleasure to meet you in person."

Goldsmith surveyed the table and saw five unfriendly faces. He turned back to Cindy. "I apologize. I didn't mean to interrupt the proceedings. I just wanted to say hello. Maybe we can get together for lunch next time I'm in town."

"I would like that," Cindy said. Her smile seemed genuine.

Goldsmith turned and walked back to his seat. Adan paused to wink at Cindy before following his client back to their table.

She paid for her meal and went to the lady's room for a final visit. When she came out, Adan was waiting for her. "Didn't you use to be Cindy Smith?"

She glared but said nothing. Adan squinted and bit his lip. "I am trying to remember where we first met."

"At my wedding reception," Cindy snapped. "You showed up without an invitation."

He screwed up his face in a doubtful expression. "No." He shook his head. "I'm sure you are the Cindy Smith I dated in college."

"You have me confused with somebody else."

He grinned. "You were a year behind me at Georgetown. You were the last good girl that I dated."

The way he said "good girl" made her stomach churn. She fought to stay in control, but when she looked into his face, and she could not help looking, she saw that sadistic grin and those predatory eyes. She could feel him on top of her. The metallic smell of testosterone made her itch all over. A scream tried to force its way out. Cindy choked it back and pushed past him. She charged through the restaurant past the patrons enjoying an evening out. Cindy caught Ellen's worried expression out of the corner of her eye but kept going. She did not stop until she reached the ticket kiosks on the second level of the Metro station. Tears were streaming down her cheeks. She leaned against one of the boxy machines for some time sobbing and fighting for control.

2

CINDY FOSTER SQUIRMED. She couldn't sit still. The voice in her head screamed, "Go home. Now." She ignored it and turned left off of I97 onto Race Track Road. A half-mile later, an almost imperceptible bend in the road put her on 11th Street in Bowie, Maryland. As she continued down the two-lane country road past farms and recent housing developments, she grew more and more convinced that she had taken a wrong turn.

The road ended abruptly at an intersection. A railroad overpass to her right led to what looked like a shopping area of sorts. On her left, the road led south to a housing development. Across the intersection, Cindy saw some old stores probably constructed before WWII. According to her GPS, she had reached her destination.

She closed her eyes and took a deep breath. When she opened her eyes, she began to scan the buildings from left to right. She spotted the leprechaun painted on a large plate glass window on the front of an ancient building almost hidden by the overpass. The words "Old Bowie Town Grille" were painted in large letters in an arc above the leprechaun.

Cindy rolled toward the restaurant. A few vehicles sat in a parking lot nestled between the Grille and the overpass. She studied them before pulling into the lot. There was an SUV, two trucks and a sporty Lexus. There was no sign of her contact, but she didn't know what to expect. The woman was supposed to be waiting for her in the parking lot. She considered going back home and calling Ellen. Or, calling Ellen and complaining that her detective was a no-show. She settled on the latter and pulled into a parking space at the rear of the lot. She turned her car off and surveyed the parking lot one last time. "Shit! Did I come to the wrong place? Or did that stupid detective blow me off?"

She was still sitting in her car wavering between going back home and calling Ellen when the sound of a car door opening and shutting caught her attention. She looked in her rearview mirror. A woman had emerged from the Lexus and was heading toward Cindy's Fusion. She was 5'7", slender with black hair and Mediterranean features. Not someone who could help with the problem.

Cindy got out of her car and walked across the parking lot. The woman extended her hand. "Cindy Foster? I'm Nickey Arnold."

Cindy shook hands but said nothing.

Nickey smiled and said, "Why don't we go inside where we can talk?"

She led the way past the counter and cash register that served as a gateway between the front entrance and the modest dining area. The restaurant had just opened for the day's business. The lunch crowd had not shown up yet. Nickey found a corner table where she and Cindy were unlikely to be disturbed. Cindy's friend and former classmate Ellen Magee had arranged the meeting. The incident at the Gal Friday get together a week earlier had left both women shaken.

Cindy took a menu and studied it. She was avoiding eye contact. When the waitress came to their table, Cindy ordered the Salmon. Nickey ordered a Chicken Caesar salad.

Nickey broke the awkward silence. "Are you okay? Ellen said the incident at the restaurant was pretty serious."

Cindy brushed her hair back and licked her lips. "It was upsetting, but I'm okay." Her voice was barely audible.

"Can you tell me a little about yourself?" Nickey asked. "You work for America First. How long have you been there?"

Cindy's hands were folded and resting on the table. Her eyes focused on them. She cleared her throat. "Almost ten years."

"Was that your first job?"

"Yes. I went to work right after graduation." The words came out in a slow monotone.

"You're married and living in Bowie?"

"Yes."

"How long have you been married?"

Cindy looked up at Nickey and grinned slightly. "We celebrate our first anniversary next month."

Nickey smiled. "How is married life?"

Cindy blushed. "Great. Are you married?"

"No," Nickey sighed. "I don't think that is ever going to happen."

"Why not?" Cindy chided.

Nickey screwed up her face and shook her head. "I'm not ready to settle down." She smiled enigmatically. "Marriage isn't for everyone."

Cindy's eyebrows shot up. Nickey pressed on. "Your husband is Eric? How did you meet him?"

"We met at work. He is the manager of the office computer system." Cindy smiled. Her eyes looked off to the right. "He's a hands-on kind of guy who will come around to check on complaints and answer questions."

"So one thing led to another, and the two of you got married?"

"Actually, he's shy," Cindy replied. "He wouldn't ask me out. A mutual friend set us up on a double date. She and her husband took us to see 'Cats' at the Lazy Susan Dinner Theater." Cindy was becoming visibly more comfortable and animated.

"When was that?" Nickey asked.

"September 10, 2006."

"You waited a while to get married," Nickey observed.

"We lived together for over a year." Cindy studied her hands. She seemed to be telling her story to the table. "We talked a lot about what was going on and where we wanted to be in five or ten years. We both wanted a family and a home." She paused to look up at Nickey. "One night, I decided that I wanted to have children and soon. Eric said if we were going to bring children into the world, we had to be committed to raising them. That was the end of October 2007. A week later he proposed and I said yes."

When their food arrived, they paused to sample the dishes. Nickey asked, "How's the salmon?"

"Pretty good. Very tender but they might have overdone the lemon. How's your salad?"

"It'll keep me alive." Nickey grinned mischievously. "Chicken salad is not an Irish dish, but it's an excellent food choice."

Cindy's eyebrows arched. "Do you like Irish food?"

Nickey rolled her eyes. "I'm Greek. I love Greek food. But, when I was in the Marines, I learned to get by with whatever slop they put in front of me."

Cindy laughed.

"Can you tell me a little bit about this guy at work?" Nickey asked. She lifted a piece of chicken on her fork. "What's he doing to bother you?"

Cindy's smile vanished. "He manages to walk past me once or twice a day and make eye contact."

Nickey took a sip of her wine. "That's it? He doesn't say anything or touch you?"

Cindy shook her head. "No. I am pretty sure that he is trying to see how far he can go without getting into trouble."

"Have you talked to anybody besides Ellen about it?"

Cindy reddened. "A couple of my friends." She shrugged. "They haven't noticed anything."

"And his supervisor?" Nickey prompted.

"I can't go to him. Adan's a senior account manager, and I don't have anything concrete." Cindy lowered her eyes and bit her lip. "But he's making me uncomfortable."

"That should be enough to go to management these days."

Cindy shook her head vigorously. Her voice was choked. "It isn't. I talked to Ellen. He can go anywhere any time he wants and claim he was just doing his job."

Nickey nodded. She asked in a soft voice, "How long has this been going on?"

"I don't know. It's been over a year." Tears glistened in Cindy's eyes.

"Why did you wait so long to do something about it?"

"I was hoping he would stop. But the way he came on to me at the restaurant was too much," Cindy snarled. "Ellen said you could take care of it."

Nickey was impassive. "To the best of your knowledge, when did it start?"

"Early last year."

Nickey put her elbows on the table and clasped her hands with her thumbs touching her lips for a few seconds. Then she asked, "Was there some sort of trigger event that you can identify? Were the two of you in a flirty conversation or something?"

Cindy's jaw tightened. She rolled her eyes and shook her head. "We bumped into each other at a holiday party at the end of 2007." She shrugged. "But it was nothing. We were just at the same table at the same time getting food. I was there with Eric."

"This guy thought it was something. Why was he there in the first place?"

"It was a company party. We both work for America First. We work in different departments, so our paths don't cross."

"But you have been running into each other regularly since that encounter?"

Cindy nodded.

Nickey eyed Cindy suspiciously. "Is there anything else?"

Cindy blurted out, "He crashed my wedding reception."

Nickey frowned. "Does Ellen know about that?"

Cindy shook her head. Nickey's eyes narrowed. Her head tilted back. "And you just forgot to mention it to her because …?"

"I pushed it out of my mind. I didn't want a scene in front of all those people," Cindy said in a panicked voice. "Eric doesn't know anything about what's going on, and I want to keep it that way."

Nickey sipped her wine as she studied Cindy. "My fee is $200 per hour with an upfront retainer of $2000. If it looks like I am going to need more than 50 hours, we can talk about a deal."

Cindy's lip quivered. "Can you get him off of my back?"

"There are no guarantees in a situation like this."

"So I just hand you a bunch of money and hope that you do something about that piece of crap?" Cindy snapped.

Nickey glared at her. When she spoke, her voice was flat, harsh. "Your best bet is to find another job."

"I am not going to let him run my life," Cindy shot back. "I just made manager and I intend to keep moving up the ladder."

Nickey leaned forward staring directly into Cindy's eyes. "Then you had better be prepared to fight."

Made in the USA
Las Vegas, NV
27 July 2024